ROOM 101

Motorbikes, Big Brother & Objectivists
Observations of an Abstract Connectionist

C.A. Reuben

ROOM 101

Room 101
Motorbikes, Big Brother & Objectivists
Observations of an Abstract Connectionist

Qualiabooks.com

Reuben, C.A.
1. Fiction 2. General

ISBN: 978-0-615-73372-2

Contents

The Narrator and the jester

The arm of a half sleeping Narrator reached down and turned off the small, bedside digital alarm clock-music player tuning in 'Working Class Hero,' by John Lennon. The workday is to begin again. It's 6 o'clock in the morning. It is a clear, beautiful Spring day, the sun rising in the east shining warm light into the window of a cottage located within the center of a small central European village, nestled between green rolling hillsides along the Moravia River in southern Czech Republic. A band of several birds bring on the day, chirping and busily gathering nesting materials. Throughout a large garden of fruit trees the sounds collide with Lennon's depressing lyrics…"by giving you no time instead of it all."

"Time?" he thought as he rose to adjust for a new day.

"What came first, space or time, are we all just dreaming every new day out? Is there such a difference between truth and belief, and what is it that drives me out of this bed?" Asks the middle aged man to himself as he slowly, uncaringly puts one blue and one white sock on before standing to look at himself in the bathroom mirror. Instantly remembering a time when he enjoyed seeing that face that now looked so foreign, unrecognizable, worn and homely, his comical balding head over his brow with unkempt long clown like curly tangled grey hair mostly hanging off the back,

9

his wrinkled skin and large belly exterior covering up a core that wasn't always consistently this phlegmatic in nature.

"I have everything I set out to get, yet not particularly excited am I," he thinks as he trims the sparse, wiry hair growing off the ends of his ears.

This is not the world our fathers said they would make it to be. It has become rather the world their grandfathers perhaps feared it would become. "Let it go, cheer up, don't stress," he says out loud, rubbing a face cream deep into his flaking dry and sun-spotted skin. He takes a half round, red plastic cap from the top of a narrow bottle of after-shave and attaches it to his nose. Now smiling back at the mirror and laughing out loud he suddenly is comfortable with himself.

Perhaps there is a little fool inside us all desperately wanting to get out and play with reality? A conscious little *jester* eager to point out that all life's illusions are being spelled out for us by unknown, unapproachable narrators, the clock ticks time away. Why do we give into totality and narrow singular beliefs furthermore gravitating to false senses of security only dividing ourselves over and over, shattering our windows of creative potential? Yet at the same time our aging series of doorways remain wide open wakening us slowly, each decade our thoughts and open minds and opinions leading us on through a thing we call time and experience. We try to become that something we reason is real, even if we feel nothing from it, proving before our last breaths and inevitable departure beyond all the matter which surrounds us and all the jumble of words and values we use and share amongst each other—to seal our characterized fate, that we are all inside and out in reality—fools in the end anyway.

It is the spring of 2011, the end of a very strange technological and political decade. The Narrator sits down with a large cup of coffee looking over his large courtyard and vegetable garden stretching out several hundred meters. The flowers of spring fill the entire yard with several colorful dots mixing in with a full pallet of green hues from a menagerie of shrubbery grasses and trees. He opens the small laptop then looking down, he adjusts the angle of the screen and begins to write.

The world at your fingertips. Google it, see it on high definition digital. Anything you want to ask it, and some things you dare...

Foreword

For lack of art commissions and a poor state of economy,
To help adjust my thoughts-I decided to write a book
I didn't know where that ascetic mood would take me…
I opted to take a look
Why is art and the artist a target for eradication?
A three-year quest to know became my life investigation.

I went on a creative frenzy that was all I did.
Fiction, characters of past and present,
Comedy, adventure, history, philosophy and commentaries
I spent time connecting graphics and illustrating drawings and
poems, too…
Some I added to this book of connected arts,
Which I want to share with you

Though politics overwhelms our lives, life should not be jaded by
thoughts of only doom and gloom.
Father first, a husband, a gardener, a painter, a sculptor, a writer,
an adventurer, I enjoy the flirt of philosophy, and of science,
Thoughts of physical super-strings and the big bang boom!

Like Native Americans, and great masters high in the Himalayas
Great academics have taught us:
The truly used muse aspire,
Evolve to levels of consciousness even higher,
They inherently enjoy the beauty of this world,
They give it due respect
Giving abstract liberty to seed the times…

Honoring life by sharing humor with intellect.

Perhaps there is a universal consciousness, a unified field
Contributing to the free flow of healing energy,
and if we find a balance
Tap into it together, all seeking hope and truth.
Use critical thought about evolving with technologies,
One day we may unite our minds through an understanding
That we have seen it all,
in all extremes and unbelievable ugliness and beauty, perhaps then
we will not be shocked into acting out of fear.
Fear of 'alternative- wisdoms' and of one another…
Are we at that threshold yet? Is it the 11th hour?
Are we even near?
Are we witnessing the turning point of humanity's
disorderly time?
Through conspiracy theories, religious fear mongering, fanaticism,
economic collapse, wars and propaganda,

State control will not override and defeat a natural
order of decay.
We say OK-go against the flow of nature, now seems nature is
going against our say.
No matter how good we think we are, no matter how rich
No matter how connected or removed from reality we place
ourselves…
Our earth perspective- physical context as viewed from the
standpoint of each piece of paper and rubber stamp- next period…
stating…to a unilateral agreement that it should be the end.
Will not mean a damn thing in time if we live in a pile of toxic
matter-
Forbidden to be freethinking women and men.

'Tis not a question of black, white or grey,
Good versus evil, or God versus Satan,

We live with all each day.
No one is exempt from one or the other,
Whether we like them or not
You do not believe? Go ask your mother...

It comes down to a of question of balance,
to which primary natural order of code- whom do
we serve and obey?
Some made a choice long ago; some are making
that choice today,
Some have begun to connect in their own abstract rebellious way
Connecting to positive energies that come from unexpected deeper
thoughts.
Through collected synchronicities, pieced coincidences,
Or is Qualia perhaps our destiny, if one leaves it to one's senses?

Some wish to be masters of slaves,
forgetting they are slaves as well.
Slaves to something more powerful
that enticed or drove them
on that particular path, where soul is an easy sell.

Some want to control or play dice with the Universe.
Some believe in nothing and find stale existence served
in forms of meager pay
Some make no contribution to build a greater world-
this world is just for play.
Some of us play jesters, fools and buffoons to help see another way.

Whatever your trip, however you deal with it,
whatever you label it,
It is a free world for you right now.
That is... if you got to read this book
Just think about potential tyranny, before you bite a Sandy Hook.

Freedom and liberty is awesome- it's a beautiful thing!
Go ask a Russian, a Chink or a Dyke?
The world is full of slang
It's your book still, your story, you can @#$%&?*
...it any way you like.
For yourself or for the future, for the family or for the foo?
Enjoy it while you have it -my hat is off to you,

If you are reading this book right now, I am honored.

A humble narrator/jester dedicates this book to you.

The Tale of the Young Narrator

A 15-year-old boy sits looking up to a door with the title School Principal written in large black paint on smoked glass. Suddenly, the door opens and a woman invites him to enter. He is lead through several cubicles and then into an office where he is asked to sit down in front of a large bald-headed man sitting behind a giant oak desk reading an open file.

After a few minutes, the principal looks up from the desk and with a stern look addresses the young man. "I have been reviewing the conduct report sent here by your first year teachers and it is very disturbing to know that you have proven to them and the rest of your peers that you no longer wish to progress in any of this. It was after the event in your English literature class recently that brought it to a head? Apparently, upon your last written mid term test in selected literature, it clearly gave you a multiple-choice question. You gave your own answer in written form with a small essay. Your professor was not amused by this arrogant disregard for the rules.

You were asked simply on that question: 'What character would you wish to be: A, The hero, or B, the villain?'

You wrote and I quote your words… 'I would choose neither, I wish to be the Narrator because the Narrator tells the story and he is everywhere and knows the whole story and controls the time, past future and present."

"Now, young man, this is not an acceptable attitude for study in this school. It is not part of this first-year curriculum. Furthermore it is not even an option. Now I will give you a chance to choose an A or B, a black or white answer to this question, in order for you to pass the test and then you can return to your studies in these subjects and we can forget about this incident. What do wish to do?"

The youth took a long pause, and thought for a moment and gathered his words.

"It was a strange question sir… how can someone answer it and be right? What was the correct answer? I feel as though when I am in class nothing they all manage to understand together as a group makes any particular sense to me, sir. Also, whenever the questions are put to me and the obvious logical answer is not available, I honestly see everything opposite and from a different side from everyone else. When I try to make myself be or think like the teacher and the others in class I become sad and confused. They tell me I am stupid and they laugh at me and they hate me for my strange ideas. But for some reason I know that I am right and they all just enjoy being the same… they don't want to even look at what I see or the way I think about something."

"This is reality, young man," said the principal looking up at him through his reading glasses, overlooking the file laid out before him.

"Young man, this secondary school is concerned with maintaining a high-level program of adherence to the curriculum and has no room for abstract ideas from young, confused minds. If you are unwilling to adopt the rules and the codes of conduct in order to fit in and learn the provided courses, then you will have to be moved to the Secondary School of Arts and Crafts. There you are open to be and choose your own narration," he concluded, turning to the boy, looking serious while writing something into a file on his desk.

"But the art school—my father said all the poor losers go to the art school. If I am going to make any money or be something when I grow up I need to study here. A friend said the art school is a place for those who have no future as anything but slaves—isn't there a school for people like me... Sir, why can't someone say they want to be a narrator and pass the test? Narrator...villain... why is it forbidden?"

The Head Master stood up and pointed to the door. "You don't understand anything...Get out of my office, go be a narrator and see where it gets you... I never want to see you in my school again; get out of here now, you are done here, you are a stupid young fool!"

Chapter
1

The Foolish Narrator
Writes His Thoughts

*A*n elderly woman is led by a blue laser beam through a long corridor of marble floors and etched glass walls emanating soft light. As she nears the end of the hall, the etched glass gives way to clear panes. Glancing from side to side, she sees several people vacantly looking back at her while she waits for a door to open. Her legs are beginning to strain from standing for so long in one place. Just then a voice is heard from somewhere over her.

"Thank you, our scan is complete and if you will please proceed to the waiting area while we run the program checks, you will be notified in a matter of time thank you."

She enters the waiting room, looking around she notices an expressionless mass of people. She scans the room looking for a glimmer of familiarity, settling on a tall thin Nepali-American man with a grey beard sitting at a table reading.

"Professor Ramadeep," she asks?

"Dr. Nova?" He squints up at her.

During their years together at the lab in Cambridge, Massachusetts, where he was a doctor of psychology, he had always been good-natured with a jolly laugh. She remembered him well. Yet now, he seemed so distant and detached. He simply stared at her now, colorless. Finally, she sat down beside him.

"Did you just arrive?" He asks flatly, reluctantly closing his magazine.

"Yes, just now."

"And you, Doctor?" she replies.

"Please sit down Katka," he continues in a tired and worn voice. "I have been here for what seems to be weeks but could only be days, I am not sure. What I have learned here has aged me. I thought I was an atheist, but this place seems to be outside of this world, could it be hell? Is it all part of some...?"

"What are you talking about?" She cuts him off and puts her hand on his shoulder.

He begins to weep, not looking at her, bent over shaking his head.

Wiping his tears he looks straight into her eyes before smiling and begins to laugh.

"My dear, humor and laughter is all we have left."

"It is so good to see you," he smiles at her… kissing her cheek. She feels relief seeing him come to his senses and begin to communicate in the character she remembered while he relaxes in his chair and starts to let his old friend in on a story.

"Many of our finest minds have just floated through here, I have seen them come and I have seen them go. I have heard so many opinions and have slowly begun to piece this puzzle together. They told you this was the enhancement process before you entered the building?"

"That's right," she said.

"That the science guild was preparing the unlocking of the PLATO Brain, something was always weird about that name, never liked it, the concept of a republic that compartmentalized humans over leaving it to natural fate that seemed a little too strange…anyway, when they started developing their version of the (AI) supercomputer of which we all had a part to play in its construction, the final unlock was to be set for this year right?"

"I remember something like that," she answers shrugging.

"Well… It seems to be the eleventh hour my friend. I saw so many (A) ranking politicians and get this, I saw the King of England come through here as well."

"You're kidding. Why would they need the English King to unlock the PLATO system? Did I miss something? Because the program we thought we were working on had the blessings of the elite body including the Monarchy," she says still looking confused, "It must be someone who looks like him?"

"No, I swear it," he says, grabbing her by her shoulders, "I had met him before when he was much younger when his grandmother ruled. I am going off; sorry… anyway I think the whole cyber system has been secretly hijacked completely all the way to the Monarchy."

"But the Monarchy gave us the go, we had their blessings and they liked our version of the (AI) connectionist construct. They said it made sense in regards to trust and transparency." She continues, "We had figured out the most difficult questions pertaining to the subjective side of the machine brain, there is still so much to complete on that and it could take years… It's not yet ready to integrate into making any complete decisions for controlling a society. This is the first time I have heard anything about the PLATO project taking over our project."

"True," he adds, "Although do you remember when we were putting the initial layout together in the late '90s we would say things like, 'Wow if you could take control of the world with one computer, you could be a God.'"

"So you're saying the demon of our imagination came true?"

She asks with an unbelieving tone.

"That's right; at least that virus-like demon is working on it right now. I know it is so because that Englishman who used to own a title to one of the most powerful nations in the world just got sent to Room 101. It really happened."

"What's that mean, Room 101?" She askes while shifting from her uncomfortable position in the hard desk chair.

"Just a figure of speech, you never read "*1984*" I take it? Many people haven't, too busy reading pro 'Objectivist fiction novels like "*Atlas Shrugged*" or the "*Fountain Head,*"…begging to be bigger than they are, living beyond means flashing riches to compensate for their absence of heart. Only the extreme selfishness of these last few tech generations of cultureless sheep harnessed with their use of larger-than-life-egos... Probably too late for society to check out Orwell's "*1984*" now and grasp its prophetic warnings. I'm sure everything will be different now. I can only imagine what is in store for all of us behind that door. From the info I got from the folks at MIT and the majors in Silicon Valley that have been through here; once the final phase is complete and all the checks have been made they will turn on the machines they determine suffice to run their new plastic utopia."

Katka interrupts, "Why would they want to bring us through here? We don't have much to do with running the PLATO project; we were working on the connectionist, unified mind projects that were preparing us for harmonizing with the (AI), then integrating it into mankind's utilities as a tool and not as a leader or dictator which would compartmentalize our society… wasn't that what the PLATO (AI) system required to be legitimate? Was that not what our research was all about? It was to give the techno-plutocratic nonsense a consciousness and a heart, right?"

"Well, now we are in for a total plutocratic new world," he says staring straight at her.

"There will be a new replication of the administration. That's right. A total copy of our walk, talk, everything right down to how we blink our eyelids... remember that spiderweb head piece that was developed in the beginning of the 2000s for video gamers. It watched brain connections with sensors and it moved the controls of the game by your neural thought process. Well, that technology was the breakthrough that took it out of the park. That and the controlling of our subconsciousness through zombie agents that they shot through our neurons via that same contraption; the whole (AI) world went upside down at that point and when the military and the politicians began to work together it became the ultimate Pandora's box of tricks." Katka looks at him bewildered.

"Who is *they* and why would *they* go through the trouble to create copies when we are cheaper as we are human. We both know this stuff costs millions?"

"*They* are the owners of this world's financial and material reality. *They* want the job of control to be easier and more functional. Once *they* have a copy of a figurehead of authority they own it and control it for as long as *they* like; it is useful to have a copy of the King of England for as long as you like to own him. He must do and say what the controllers wish of him because *they* will control his brain. Would you need the original any longer? Those that can be turned into robots will be programmed through the neurotransmitters and those valuable to the party who cannot be programmed will be replaced by a machine."

"This sounds so unbelievable," she says as tears well up in her eyes. "But there are members of the monarchy and ruling class who respect human intelligence and love the beauty of nature throughout the world and they understand very well how sensitive the brain is and how important it is for the world to maintain a transparent, artificial intelligence-united-world mass created super computer. Many of those folks have donated and promoted our research for years."

"I am guessing some have given in to the powerful Joker's plans and the ones that fight the Jokers carved out concept of reality, we probably will find in here, or on the other side, or perhaps never see again?" He shrugs and points to the sky. "Heaven knows at this point my dear?

"So what you're saying Doctor," she asks looking around the room to see if anyone was noticing their conversation… "So the Jokers have turned on their lords and masters tricking them into a false sense of control over a matrix that has shunned the values of respected higher thought and moral reason, truth and reality. They now leave it up to objectively programmed calculators to do all their mental work?"

Nodding his head up and down he continues, "Exactly, Katka. Remember how they used us, and as the years went how they started to cut us down, the big paydays were few and far between as they consolidated all the departments under the World Central Science Guild that runs somewhat like the UN and even less efficient. Then the Joker politicians and accountants started to get involved with directing our programs. I knew we were not able to keep even our own research secret any longer and the corporations took over owning even our thoughts before we had a chance to bring them out for fear that many of those thoughts could actually harm us. Then, when we did hold back the brilliance of our creative endeavors... Because we saw those theories as harming... They chastised us and many lost their projects as well as their positions. The big cloud of fear took over forcing us to give in to all of their demands."

Shaking her head, "I was working on a completely different project with some of the world's finest minds; we knew one day the party on Earth would have to end and order would have to replace total devastation. Dr. Ramadeep, perhaps it was meant to be because there is not enough room with all the rape and destruction to nature. What if no one in charge thinks about their role in taking charge of fitting into nature? This planet is divided, and we have overgrown our resources so it has finally come to an omnipotent rule to bring a type of order to survive, that is a natural process in itself, is it not?"

"You're absolutely right, Katka. I respect your open approach to understanding it for the facts. We all are to blame, we turned off our own brains, our own consciousness to reality, and we also stopped questioning authority. We gave in to the Corporate Omnipotent Authority and its order because it seemed safer for us to thrive as well. This mass complacency spread like a disease through the free world and now this world is left to a selfish corporate collective of idiots and their objectives and profit directed machines with very little respect to the resources of which they rape. We were too busy working and consuming the junk ourselves to see all the corruption develop into a disease hijacking our own futures. Thus forcing these technologies into controlling our children's future; we were the greatest of our fields yet blinded by our own need of life's trivial materialism that we hungered for at the time. The art of technical science is richer than ever, almost over-funded, yet dead because liberty, reason and truth have become chained again."

"Dr. Ramadeep, we were Respected Masters,' we made our way up the ladder of success and now you're telling me we are to be feared for our talents. That is very hard for me to believe. The (AI) can't do what we do. It is not human; it is just a baby yet in relation to our minds' capabilities concerning subjective nature?"

"But, the Jokers own fear now." He says while taking hold of Katka by the arm, "They use it as a tool against our subconscious. They live for power and money. The Jokers are the masters of hate, torture, and tyranny as well; some of the contradictive formulas of the natural brain that the 'Abstract Connectionist'

25

built (AI) was not able, for lack of logic to build into itself, or program into their model of a machine brain. So now they have a phony dictatorship of ignorance holding the keys to an overly rational objective driven (AI) brain, unable to comprehend across the field's abstractly at all. Had the machine been programmed properly the (AI) would no doubt find their masters humorous bards, and idiotic clowns."

Katka, nervously pulls her hands through her hair at the top of her head, resting her elbows on her knees:

"This was our fear all along… We and I am speaking as one member amongst a giant powerful scientific authority… We thought we had a handle on it. How could they have taken over, out from under our eyes this way? We are still constructing the formulas and have just now begun to test them. We had been getting great results, Doctor, besides our volunteer co-operated social networks and search engines have been proven to be more trustworthy than the original privately-owned ones. Our movement and community is gaining ground all around the globe because of our community's maintenance of Internet neutrality. Humanity is slowly waking—honestly, I can't believe they have taken it over; I don't know what is behind that Room 101 door you're talking about, but I won't believe that a conspiracy of corporate-greed-driven idiots will be running this thing when we go through it. I can't fathom it, Doctor. The members of the ruling class I have been in contact with are too strong and brilliant to let human evolution be overtaken by a Death Star full of Darth Vaders and robots. It is beyond comprehension. Besides, conspiracy theory only creates more fear and distrust."

"A powerful virus-like manipulation did take over, Katka," he says, throwing up his hands. "This Jokester machine has harnessed the power of total negativity. The unconscious masses living today, unbeknownst to them are pushing, and supporting this new world (AI) takeover as well because they have no keen senses and broken subjective consciousness. They have their Hollywood action films, fast food, salt, soda, sugar, and the virtual reality and video games. The Jokers are pushers of several diversions wrapped in pretty packages and, frankly, that seems to be all the public wants and lives for in this modern era. This stuff is their new symbol of liberty. Most have no care for the natural reality or the appreciation of the mind, true subjective modern art and unique thought or a positive evolution of mankind as a moral and sensitive caretaker of the natural biological world. Every generation is destined to become more reprogrammed obedient machines who take their orders from brand names and corporations.

Our natural subjective senses, our 'Qualia' has been broken down by years of marketing masters mainstream programming further simplifying our languages and numbing us to violence and mediocrity, and slowly tightening and manipulating the laws. Our new Bandito-Totalitarian lords will turn their spoiled children into gods ruling over cultureless Zombie consumers. They intend to bring us up feeding us their processed artificial concoctions, and then kill us slowly with their expensive remedies profiting from the whole cycle. Anything it takes, breaking a rule or law or destroying democracy, a government a country or constitution... Anything to keep their beyond-belief extravagant materialistic lifestyle in tact."

"Qualia are a special property of massively parallel networks. This framework also explains why Qualia are private and why their full content cannot be communicated."

-Christof, Koch and Francis Crick, *Quest for Consciousness*

Qualia

Subjective consciousness: sounds, smells, taste, pain, love, experience of recreational drugs are a few examples. Qualia are our own experience, our own story uniquely painted by our own minds artist within us, using colors, shape and symbols only we see. Qualia are symbolic representations of fast-moving scattered information. Qualia is instantaneous consciousness... light speed and critically necessary... Qualia is our mental driver. One could not ride a motorcycle down a dangerous dirt road at 80 miles per hour without first adjusting for changes of condition, curves, changing gears and listening for trains, cars and adjusting speed.

Qualia: the game

Objective... Protect and maneuver as many Qualia into the brain as you can before a Mouse or TV enters your brain. If a TV enters, you lose your Qualia points. If a Mouse enters, you have ten seconds to drop a smart bomb by answering a life-saving question that should blow its head up before it eats your brain, slowly turning you into a full-time Zombie. Once you have been turned into a Zombie it is Game Over!

What if we try to line Qualia up?

What if we catch them, connect them, draw them-write them down mainly-linking symbolically with art, poetry, stories, history or even topics of politics mainly piecing them together? Connecting these many fields and genres deeper abstract structures which combine them as if they were flakes of golden reason in a puddle of catalyzing mercury, just waiting for that moment when the torch of combined understanding, truth, and action should arise burning away the ignorant toxic unrealistic haze? What if we utilize, value and protect those Qualia as if they were more precious than gold?

Chapter
2
Introducing Katka, Ammo and the jester

Katka

It is spring 1990, Katarina Nova is finishing her final thesis: '*Semantics for the Social Linguist,*' for her first of three degrees she will receive from Charles University School of Language and Humanities. At 18, she is the youngest of her peers to graduate and with high honors; her focus of study was English linguistics and philosophy. She devoured books and any new theories, on semantics and contemporary visual arts and technological perspectives coming out of the rapidly opening western world. Everything was brilliant and ready to be tapped that linked our world's thoughts and symbols together. Katka was also interested in linking science to the arts. She felt they provided the roots of humanity. "The arts were the driver of thoughts which separated us from all creatures," she would say to her professors that were often very one-sided or unable to break out of their daily objective grind. She often opened their minds to fresh ideas. It was easy to see how she quickly became the young darling of the intellectual brass in the old Prague university.

It was an accident that she came to study English and philosophy. As a teen, her parents were unable to get her into a

University-bound program right out of grade school because they were not members of the Communist Party. Those exclusive spots were reserved for select Red-Card-carrying members' children. Katka's father, however, noticed she had an ability for drawing and making creative art. So he showed up at the principal's office with a bottle of his best homemade slivovice (a home made plumb brandy), at a secondary trade school for graphic artists and book illustrators, and managed to convince them that Katka had artistic potential. This art school was the only option for a poor family from Brno in Central Moravia, but this practical mechanics foundation in art would prove to provide a special foundation compared to the one-sided players she would join later in life.

Katka's grandmother was an English teacher, a rarity in those jingoistic times. Every Sunday, Katka had English lessons, initially loathing them, preferring to draw, play or watch TV as any normal child would…yet eventually she set to task on her English, and before she graduated from art school, Katka was fluent in reading and writing. Through pure serendipity, she won the random open spot for non-party members to study at one of the oldest Universities in Europe, The Schools of Language and Humanities. At age 15 she left her art studies halfway with honors, however; with a certificate of graduation, having passed all the required tests in order to qualify for entrance to study at the University.

Prague in the late '80s and early '90s would awaken Katka's spirits and feed her curiosity. Witnessing the Velvet Revolution, she experienced her country change and transform into a new democracy. She felt a strange and overwhelming high along with several others, a drunkenness of freedom; freedom for the first time since the Russian tanks began their occupation in 1968, an occupation that seemed as though it would take over all logic and wipe out any thought of a free-thinking Czechoslovakia. Now after the revolution within the old broken-down warn facades of the

31

grey Gothic and Baroque city of Prague, people acted as though life had become a non-stop party… Everyone was suddenly kinder, as the borders put down the iron-clad guard. The long forbidden things from western worlds began to show up wrapped in fancy packages. New foods, and drugs and the unavoidable western technological corporate world made material addictions come to a hungry new market. However, it was mainly the western thoughts, theories, and Scientific technologies… This is what Katka lived for, and this gathering of understanding consciousness, with new abstract connections to her own creative destiny intertwined with the philosophical and scientific academic world. This is what she found to be her most natural chosen life purpose.

Ammo

Amon A. Lawrson, his friends called him "Ammo," was born in "The Biggest Little City in the World" located in the "Battle Born State" of Nevada in the USA. Reno was a town of 24-hour bars, gambling and prostitution, and every kind of drug imaginable. Ammo was educated according to the system, by the system. He left town at 18 in 1986 on a 1975 R-Series Toaster-Tank BMW motorbike and headed to Canada and Alaska. He started searching the world for a purpose. That inner drive, and his experiences took him full circle, connecting him to alternative ways of seeing through the minds of other cultures and lands. He found his purpose by discovering time itself, through living a moment- to-moment experience.

She Calls

700cc motor humming, ferryboat tong-spits out
impressionable youth
Baboom, baboom, wheels on an off ramp,
bind broken free at last
Over the Chilkoot Pass, through white glacier out of Skagway
Over the golden steps, iconic Northern route they say.
Over the steep incline gate of the Yukon gold rush
Carcross, Alcan, White Horse, Anchorage, Denali, Homer
'Tis nether lie nor misnomer
More than words upon this paper
Now he's hooked he won't escape her.

The Day Viking Arrived

Ammo was hard at work in his shop when he heard the sound of a motorbike outside. He went out to meet it. Straddled across the teal blue '91 Paris Dakar BMW, just setting out his side stand and standing up strong, was the Viking, a tall, lean, red-haired master of alpine sports, and ex-rock star, engineer, family man-hippy.

"Hey, Ammo, brother how would you like to start a bad ass motorbike gang?" He said laughing at Ammo, with a big smile knowing he was surprised to see him. Ammo, returned the smile and with feeling a tickle to his senses exclaimed, "What took you so long bro? I was wondering if I was going to go down the old age drain feeling like a washed out jerk calling for my *"Rosebud?"*

"You Kane-t do that, citizen douche!" Viking exclaimed... Ha Ha, they both start laughing.

"Awesome bike, Viking. Perfect timing dude, I have to get out of here, this place is strangling me. I thought of getting together many times to ride with others but I am such a shitty communicator man."

Viking laughs, "I am not much better... anyway...I just got this insane enduro bike and I knew you had one just like it so it made sense to hit you up for a ride first. After all, we ski and rock climb together. So why not ride right?"

"I am stoked you did, Viking...I need to get out of this crazy town and ride more out in the desert. That's the most wonderful aspect of where we live, the wide open spaces, the smells of the sage and the pines. Nevada is home to endless remote dirt roads surrounding us in every direction, calling me for some time now. Except for a ride or two a year and of course a few trips to the Burning Man festival, I have been too busy."

"Ammo that's where it's at. The dirt is what these machines are made for. Doing miles of dirt, and getting lost in it completely. We can go almost anywhere on these. At least, I sure want to try to. Let's test the machines to their maximum, and find out the extreme limitations. After all, I believe Reinhold Messner once said... "*It isn't much of an adventure unless you get lost.*"

"I'm good at that," Ammo said laughing.

What Ammo was not good at was organizing all of the things on his life's mentally conscious wish list; he tended to let the moment and experiences come to him. When the right options presented themselves, he could somehow recognize them as being signs pointing direction. The feelings relating to the signs spoke to a higher part of him. If it felt right, he went with it - moment to moment. Viking's timing could not have been more perfect. Ammo did need a way to get away from the constraints of his personal life at that moment. His wife had been getting on his nerves, pushing him to become perhaps what he was not meant to be. The ride represented a release valve to facing some of his depressing home life reality.

Adventure was always a means to deeper truth, both Ammo and Viking lived for cliff hanging and stretching limits to find extreme life-and-death heart-pumping reality. Both would lead and follow each other equally balancing out reason according to the feeling of the ever-changing abstract road, never pushing the moments they shared high on mountains or deep into deserted valleys they let time and landscape take them. Besides having had a professional life for several years playing drums for hit-up beat art music bands such as the 'The Wangs' and blue grass bands like 'Rock-a-feller and the Down Street Boy's; Viking was a multi-talented electrical engineer mathematician and craftsman by trade, very clever with mechanics as well as a valuable knack for working on bikes. Viking was a fearless rider with a great sense of humor, always ready to tackle any abstract problem on the road or under the tank. In 2004, Viking planned a ride from Reno, 450 miles south to Death Valley, California, using primarily dirt roads through mining country and ranches on their classic, airhead, BMW R-100 Paris Dakars with 9.6-gallon tanks. They liked to brag about the most appropriate Enduro-GS 1000cc bikes for the money and what would best fit the long distance terrain of the high desert they called home. These bikes were as close to having an airplane as you can get as regular folk. In fact, they were developed into reliable touring machines by what was left of a defunct, yet efficient German aeronautics industry in Munich after the Second World War. BMW created well-designed carbs, shaft drive and minimal electrical systems; straight forward, you-can-fix-'em on the road with bailing wire and duct tape. Flat twin, two–cylinder, internal combustion engine the cylinders were arranged on opposite sides of the crankshaft. It is also referred to as a "boxer."

It was an intense feeling with the wind in their faces and a 360 -degree view, at 65 miles an hour through the warm Nevada desert in early April. One is left for hours totally alone with a helmet full of thoughts, only an occasional stop to discuss the scenery and, or new methods of riding on endless dirt. Viking and Ammo shared a fierce outlook to problem solving… all was positive and possible on the road. Everything could be figured out with pure perseverance and they finished each adventure in style.

Those early rides were particularly meaningful to Ammo and Viking. They were both enlightened by the absolute beauty of the vast, remote nature that became their literal playground. It was a transitional time, 2004, at 37 years old. Ammo was not getting any younger… it was time to make some life-changing decisions. Things were changing rapidly in the world. War escalated in the Middle East and the general public became more cynical and depressed every day about the state of political controls and media-induced political correctness changing the daily lifestyle in the states post 9/11. America was becoming paranoid and fearful of everything it seemed… mostly war, and terrorists-murderers, and Muslim extremists and many even started fearing our own government. The 2004 U.S. presidential elections were gearing up between two Elite Yale privileged fraternal club Bonesmen, G.W. Bush and John Kerry. The news was all diverted to the election full of repetitive stump speeches and spin doctors lying about the differences these two elite privileged puppets represented to the two-party system. The bikes provided an escape from all the political bullshit. Ammo fortunately for himself was too poor and impatient for a mistress, with an intense love of much deeper intensity for the mystical desert roads that called easily such bored men toward imagination and personal adventures.

Contemporary Nevada Cowboys

Viking and Ammo, in full gear and overloaded with food treats and artillery, rode over the Westgard Pass from Big Pine to meet Cyclops, who rode from Las Vegas where he had been trying a case. Cyclops was a thin strong healthy 60-year-old criminal defense attorney who rode one of several of his collected hive of black and yellow 92 R-100 Bumblebee GS's to courthouses all over the cow counties of Nevada. Cyclops had one eye, but no one could tell because for some reason he could see with that one eye better than so many who have both; he had a deep wisdom and loved to help the unfortunate, a true altruist.

A less afflicted man should hope to brag of accomplishments equal to that of Cyclops. He graduated top of his class in law school, one of the best criminal defense attorneys in the state. He was also a rock climber and windsurfer and he rode a tandem bicycle with his second wife across the United States and then through west and central Europe, and explored with scuba tanks the oceans of the Micronesian Islands. Cyclops rafted the Colorado on his own raft and climbed Mt. Rainer, Shasta and Whitney and trekked the Himalayas. Cyclops, by perspective of the gang he rode with, was the model of fearless optimism, a favorite comrade and role model of the young. It seemed he would never grow old.

The three decided on a rendezvous at Scotty's Junction where U.S. Highway 95 meets California State Route 267, just outside of the Death Valley Park on the way to Scotty's Castle. Orange, yellow, and purple mountains surrounded them on all sides and the sun was in the safe low hanging position for the right time of year for cooler riding.

Cyclops arrived wearing penny loafers, jeans and a Hawaiian shirt. Viking said, "Hey it looks like Hunter S. Thompson just showed up on a bike. You just need a long cig…man!" They all start laughing.

"Good idea," Cyclops said pulling a mason jar of fresh buds out and began to roll a large joint. As Ammo and Viking looked over Cyclops's riding gear shaking their heads.

"You don't have any leather boots Cyclops?" Ammo asked, looking at his old loafers covered in dust.

"Boots are overrated, "he answers." If it's so important to you, why don't you give me yours?… I like those. Those are cute. What BMW jewelry store did you give your life savings to for those babies?"

"You're a non-conformist to the end. We all know you have enough money to buy a complete wardrobe from BMW. As your riding partner and friend, I advise you to start dressing like an attorney, Cyclops," Viking said chuckling. "By the way, how was the trial? Did you win?… What was it about?"

"Boring case in Vegas, slot machine cheats and thieves, the usual riffraff clogging up the Nevada court. Basically I am just a plumber who shows up to push the clogged shit through the tube of the justice system. I didn't exactly win. My client had to plea to a misdemeanor, at least we avoided the felony."

"Well, that sounds like a good deal."

"Not really… a good deal would have been to go to trial and prove the case."

"Why didn't you? Ammo asked.

Cyclops turned to him smiled and asked, "What's the difference between a good lawyer and a great lawyer? A good lawyer knows the law. A great lawyer knows the judge. The prosecutor golfs with the judge in Vegas. They all golf together down there. I am odd-man-out in Vegas, a stranger. I take what I can get. Settle quickly and move on, thus saving myself, and the system money in the process. Besides, it gives me more time for rides."

Viking questions the logic of the topic, "Sounds a little jaded, Cyclops. What about your clients best interest? What if you could get him a better deal by going to trial? Did he want you to go to trial?"

As Cyclop's finger rolls the spliff and licks and twists its ends, he looked up at Viking nodding. "I explained it to him the same way I just explained it to you. If we went to trial, he would most likely have gotten the felony. Not the best idea, in fact the worst, but he got to take the lesser stigma that will follow him in his life, written into his records. You can feel the system out based on experience. Why waste time trying to be a star?… Overly optimistic lawyers who want to fight to the end for their ego and not thinking about the client's best deal, don't often live long, happy lives. Trying to be positive about a no-win future is foolish…It's the power of negative thinking, that ripe utility called pessimism that keeps us from wasting the day, gentlemen. I have learned to master it."

He then placed the tightly rolled joint between his lips and lights it up and passes it off to Ammo. Viking pulled out a map.

"I was thinking we could head down to the southern tip of Death Valley, to a BMW motorbike gathering at an old mining ghost town called Ballarat, off the Panamint Valley Road, where other Enduro BMW riders would be camped out?"

"That sounds cool," said Cyclops. "I haven't been down to the end of the valley very often. A big BMW camp out sounds like a trip, let's ride." He then immediately put on his helmet and tore off in a cloud of dust before Ammo and Viking could get their stuff together.

Ammo yelled! "He always takes off, that one-track mind, it is amazing we can stay together at all… we better catch up to him before he gets off on the wrong road. I don't think he has a map, does he?" They both hurried to put their helmets on and chase after Cyclops.

The BMW gathering was a real disappointment because out of about 200 people with RVs, bike trailers, generators, food catering etc... this threesome were the only ones who showed up with camping gear strapped to their bikes. Nothing seemed natural about this BMW club; it looked chaotic yet at the same time over organized, something like a small materialistic government. One of them should have probably asked what it was all about. Too tired to socialize, they just wandered around and kept to themselves for the night like silent observers who were never approached, accepted nor denied. Something anticipated as an eventful experience, rather-passed into the night with each rider reflecting on his own social perception. This Northern Nevada trio knew they did not fit in and the host California gang of weekend warriors sporting the newest high-dollar water-cooled and oil head toys

41

never asked them to.

In the morning they rolled up their bags, packed their bikes and headed north toward the Enilas Valley Hot Springs, a 150-mile journey into the unforgiving enclosure of hot wild desert off 190 to Lone Pine.

That night as they soaked and relaxed in the geothermal mineral baths, Ammo asked Cyclops… "Hey what did you think about the BMW camp out? I was a little let down myself."

Cyclops explained, "Most clubs are important usually for the weaker of species. Clubs tend to always ruin good times with rules and 'dogma-for-me,' kinda like religion does."

"Spoken like a true atheist, Cyclops." Ammo said, then asking him if he'd ever joined a club?

"Oh, yes, when I was a about seven we had a club called the Double Dukes… it was serious stuff in the '50s we were inspired by the Little Rascals. We did harmless stuff, threw hatchets in walls and vandalized things, got in fights over marbles and we had our own language even."

"Tell us something in the language Cyclops?" asked Viking."

"Hmmm!" he thought for a moment …"OK, E, A Tutti, selfi, Hi, Pi Tutti…

"What's that mean?" Viking asked, "It sounds almost Chinese."

"It is just like Chinese that's how evolved we children were of my generation, it means 'Eat Shit'… Hey, pass me that doobie Ammo... Thanks man," he said sinking into the warm water and staring up at the giant palm trees that surrounded the pool.

"Hey guys," said Ammo, "About the idea of clubs and what any potential organizations do to the concept of good times. What kind of club would you perhaps be willing to join?"

Viking interrupted laughing, "Hey! Groucho Marx once said,

"I would never join a club that would want someone like me to join," and they all laughed.

Then at the same time they clicked on it, as if it were as relaxed and destined as breathe itself, "What about a club that is no club?"

"Hey, what if we had a logo, what would it say?" asked Ammo.

"NO RULES!" shouted Cyclops, taking a long hit off of the joint, then blowing it up into the starry night sky.

"Ya, and no fees,"… agrees Viking.

The 'Club No Club.'

The CNC Logo reads: no rules, no fees, no code, just road.

Over the next several years, Viking and Ammo made it to every April ride from Reno to Death Valley together. Cyclops would try to make every other when he wasn't in court or fending off weird, needy girlfriends. He had many, the poor unfortunates who liked to cling to him because of his stable, dominating, and philanthropic character. His heart was pure and it was hard for Cyclops to say no to a young woman in need. They saw his weakness and devoured his heart and his pocketbook every time.

Over those years, the threesome would make many interesting friends, always inviting more people to join on the riding adventures.

CNC has no leadership at all, only a philosophy that minimalist pleasure can be exchanged between individuals and shared from the backs of their motorbikes under the stars. The CNC sounds subversive to an outsider, as though it begs to be something almost cult-like or threatening. However, it is absolutely void of any organization, or charters because to do so would be a contradiction of the total idea implied. No rules yes, but what is held as secret on the road stays on the road. Everyone shares the itinerary and choices of route, and everyone keeps an eye out for the last man. No fees, but everyone shares in food, extra gas and party treats. No code, just be careful. If you try to be a leader you might be the first to fall in the ditch. A rider also should want to be friendly to his partners because he might need them to help him get out. Getting a 500- pound motorbike over some of these roads in the middle of nowhere is a task requiring serious focus. Everyone works together in bad spots where the sand is thick or the water fast and rocks too high. The idea is to get there and back home again. Everyone will fall and get up and get back on the bike. No one will quit, you're not allowed, in the desert you stay on the quest, you rest at the oasis.

Over the years the CNC had improved their gear and skills and respect for the humbling ride and mostly towards each other. They also gained members from ages 30s to 60s and all of different characters and backgrounds, all interested in the moment at hand and sharing the experience of the beckoning road ahead.

It is a strange feeling one has when alone flying through the desert landscapes. Endless thoughts and memories that come into your little world within a helmet and the faint sound of wind passing as the sound of poetic music like the Doors plays '*Riders On The Storm*' from an ipod molding a living movie in motion. To watch the CNC ride through the desert from above, almost resembles a fleet of fast-moving road runners spitting out lines of smooth dust trails in a buzzing wake that they leave behind on the dry earth behind them.

The CNC are living history as they journey. It's their story. Yet, these modern day cowboys travel the same roads that only a handful of past travelers shared, and the places they will see being learned as described to them by rusty historical markers and vandalized bronze plaques of booms and busts on almost all but forgotten dirt roads.

Late one afternoon in April 2004, the threesome pull over at Panamint Valley road out of Panamint Springs to look at a spot on the map, called Barker Ranch off Wingate road near Trona, California. Cyclops explains that this was where Charles Manson hid out with his group of cult followers. The sun sinks in the west as time becomes drawn out. This significant yet insignificant at the same time sad part of history. Like all history that was once so important in a period of time in matters of life and death, have managed to stay harbored in our memories for some strange reason... if we saw news from any part of it we could never forget it. So, now what is the necessity for history's sake to see a ranch on the side of a road in the middle of Death Valley? They all decide the road and time of day and gas is not worth going out of the way to see a deserted hideout.

Viking and Cyclops put the maps back into the tank bags and Ammo takes one last look in the direction of a long dark desolate road, to a place he can only imagine was bigger than life at one time, yet for now as he sits on the most versatile of off-road time machines feeling the thumping power between his legs as it idles. Ammo is in the center of the universe when he lets off the clutch and gives it the throttle. He rides off into a different direction lit up by the suns cascading spectrums of colorful light on vast miles of sagebrush, Joshua trees, olive green grass, and purple and yellow wildflowers.

Contrast & Comparisons of the Four Year Olds

On or about August 3rd of 1970 while a little four-year-old boy, sits on the floor in front of an RCA 30-inch Technicolor screen. President Richard Nixon speaks on behalf of the American people condemning the acts of Charles Manson and his hippy cult-like family of followers, which hastens their prosecution.

45

What was it all about, why were Mom and Dad so intrigued by all this? The young boy looked on in awe.

"Why do such beautiful people that look like my mommy and daddy kill innocent people just because?" He sat staring puzzled, confused, intrigued.

Helter Skelter was Charles Manson's slogan. His psychotic fear was of a future where Helter Skelter or hurried disorder and mass confusion would arise. It is so unbelievable how this man was able to persuade with his own use of mind control such seemingly normal gentle good and loving flower children to kill for him and his paranoid psychotic delusions. Yet from this act was born a slew of conspiracy theories about government mind control, some implicating Manson as a juvenile test child with an unfortunate past in and out of federal reformatories and under some higher secret government control himself. There is so much written on this topic one can get lost in it completely. However, beyond the intrigue and temptation to go into it, let's leave it up to those who wish to find it on their own. For some, the ultimate occurrence or the ticking of time and the waves of change to society, that is what remains the saddest part of this particular story. The fact that the 'Manson Family' by use of an evil planned plot brought on by drug-enhanced mind control and manipulation closed the decade of peace and love; hippies, and free, intellectual, thinking about art, culture, community, and recreational drug use for their generation, some would say. Some could also philosophize the notion that the conscious mind having freedom of choice over reason, truth and reality, within a social political context was to be more controlled and monitored from then on.

Others can, and do deduct from this, that there may have been a conspiracy or that this was all planned in some way or because Manson spent most of his life institutionalized, that somehow the system could take some of the blame or all.

That all being said, 'tis neither here nor there: Whether he was prior to the event an experiment. He and the "Family Members" of the cult he organized most certainly have become one of intense study.

Take the four- year-old's parents in the Charles Manson headline news scenario. Imagine the couple watching the nightly news show in the early '70s; imagine also for a moment just for fun that you are in the room with the couple and the 4 year old boy, and you're all watching the news together:

The jester enters wearing a white doctors smock carrying a clipboard and sits down to observe the four-year-old.

A serious look comes across the jester's face as he begins a topic for which there is no right or wrong but only an 'open opinion'- 'an open mind' perhaps "Can both be one and the same he jests?"

One must take into context that a 4-year-old is unable to grasp combining a series of events, such as Charles Manson's cult, U.S.-lead forces against North Vietnam and movements into Cambodia and the National Guard opening fire on innocent students killing four and injuring nine protesting at Kent State University, the rise of inflation and debt and the start of the middle class squeeze.

The 1970s felt the pressure of tensions brought on from the cold war as well as Watergate, witnessing of the first caught-red-handed corruption case against an American President. Who to some could be likened to connecting Nixon's circles and dots, seemingly as if only fall guy for more delinquent string-pulling-elite-connected saboteurs who manipulated the executive branch during that period of time. The only thing this child recognizes is that Mom and Dad are feeling more frustrated when they look at the images on the glowing box, he sees it in his parents eyes... the imprint passed on to him from the box, which he sees as a threat and logs it into memory as such. A memory that could shape the child's future in one form or another, for good or bad, or both?

The jester pulls out an iPod and scrolls across the screen and declares this is not a unique conversation; we have been playing with this notion for centuries... Try this thought?

A Confutation questioning: *"Those mathematicians, then who say that the eye has no spiritual power which extends to a distance from itself, since, if it were so, it could not be without great diminution in the use of the power of vision, and that though the eye were as great as the body of the earth it would of necessity be consumed in beholding the stars; for this reason they maintain that the eye takes in but does not send fourth anything from itself."*

-Leonardo da Vinci

In fact, it could be debated that the child sees deeper into the eyes of its parents and feels the energy of the moment and that sweet moment is where the learning begins. Not from the singular experience directly learned later in age first hand; it is possibly the validation of the parent and the acceptance or denial that the child sees through the quiet movements of the eyes and energy of the adult it trusts to interpret for it. Maybe this telepathic language through deep connections is the way most of us all learned prehistorically and through the ages, as a means of survival, perhaps it is natural even today although not generally understood. It is a challenging topic of inquiry weather we are presented the true abstract mathematical formula via our subconscious feelings from birth that guide us to do the right moral act, and find the correct answer to please our host, those who give us life and feed us in our helplessness. Needs are the first feelings we have, need of love, nourishment, and direction. Perhaps all of what we get once we begin to understand human language is only that a second product produced, transferred, and reasoned out by the instinct of a mortal mankind in charge of the next generation. Many animals do speak with eyes, as well as some native cultures.

When influential technology or an unloving, or uncaring surrogate is used in place of the code transfer passed on by the silent biological parent, what then? We are deep into the visual age and our animal, natural processes are most likely at this point becoming threatened. These are the questions many have no time to ask. The math and competition for self-driven superiority in a growing technological world is moving faster and this state-of-the-art technology requires our speed to understand at an ever younger and younger age. Our sons and daughters are fulfilling computer and smart phone tasks in a matter of minutes with relative ease what took our fathers with master's degrees days to figure out. The corporations and brand names are eager to take over the role of parenting and it becomes easier for them to do so with every year as Mom and Dad spend their lives away from home, chained to debt and forced employment, a life in which they were programmed into by themselves because the joy to have your own castle full of stuff to play with has become truly addicting.

jester enters wearing headphones connected to his ipod:

jester's tip

This is an experimental random mix
Romantic science fiction story collides with art, science, and
philosophy play with linguistics,
poems symbolism, and observational-politics

The idea is to 'connect' the Narrator's/jester's narration,
stories and poetic mood,
Or 'jester's abstracts'- if you may
Brought in as pieces of a chain of events
in a linear sort of way

Read with search engines if you like to find new food
A treasure hunt of thoughts, keep them yours... stay in the mood!
For the reader to grasp the final purpose of the story
Hypothetically turning circular
If this abstract experiment should work
Go back reread find the quirk

From any chapter or skip
Grasp historical time frames, symbolic villains,
Hero's and characters, just a tip.

Draw your own conclusions make connect info
summed up to an end
Don't forget the jester's goal: understand a joker-jokes
Sometimes their jokes on us;
perhaps he's not a friend?

jester Logic
The Tale of Brother Jack

The jester's older bro, Jack, was an out-of-the-closet *heteroglossia*. After many years stuck in a cubicle, Jack suddenly popped out and became a famous franchise corporate spokesperson for fast food America. The first proving to humanity that the obedient consumer would rather take novel milkshake and cheeseburger advise from a giant toy head in a business suit and tie than from an idealized expert or average narrator. Jack's father collected '*Fabulous Furry Freak Brothers*' comics by the genius cartoonist Gilbert Shelton. When Jack was four, he remembered loving Shelton's art, and mostly the drawings and characters. One story stuck out so much as absolutely hysterical to Jack about a Cat named "*Fat Freddie's Cat.*" Anyway in this story the cat playing a part as an FBI agent who got stoned smoking grass, found himself lost and stuck in a hippie nudist colony, where he went on a rampage and shot a bunch of the nudists.

This sounds horrible? But if one were to read it and remember the demonization of the times regarding the dangers of smoking pot and intimidations felt by the conservatives and religious groups over hippies and nudists etc., it was a comic for adults, and it addressed the times. Jack's parents were open and let him find his way through what interested him on his own. They never made a big deal when he flipped through "*Playboy*" or the '*National Lampoon Papers.*' They looked the other way. Jack never asked questions about those images he saw. He didn't question, "why did the cat shoot all those hippies?" His parents preferred to ignore that he was reading it, rather than having to try to come up with words of reason to a four year old, whom they figured would forget all about it the next day anyway.

What Jack did remember was how cool the artist drew women's nipples that looked like 'Etch a Sketch' knobs and bullet holes that literally were see-through holes in people like Swiss cheese. This was what was funny to him. The Mickey Mouse character of the late 1960s and 70s seemed to evolve into a fluff of commercialization and plastic. For Jack the whole idea of Disney had blown up into a corporate profit-driven, heartless brand of money-churning sludge. Mickey somehow transformed into a Gene Simons' rock character from the 1970's rock band '*KISS.*' and, Mickey had lost all appeal to a depth-craving intelligent observer that needs a feeling of evolutionary meaning or motivated purpose in his professional opinion.

Jack was referring to commercialized, pop content. Gene Simmons, as a person on the other hand, seemed to Jack to be an intelligent, good father and family man. As far as sexual depth he was the Doctor Love. He had that, women loved him, at least they loved that pink organ he trademarked that flops out of his face. Jack being familiar with all the corporate comic riff raff around Los Angeles, thought Gene beats that do-gooder monoga-mouse Mickey hands down in that department. Besides, Gene says he is a drug-free music-making businessman and for the son of a Hungarian Jewish Mom-refugee from a family who lived during the Holocaust to make it as big as Gene, commands respect.

Gene Simmons seems to be a very wealthy, powerful, ego-driven man and he apparently made it all himself by becoming a jester, or a clown like Ronald MacDonald and Mickey Mouse and he's honest about it, not ashamed to tell you when ever interviewed. He lives it up and laughed his way to the bank. Gene cashed in on the long tong bloody mouth and evil-bad-boy stereotype brand he sold a lost generation of kids that wanted something different. In 1978 some born again Christians would say: "Burn them records, that Gene Simmons, he works for the devil. He's an evil Jew devil worshiper." "'Nasty that 'Bad Gene' We need to protect our children from this 'Bad Gene.'"

Problem with Bad Genes

Jack is an expert authority of superior quality and he knows the problems with Bad Genes. When Jack speaks people listen:

"There will always be an endless supply of 'Bad Genes'
"Why try to hide it from the kids?
"Who is going to be the judge of 'Bad Genes?
"Kids eventually get what kids want anyway.
"What usually happens when you try to keep stuff from the children?"

> *-Jack*

Jack, being a well recognized fast food market critic by nature, having a gift of the gab that places him alongside some of United States greatest contemporary talking toy head pundits, such as Bill O'Reilly and Rush Limbaugh on critical issues…

The kids are often much brighter than we give them credit for. Once, Jack's daughter, age twelve and a half, was watching the brilliant comedian Jon Stewart do his parody on "Fox News" talk show host Glen Beck's chalk board- drawing conclusions that finally lead to the Sesame Street character Bert as Hitler. Jack thinks to himself… "She can't possibly understand this humor?"

Think again, she explained it all quite clearly that "Glen Beck is drawing conclusions based on using peoples most simple and basic fears to gain their interests in his stupid show through shocking them." Not only is English Jack's daughters' second language, she also has been interested in jokes and how the world works, from age four in two languages mainly because she wants to understand her parents and what they are interested in. Jack has been watching the news sources of 'Comedy Central's Daily Show' and 'Colbert Report' on the Internet because, as opposed to the mainstream media, this type of faux news-real news has a strange effect. It has been one of the only news sources that truly keep some of us informed about the realities of a corporate media-controlled Republic. This sounds suspect of course, but these programs do it by poking fun at the entire media establishment, creatively showing absurdities through mistakes and hypocritical blunders. Everyone is targeted from the far right, the marginal and to the far left, as well as all races and religions... mostly politicians and pundits just delivering the news happening in the world every day, keeping it all humorous and sometimes provocative all at the same time.

Both Jack's twelve and ten year old children are hooked on seeing news that is silly.

Jack likes observing his children as they watch parody to see what they find funny. It is in fact the adult bathroom humor, and sexual innuendo that usually supplies the least interesting elements to these faux news programs even more so to children according to Jack. Again, the strongest and best aspects of this fake news parody lies in its intelligently motivated uncovering of political hypocrisy-through the use of creative off-the-wall "jest," and well-written twists constructed via-'abstractly connected' presentations of true life human contradictive insanity that makes one think.

Note to reader: This original parody artwork copyrighted titled 'Bad Gene' expresses an idea. It is an illustration of the extreme corporatized character called the 'Bad Gene' describing many modern era cultural questions in one symbolic design. The intention of this graphic is aimed to open the mind on topics of original thought. True art comes in many abstract forms and should never easily be belittled by heavyweight corporations when individual vision, speech and freedom are at stake. The very idea of the Retroactive Copyright Extension (Mickey Mouse protection act), a campaign the mega wealthy Disney Corporation continues to pressure, could be leading to dangers facing all artists in the future. Fair use concerning true intellectual art vs. Commercial Corporate-mass produced art, as Intellectual Property (IP) becomes a more tricky issue in the face of building a modern and freethinking technological age. The respectable Judicial branches must maintain opinions from both sides if fair controls are to be written by Justices that want to prove they know Jack.

Katka's Central European Upbringing

It's 1995, and Katarina Nova walks up the five flights of stairs to her parents' small two-bedroom apartment at the giant communally built block of flats, outside the city center of Brno Czech Republic. On the wall next to the door is a paper dial with cleaning duties and a moveable arrow pointing to family Novakovi. While turning the key as the door opens, Katarina is furiously greeted by a jolly robust woman in an apron who instantly helps her remove her jacket and shed her of her material worries of the moment.

"Hi Mommy, looks like it's your turn to clean the hallway."

"I know, I will do it Sunday," her mother answers.

"Katka," her father calls from the living room where he is reading and watching championship tennis on the local commercial-free Czech State network.

"Hi, Taty," she says, flopping into a large couch across from him.

"You look tired, did you get all of your lab work complete and up to date?" he asks looking up from a copy of '*Young Front Today,*' a local Czech newspaper.

"For the most part, but I have more going on than just the lab, so much it is not even worth going into."

"OK,' he said, "I won't pry."

'Thanks, Taty," Katka says while looking around. The only home she had known growing up in this little two-bedroom apartment and as an only child of a Civil Engineer mother and a business machine repairman. She is the centerpiece of it all. It's almost 7:00.

"I think '*Vechernicek*' is on right?" she asks.

Her father turns the channel with the remote. Up pops a little light blue cartoon character, the graphics resembling the 1960s style of animated art, the character takes off his paper boat hat.

"Good evening," he says in a nice child's voice and spins around in a spiral of stars and disappears. At this time Katka's mother enters the room and sits down next to her with a pot of tea and some open face sandwiches. They all quietly watch the fifteen-minute animated program together smiling and laughing as they have done since Katka was four years old. This was the child's program on state television developed in the 1960s, which came on every night of the work-week to put the children to bed, although resembling a tool. It seemed a most logical one that parents embraced as habit and lived by as if it were a form of ritual. Its multi-character story format was always sweet. Beautifully and peacefully designed, it uses several styles of artistically unique programs with gentle intellectual subject matter and masterfully created with various forms of hand crafted technically difficult puppetry and animation. *'Mat and Pat,' 'Krtek,' 'Bob and Bobek' Josef Lada* illustrations made into cartoons are a few examples of this great handwork done by small artists studios that were scattered throughout Czechoslovakia. It appeals to children primarily although adults easily fall into the soothing trance as well. This closing of the day calmed Katka as a child and took her away from her anxiety then same as it does now.

Today, this Czech families evening is complete. Today everything is as it should be and tomorrow is another day. Mom looks up at the small clock near the telephone, picks up the clean plate and tea pot returns to some work in the small kitchen quietly humming to herself. Father changes the channel and lowers the volume to a rerun 1970's Bohemian musical comedy, then picks up his paper and reads quietly. Katka lays back perfectly calm and falls fast asleep having returned to the center of her secure and perfectly adjusted world.

jester's 1ˢᵗ observation of world politics

   As the jester enters the scene he is wearing a black
top hat with dark glasses and black and white spinning
spirals over the eyes and a long black trench coat.
   History:
We all have our own eyes to see the strange forces
emerge.
We see experts shape world and history.
Explanation of past to present a mystery
Social times well sheltered, holds few truths.
The historian may paint it true and clear as day-
Or try to drive an opinion meant to blow it away-
History has a 50/50 chance

jester smiles wide like the Cheshire cat and lifting his
hands, palms up into the air he adds...
To know this present social reality is happening the way
we think we see it, furthermore to share together the
world's feelings from moment to moment via the intricate
new Internet tech mega share that is transforming the
entire world. Descriptive shared reason and truth is left
to a local attitude and perspective at that moment in
which shit happens. Reason and truth left to a divided
attitude as consistent as a wind in the eye of a real
twisting, expanding storm.

On the 13ᵗʰ of November, 2009, the Lisbon Treaty was finally
ratified by Czech Republic. Slovakia, now long independent
from Czech Republic, had already signed it and had even already

adopted the Euro currency. The Czech president held out the longest in the European Union because apparently, "I read it," said Vaclav Klaus to a local news journalist on Czech TV. Klaus was the last president of the completely sovereign and Independent Czech Republic. The headlines of the time told us he was forced to give in out of pressure from European leadership as well as his fellow members of Czech Parliament who were bought off by the elite Euro powers that wined, dined, and dazzled them. The Czech Parliament forced him to give the European Union the last signature they needed to enforce the treaty to push the Eurozone agenda without opposition, political blockades or referendums. The treaty would mould member states' futures in economics, defense, and environment without pesky interference from small state parties. This focused mainly in accordance with a direction passed on via a strong arm of authority controlled from non-elected Jack surrogates operating in the Joker-designed facetiously-shaped new Babel building in Brussels European Union Headquarters.

Some of the problems President Klaus had with the emerging new Union were mainly related to a new governing system where member statesmen are only given time and attention if they submit to the higher power structure. Any opponent who fights that powerful elite circle will be walked out on literally and-or made to look like an idiot until they give in and join the objectives of the ruling body in Brussels or quits.

The Euro was at an all-time high throughout this period, with investors confident in the new Union. Many of the investors in the states suffering from the housing and bank loan meltdown began moving their money into the Euro and EU stock market as well as other currencies, and gold and silver. This made the Euro climate seem all that more favorable and Europe seemed to be surviving the bank crisis that had started in United States, as was Asia and east Europe and Russia who were seeing their currency rise suddenly as well.

Super Europe Lasts for Almost One Year

Then, out of the blue in the end of that same year, beginning in 2010, with Greece declaring bankruptcy and the European financial meltdown was to begin to look ugly for everyone in this brand new union. The Euro value began to fall fast as banks in stronger EU states tried to help Greece, Portugal, and Spain from going broke as well. The EU, in a politically correct fashion, suggested and demanded austerity measures be implemented into states that had larger problematic social systems. They hoped to save them rather than dissecting some of the banking failures and holding the real debtors and politicians surrounding the banking and economic systems accountable for creating the problems that no one wanted to stand up to, forcing the money changers to take the hit. This blatant attack against the rising unemployed, disgruntled students who were unable to find jobs upon graduation, started to send masses into the streets protesting.

This is the news that took over the European mass media headlines.

In winter 2010, a new tool emerged and caught the whole world off guard... it spread like wildfire. In Spain, people used social media to call friends and family to the streets, joining in movements of labor protests against the economic ruling elite bankers and stock exchange firms, blaming them for the unjust division of wealth. Spain's 4.9 million unemployed and mostly young vigilant students used Twitter and Facebook to start a revolution that spread worldwide before the end of that year. Then into 2011, the growing movement started exploding into even larger ones that began to transform whole governments, ousting leaders and dictators in Libya and Egypt and throughout the Middle East. Journalists called that one the Arab Spring. Then, by the end of summer a wave of revolutionary spirit spread to New York City and Wall Street where masses began to call themselves the 99-percent, furthering the wave of energy back to Europe and worldwide. Protesters called for the 1-percent to take a long needed introspective look at how flawed their precious crony created "globalism" truly had become.

"jester Yells!"

"But wait, some question whether social media and Google are a means to a more threatening tool of totalitarian control. While other schools of thought maintained it could be a catalyst for greater Democratic Freedom."

For the late 2000s, the mobile phone/video/camera and YouTube, potentially may be showing us the key to our survival as a free race of Human beings, connecting us and protecting us from tyranny. We start to open our eyes and our minds collectively. Abstract gatherings of world ideas in thousands of cultures and languages, linking us into one connected movement, one giant community of unified thought all understanding the nature of shared skepticisms of our world's leadership now regularly being referred to as the "99-percent." Now a new kind of protestor emerges with a tool to fight the batons and teargas. A new movement begins with no declared leaders.

The technology race to own the ultimate internet-connected mobile phone gave a power to millions worldwide instant communication and a 3-to-8 megapixel video camera that can record and document and describe events as well as protect the protestors from police brutality as they unfold visual, violent and undeniable truths before our eyes via the Internet.

The division of the world's ideals and philosophies has begun to shift. To control it will take a huge sacrifice by the newly-titled "1-percent" cast structure, because the fingers of blame are beginning to slowly point upward.

What's keeping balance and sanity solid among the protestors?

What's keeping them from total violent revolt? In America, it's the amazing belief in truth and the Constitution. This great document still serves as a solid monument and as a symbol created by a highly intellectual group of unified thinkers, during an era of great enlightenment and reason. When knowledge of philosophy had evolved relative to a democratically driven moral reality of the times. The USA's founders wrote this document based on The Declaration of Independence and a premise that "we are all created equal and have a right to liberty and free speech and assembly," and that no free man is above the law and that "we hold these truths to be self-evident."

"Strong Stuff" yells the jester!

Democratic reality scares the Jokers
Those manipulative I doters' and T strokers
They dig, divide, draw lines and concur structure
in their favor.
Cheating, tricking, pushing opinions right left to suit

their flavor.
The cloak is ever thinner.
Their mass info spin of confusion bet
The prize to control reality a code of order fear has set
Some becoming immune to the spin
truth wakes some from their spells
The race and search for truth is on-pump fast!
Before a Joker drains the wells.

"God forbid," sarcastically swears the jester
When and if the military authorities and the police begin
to turn on their lords and masters."

In the fall of 2011, the United States of America watched as class warfare began via YouTube and independent Internet news networks. The mainstream media news outfits refused to pay serious attention to the civil unrest sweeping the country. The large media firms quickly found out it would be a mistake because it further lead to the distrust of the giant news corporations. This realization motivated back-room joker loyalists to push for the passage of bills like ACTA, SOPA, PIPA and TPP on both continents in an attempt to control the Internet. Jokers insist by taking away 'Net neutrality' they may disassemble Internet free speech, eventually controlling it as they have already done with the television.

Jokers scramble to rein in their loyal mainstream television and radio press, politicians and pundits and school them on the do's and don'ts regarding "acceptable information."

The Internet provides a completely different perspective contradicting the mainstream media; audio and video truths unfolded about what really happened to the economy and how badly the jokers had played their hands at it. Various Websites disclosed the truth that the ruling class had to use police force to calm the non violent protest movements of the new 99-percent which has spread and grows angrier worldwide.

The world's massive alternative information system awakened various social causes. This ignited panic and fear among certain mega-wealthy elite circles and ruling bodies, unable to control and easily subvert this ever-evolving unique new multi-sided movement. This in turn, sparked an invigorating effect throughout all walks, ages and races of humanity wordwide.

Talk of repealing the 17th Amendment began to circle Washington, perhaps in order to keep Senators loyal to the 1-percenters from losing future elections. A Supreme court symbol of modern Crony-Justice, Antonin Scalia, said regarding the Amendment in question:

"We changed that in a burst of progressivism in 1913, and you can trace the decline of so-called states' rights throughout the rest of the 20th Century. So, don't mess with the Constitution."

However, according to journalist Ian Millhiser's research... *"Before the Seventeenth Amendment was enacted, corporate interest groups were able to lean on state lawmakers and thus effectively buy U.S. Senate seats."*

-Ian Millhiser on Think Progress, Nov 15, 2010

Fear Itself Brings Out the Best of Them

The resulting situation became something of a circular snowball rolling down a steep hill of strange history, growing undeniably larger by the second, although poorly publicized on major TV news networks and ignored by the world's most prominent leaders. Millions of non-violent protestors started calling the elite 1-percent out. The movement interrupted political and economics speakers and pundits worldwide exposing them for what the activists and movements call "out-of-control greed driven by corrupt practices bent on favoring Wall Street, corporations and giant investment banks. Some arrogant political egotists made rhetorical comments against the peoples' protest movements, passing over them as though they were unkempt, ignorant, and unimportant slabs of meddling meat-monkeys…

The jester enters a kindergarten of small children wearing a purple psychedelic metallic lizard costume with a big round blob head made of a colorful combination of recycled plush stuffed toys. Bobbing up and down, suddenly the confident puff head sings out loud.
Praise Us!
Let us have their cake and eat it too…
Let them eat nothing and like it.
You must praise us for nothing as well
Praise, praise, praise,
We praise us for being so swell.
You kids praise us on a great job building your future hell.
"Boys and girls, I am afraid we have been invaded," He announces looking serious as he reads from a scroll he pulls from a pocket located at the center of his rear end. Pulling it, he extracts an ancient looking scroll. A foul orange toxic gas fills the air causing all the little children to run crying and screaming for cover. Rolling out the scroll he reads the following:

Invasion of the Newts

Like Machiavelli
The future American elite children
need a symbol of Conservative Capitalism
A man Symbol, who valued not,
Ike's post WW2- Moral Americanism
Rather embraced an era of true unified
world global Crony Egoism
A treacherous man who will show the world

he's the priori of that fallen fig
A man that should have been as smart as his head was big
A man that is cool as breeze and as bear as a brute
History will know his name, the great and powerful

NEWT!

If Newt were asked how to deal with the 99-percent, we could easily hear him using a historical quote from Joseph Stalin with applause to the oil corporations and military arms manufacturers and Wall Street banks who line his pockets. He could easily just smile at them…

> *"A death of one is a tragedy, the death of millions a statistic."*
>
> -Stalin

Newt is the kind of man who smiles when you ask him about his angry aggressive ideas.

One of the harshest unsympathetic politicians of our time and a perfect summed up example and symbol of the 1990-2000s era's neo-conservative was Newton Gingrich. Newt was one of the hardest hitting hypocritical Republicans who shamefully bashed President Bill Clinton for his private sexual affairs. Newt later had to give up his position as Speaker of the House of Representatives because of his own twisted affairs. In November 2011, Newt briefly became the frontrunner for the Republican Presidential nomination to run against President Barack Obama, a Democrat. But the politically correct Religeo-Republican public did not receive Newt favorably. His true-life story unfolded the veil before a symbol that painted Washington's worst in one package. It is no wonder why. Newt had Corporate Elitist Puppet written across his literally very large puffed-up cranium. He would not have represented even 25 percent of the country if elected. In fact, Newt Gingrich had been in Washington a long time doing his best to prop up the illogical systems. He was part of a revolving door political lobbyist bribery process that lead to crooked deregulation of the stock market and of banks as well. This corruption generated questionably legal, loop-holed, 'joker-cursed;' government policies that favored his corporate lords.

It made total sense that when the elites had their backs to the fire, they better get a real smart yet, nasty bad, bag man behind the curtain ready to do their bidding.

Newt was more than happy to present to the media his long list of previously well thought out "Newtisms," stuff like if he were the president:

"I would rather plan a joint operation against Iran than push the Israelis to a point to where they go nuclear," Gingrich said on the Wolf Blitzer show on CNN.

Newt used this rhetoric consistently with a gleam in his eye and total belief that he was right. He even weirded out some of the world's creepiest right wing news interviewers who usually don't blink at the absence of care that comes out of Washington. You could almost hear him saying to himself when he spoke to a camera. "I am so smart. Mess with me and I will intellectually screw you into total submission."

He was truly the evil type of Joker who likes to make others feel stupid and lesser while pumping his ego with their failure to keep up with his jaded mental capacity. Using his typical cold, shrewd, snide tactics, this man never showed any empathy for others or for their alternative points of view. So "Newtavellian," but if we watch world news and really listen to the rhetoric, every country has its Newts, far right, nasty, stuffed, egoist puppets from Europe, Africa, South America, Asia, China and Korea and out to the smallest little islands in the Pacific. Aggressive postulating Jokers all say the same things, pushing against the will and best interests of their public, towards enterprises that benefit selected minorities in high places of power and corporate infrastructures.

"**B**eware the Scali-Newts!" The jester yells, "Why do they dangle this never-ending Punch and Judy show? So have we come full circle? What is ahead for this "Brave New World" left crumpled in the hands of selfish Jokers lost in a wealth of drunken vociferous laughter? Are we truly as stupid as the 'Scalias' and 'Newts' think we are?

Is it this planet's destiny to be run over by a minority invasion of pig-like men; bloated up 'Scali-Newts' with massive egomaniacal plastic, corporate programmed brains to do their bidding?"

Chapter 3

Burning Man
"Newspeak" and "The Tool"

Before the birth of Club No Club, Ammo rode solo...let's travel in time, perhaps even take a peek into the experience of one lone wolf-rider's subjective reality.

Important is the time and date,...the last weekend of August 2001.

Our hero Ammo is covered in dust and dressed in an all- black leather jacket and old cowboy boots. He pulls up around 10:a.m. to Hugo's Bar and Café in Gerlach, Nevada, on his R-100 red and white Paris Dakar Enduro. Ammo was on his way back to his camp, his friends sent him out to Winnemucca to get some grass so they can have enough for the Burning Man festival. It is held every year through the Labor Day weekend not far from there out in the middle of the high desert playa of the Black Rock Desert. Every native Nevadan knows that Gerlach is the place you stop to fuel up because there are not any other chances when you get out this far into the vast big blue sky terrain. It is also well known for Hugo's Bar, and its homemade raviolis, with famous red sauce and garlic bread.

It's busy and he can hardly get a seat at the café, it is the start of chucker hunting season. All the dusty tourists and city folks mixed in with the desert locals and gypsum miners makes for some incredible people watching.

For this one-month period, as the festival usually takes all of the middle of August to the beginning few weeks of September to set up and complete, this little café in Gerlach makes more revenue than during the course of a year of regular business. Every kind of creature walks in and sits at the bar. Typical for this venue's social settings, rednecks in hunting camouflage laugh and buy beers for half naked hipsters with pink hair while a truck driver plays pool with a lady dressed in a white fur bikini, Sasquatch boots and goggles cover her dusty hair. Next to them even filthier playa-covered dreadlocked, black and white lesbians embrace each other. The local town drunk introduces himself to the women and asks if he can have a dance near the jukebox in the corner that is stuck on playing Dean Martin's "Volare." After the plate of delicious raviolis, Ammo takes a vacant seat across the hall at the bar to wash the meal down with a Basque pecan punch and a beer as a chaser. He orders and pays the longtime owner of the bar.

"Thanks Hugo," Ammo says handing him a fiver, thinking to himself, "Shit!" This guy is still alive and he looks great. He looks the same medium height, buzz cut, grey hair, light blue-short -sleeve-collar, buttoned.

Ammo has a flash of memory of his grandfather taking him on chucker hunting trips out to Gerlach when he was 12 years old. In those days it was either Hugo's or Josef's Bar and both places he remembered as fun even for kids. As the story goes, Josef was Hugo's brother and the two of them didn't get along that well. Ammo remembered town's people said they never talked, something about a woman in the middle, at least that was the type of gossip they throw around and expected everyone to be up on out in the one-horse towns in the calm remote regions of central Nevada. Josef died and the bar closed but Ammo always recalls the fondest memory of the only time he saw his grandparents swing dance next to the juke box at Josef's. This time Ammo watched the town drunk flop around the tourists and local miners all laugh at him spilling beer all over himself and bobbing up and down like a wild turkey. Ammo thinks back like yesterday to camping at the Gerlach city hot springs during the hunting season. "This place sure has come a long way."

Ammo remembered how the grandmothers would round up all the kids as though they were a flock of little ducklings when the hippies and nudists showed up to soak in the pools. The old women sporting conservative 60s big hair styles, puffing thin cigarettes would sit in their small silver Airstream camping trailers playing card games while the old school Nevadan males grumbled, swore out loud and shook their heads, all the time peeking through the window at the display of youthful freedom going on outside in the pools of warm water. It was a different generation that's all, but the forbidden fruit intrigued young Ammo all the more because, although he loved hunting and fishing with his redneck grandparents, his parents belonged to the tribe of the nude-bathing, acid-experimenting free-love generation.

Gerlach has since closed down the free downtown hot springs campground, but considering all that has changed this town is now known worldwide because of the festivals and land speed records and garage-built rocket contests that take place on the playa. Too many tourists now, and not enough room for a free campground. As Ammo looks to his right side, he can't help but smile and nod his head at the same time at a beautiful young plump blond dressed in a black leather bikini and a skimpy pair of black leather shorts with small feathery black angel wings. She sits on the stool

71

next to Ammo, noticing that he also enjoys the people-watching experience. She moves closer, "Are you going out to the playa?" the angel asks.

"I am as soon as I finish my drink," he answers with another swig of his beer and another smile as he looks into her young blue eyes.

"Have you gone out to a burn before?" Ammo asks her, already guessing she has because she doesn't look like a virgin, the title given for making your first visit to a burn.

"98, 99, 2000, and I was out last night," she said, long story how I ended up here some of it I can hardly remember."

"Of course not," he answered, "nor do you want to remember right? I know that the moment- to- moment experience grabs you out there, at least it has for me the last few years since I started to attend?" he asks, lifting his eyebrows.

"No, not so bad as that." She went on... "It was a harmless evening. We ate some Ecstasy." She explained looking into his eyes for a response, "Then I got a ride out here to get a real café meal and see what the civilized folks of the one-gas-station town were up to. It was cool, but here I am and I don't know where the rest of my camp friends went?"

After a long silence he takes another glance around the bar and café. Ammo picks up his black leather jacket and camel back which made him look a little like a futuristic cowboy of some sort, adjusted the collar nodded and smiled at the Angel and made his way towards the door, but then hesitated. Then, he turns back toward the young woman who watches him. He looks straight into her eyes. He sees she is also looking deep into his. He then returns to her side.

"Do you want a lift to the playa?" he asked.

She nodds, saying nothing just looking at him with a "What-took-you-so-long-to-figure-this-one-out" smirk on her face.

72

"OK, that would be great," she says with a sweet excited bounce, black angels wings floating in sync with the wail of Dean Martin, oh la la la, in the background. She hops off the stool, landing firmly on the floor in solid dust-covered combat boots. She grabs a small backpack made out of a stuffed animal cow toy from the table next to her and follows Ammo out into the day.

As they step out from the Bar into the one road-town and the door gently shut behind them, it seems suddenly quiet, almost like time has stopped for a moment, having gone from such a hysterical saturated social mix of characters into a void. The contrast is sense provoking, for that moment no cars went by and perhaps because it is getting on to the prime time of the lunch hour, so no one is in the parking area or the street. The heat rising from the pavement and the air still and dry, the middle-aged character in the center of his own fantastic movie, the hero Ammo stood beside the plump-breasted, blond, soft skinned, blue eyed, half naked, black angel in combat boots. Naturally, she goes right over to the dirt bike, somehow even though there are other bikes in the area, she knew which one is his. Ammo nods and puts the key in, turns up the petcocks and fires up the baby. Ammo then gets on the bike, reaches back to set down the passenger pegs for her and she jumps right on as though it isn't her first pony ride. Ammo feels glad because she only looks about 20-23 years old and he is not in the mood for a drama at the burn this year with an inexperienced playa friend.

At high noon they pull out off the main black-top road onto the playa and shoot out towards the center, a trail of dust floating behind them as they drift across the vast flat alkaline smooth surface. The young intriguing angel embraces the modern middle-aged cowboy, wind in their faces and energy driving their adventurous hearts. You can only imagine what they both think. It should be an intense day today with the hot sun shining and two days of parties, camping, drugs, art and play until the burning of the giant neon wooden man with fireworks show and then another day of partying before partyers burn the temple.

Ammo figures he is in the center of the playa now so he comes to a sudden stop, turns off the engine, and listens to the subtle wind. The angel seems as though she was hardly even there. He enjoys the fact that this silent stranger, even as young as she is, looks appreciative of nature. They sit here in the stillness together for a few minutes looking out at the amazing view of solid mass colored mountains and blue sky and tan cracked alkaline playa that surrounds them in every direction. Ammo then pulls the hose from his Camelback, takes a few sips while hearing every sound made by water sliding down his dry throat. Then he passes it to the angel. After drinking she asks him calmly, "You want an ecstasy tab? You ever tried it?"

"Never had it," he replied. But, I have heard rumors about this famous happy troop-numbing drug of choice said to have been used by Germans in WWII to keep them sedate and happy to be at the front lines, so why not?"

He takes it from her and without any question tosses it in his mouth and washes it down with a hose full of water. He then fires up the bike and they head in the direction of a small ant-like city in the distance that grows bigger and bigger as they approach it. Black Rock City for one week every year becomes the fourth largest city in the State of Nevada. It has no permanent infrastructure, however it is complete in all major necessities. It has firemen, federal police, and rangers, medical emergency assistance helicopters for evacuation, sanitary outhouses... enough to accommodate 40,000 people and a post office. It is the ultimate camp out just so long as you bring enough food and water to last your stay for one week. One can party and dance and frolic in every manor of creativity all for the rather lofty price of $180 per ticket in 2001.

Ammo enjoys entering the city from the privy locals, playa entrance... via the Burning man BRC Airport, which in 2001 is easy to enter and free, that is, if you don't get caught. Besides, he has the ultimate enduro made for this type of entrance. Most tourists enter from the main gate and went through all kinds of waiting in lines of cars and dust storms and police harassments. It's time to find a place to get out of the sun and heat and shed some heavy clothing. Angel is fine, perfectly dressed for the mid-day playa, and she knows it, angel wings flapping in the wind on the back of such a cool bike as they ride along the streets of campers she feels right at home, and as they circled the area, Ammo thinks his friends might be camped in the 3 o'clock area but was unsure.

The streets were all laid out from the promenade like a clock. The man was in the center thus 12:00 north and so 3 o'clock is in the eastern side of the city. Ammo decides to go to Center Camp or 6 o'clock down to the center of the city and see if there is a message for him on the greeting board. On the way as they make a turn they end up caught in a parade of thousands of women all riding bikes and contraptions and some walking all bare chested and some completely nude, every type of breast was able to be seen... large, round, artificial, small pointy and hanging, some painted and decorated-giant nipples, small nipples, nipples with things attached to them including many being played with all over the place. This emerges as a total boob fest in every way, all the women are so proud to be here, as angel bends over and whispers...

"Hey this is the famous Critical Tits Parade." Then she pulls her top off and joins in the fun, waving her hands in the air, wiggling her chest while standing on the pegs in full display as this pair moved into the massive shirtless group on the way down 6 o'clock to Center Camp. Then Ammo and Angel leave the area as the parade continues out into the direction of the Burning Man.

Ammo has a favorite place to park by a camp that sells ice near the coffee shop of a giant tent, those are the only two capitalistic enterprises allowed at Burning Man, the profit goes to the Gerlach High School to help them get whatever students need. As Ammo pulls up a guy dressed as a native from Papua New Guinea with a long carrot-shaped extension covering his genitalia comes towards him. This guy has many tattoos and piercings and a large horseshoe-shaped bone hanging from his nose.

"Hey man," he said nearly falling onto the motor bike laughing, that is a great sticker man, ha ha yea, dude, ha," then he waves into the distance while wandering on down toward a guy in a coon-skin hat wearing a skirt and flip flops. The men embrace and walk on down to view the thousands of Critical Tits massing beyond the central entrance to center camp.

"What was he saying?" Angel asks.

"Oh I think he liked the sticker on the front mudguard on my bike,' At least I think he said "sticker," Ammo rolls his shoulders and shakes his head.

"What is the sticker?" she reads out loud, "my other bike is a bike."

Ammo and Angel enter a tent almost big enough for a circus yet with much lower ceilings. They head towards the 100-foot-long coffee bar near the back of the tent, where Ammo soon throws down two dollars and orders a large mocha from a heavily bearded man wearing a dusty orange ski cap with horns on the side. They find a large unoccupied plush couch near the stage side of the tent and sit down together sipping on a shared mocha while watching all the hipsters and dusty characters wander in and out. Angel and Ammo begin to feel the effects of the ecstasy work in, relaxing their bodies into a laid-out position as they begin to undress and shed the heavy hot clothing. Each feels the cool breeze coming from the edges of the tent. Now Ammo sprawls out in purple shorts and bare feet, finally feeling the tension of the long journey, unwinding and taking in the colorful human display going on around him. Slowly and naturally within a matter of minutes they move into a spoon position and begin to look into each others eyes as they start rubbing each others arms and legs slowly.

"It was nice of you to give me a ride," Angel exclaims with lifted eyebrows, "that's yummy mocha!"

Ammo just smiles and sinks in a little closer to her.

He looks into her eyes. "This is interesting stuff Angel, can I call you, Angel?" he asks.

"Of course you can," she says holding him even tighter.

"Are you an angel?" he adds in an inquisitive tone.

"I am today," she replies and they both chuckle. "What can I call you?" she asks.

"What would you like to call me?"

"Humm! I think I would call you 'Side Car.'"

"So in other words, you are saying I am not the central motor of your perceived adventure?"

"Something like that. How often do we get a chance to ride in a side-car? Think about it."

"That sounds perfect to me, you're quite clever although I am afraid to ask your age?" he said.

"Old enough to know better," she says with a sly smile and a wink, "legal for you, but you don't scare me."

"Sweet!" He exclaims.

Now they are cheek-to-cheek looking out at the talent show being performed in front of them, as amazing dancing girls throw themselves around the small stage while drummers beat in rhythmic deep sounds that start to penetrate Ammo's whole body.

Ammo feels a relaxation so profound and yet he can't help but experience some anxiety at the same time because he just arrived and the taste of the experience is fresh, and this young woman is also. He remains cautious.

"I liked riding the bike," she says, still watching the performance. "It is such a fast journey to get here with a whole other perspective and almost like flying."

"You were the flying Angel today, I guess," Ammo says kissing her cheek.

She looks back at him, smiles and rubs her nose into his long hair, kissing his neck before focusing on the performance again. Ammo thinks of the randomness of this event. Here we were within a city of constant creative volunteer spirit, everyone focused on being a performer in the ultimate contribution. All who entered the Black Rock City receive a free gift of art form, but only if they open themselves up to it. Everyone does their own thing and shares it with whoever happens to show up and connect with their own abstract concept and everyone becomes a part of the exchange.

The dancers begin to move into very erotic positions in and out and back and forth they sway in time with a heartbeat bass drum that seems to shake the whole tent. The audience watches quietly engrossed. Ammo begins to feel something deep within him. He has to control himself. He is still a different person outside of here and away from Angel's arms. He has another life, although here to play. Guilt is not an option, only to savor each moment of value on this dusty dehydrated landscape. At least 80 other people in this corner of the giant tent at Center Camp surround him as a projected image of war and violence comes up in full color on a screen behind the dancers. Other dancers dressed in military uniforms and war helmets begin marching behind the two prettiest girls as animated tanks and planes fly over the entertainers who make dry sexual-thrusting gestures... while the drums and flutes wail in the background. Scenes from the film version of Orwell's "1984" are then projected with the words in bold lettering **"THE BROTHERHOOD OF MANKIND. TIME IS RUNNING OUT."**

The words stick to Ammo like glue, driving deep into him, for he took strong symbols seriously...nothing happened by chance from his perspective and never did. Life is always about living for the moment linked by seconds as they come at him through the journey of life. He did nothing that felt untrue to his heart-felt convictions. This time under the influence of a foreign and threatening yet intriguing substance and in the arms of youth brought on a powerful feeling. He began to think, "Who are we, what are we, and why are we the way we are? Why do we make the same mistakes on topics of love and war over and over again?" Ammo began to dwell. At the same moment, the drumming began to get louder and the whole room seemed to be connected, everyone looked paired up and some on couches in the front row seemed to be making love unable to control the energy or was it induced imagination that made this unfolding scene before him look as if feelings of sensuality were tuned up to lofty levels. Ammo and Angel just sat embracing the frequency, taking it all in. The freedom of that random moment was almost orgasmic in itself as though floating in a galaxy of stars, one complete moment where everything imagined and unimaginable conscious and subconscious seemed to fall into place. The heat, the sweat, the cool breeze, the smell of coffee incense and old re-cycled carpets and thrown-out used couches. The projector flashed one last reference to "1984" in large bold letters surrounded by several symbols and logos of the world's religions and corporations as the drumming and flutes slowly died out in the background and the dancers slithered their way off the stage while a blast of playa dust blew across the stage and a cold chill entered the tent as if it were a code of warning. Ammo questioned if he was truly awake as the projector ominously flashed up on to the screen overhead in large stenciled letters as the dancers silently exited the tent and the music faded away:

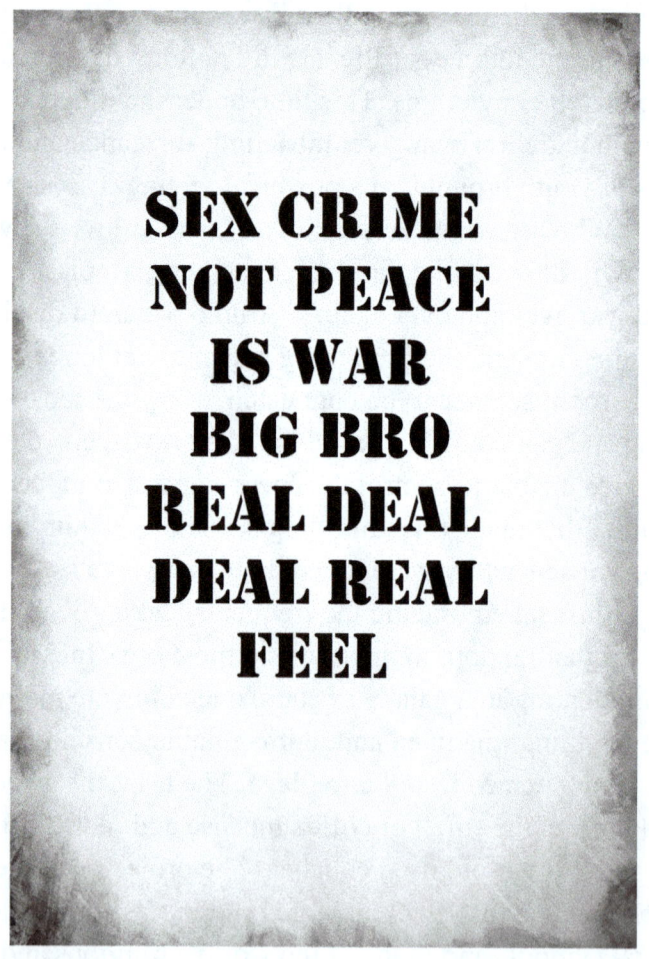

SEX CRIME
NOT PEACE
IS WAR
BIG BRO
REAL DEAL
DEAL REAL
FEEL

A Tool That Replaces Books
and The Parent Is Born:

So, while our four year old watches "Sesame Street" in 1970 (a children's educational TV program in the United States) he begins the journey of visually enhanced education through the use of a new medium.

Around 1926, Scottish scientist and television inventor John Baird created the first grey-scale image of a moving person sent long distance.

When the first TVs were suggested at the beginning of the 20th Century however, many people disliked the idea and became wary of it as they felt an uncomfortable feeling of distrust that the government could look at them through the new invention. The race for new technology moved forward by this time and the images were not so good with the first tests. People actually lost interest yet the potential of this concept kept the research moving forward. In 1928, improvements emerged based on an idea discovered by an un-manipulated open-minded American teenaged farm boy, Philo Farnsworth, while he looked at rows of plants in a field.

This "abstract connection" of thought between agriculture and mechanical electrical science inspired Farnsworth to use a cathode ray tube to project lines of several light and dark small images. To display these in a manner that people could see and visually decipher, the images were projected onto a glass screen tube close to itself as if like the irrigation system of a meticulously laid out crop. Thus the "tube" revolutionized and gave birth to the technology of the television, introduced to the public at the 1939 Worlds Fair in New York. President Franklin Delano Roosevelt gave a speech to everyone who attended via the new

RCA corporation's TV, which by the way had quickly taken over Farnsworth's patents and technology.

A visual tool the likes of no other in history

George Orwell, ironically finished his book titled "1984" in 1947. No doubt the explosive addition of the television era played a big part in the way he wrote that book. Orwell painted us a picture of the future in the form of a large TV screen in every home with the face of "Big Brother" looking over the masses with the all seeing-eye of authority. Orwell's creative definitions of the future state used *"Double-think"*, "molding two contradictory beliefs in one mind simultaneously." For example, peace is war and war is peace... further confusing an acceptance of both. It is a way to inform the public of that which the state has no clear doctrine, all in order to deceive the citizens into obedience. Big Brother also uses *"New-speak,"* which Orwell formed as the basic "mutability of the past." These devious manipulators simplify the language making it smaller every year in order to remove unnecessary vocabulary, transforming communication into a more colloquial easy-to-grasp-version. All this is done in order to make the proletariat gradually more dumbed down and easier to control.

Perhaps Orwell was experiencing that tragic depressing time he lived in at the end of two world wars with all the destruction, fear and manipulation as natural progressive cause and effect. Or did Orwell know something he could never say out loud unless it was in the form of science fiction? Naturally, the prospect of a "telescreen" in every home projected an ominous threat. In fact, the fear of the TV in the early 30s and 40s possibly was not only of a projection into the homes of citizens, but also the chance of retrieving images taken from private homes that this possibility upset post war survivors. That was perhaps the fear then as is the fear now. Orwell tapped into these frightful concerns.

"1984" did not literally arrive on time as prophesized. However, could it one day if we give up and forget to keep these wonderfully written symbols alive?

With world conflicts relaxed, for a short time after WWII civil rights made a move and it came from the ground up. The world began to think again outside the box. Fear of race and color took less time to alleviate with a new television technology. The demonstrations and its illogical-unevenness, could be seen by all.

Technology steadily became a force used both for good and bad intentions at the same time, knowledge and truth as well as for deception, corruption and lies. Suddenly we are bombarded by a mass of information in a new visual/consumer age, and it's all requiring our attentive critical reasoning. The peasants are eating it up excited. Yes, excited about who is supposedly winning and who is loosing an election to rule over whole nation's thirsts for oil, booze, and football, and for what is new at Jack in the Box.

Baby boomers, and black and white Television
The end of WWII 1950s gave way to a thriving economy
Most gluttonous time period in United States history
Much of the rest of the world was dealing with
takeovers and revolutions
Life was so good for the average American
Why be concerned with earth rape-destructive profiteering
institutions

Or for what shenanigans that were going on outside her lucrative
borders
War machine on hold for a spell, new conflicts wrapped in an
American flag Pentagon gives the loyal orders
The Korean War, then Vietnam in the 60s
Both wars financed, fought with fewer lost lives than,
Previous wars because of new tested technologies

A General should know that Peace is Real
However, A no-bid death machine is too lucrative to
turn off or break a deal
You're out of time you made your rhyme
Say the "Christian Jack bought by Jewish AIPAC
Arms a well paid Muslim hack."

Blood must pour, so drain the whore
It's up 3 points trading on the index
Despite In 1961 President Eisenhower gave his speech
The "Military --Industrial Complex":

"In the councils of government, we must guard against the
acquisition of unwarranted influence, whether sought or unsought,
by the military industrial complex." -Dwight D. Eisenhower

This was not just a warning to the US but to the entire world. President Eisenhower's speech was very informative. However, the average busy working American had difficulty understanding the nature of this warning and his full implications for decades to come. It wouldn't happen until we were so deeply abused both by involvement in the battlefield and completely economically bankrupt by a 1-percent virus at home due to the abuse of power that he so eloquently prophesized.

Jester's 2ⁿᵈ Observation of World Politics

A true jester surfing the accounts of tragedy won't forget or forgive Dick!

Today we read the headlines from the Internet: The BP disaster, one of the largest catastrophic oil spills in history in the Gulf of Mexico. Tons of crude oil leaking into the gulf and no one could cap it. Leaking for several weeks, gulf marine resources will be negatively affected for hundreds of years. As we read on, it stated that in 2005, at the urging of Vice President Dick Cheney, Congress created and President George W. Bush signed the Energy

Policy Act, written under the guidance from the oil-chemical companies themselves. These devilish regulations retained the focus of Cheney's Report into law. These new rules included what has become known as the 'Halliburton Loophole,' " which removed the authority from the Environmental Protection Agency to regulate a potentially dangerous deep oil drilling process invented by some companies including Halliburton." These self-serving regulations gave them the go-ahead to overshoot and commit environmental rape literally on land and offshore.

Halliburton was one of the largest providers of products and services for oil and gas and military contracting industries. Vice-President Dick Cheney was once the chairman and CEO of Halliberton prior to becoming VP.

A jester enters a nicely dressed crowd of international scientific dignitaries holding a huge glass of wine in one hand and a filthy black bucket in the other. He is dressed in a pin-striped suit with yellow rubber boots and grapes and leaves on his head as he dances spilling the wine and throwing fish heads out at all the spectators who cover their hands in front of them so not to get hit by the flying oily dark blood and guts hurling towards them.

"Dig it," he sings laughing loud at them...
Simple orgy of the Bacchus like
New Roman and Greek gods
Oil it up, HA Ha!
Stick in your guns
Protect us, you-we do
Drink everyone...drink up!
Up on top are we, just a small corner
of the US garden-Umm!
Now try the taste of Asian Fish full of aluminum perhaps...
Did that British Petrol Company fuck up anyway?
Conveniently you forget.

"Forget everything...
We make all the bad news and history vanish." The
jester laughs. As for your soiled garments your exterior
subjected to the wake of our elaborate illustration.
I suggest, perhaps 'Ross Dress for less.'
Get your 10% off coupons on your way out.
By the way everything is on sale.
Everything!"

Just Forget Everything

On September 11th 2001,
A happy little family had just begun,
When the twin towers fell straight into the ground,
Everyone was confused and angry... the news media went ballistic
Yet our U.S. President and Vice President seemed so cool
at the same time nihilistic
As time changed the big story continued to
unfold quicker and quicker
Because of the Internet age it became increasingly apparent
That perhaps the truth be known might resemble something sicker
That an agenda to push for a war with Iraq
to set up bases to poke Iran
Was more necessary than chasing down invisible terrorists
Camped out in caves in Afghanistan
Faster and faster this illogically portrayed recourse
Geographical position covered by creative spin took over the
political discourse. Suddenly the Jokers, Jacks and Presidents
Of our great 'Constitutional Democratic Nation'
Are seen making gestures, even bowing to
Kings and Queens... A true abomination

Chapter
4
Ammo; the Rabbits, Indians and the Whip Man

Ammo comes out of a deep and powerful dream. So much has just happened, he wants to recall the episode. But as all dreams invariably come and go, his awakening takes over the moment as he adjusts to an entirely different place where he is surrounded by colorful pink, white and light blue pillows. Above Ammo and all around are several LED white lights attached to a geodesic dome covered with some kind of clean white cloth. The bright place seems, almost heavenly.

He looks down to see that his black-winged Angel still lies next to him. She remains fast asleep. Behind him, a small triangle shaped opening in the dome reveals a beautiful mountain scenery. The sun in pastel color is starting to rise in the east and from his estimate of direction they are somewhere in the eastern part of the Burning Man camp city. Next to him, two men and a woman, all dressed in white rabbit costumes, lay around a coffee table on pillows having a conversation on conspiracy theories and such. While at the far end a tall black man behind a bar wearing white rabbit ears whiskers, pink nose, a bow tie and no shirt pours what looks to be mixed martinis for another person in a rabbit costume. Held by a tall blonde white angel with feather wings this customer sits on a stool with a man wearing devil horns with a chain around his neck, held tightly by the angel.

"I'm in a rabbit camp, hmmm!" Ammo thinks "What happened last night?" Far too tired to get up or talk to a stranger or even move, he just sits there taking in the moment and slowly waking himself. He listens to the far away sounds, distant mixes of techno music from dawn parties still going on all over the playa.

This is a rich camp he notices. There are bottles of Dom Perignon all over the floor, and trays of half-eaten open-face brie and caviar on French rolls. It must have been a good time. Little memory comes back to him of the night before. The champagne probably destroyed what memory he had left. Ammo hates champagne, even from a $650 bottle. Ammo just continues lying there relaxed and calm, his eyes closed listening as he awakens to a conspiracy theory that had been going on all morning.

"You're smoking crack, Ibrah!" Yells a big hairy bearded guy in a bunny costume at the coffee table next to Ammo. A thin half naked girl in a slim-cut Playboy bunny costume and a fuzzy tail replies…

"Shhh! Tone it down, man. "

The other forty something skinny rabbit, a male, with one ear flopped over his face and expensive gold-rimmed glasses says while forcing a toned down voice...

"It's true. I heard it myself from a friend at the country club. that's why I decided to take some time off this month." This man bends over to snort a thin three-inch line of cocaine laid before him on the long coffee table switching nostrils half way.

The girl pipes in. "Our investment firm was told to close temporarily by Labor Day this month, and all of our operations are on hold until after October first. Shit! They gave us all paid leave."

"That's weird, something is up," says the skinny guy with gold glasses. "Under normal conditions I would never be able to take this much time off. I mean, this is awesome a whole three weeks

88

off and only one great party after another. Have you been watching the stock market? Up until I left for the Burn, it was acting strange as hell."

I have noticed some jumps and several of our clients stated they were interested in particular put options and short sells, and get this. They all seemed to be interested in placing trade orders the same weeks in the beginning of this month, September, when we were all to go on vacation. Honestly, that is why I was confused because our firm had to place several time-activated orders. Something strange also, they were very similar plays.

Skinny Bunny continues, "Well, just before this trip I was noticing the market act strange again with big dumps and big buys being made suddenly for no reason and by some of those majors who pull the strings. I always get nervous when that happens because it usually means a surprise is coming. My father trained me to watch out for these bubbles. He said we take care of ours no matter what the world's brass have up their sleeves. He made his fortunes keeping an eye on them."

"Also there are some crazy theories out that there is some "event" and it might be an attack." said the big Bunny.

"In the NY Times, last month there was an article about a guy who ran the FBI's counter terrorism in New York who lost his briefcase containing a mountain of info on counterterrorism and espionage, being put together to do harm," added the skinny Bunny as he taps a Deutsche Bank credit card on a mirror forming thin long lines of white powder.

"Oh right, I saw that as well," the girl said, taking a snort from off of the coffee table. "I always make note of those when the market is weirding out. It was some FBI or CIA cat. Not much went public from that one story though. Have you asked your friends in high places about that incident? It sure seemed like a game changer at the moment. They should know what 'Event' the mystery men have planned, their right up at the top of the club?"

"Shit, we probably know more than they do about it," the skinny guy interjects while placing the rolled-up dollar bill down on top of the glass next to the lines of coke.

"We are the futures traders, it is our job to worry about what could be. Anyway, they just take orders; they don't care. They don't want to know the detailed plans, none of them. They just want to collect on what ever goes down. They stay in line with their tongues hanging out drooling. As long as they keep their positions of power, they could care less. We care because we shift all the funds around. No one wants to put them in the wrong spot or make a bad bet. Everyone watching the flow stressed out, though, that's for sure. It is good to be away from there right now. I was getting sick of the phone calls; something is truly weird about the NYC exchange right now. That's all I know."

"I got the same info from our side. Glad my office is in Connecticut just the same," said the fat hairy rabbit as he took a sip from a fancy looking bloody Mary.

The girl leans down and in almost a whisper she said, "You know if a sizable "Event" goes down all the players on all sides are going to be filthy rich if they are betting the war card. Everything I have been following is gearing up for it."

The fat rabbit comments: "Well, that is if they made the right bets. It is still anyone's game. We all have our theories and no one knows anything for sure."

At hearing this, Ammo began to feel a little uncomfortable but remained quiet, playing dead so not to let the rabbit threesome in on the fact that he was eavesdropping. He stayed there in his own thoughts that continued as the strange conversation went on next to him. Angel awakened, yawned and looked around.

"I love this place wow, cool dome," she said, conveniently alerting the threesome of rabbit-conspiracy theorists that they were no longer alone in their discussion.

Ammo saw this as a perfect moment to act out. So he rose up, yawned, and said something to the same effect, looked over to the threesome and smiled and they smiled back and said nothing.

"What a night." Angel exclaimed!

"Yes it sure was," replied Ammo. He paused...

"Can you tell me what happened?"

"Oh you were fine," she said. "You were just real happy and all the rabbits loved you."

"What does that mean?"

Angel laughed, "Oh nothing too crazy. You were very sharing with your grass and they all wanted to share their expensive drinks and food with you in return, and we danced and had long conversations, and it was all super dooper fun!" Still with a hang over, she said this in sort of a giggle.

Ammo should have felt good about this news, but in reality he was a little drawn back because he liked being in control. He liked knowing what he said and did. "It's the damn alcohol!" he told himself.

He had a problem with it, although he hated to admit it.

"Don't be bummed," she said looking into his eyes and giving him a big smile. 'You were fun. Everyone liked you."

"What's the plan?" he asked as the black bunny from the bar put an Irish coffee down on the floor in front of them.

"Good morning and thanks for the ride around on the bike last night. I will always remember that. It was just like flying! By the way, there is a great juice bar on the Esplanade between 9 o'clock and 11 o' clock. Between two big palms, it's called The Oasis. I will be heading there soon to DJ a noon mixer. Drop in if you have the time." The black bunny added with a nod and a smile. Ammo looked at Angel telling her, "Now it's coming to me. I gave him a ride yesterday afternoon, after we jumped around on the trampolines with that blonde cave bear girl from Hollywood and the gay dwarves from Idaho. Now I remember, he was the one who invited us to this party. Now I remember," he said, feeling better.

Angel asked him, "So, shall we make for the juice bar after we finish the coffee?"

"Juice sounds good," he replied. "Who knows, Angel, if we take the bar tender's tip after all it is from a supplier of a key Irish Java, perhaps by following the dark rabbits directions through the tangle of mysterious paths which surrounds the endeavor of our temptations, perhaps we will find the juice provider of the 9/11:00 Oasis?"

With that thought he took one last glance at the threesome still engrossed in their little toot fest. Something gave him an uncomfortable feeling about that party.

On the way they toured the several central playa art installations spread out all over the alkaline dry earth bed. One art piece was a solitary phone booth with a sign that read "Talk with god." Angel spent a long time on that call.

Ammo wondered if she was asking how long she was to remain fallen. Then they climbed up the tower that held the giant 'Man' and looked out over the Tent City which seemed huge, at least three kilometers square from end to end counting the orange fence that circled the entire area at its boundary. The orange fence kept all the trash in, both animate and inanimate. The animate playa trash was busy with everybody showing up thousands by the hour; lines of cars enlarged the camp by the minute, because that day was probably the single biggest amassed, all-inclusive, free-volunteer party held in North America and perhaps the entire world. Every spectator was in some way a creative contributing part of a giant natural buildup to the anticipated lighting of the large 150-foot structure of 'The neon giant wooden stick Man.'

People were flying in on parachute, paragliders and ultra light planes, Cessna airplanes, playa windsurf boards and sand sail-rails, and every kind of strange art car, art bike imaginable from solar powered space ships, to Spanish Galleons with dance hall-sized decks to trains made from salvaged school busses pulling DJ party bars, and scrap metal dragons shooting 20-foot-long flames of fire.

Ammo pulled up to the sign that read Oasis Juice Bar, right where the rabbit told them it would be. Very cool set up, meticulously laid out, the all-canvas giant tent had two towering palm trees out front and looked like a Lawrence of Arabia Saharan oasis.

Everyone was smiling and friendly, welcoming them as they entered through waving white curtains. Inside all over the floors were colorful eastern-themed carpets and eastern art hung all over the tent walls. They found a nice place to sit together in the back as a sweet girl noticed them and brought a small clear plastic cup containing something like a non-alcoholic pineapple, orange, mango, concoction with ice plus a plate of hummus and pita bread. Fabulous and spicy, it tasted as good as anything he had had out in the real world. This was exactly what Ammo needed.

The Black Bunny bartender from Rabbit Camp stood behind a table upon which turntables handled the music. He had taken off his rabbit hat and whiskers and pink nose and traded those for a tan and white turban which made him look like an authentic Arab sheik. He noticed Ammo and the Angel and waved. People danced near him, and the whole place emitted wonderful incense aromas amid enchanting music and everyone seemed to be very relaxed. Love permeated the air, and you could feel the energy swirl around. Angel reached into her cow bag and pulled out a small plastic container shaped like a monkey head with a big mouth.

"You want another?" she asked, placing a tab in her mouth.

Ammo took another sip from the juice. "Sure," then he held his hand out, took the pill and acted as though he put it in his mouth. Then he clasped his hand and found a pocket in his shorts to dispose of the drug for the moment. He was enjoying a clear mind and wanted to catch up, but didn't want to miss the opportunity to have a chance to experiment again in the future.

Ammo seemed a little more attached to this young thing than he would like to let on, but knew it could go no further than this momentary friendship they shared, a special happenstance that would eventually be broken down and removed and burnt into time and space. Only the memory would prevail. But this is the nature of the 30,000 people event... no permanence and the acceptance thereof.

On this Saturday, Sept 1, 2001, within two weeks there wouldn't be a trace of human existence left on the playa. Not a center tent coffee shop or a parade or an art installation or a geodesic rabbit camp or juice bar... not even a piece of chewing gum wrapper or a tooth pick would be noticed anywhere around, that is how an organized and enjoyable happy-to-be-living event is taken down with as much care as it was built up. All that will remain is the alkaline playa with a few burn and tire marks scratched across its surface.

Angel started talking to a tall brown-haired fellow who looked like d'Artagnan sporting a goatee and long mustache, wearing a pirate hat laying next to her. She had begun to have the love need. This time, having refrained from another dose, Ammo was more contemplative. Thus she moved closer to the pirate who seduced her with his inviting quiet voice and advancing smiles. He seemed nice, and looked closer to her in age. Ammo returned to his thoughts, lying by himself, listening to the calm Middle Eastern techno electro rap music and comfortably watching the cast of characters who came and went from the tent.

About an hour later a gay couple, one dressed in aloha flower skirt and the other bare-chested in a grass skirt came in looking for a place to sit. Naturally, they looked like they deserved to be there more than Ammo. So he gave up his spot, took one more look at the Angel with black wings. To him, she looked content in the arms of the handsome pirate. Angel and this swashbuckler kissed and held each other tightly. As Ammo walked towards the exit, Angel looked up noticing her ride was leaving.

"Excuse me," she said to the pirate, and then stopped Ammo at the door... "I want to give you a thank-you kiss, Sidecar." She threw herself up into Ammo's arms and drove her lips up firm against his.

"Thank you, enjoy yourself, Angel," he said, looking over and nodding at the pirate, who watched them with a concerned look on his face.

"You are an Angel. Keep being you, Peace and Love," Ammo said with one last smile then turned and let go of her hand.

"Peace and Love, back at ya," she replied as Ammo slipped through the tent curtain and was gone.

As Angel turned and walked towards the back of the tent toward the pirate, she suddenly stopped and pulled the cow backpack off her back, took her black wings off, folded them and stuck them into a large 'Ziplock' bag. She began to strip while some in the room started to notice and some whistled and yelled and prodded her to take it off. Animated by the encouragement, she began to dance while taking off her combat boots, throwing each one ever so carefully to the pirate who was laying down completely bug eyed. She then peeled off her black leather bikini, releasing two well-shaped natural soft breasts with large pink nipples and put the garment into the "Ziplock." Then she reached back deep into the bag and revealed a long sapphire satin nightgown and a fake diamond and plastic gold tiara and lace gloves and a long pearl necklace. She then began to shake and wiggle her belly and plump breasts and rolled her body in wave motion to the exotic Turkish-East Indian techno-rock music that the DJ kept splicing into as if he already knew her dance style. Her voluptuous rump rolled in a round circular motion. She had nothing on but a g-string, then she tastefully slid the sapphire gown over her privates, while pulling the g-string down her leg before throwing that into her cow-bag. She put on the tiara and then slowly each lace glove and necklace with fluid grace and class she bowed to a large applause and then slowly made her way towards her pirate who was smiling and shaking his head as the crowd cheered and the young server placed a new giant cup of deliciously spiked fruit juice into her hands, adding a hug and a thank you for the fine show. She lay down next to the handsome pirate and fell into his arms.

He then asked her gently, "Are you a Sapphire Princess?"

"I am today," she replied with a sigh and a big happy smile while snuggling closer to him.

It was getting into the evening when Ammo left the Oasis juice bar. On the playa, the sun fell in the western sky and a dust storm blew in from the south. By himself, Ammo felt a little alone and lost suddenly but not for long. The minute he threw his key into his R-100 and hit the ignition, the sound of the bike and the thumping of the exhaust through the tail pipe reminded him immediately who he was and where he was going. He was home already, this desert was his home and this mass of creative-world tourists that happened to camp in his back yard every year made it all that much more exciting.

Magic Mik and Harvard told Ammo via a note left on the Playa Greeting Board that if he was lost the night of the Burn he would be able to hook up with them at Cowboys Space Camp, somewhere around 1o'clock or so on the Esplanade. So wearing nothing but shorts and cowboy boots, Ammo rode off towards the east, past the busyness mounting in the center of the playa where many people kept busy setting up the giant Man for the Burn. Ammo thought to himself as he rode by: "In about four hours, this place will be swarmed with people going nuts as they light that big wooden bastard on fire. This is the life."

As Ammo pulled up to the space camp on his bike, some busy guys in cowboy hats worked on a giant truck that had huge projector screens and an amazing sound system. He turned off the engine and asked one of them wearing nothing but a Speedo and dirty-shit kickers if he knew Magic Mik and where he might be.

The cowboy looked around and asked if anyone knew him?

They all shrugged.

"Check in the dome." One of them suggested.

The dome they were referring to was also a giant geodesic where it looked as though a huge party appeared to be going on. Ammo parked the bike and walked in. It was well shaded inside and cool. About 30 people were scattered everywhere dancing. In the back of the place up on a large platform shaped like a hot dog there was Harvard in full skinhead and a wizard's robe turning records and projecting amazing images that he had taken of native cultures wearing tribal outfits from all over the world where he had toured as a special guard for diplomats. Ammo took a seat where he could get the best view of the show.

Harvard was a well studied, talented photographer. Before that he did special combat missions as a professional Navy Seal who was always more than happy to inform anyone that the elite combat troops like the Seals and Green Beret commandos and special forces military would never allow a dictatorship or monarchy operating rogue to rule over the United states military; a military loyal to an American code of realistic conduct, order and truth that defines our country. Harvard impressed Ammo as the truest and most serious American-loving patriot he had ever met. Harvard knew the inside of the war machine and saw all of its strengths and weaknesses, and he was an artist and realist at the same time.

He would say the new president and vice president are gearing up for something. Everyone he knew on the inside at the Pentagon got promotions and larger checks so long as they went along with the new executive direction headed by the military contractor King Dick.

Ammo sat thinking about all the long conversations he had with Harvard on the topic of being able to sense that something just didn't seem right about the new Republican Executive Branch. Both could feel it in their hearts. The men became suspicious of how the election was decided and all of a sudden so much strange friction started brewing in the Middle East. It also was good for Ammo to know that an intelligently balanced soldier remained skeptical of the leadership.

Around this time Harvard put in a techno house music jam and hit the switch for the smoke machine. Magic Mik popped from out of the large crowd, emerging from foggy pillows of smoke floating out into a sea of wobbling waves of colorful dancers. Magic wore a white doctor's smock and a silver wig, dancing his way uniquely into the center of the dance stage. He slid into an amazing almost robotic dance. Awesome, everyone cheered him before he noticed his friend on the sofa at the side of the room and moved over to Ammo and slinked down into a flop on the couch next to him.

"Wasssup!" he said in a long slow groaning sound, grinning ear to ear.

"Where have you been? All our peeps have been wondering about you, Ammo?"

"Out and about Magic, just following rabbits and angels, stuff like that."

"Cool, I like both," Magic reached behind the couch and extracted a large Mickey Mouse-shaped balloon. He started afresh to inhale long deep breaths from it, then passes it to Ammo.

Ammo took the navel of the balloon to his lips. "Suuuuus –psooo," went the sounds as the air escaping through pursed lips.

His head became heavy and static. He flopped back into the sofa then numbness shot towards the rest of his body. Feeling as though someone robbed his bones as he lay limp in the sofa next to the silver haired robot dancer in white, who suddenly in somewhat the same position fell fast asleep with his mouth open.

Magic was a genius computer geek, professionally diagnosed with what his parents assumed to be A.D.H.D. Magic hated *Ritalin,* however he was more than happy to give it away freely to folks that he figured were more in need of it. He was also a veteran hacker who worked in cyber security, and new almost everything about the latest Internet firewall technologies. He had the inside scoop on all the strange antics the new Internet security and high-speed surveillance systems being programmed and prepared to offer this new concept referred to as a "New World Order."

Ammo, Harvard, and Magic would spend long hours into the night discussing the strange reality and ominous threats that a militaristic-tech empowered world posed to humanity. Although very confusing to understand, this language became symbolic of a powerful change happening faster and building by the second. Magic was an all around unique creative individual in his mid 20s, with amazing amounts of high energy, but unfortunately suffered from a severe addiction to nitrous balloons at that time of his life. He always had a surplus of positive upper directional, motivating, mind-altering magic goodies, always happy to dose a friend in order to liven up their experience a notch. Personally, Ammo couldn't understand how anyone could get addicted to such a thing as nitrous without getting severe headaches, usually developing one if he had more than two huffs.

Ammo awakened on the sofa, and looked around, noticing that Magic and Harvard had gone. The whole empty place seemed dead, the sound of a huge party off in the distance.

"Shit! I missed it. I must have slept three hours," he said to himself. "I shouldn't keep mixing all this stuff when I haven't slept." Next to him was Magic's white smock. He threw it on, jumped up, and headed out into the cool evening. It was dark. From a distance he saw the giant fire blazing. Upon observing dim, quiet, still camps, he left the bike not wanting to ride. He walked into the madness and headed towards the fire.

Ammo approached within what looked to be the halfway mark at the time. The man was already crumbled down into a pile and the flames were only 20 feet high off of a clump of debris gathered at its base. Everyone had already started to leave the center and move about in their eclectic menagerie of lit-up art cars. People by the thousands went past him back towards their camps to party all over in the other directions. By the time Ammo got to the flame it had become so small that some characters were already roasting marshmallows from it. Although having missed the burn, he felt completely sober and full of energy, following a long needed sleep. So, he headed out on a walk-about. Within a half hour of leaving the fire he headed toward a large white cloth fence in the shape of a ring. At the entrance was a message:

WELCOME ONE AND ALL TO OUR FIRE CIRCLE, PLEASE COME IN AND JOIN US WITH YOUR ENERGY AROUND THE LARGE FIRE, PLEASE CIRCLE THE FIRE CLOCKWISE AND JOIN US IN PRAISE OF THE GREAT SPIRIT AS WE PERFORM OUR RESPECTS TO OUR UNIVERSE TOGETHER.

Ammo joined a circle of hundreds of dancers around the large wood fire. He circled a few times in the clockwise direction, but it felt so strange to him, until suddenly he closed his eyes and found himself spinning into an overpowering trance that reversed his polarity causing him to travel in the opposite direction from the rest of the dancers. It became more natural, and as he danced he felt extremely powerful. He danced for hours circling and reversing directions when it suited him without rest or water and no one bothered him. He danced until workers took down the fence that surrounded the fire. The sun started giving color to the eastern horizon.

He danced until there were only about 25 people left dancing around a very small fire. Suddenly the drumming died down and all dancing quietly stopped. Without a word, all dancers stood still looking out towards the rising sun. A man in a top hat with feathers stood out between the sun and the dancers and spoke to the ethnically mixed varied people who remained. He credited them for carrying the fire with strong spirit that night.

They stayed and kept the energy moving and the music remained strong, the night magical. However, These were only a single handful of the hundreds or perhaps thousands who had passed through, having danced all night for hours till dawn. They were the givers and the receivers of the blessings of the Great Spirit on that night as well.

The gift of the sunrise was theirs to remember forever. They all started to hold each others hands' in a circle, looking at each other and smiling. Not saying a word, they all had a powerful moment: some laughed sweetly and some cried quietly. As the sun rose higher, everyone began to hum in unison. Frequency getting louder with the heat raising their tone, intensifying with the increasing rays of light shining at them. After the whole sun became visible, the shaman with a black feathered hat spoke again, thanking everyone for coming and sharing in the fire, the music, and the dance. Then everyone smiled, made their own subtle goodbyes and departed in different directions toward the camps.

It was Sunday morning, Sept 2, 2001, the day they burn the temple. Ammo wandered into Fish Camp at around 8 o'clock, a gathering of about 20 people laying around outside all over the Esplanade. Some crazy *Hooligans* played all Black Sabbath songs, like karaoke lounge lizards throwing the mic to whoever wanted to sing one. At the same time another group busily made breakfast for whoever showed up. The smell of sausage and bacon sizzled steam into the fresh morning air. Sober, smiling and friendly, everyone cooperated on a volunteer task of giving life and nourishment to the soul and the stomach.

This connected moment-to-moment construction of time marked a placement of life, as if a puzzle piece landing for that moment into exactly the spot it was destined for Ammo laid back and took in the slow BRC Village Morning Show the sounds, a sweet melody, rhyme, lyric, a symbol not by accident, precise to the moment of time. As the flawless band played out...

> *Red sun rising in the sky*
> *sleeping village cockerels cry*
> *Soft breeze blowing in the trees*
> *peace of mind, feel at ease*
> *"sleeping village / a bit of finger"*
> -Black Sabbath

On Monday, Sept. 3, Ammo road to camp at the Dog Pound Hot Springs on the east side of the playa and camp a few days alone to reflect on the whole heavy experience and soak in the healing minerals. Then he made a restful calm ride past Planet X through the Joke Creek Desert, taking another stop at Pyramid Lake for a few more days of camping, swimming, meditation, and yoga.

Ammo got so high on nature and tuned into a peaceful feeling while riding his bike over all the ragged back roads. He hadn't felt freedom like this for years. So much went on in his head with so many mind-altering experiences, and so many interesting people as well, but he took his time returning to Reno. "Why rush," he thought, "Just go with the flow."

Ammo watched the sunset from the shore at Pyramid Lake on a still and quiet evening. While he sat there looking out in a trance to the multiple display of magical color laid out in front of him, a group of young weekend partiers pulled up in a pickup truck. They blasted loud music, and yelled and drove in circles, kicking up dust on the beach. The moment they stopped the pickup about 100 yards down the beach from where Ammo sat, one or two jumped from the back bed.

A sudden violent windstorm sent dust and sand in their direction engulfing the truck and the visitors before they had a chance to even set up their camp. The strange thing: although only 100 or so yards away, the wind was just a calm summer breeze hitting Ammo. Within minutes the group packed up their camping chairs and beer and left. The wind died just as the pickup went out of sight, and it was again calm and quiet.

Ammo was not surprised. He knew the powerful spiritual nature of the desert lake. Many Native Paiute mysteries and myths surrounded this ancient mass of pure water. Ancient teachings from hundreds or thousands of years ago tell of the connected Grandfathers and Grandmothers who guard her and keep this natural gem mostly undisturbed. Which she is, and has remained. You either love her or you hate her. Those who loved her respected her and gave thanks and were welcome. Those who came to only take… beware, she will torture you some way or another. Furthermore, one must be careful of what one takes home from her. It could be the thing of destruction.

It was Sept 9 when Ammo arrived at the Pyramid Lake Indian Reservation to visit his good friend, the local medicine man. Ammo drove up a dirt road to a large two-story tract house surrounded by sagebrush, old cars and campers, two scrappy looking dogs came out to meet him.

"Hi white boy," Ammo said to the one that seemed to play the Alpha male. "Where's the crew?"

"Hello," said the medicine man's father who came up to the screen door…

"Come in, it's open," an old man about 5 ft. tall with a straw cowboy hat answered, as he greets Ammo at the door.

In his late 60s, the medicine man's father, J.B., impressed Ammo as a wonderful, positive man with many great stories and the kindest heart. J.B. always invited guests to the kitchen and offered coffee or cookies or Indian fry bread with beans, what ever food happened to be around. You were expected to make yourself at home.

"Where's Warm Bear?" Ammo asked, taking a bite into a giant Indian taco covered in beans.

"He's down at the sweat lodge preparing for this evening. A group from Reno is coming in whose mother passed and they asked him to help them with some medicine."

"How was Burning Man?" J.B. asked smiling, his white teeth showed wide next to his soft reddish-brown skin.

"It was great man, I had so many good times. I don't know where to begin," Ammo said shaking his head.

"So, when are you going out to see it, J.B.? …I mean you live only right next to it."

"Oh d-know, I think it'll be too much fun, cuz they got all

104

them necked girls out there. I don't think I'd make it back home alive."

"Perhaps, but wouldn't that be a great way to go out?" Ammo answered as they broke into a good laugh.

Paiute as a culture are not very talkative, but when they do talk, they prefer jokes and funny stories to just about any topic. Risqué jokes are preferred above all others. Ammo then took the last bite from his taco and washed it down with a final swig of black coffee and went to the back patio door. "I think I will go down and see if your son is down by the sweat lodge."

J.B.'s house was quite a ways from the lodge, down near the edge of his large farm. Ammo got on the bike and road in the direction of smoke lifting in the distance near some large cottonwoods. Getting closer, he noticed that the fire had just been lit and the logs were stacked up over several volcanic rocks being heated in preparation for the sweat. Warm Bear sat in his usual seat on an old metal folding chair near the entrance to the sweat lodge. His cousin Skippy tended the fire poking it now and then with a pitchfork. In following Paiute customs Ammo remained low key around the stones and fire, in respect to the Great Spirit and the grandfathers, who it is believed watch over all things in relation to the ways of the sweat lodge teachings. After parking the bike some distance from the ceremonial area, Ammo walked around the fire and took a seat next to Warm Bear by the fire, greeting him with a nod and saying nothing.

"How was the Burning Man?" The large 6-foot-tall Indian asked with a smile.

"It was cool, but I got drunk and stupid and lost my way a few times, but then found my way again in the end. So, by and by I guess it was a success, much more on the positive side."

"Did you find a soul mate out there?" Warm Bear asked.

Ammo contemplated the question for a second: "Briefly

yes, there are so many out there but I just keep going back to 'my baby.'"

"You like that motorbike, don't you?" Warm Bear asked while rolling a cigarette on his lap.

"I do, she is the symbol of all that I have in the world. She keeps me on track. She makes me return to where I belong."

"This is good." He said, "Everyone should know the limit and probability of one's wishes."

As Ammo looked into the flames, he told Warm Bear the story of the fire dance he experienced on the playa, and how he felt in a trance throughout the night of the burn. He told how he felt more comfortable going in the other direction than the others around the fire.

"Is it weird," he asked, "to dance that way against the flow and energy coming at you?"

"As the soldier, also known as a 'whip man'," answered Warm Bear, nodding his head. "It is normal in certain native cultures, for only the whip men can dance opposite. They are like experienced warriors."

"But I am no experienced warrior," Ammo said, shaking his head. "I am a peace lover."

Warm Bear put the cigarette into his mouth, lit it with a stick from the fire, took a drag, let out the smoke and then continued: "You are a spirit of the stars as we all are. Peace is part of war and war is part of helping to create peace. Both are a part of the delicate balance of life. It has always been this way. There is no escaping it. Our people know this too well. Unfortunately most of our race lost the colonization war that forced us into unfavorable treaties that continue to be violated by the ever-hungry white thieves. However, the elders spoke of an end-time that would come."

"Not an end of the world?" asked Ammo?"

"No," he continued shaking his head, 'an end time that would bring with it a great shedding of tears and sadness and divide the people for many years. We on the reservations have been living that reality for many generations and now the white men themselves will feel this reality for the accumulation of disrespect to the Great Spirit and the order of nature. The warrior spirit will return to retaliate and wash the virus-like evil human away. It happened before, long ago. That is why our people respect the Earth and its creatures. We remember respect and value true reason and reality."

"Who will be affected?" Ammo asked.

"Everyone will, again, it started a long time ago and has been building… And those who stay close to their un-labeled non-extremist spiritual convictions and follow and respect the ancient medicine will go on to where they belong. And those who play games and use fear and harm other creatures and this Earth out of pride and unwarrantable privilege and ignorance of care, waving symbols and religions and false Gods. Those who try to play warrior chicken hawks disregarding history, will go to meet their appropriate ends as well."

"Wow that's heavy man!"

"Yes, but it is nothing new, it is a shaman's dream yes, but many of our native Brothers and Sisters throughout the world who have kept the old ways alive, hold on to this to give them hope. "Hope that the old way of honoring the four directions, return to the lands and colors of people, for whom those four directions of conscious-connectivity represent. It is the only way we will heal the land's pain with intelligent-connected ideas protecting the Mother that make mankind one again as caretakers of the Earth and all her delicate and important creatures above all. "So will you be joining us tonight for the sweat?" He asked as he put out his cigarette and began tying tobacco offerings.

Ammo shrugged, "I have been clean the last few days but,

I drank and did some mind-altering drugs out on the playa. Not sure if I should go in, I am a little afraid. I have been partying and playing so much lately I think perhaps it would be better if I stay out and help tend the fire. I can bring in stones for you."

Warm Bear, a very tolerant medicine man said nothing, a sign for Ammo to find his own way.

People started showing up, as the time came to start the sweat. The sun set in the hills to the west. The lodge door faced east, the fire perhaps ten feet from the entrance, although flames subsided, the coals had been built up, having cooked for several hours. Warm Bear set out tobacco ties and his stone with feathers near the skull of a buffalo in front of the lodge door. Other people gathered and since the ceremonial chalice was out of its sheath, no one spoke as men in skins and women in T-shirts wore only towels around their waists. Participants entered the circular dome made of willows, old blankets and canvas tarps. Each turned clockwise honoring the four directions before they knelt down and crawled inside.

After everyone made a circle inside and the medicine man gave the word to bring in the stones, Ammo and Skippy took turns picking the glowing red stones up with pitchforks and placing them through the small opening and into the center of the lodge. After the last stone went in, Ammo knew that his visit there that night was no accident and everything leading up to this moment had been just time and life experience unveiling itself as it always had. Instinctively he began undressing down to his undershorts, removing his watch and gold ring. He turned in a spiral and slid inside and sat near the small opening.

"OK, let's close it up," said the medicine man. Ammo pulled the blankets down and sealed the door to complete blackness, so not a single beam of light could enter the lodge. Nothing could be seen except the dim red glowing pile of hot lava rocks at center.

On Sept 11, 2001 Ammo had just pulled up to his office garage from his long two week motorbike vacation. He noticed hardly any traffic on the roads at 8:30 in the morning. Ammo felt used up from so many days away. He wanted to go home but had an important business meeting that he needed to prepare for later that day. His next-door neighbor, Kelly, a talented professional blues musician, met him in the alley as the garage door slowly closed.

"What's up, Kelly?"

"Hey man, you have to see this! Come quick," replied Kelly.

Kelly lived in a two-room, two-story small Victorian rented shack that looked like it could fall to the ground if you blew too hard on it. He liked to say it was "Jethro Bodine on the outside and Donald Trump on the inside."

"Hey what the hell is on the TV that's so important? You have an end-of-the-world-thriller Hollywood epic, planes flying into the trade center, shit! Looks like real... good computer graphics... Cool, hey Kelly got to run, catch you later. I have so much to catch up on."

"Wait! Wait, no it is real." Kelly said grabbing Ammo by the arm. At that moment Ammo finally noticed the CNN logo across the bottom of the screen.

"What the ffffu!" Instantly Ammo felt nervous and his heart began beating hard. He had to sit down.

"You want a beer man?" Kelly opened a Miller High Life and sat down next to him to watch.

"No thanks."

"It was a replay of what had happened in New York Eastern Time an hour or so ago," Kelly said, sitting down next to him on the couch.

Within what seemed like minutes the first tower collapsed. Everyone from the East to the West Coast watched live. The memory was burned into him as it did for everyone worldwide who turned on TV's to see live coverage on that day. Many disasters and events have come and gone that destroy innocent lives. This one was different, live and in full color on a 48-inch Sony, the pain and agony of visual death so real, graphic and perfectly orchestrated. It changed the human frequency of the planet for a day. Phones rang, traffic stopped, and time itself went on hold for an entire world.

Ammo's cell phone rang and his meeting was canceled.

"My meeting canceled, do you mind if I watch a little of this?" Ammo asked.

"Are you sure you don't want a beer, man?" replied Kelly.

Ammo said nothing while Kelly just opened one and put it down on the table in front of him. Ammo spent the next hour and a half just watching the whole thing live sucking it in like a sponge into his mind as if he were supposed to figure it out himself…as if it were a puzzle of time that made no sense… Perhaps this is what the white-powder snorting Rabbits in the desert had kept talking about. Now, their statements kept returning to him as he sat hardly sipping his now warm beer.

Just then the Jester walks in and sits down for the first time next to Ammo. They watched the show together and from that day forward. Like a little skeptic untrusting twin or alter ego interloper, the jester enters uninvited and constantly piping in nodding, smiling and pointing out every nonsensical jest.

And the cheeky bastard won't shut up. And, he never will.

"Event"

This one "Event" may change the whole concept and direction of democracy further projecting, confusing and manipulating our world's leadership by painting a picture of a new kind of invisible enemy that could be anyone-anywhere-anytime and is an enemy of the entire world.

One "event"
One "event" despite all the conspiracy theories
Or accepted professional blessed political points of view
Surrounding it, or shrouding it, or shielding truth from you

One "event" would show the world the power of the corporate mainstream blues
CNN says one enlightened surfer, "is a tag for constantly negative news"
Giant, corporate news corps, commercial monarchy use of digital cable
Endless ads while the loyal public plugs it in and pays the dues
One "event" proves beyond all doubt a conspiracy to go to Iraq was used

Arranged out of retaliation they say-to this one "Event," like sheep the useful pundits bleat "Iraq-nukes-Al Qaeda–Terrorists-Saddam," "Our American ego has been bruised."
Pull in the Generals- send out the Jokers, the Jacks will spread some lies
The facts: a corporate, constructed propaganda, spin-machine implemented this Iraq War's demise.

"A popular government without popular information or a means to acquire it-is a prologue to a tragedy or a farce or both."
A warning from... James Madison

Yells the jester as he dances out into a street ringing a large hand held-bell joined by several other jesters, all yelling and shaking signs and looking serious but cheerful. The streets are full of busy people going about their workday, our jester now holds a loud- speaker up to his mouth:

"We are told to hate them, they tell us things that sometimes make more sense. -But they are lies so say our leaders, the men calling themselves our democratically elected brethren..." As he dances and sings his rhymes, the busy mass passes by, some smile and some frown, some shake their heads up and some just look straight down.

Yet he can't seem to stop. Nothing will stop him no matter what he has to sing.
A baker bakes a shooter shoots and a jester jests, the bell we must ring."

Decade of Conspiracy Theory

Don't blame me it's what you see pick it out on YouTube and it's free
Hard to believe, thus...
This is what they tell us:
That we are nothing more than a commodity
Just like vegetables, livestock, or Bio-D

Every year ruling body gets closer to handling all of us at all the corners
The all-seeing eye, Big Brother, "Atilla," "Ingsoc,"
Builder-ham-burgers
Growing us up and extracting from us and feeding their mergers

When we are strong and buy more they love us
When we are weak and poor
They find a way to weed us some more
Use us to kill each other off, the money always stays in their big
troth

If the conspiracy theories are true
Endless power, wealth, security for a chosen few
Internet news says that it's true
They say we are run by a mysterious secretive elite power structure.

Who use a cloud of defense top-secret demand it is safe
US Air force blasting electro magnetic pulses into the ionosphere
with a HAARP
Was the 'A Bomb' test safe? Ask families of soldiers behind
the Ground Zero tarp.

'Geoengineering,' of Aluminum, Barum, Magnesium
Cooling our atmosphere their spokespersons
say is the purpose
As our soil PH degrades becoming ridden with metals
rendering it worthless
Monsanto develops genetically modified seeds, which can
grow in the horror
A divine plan; fit us into a trickle down loyal consumer-based
insect like order

Follow jokers on up, through series of strict direct teats they
say they draw the boarder.

Big heads give plans to a body of fake Experts of brown
nose cushy weak clans
Blatant theft from the masses, greed driven hypocrisy
Selfishness Objectivist or emigrated-Austrian econ run aristocracy
Capital, Crony Intellectual Jacks worship refugees like
Friedrich August von Hayek

New School University "Geistkreis" the rich- Reich write
the book run the psych

They should shower- get jobs say these New World Order freakers
Use NAFTA and let them eat more cheep Chinese sneakers
Buy rights and drill steal oil and now water
Sold back to us in plastic toxic bottles marked up 100% profit on
the dollar

When Corporations are asked to provide their fare share in
proportion to earning
The CEO cries "please!" For handouts to toss on the
flames of debt that is burning
Such Egoist-Egotistical disorder,
Where is Evolution of mind?

Think, has that not been the goal of mankind?
From the start of creation
Evolve from a primitive state to supreme
elite thug incarnation
One with aspirations to become as like Gods
to rule the Earth
Abundance belongs to the ones strong and intelligent enough
to seize its worth

Hold on to it... fight hardest for domination to maintain
The dirty needles in the vein,
the power to control its very flow
Tighten the rubber, drill deeper put in the screw
More oil and corporate money buys more intellectual
power to drill for more goo

Intellectual power to corrupt more... in order to make more
They continue a plan to build hell,
Huge profit from pills for Alzheimer's, and children with
ADHD and cancer as well

Joker's profiting from this show must
have a one-track brain
If they can't see there is no healthy natural future in gold
surrounded in plastic
Chemically saturated, electro-magnetically
confusing and toxic terrain.

This time the jester enters wearing a Native American headdress full of eagle feathers and he is seen holding up a roll of toilet paper in one hand and a turtle shell shield in the other. "Did the European White Man revered for his ingenuity and prowess for stealing and raping the Earth ever expect to loose control as times of enlightenment encouraged spreading out wealth and sharing resources?" Everyone gets a little of his own shit on his finger now and then and everyone hates it when it happens. It is a human mistake. No longer do the checks and balances of a once-organized superpower of experienced connected intellects guide and notice a sham. Because those who go to Washington or Brussels to represent their flock are more interested in wiping each others anuses and washing other members of Parliament or congresses or the Executive Branch or Judicial courts systems. This results in foul shit on their fingers because we accept looking at this shit when it's from our own baby and or our own buddy, but not and God forbid it be from your own hands... Phooey!"

If Orwell Were Alive After Sept. 11 He Would Probably Say

The USA Patriot Act was developed by the "ministry of love and thought police using methods of manipulation like "newspeak" and "doublethink" in order to supersede our Bill of Rights and go around the Constitutional Amendments that protects us from unwarrantable governmental abuse against the common citizen.

Wikipedia Definition:
A patriot: is someone who feels a strong support for his or her country.

Would a real, intelligent, true patriot sign such a thing as the Patriot Act? Would he be positive about directing the country towards such acts against the U.S. Constitution, and Bill of Rights? Naming this a "Patriotic Act" is a farce. There is nothing patriotic about this act. It is literally about one thing and one thing only... More control and power stolen from U.S. citizens. The Supreme Court, Congress and Senate in order to consolidate them into an executive-singular-branch of government.

The jester goes into a juggling act as he sings out!
"Mordor
More-odor!
More-odd or
More-order?
The building of Mordor has begun:
An evil wizard gets down and dirty
They Stick in your fingers-ground off-
They pull out their plumb
You thought they were smart
Think again
We are just dumb."

March 17, 2003
(Bush's Address)

"Intelligence gathered by this and other governments leaves no doubt that the Iraq regime continues to possess and conceal some of the most lethal weapons ever devised. Before the day of horror can come, before it is too late to act, this danger will be removed. When evil men plot chemical, biological and nuclear terror, a policy of <u>appeasement</u> could bring destruction of a kind never before seen on this Earth. Responding to <u>such enemies only after they have struck</u> first is not self-defense, it is suicide. The security of the world requires disarming Saddam Hussein now."

-George W. Bush, 43rd President of the United States

President Bush used Orwell's "newspeak" and "doublethink." He uttered the word "appeasement" as if it were a dirty word. In other words diplomacy is not an option.

Bush's speech strived to instill widespread public fear of a hypothetical future.

The administration wanted to prep us for the "Ministry of Love and Thought Police," in order to punish actual potential opponents and political critics for a thought crime.

Unfortunately, on March 1, 2003, that same month Congress, with Bush's blessing created the Department of 'Homeland Security.' Why is it different than the CIA? Its international and domestic policy is coordinated and directed by the White House.

Chapter 5
Katka's First Lecture on 'Abstract Connectionism'

A beautiful tall woman with long auburn hair stands before a large lecture hall filled with students of various ages. In the spring of 2010 Katka gives a lecture to her students on the concept of semiotic use of symbolism in her class at the Harvard School of Law in Cambridge Massachusetts. "She explains how societies worldwide at various times have used artistic symbolism in efforts to manipulate language... Always attempting to control and to manipulate political thought." Katka finishes writing a passage on the chalkboard and looks out at a vast 200-seat lecture hall.

"Thank you all for being here today. I am very excited to see so many young law students interested in these theories. This is the future as we head into the 21st Century. 'Abstract connectionism' is basically the joining of two fields or forms of thought or more... in fact the more the better. The more abstract the better, thus creating anything unseen or heard of before from it, material or immaterial, thought or pure phenomenal feelings...The key is an open, child-like, playful, creative, conscious mind."

She clears her throat.

"Now, let us look at today's topic the 9th Amendment of the Constitution... my personal favorite because it is written in an 'Abstract Connectionist' manor. It is truly a work of clean minimalist art in written form. Yet it must be viewed via pure holism, and should never be viewed abstractly by less than the sum of all its parts. I have written it here on the board."

The 9th Amendment

"The enumeration in the Constitution of certain rights shall not be construed to deny or disparage others retained by the people."

Katka continues, "Although it sounds difficult, it really is the backbone that holds up the previous eight amendments that make up our foundational democratic principals, almost Gestalt-like Principals that helped this country to maintain control of re-occurring tyranny for centuries.

"The verbiage is quite specific; the hard one is the interpretation of the old almost revolutionary French word 'disparage'... meaning many things simultaneously. At the time this document was written, how was it interpreted most directly? There are many ideas, that is the problem when left up to authorities.

"This Amendment stumps the best judges; some might say could it be literal. Perhaps that was the point because the wording somewhat vague yet at the same time this statement stays synonymous with our changing language, especially when directed at minimizing rights within the society. The verb is direct and protective. If an open and democratically interested mind reads this it might sound like this,"…Katka points to a specific phrase on the chalkboard: "The counting or determination of rights via the viewpoint of government shall not be grammatically interpreted or explained in order to deny or damage, belittle the reputation, nor minimize, tear apart opinion or speak contemptuously of others, primarily the constituency this is to be maintained by and held in place by the people.

"Your homework for today: Write your own opinion of what you think the 9th Amendment sounds like to you.

"Are there any questions?

"OK, then lets move along…If snow is white, then is white snow also?

"White is a code word for the color of white. White is symbolic and draws many conclusions about many more things than just snow. Therefore logic concludes that white is not snow nor is snow only white in color."

Katka Continues:

"If snow is always to be seen as only white by the authorities because it seems safer for them to control... how will we ever enter a new intellectual era?

If our understanding is always carved into our heads from a top-down direction from an authoritative illustration of truth, then how do we return to a cave of understanding not unlike Plato's? How do we lock ourselves in and see the images for what they are with new understanding, but also interpret what the images are for ourselves... again via our own conceptual articulation of our previous inference enhanced by our own real grasp of the experience, and not by those provided for us by authority?

"I love painting and, when I paint a picture of snow, I use white, yes. However, I use so many other colors in the shadows

120

and reflections to bring out its values and plasticity. That means that the snow is colorful according to my own colorful observation. I saw a painting where the snow was all blue. Perhaps that artist is colorblind or just likes blue. In this case the artist is saying something abstract that may not even resemble the authorities' concept of what snow should look like. He is perhaps not saying that snow is blue rather just illustrating the idea of blue snow with an alternative perspective.

"Do we kill the messengers that provide us with alternative thought or reality? Van Gogh painted in a way that was far beyond his time. He died feeling un-appreciated.

"Today his abstract way of looking at nature and color, light, and texture has made his paintings some of the most valued and treasured in history. Van Gogh became an inspiration also to a whole new form of artistic creative thought. It takes time to understand great thought and even masterpieces that leads in time to unanimous polyphonic truth such as the U.S. Bill of Rights.

"There were so many successful artists smothered by their own misfit into society, Mozart, Henry David Thoreau, Jim Morrison, Hunter S. Thompson, just to name a few who come quickly to mind."

One student asks, "What does all this art stuff have to do with the topic of constitutional and contract law and the 9th Amendment? Everything has to be laid out in a legally acceptable and clear way for all parties to agree anyway?"

"Well," says Katka, "let me give you an example from where I grew up. In 2003-2006 or so, the Parliament in Czech Republic gave the go-ahead to subsidize a European Union-endorsed green energy plan. This encouraged electricity providers to buy back from the public at a high rate of 12 Czech krowns per kilowatt through net metered power converters returned to utility companies. The wording on the government public utilities contract was not properly stating what the objective was. The objective initially was designed as a policy to provide solar cell converter systems for small homes throughout the country for the rebate. At least that is how the politicians sold the "fancy idea" to the public.

"What happened was that giant corporations bought tracks of land and created huge solar farms taking up agriculture lands and sucking up all the space that was left over on area power grids. Thus the regular folks at least very few were able to compete for the left over spots.

In this case the Green environmental carrot that enticed the parliament and got favor from the public and grants from the EU was a facade that covered over the fact that the corporations glad-handed their way into profiteering off a well disguised hidden agenda. No one noticed until it was too late; the power grid was maxed out taken over by the insiders. There was no room for regular citizens to get on. Then the politicians that overlooked it just said, "Oh well, we didn't write it; it was an EU plan. Should we cry over spilt milk? Life goes on." A large family of cheaters connected to the swindle, all got rich and laughed at those powerless who criticized them and continue to this day as average Czech citizens ended up paying even more for their electricity so the power company could keep their profits un-affected thus paying a premium to the money churning fly by night solar companies. Something they were told would become the opposite if they embraced the green solar energy plan.

"Katarina looked out at a still audience that looked like a bunch of deer staring at headlights, any other questions?" She asked.

"This example teaches us an essential lesson about the Abstract use of artistically manipulating agendas or critical text. The green environmental case involving the Czech Parliament teaches us of the critical and essential need to consider only clearly written, and concise legislative proposals. Using flimsy, open or general verbiage and weak language will always be left to the interpretation of the ones who wish to manipulate its outcome from the top down.

"The idea of going in circles is nothing new. We are experienced in it.

"After communism failed to find a solution to control bureaucratic disorder, you can see through the solar example I made: even in the Czech Republic a new 'democratic' central European seven-party Parliament using a well intentioned capitalist "Euro Zone" objective approach will bring out man's natural greedy will and ego. That always takes over and rewrites the definitions. This is the very essence of the history of mankind.

"Life, Birth, growth, love, confusion, hate, corruption, war, death, again-life, birth, growth, love, confusion, hate, corruption, war, death, again..." Katarina drew this on the chalkboard in a spiral shape-

"Like a dog chasing its tail.

"The 'Dog' it may as well have been. Politicians never launched a more thorough investigation. To them the agenda became more important than the facts. A smoking gun came in the form of a smoke screen rather than a mushroom cloud. The U.S. news media, the frightened

Congress, the oblivious Judicial Branch and the United Nations in cooperation with then, British Prime Minister Tony Blair and certain members of England's Parliament all seemed to be on a fact vacation from reality."

The Jester Laughs
"Somehow the dog ate the weapons of mass destruction."

For the first time since television was created, a whole team of Jokers in the Executive branch from the president and the vice president right on down to advisors and generals could literally lie and commit countless acts of manipulative fraud. They did this openly and literally while laughing at everyone and nothing would ever emerge to bring or hold a single one accountable.

We all know this story and around the world we all shook our heads because we didn't get the joke. Yet that garden in the Middle East called Iraq full of premium crude oil and a central strategic base for future Mideast, U.S., NATO manipulations had to be secured. At least the western world's corporate-political dogs, having a steak in the war and oil games, were set to plow through Iraq no matter what. The (MSM) main stream media actually helped set up a war possibly without even knowing they were doing so. The world began to notice that the free and open press had disappeared. People worldwide started to look elsewhere to get the truth. The corrupt and inept news media started to look like 'Ministry of Truth' within a brave new world as once described separately by the late authors Huxley and Orwell. These authors started to look like prophets. In so-called "real" life, those of us cognizant of this transformation felt as if we were being told: Turn on your sports. Eat your soma, get in line, repeat after me "War is peace, freedom is slavery and ignorance is strength."

Around this time someone said, "A person who watched absolutely no news was much more informed than someone who watched Fox News."

The sad thing is that for 2010 in a USA Pew Survey the American conservative Fox News Channel was listed as "the most watched television news source for the United States." The rest of the giant news organizations start pointing to the divisions and one sidedness of Fox. Yet they start to program with the same bias projections to support their side spinning their own form of what comedian Jon Stewart calls "Bullshit Mountain." His comedy news show for some reason had become the only source of true reality for the intellectual demography of the United States during the early 2000s. One hour, if we include Stephen Colbert, who plays the Objectivist Right-Wing side of issues, ensuring that we see the reality of the "newspeak," "No-Spin-Zone-Fox style." One hour is all we get in a workweek against all-day programming and back-and-forth split and distraction of turd-and-vomit social issues, a tool to keep society calmed and controlled.

The media Shadow-Hand Plays Fear Card

So guided by an MSM news presentation of fear and accepted by the establishments of governmental powers as the only true source of information, we are left to accept ourselves as a generation aware that the Omnipotent Power rules and runs most images. The Media shows propaganda to us via the privately-owned-corporate profit driven conglomerates' discretion within the mass controlled societies we live in.

We now also know that we are to be managed like sheep and have little chance to voice an opinion beyond ground level if it should upset the function and flow of the program. The Shepherd is watching over us, our new strict mother and father giving everyone our vision of how we're supposed to understand reality. This is done via the program of spin in order to override our subjective consciousness. Now the Shepherd has begun sharpening his blade before our eyes, what used to be done in private. The Shepherd selects who will be fleeced and who will be sheared and all by a new strange design.

Today, Watergate seems to many a fragment of a stolen cookie.

"You're either with us or with the terrorists."
-George W. Bush

Big threatening words for a man never popularly elected to his first term i.e., Diebold, bro-Jeb, Florida, hanging chads, missing ballots, the crony Justice Symbol Scalia re-boot? Who can forget: The GI Joe, superhero image of Tex on the aircraft carrier in a jumpsuit. Behind the Hero Reads: "Mission Accomplished."

"A banner, for whom?" The jester yells as he raises his arms into the wide-open air!

Now pointing to his head, **"can planet Earth survive this takeover of our minds?"**

Check Out the Use of Doublethink

"Simply stated, there is no doubt that Saddam Hussein now has weapons of mass destruction. There is no doubt he is amassing them to use against our friends."

"Yet if we did wait until that moment…And many of those who now argue that we should act only if he gets a nuclear weapon… that argument counsels a course of inaction that itself could have devastating consequences for many countries, including our own.
-Dick Cheney Speech to the VFW Aug 2002

It is also easy to see that former Vice President Dick Cheney is not a conscientious person, because he shot his own friend in the face and chest while hunting. Worsening matters on a much more serious international scale, Cheney uttered rambling "doublethink" so many times through his own statements on national television. It is difficult to value and respect this over-estimated pathetic, unapproachable character. He is the worst type of 'Zombie Elite,' a lowclass dog-eat-dog monster who feasts on the profitable destruction of democracy through providing and creating profitable crony totalitarian control on a grand scale... Dick serves as a symbolic representative of many who run the bloody conflicts surrounding the world's resources. We become numb to the facts as these wizards present their sinister characters as if evil villains of fantasy and science fiction.

The jester sits down, crosses his legs, puts his elbow on his knee and his chin in his palm.

Propaganda 101
The Protrusion thinks he's funny!
The powerless public thinks he's lame.
The programmed broadcaster just takes the money.
The reality is, they are all insane...

Is room 101 on its way?
Is this distension a form of conditioning,
a mental play?
Is a narration trying to numb us?
Why would Dick admit his guilt and evil?
He is retired and old.
Why is Dick leading a campaign to validate acts of torture?
This brutal bulge is bold

His progressively harsh statements over a stretched-
out period of time
To only one specially chosen interviewer?"
The poem he lays out somehow does not rhyme.

He is serious, yet we laugh at him
Dick laughs at himself with a half-shit grin
We call him a stupid, Darth Vader Dick?
Ma ma ma bla bla bla!... That's all folks!
Yet that silly dick changed the rhetoric.
Now torture is referred to by the American Executive
administration as "Enhanced Interrogation Techniques"
what many concerned consider a euphemism.
Orwell called it "Newspeak."

From ABC News Transcript of
Jonathan Karl Dec. 16, 2008

Jonathan: *"And on (Khalid Shaikh Mohammed) one of those
tactics, of course, widely reported was water boarding. And that
seems to be a tactic we no longer use. Even that you think was
appropriate?"* Cheney: *"I do."*

ABC News Transcript
Feb, 14, 2010

Jonathan Karl ABC: Cheney comes out of retirement to
criticize the new Obama administration for being less strict
on the interrogation issues, and for their attempts to close the
Guantanamo prison, which was an election promise President
Obama had made.

Karl: *"Should the U.S. have the option to use enhanced*

interrogation techniques such as waterboarding?"
Cheney: *"I think you ought to have all of those capabilities on the table."*
Cheney later same interview:
"I was a big supporter of waterboarding."

Amazingly, half way into the Obama presidency's first term, and Dick Cheney criticized the Democrat's diplomatic strategies and policies.

The jester screams! "Wake up friends! What is considered war crimes?"

"Waterboarding holds a victim down on a table or board as you pour a large continuous flow of water onto his face as the victim struggles to gasp for breath from drowning. This torture listed as a war crime under agreements reached in the 1949 Geneva convention and has been understood as such to this day. According to an unclassified draft dated February 25, 2006, the McCain Amendment article 16 of convention against torture: Conducted by U.S. officials anywhere in the world cruel and inhuman. Article 16 states, the techniques least likely to be sustained describe as "coercive" especially viewed cumulatively such as waterboarding.
Yet acts of torture and atrocities against human, animal and the disregarding of environmental rights are used all over. These details get swept under the rug of spin every day by the world media to protect certain Zombie elite Joker parties."

Jester announces
New millennium Political erotica Porn Show
Brought to you by Viagra
Host: C. A. Johnson
Written by Carrie A. Koch
Directed by: Hairy Peter
Art: by Phill Gaps

The majority of Americans hated Dick after eight years of power and leaving the White House in his wheelchair of symbolic pity with a less than 30-percent approval rating. Cheney probably became a multi-billionaire via un traceable profits made by his collusive orgy of deep, penetrating friendships with no-bid mega corporation whores such as Halliburton. Right in the middle of a stock market crash and trillion-dollar bank bailouts, didn't Cheney emerge from perhaps some cushy warm-island mansion in order to pull his postulating assertion out... spewing and shocking us? For most, he had lost his democratic, patriotic credibility. Why did he pick on the poor little one-legged impotent Democratic Party Executive Branch for being weak on the terrorist threat? President Obama had every right to have the attorney general open the nasty political drawers and cabinets to build a case against Bush Cheney's Executive Office deceptions, but chose not to.

In the turn of the 21st Century we will remember that Dick Cheney for some strange reason, seemed to be mutually feared by literally all media and politicians worldwide. Why? He was just a man, such as Nixon, "Tricky Dick" taken down for corruption three decades earlier.

Sounds like a conspiracy theory right? We are so trained by the spin doctors to keep from believing. Yet dare we try to seek the truth, lest we fall victim to understanding the reality. On a broad scale, society needs to realize that we are beyond the mega-prick conspiracy. Even so, we have become immune to the porn show, as the dicks surround us in all directions.

We call it "political correctness," or "attitude control,"or "conservative value facade," or being "non-provocative" or "non-confrontational," or "remaining falsely comfortable," or sadly I jest, an "(MTAP) Media-Trained American Patriot."

Orwell Called this in Newspeak One Word
"Crimestop"

"Means the faculty of stopping short… any dangerous thought, analogy, or criticize logical errors, or misunderstanding simple arguments capable of leading one in a heretical direction… 'Crimestop,' in short means protective stupidity."
-George Orwell's "1984"

Note to the Reader

Don't worry if you've found yourself committing a "Crimestop" while reading this book prior to the description of it. It's OK. Don't feel bad. It happens to all of us. You're OK... This happens because we are most likely being automatically programmed to do so. Think of this as the jester's cure for us as we awaken and realize that we are being fooled by fear-mongers. Why Fear?

As Crimestop intensifies today, the Wizards are right out in front of our eyes and they seem to want it that way. They keep selling us their lies long after the caper, turning a cover-up into a bestseller as they redesign history and reality for us. Just read their new 200-page ghost written biography and let the Executive Branch's hacks or what jesters might call our new watch-out-for-more 'scali-newts' like symbols. In this case we may call them" the "three R's," Rumsfeld, Rice, and Rove.

Enjoy the Turd Shuffle Show, on TV and radio. Such skullduggery points out and validates why he or she had to lie and rip us off. The booty goes to repay their round-a-bout lords campaign debts. This is all done under the deceptive bogus guise of keeping us free and protecting us from something that never happened and may never have? Perhaps if they lie enough we shall start to believe everything they feed us. It is good to note however, that the 2011 oil spill in the Gulf of Mexico points to Dick's involvement through his long-time close affiliation with Halliburton and other oil magnets. He has finally disappeared from the bigger "Republi-con Power Scene Show."

Perhaps this huge farce screams corruption from the highest and most disgusting and pathetic and embarrassing levels. The mysterious ex-VP, who for all we know could have gotten a new anonymous black market Chinese body part heart, is probably sitting in his velvet chair somewhere in the Caribbean or Dubai. He undoubtedly sits in the lap of artificial luxury, sipping his last day's elixirs made from specially crafted aborted infant stem cell placenta under the watch of a huge, expensive, publicly-paid for armed guard.

"Is a love of pure evil the key to becoming a bad-ass, 'Al Pacino-scar face like hombre?"

Living in Giant mansions that were built on the death blood and oil of nations. Knowing what great sins one has committed to every walk of life in the world, it should make it easy to keep a cold faux heart beating. The devastation to ecosystems and the overall balance of nature around the gulf is connected to the stream that flows like blood through the whole world's oceans, not to mention the lives Rich-Dicks have destroyed and relatively calm countries they continue to upturn by waging wars for stolen resources in the name of a minority corporate greed rather than principal to benefit a building up of a stronger third world and a better overall collective world economy.

To take Dick down would have been like removing a star player from the massive corporate political game... Preventing him from scoring critical goals for the world's top fascist cartel. Cheney's corrupt allies will no doubt put his face in a granite mountain someday and rewrite the history books, pretending that he was an "American Patriot."

Earth lesson #1: Don't negatively affect standards of living of the ruling class.

'In March 2009, Bernard Madoff pleaded guilty to 11 federal crimes and admitted to turning his wealth management business into a massive Ponzi scheme that defrauded thousands of investors of billions of dollars. Madoff had served on the board of the NASDAQ securities trading exchange, which he helped create.'

The Jester asks wearing a white suit
and a sombrero while smoking a big cigar:
"Que es mas macho, Richardo or Bernardo?"

I ronically, when you contrast these two nasty bandito-like characters, little difference emerges. These greedy characters that dig having power to turn big money gears on and crank out serious cash for their closest shareholders.

To feed his greed, Bernardo **made off** with the investment capital hurting some of the rich and powerful. Conversely, Ricardo swindled the innocent and defenseless earth's law-abiding, tax- paying citizens. Ricardo did this in the name of freeing and democratizing the heathens of the Middle East and protecting us from phantom fictitious nuclear, terrorist threats. Thus, he supposedly saved us from inflating resource doomsday scenarios. His ruthless party dreamed up whatever bogus story they needed.

Madoff used his close ties to the U.S. Securities and Exchange Commission to jack his clients off for awhile. He stroked the SEC long enough to fleece billions. Meantime, Cheney remained close to ultimate powers that run our entire federal government and Pentagon. This helped get his elite cohorts no-bid-back-door war contracts to fleece countless pallet loads of undocumented trillions sent to Iraq from the American people.

Madoff is serving a 150-year sentence. Dick, finally retired after two terms as vice president of the World's most powerful country. Cheney remains a hero to a 1-percent international minority. Who became multi-billionaires and millionaires thanks to his cartel, a true comrade.

Madoff's sons apparently turned him in, exempting themselves from having to give up all their holdings. Madoff checked out at the right time, in his seventies. Regular folk non-elite low end millionaires and investors got fleeced primarily, no bank bailed them out.

Even after being pre-warned by an independent whistleblower, the negligent U.S. Securities and Exchange

Commission took six years to investigate Madoff's Ponzi scheme. Afterward, the hot question remained around Wall Street jester circles.

The jester Asks
"Can he be the only one who was running a scam like this?"

Interestingly, many big people retired during the time leading up to and after the 2008 banking scandal and bailouts and stock crash and literal fall of the American economy. This placed a $4,000 debt instantly on the head of every American citizen.
Only the most affected and powerless will look into it? Some will write about the strangeness of those times, the mega-wealthy will call those the greatest years.

The class and character of mankind shifted yet again as wealth and power faced slowly awakening reality. World economists started using the term "Crony Capitalism." They described this as the key factor in ruining the economic terrain of the average world citizen. Not altruism or socialism or communism or public governmental mismanagement. That was left to propaganda, put out via the mainstream media to cover up and protect their lords.

Crony Capitalism: Self-interest and greed among close friends and partners over principle pure and simple.

Just then, the jester holds up a sign...

Hey, Vice dick!
Symbolic war criminal traitor of humanity:
The ultimate trick
The Model, the flaw, fly in the ointment
Corporate virus of greed and power total omnipotent
Will he shut his hole it starts to make us sick
dick likes torture, he's a fan, thinks it's function suffice
So lets put this dork in a vice
Turn the handle thrice
     Tell us your truth dick, who makes you kill,
     who cuts up your slice?
      How you like it now? Not so nice?
               Hey, Vice dick?

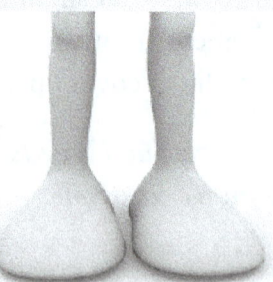

Chapter
6
The Crossover

The jester calmly sleeps in his bed when two dark unrecognizable figures suddenly awaken him, grab hold and pull him from his sleep. One holds him from the back as the other forces him to thrust his arms into a white canvas straitjacket. The two pull him from the bed and escort him, although half asleep, down a long corridor towards an open door. Half way down the hall, he sees a man in the distance resembling himself. In fact, now as he is just passing the man walking past him going the opposite direction, is a complete duplicate. The man walks past and smiles. The jester smiles back confused, but feeling strangely unaffected. As he turns and glances over his shoulder, he can see the copy heading for an open door at the end of a hall in that other direction.

Arriving at the room, the three men enter slamming the large metal door behind them with a loud echoing clank. The jester focuses his eyes as he looks around the room. He notices a large stainless steel chair reminding him of a dentist's chair, but much colder. Attached to the chair hangs many different-shaped leather straps, wires, ropes, spikes and metal objects and bizarre apparatus's attached to it? Next to the chair on the floor is a bucket of water and some wet towels, and above the chair an old metal lamp with a single bulb dangles from the ceiling..

The two men push him into the chair and strap him in. Then, these two attendants step back and exit through a side door as a tall, attractive, thin woman with red short hair in a black suit enters and stands before the Jester.

"Do you know who I am?" she asks with a calm cool soft voice.

"No I have no clue, I have never seen you before... who are you?"

"That is something you will never know. Many have tried and failed to capture me and make me their servant. They have no clue, I go to where I can when I want and as long as I like, I take what I want and I rule over time and history. 'Do you know why you are here before me?"

"Not a clue honestly...why am I here? What have I done? This is some kind of mistake. I think you have the wrong person?" he asked nervously.

"No you're the fool we are after. You are playing the game of connecting the physical negative complexities of the universal cyber system and now you have entered the crossover."

"What is the crossover?"

"It is the place in which illusion and reality collide. It is your mind and always was, your thoughts your dreams and your ideas, your hard-earned labor and vision that brought you here to this moment and put you into that chair. Did you see that other individual walk past you, going in the other direction?"

"Yes, who was he?"

"He was you. You see, you are now sitting in between layers of dimensions, and that other 'crossover' you is going to a dimension and time as well. Do you doubt it?" She asks smiling. "If so look around."

As he looks around, he sees several doors surrounding the small room. He looks down, noticing himself floating in the chair. When he looks up the light is gone and above, he sees several more doors leading in every direction.

Suddenly, the woman stands and walks to the edge of the chair pressing a button. This sends the electric seat back slowly while she explains an age-old philosophy: "Jesters come and go, the only true and real history one can study is the study of ancient artifact and art history. Time was great when the artist was free. Knowledge and truth are passed down from power relative to the security for those who ink a period at the ends of texts. Reality and the narrative are controlled by the owners of time. Now, you are most likely wondering why you are sitting in this chair? Everyone has and will sit in this room and in this very chair and everyone will have to face his own actions that changed the reality of the dimensions from where they were born. All will be tortured for crimes committed against that which they will never be given a label… eventually if not this moment… one day.

"You are a jester and you're not alone. There are many and they are not a fearful lot. They see things and feel deeply about connection, unification and collective positive ground-up directional movements. Jesters point to alternatives. When they have power and join together and unite they can be extremely effective or dangerous witch ever way one looks at it. Most want to keep logical humor free flowing in order to maintain the balance and sanity of Camelot.

Conventional torture usually fails to convince a jester because he knows that life is an illusion and his purpose is more important than the pain and fear he will suffer if he fails on one dimension. This is also why a jester is considered a fool. History is full of hero fools who battled against the light or dark reality of their times. However, today I want you to just sit back and relax, look up to the dome screen that surrounds you in this Imax observatory of your imagination, and watch a torturous story unfold."

"By the way can I get you some popcorn and a soda?" she asks, looking down smiling at the unamused helpless man."

Suddenly large letters flashed across a screen above the jester as he laid back into the cold chair.

The Adventure of the Objectivators
a.k.a. INGSOC*Independent of Nations Governments Social Objectivist Cults
As Told by the Crossover jester
Staring Female Lead jester-joker hero Ayn Rand

This adventure was based on reading quotes from The Objectivist magazine, published from January 1966 to September 1971, and then replaced by a biweekly newsletter called the "*Ayn Rand letters.*" Rand's other works were "*The Fountain Head*" and "*Atlas Shrugged.*" This new 'crossover' jester contrasts the Rand philosophy with George Orwell's predictions.

"According to a nationwide poll by the Library of Congress, the 1,168-page Atlas Shrugged is the second most influential book in the U.S., after the Bible." -George Gurley, New York Observer

"There are no blacks and whites; there are only grays"
                                                        -Ayn Rand

*Ingsoc (English Socialism): The controllers are termed "The Party." The Party is divided into two sections, The "Rich" and the "middle-class." The third group, low class "The Proles," or A.K.A., "The Proletariat" the poor, and considered animals by the Rich party. The main leader, The all seeing eye is Big Brother... the Omnipotent Leader.

"Objectivism became a very talked about and pushed philosophy during the end of the 20th Century. This viewpoint continues to gain momentum even today with working clubs and groups of future philosophers, and businessmen, plus economics and political science majors, gathering in major creditable universities. Although Rand portrays the ultimate mathematician, she lays her argument out in a very abstract mathematical way. This social philosophy that excites her practitioners personal wish to validate their wants and desires. Her concept continues to be an objectivists eternal flame by enabling application of a mathematical answer for handling morality, something entirely open and subjective. In other words, her quotes are mostly wide open for interpretation. But the catch is you have to be a member of a "new intellectual cult" to know the answer. According to a Rand follower, or a lover of objectivism, when one is asked if he or she believes in morality in terms of black and white, the answer should be: "You're damn right I do." Ask an objectivist to which camp he or she belongs to. The person can lie to whomever, black or white, good or evil. The objectivist twists logic and plays the part of a joker whose character is nothing but hypocritical gray matter in the end, and have no idea what a true answer is or should be, because it is not a game of truth seeking. Rather this is a game of fitting within the strongest leveraging niche for any particular moment. This is done to land on top of the power and money heap, which in turn gives a stronger illusion that one has total control of Reality. Big competitive people who like climbing the ladder of success love this philosophy. It is easy to get wooed into its magic spell.

Rand's Other Quotes Include:

"Just as in epistemology, the cult of uncertainty is a revolt against reason -- so, in ethics, the cult of moral greyness is a revolt against moral values. Both are a revolt against the absolutism of reality." "Cult of Moral Grayness Objectivist Newsletter," 1964

*"Ethics is not a mystic fantasy -- nor a social convention -- nor a dispensable, subjective luxury, to be switched or discarded in any emergency. Ethics is an objective, metaphysical necessity of man's survival. "-*Ayn Rand in *"The Virtue of Selfishness"*

Objectivist Top Calls Kettle Black

"Objectivist Moralism" may often sound like a plausible replacement for alternative ethical guide-stones normally achieved through one's own deeper connection to beliefs, senses and subjective consciousness. Many critics say this controversial philosophy often leads to a contradiction in itself and encourages repression, self-alienation, and guilt. Rand gives no clear direct article describing who belongs to the "Cult of Moral Grayness." Although vague, one easily assumes Rand abhors all of this, which she describes as "altruistic, socialized and morally grey." She says that, "moral grayness is a revolt against absolutism of reality."

"Right here she commits to saying that being in the center, the grey, liberal, social or moderate level, equal the understanding of two sides, which contrasts with absolute true reality.

Give Us Moral Reality, Great Chain Smoking Shaman!

Although she will not say this outright, Rand simply expects that one's use of ego, and selfishness whether all black or white...

makes true character. Her concept of a "Metaphysically," given strength to go forward, unconscious of its perplexing contradiction to humans symbiotic natural intelligent and socially collective moral evolution.

According to Rand's philosophy, an objectivist should use self-driven determination to climb to the top of the intellectual ladder, learning to master the past great strengths of the ancient philosophers like Plato and or Aristotle, or any Joe who became something in ancient civilizations. Now we use our mix of it to copyright the future of mankind under a united selfish brotherhood banded together black or white, good or evil and referred to by all as a privileged and a special breed. Socially recognized achievements provide an illusion of stature. This Social Darwinism drives forward any number of definitions to what absolute truth reason and reality means for those less special laymen, or in the objectivists' opinion knowledge-less who believe in subjective feelings, altruists, socialists, morally confused and mainly poor underachieving idiota.

These definitions are therefore colored black or white based upon necessity of the supreme survival of the superior owners of the code of realities definition. This magical flip-flop of contradictions changed as necessary any word so long as it achieves the goal to subdue the inferior classes not privy to the intricate grey code.

Suddenly out from the past a time traveler enters in a half white half black suit. He holds a ninja sword while flying across the screen, landing strong and secure in front of the giant powerful two-headed smoking dragon of mass delusion.

"Is that Saint George Orwell?" the jester asks, puzzled looking up to the giant screen? **"He looks so young, cool, fresh and alive next to the corrupt timeline of the last several years."**

Ironically or by coincidence, or by adoption and stolen design, Ayn Rand's concept of black and white exemplifies her within her complex layout of moral grayness. What George Orwell defined and designed nearly 20 years earlier in his symbolic warnings to watch out for in his book "1984" ironically termed "blackwhite"as a code of tricky grey matter in his explanation of the use of 'Newspeak and Doublethink."

The order of the Ingsoc "The key word is 'blackwhite'… has two mutually contradictory meanings… it means the habit of imprudently claiming that black is white… in contradiction of the plain facts. Applied to a Party member… to say that black is white when Party discipline demands this…means also the ability to believe that black is white…to know that black is white, and to forget that one has ever believed the contrary. This demands a continuous alteration of the past…known in Newspeak as Doublethink.

"Thus history is continuously rewritten. Falsification of the past… The mutability of the past is the central tenet of Ingsoc… Doublethink means the power of holding two contradictory beliefs in one's mind simultaneously… The party intellectual knows in which direction his memories must be altered; he therefore knows that he is playing tricks with reality; but by the exercise of doublethink he also satisfies himself that reality is not violated… It need hardly be said that the subtlest practitioners of doublethink are those who invented doublethink and know that it is a vast system of mental cheating. In our society, those who have the knowledge of what is happening are also those who are furthest from seeing the world as it is." -Orwell, "1984"

The crossover jester now enters the screen wearing a pirate hat and a patch over one eye and with his best Scottish accent he yells, "Haarr!"

Remember Ragnar Danneskjold the capitalist,

anarchist/pirate hero of the Capitalist Objectivists, the spunky white-collar self-validating Robin Hood character of "Atlas Shrugged?

False Heroes Emerge

After World War II and the departure of President Eisenhower, one can only imagine how the United States strived to even the economic playing field. False heroes and self validating pirates were bound to emerge and change the world power reality game in their favor, further squashing the populist free market before it had any chance to create a healthy even playing field.

Former Fed Chairman Alan Greenspan voluntarily left that job shortly before the catastrophic 2008 housing and loan crisis, a devastating domestic and international economic meltdown that he should have warned us about. Proving himself as among the world's most sinister objectivist pirates. He created Greenspan and Associates LLC. This firm specialized in protecting investments, obviously knowing how to profit thanks to insider information regarding the up-and coming Recession. Greenspan had managed the U.S. Federal Reserve since the 1980's during the presidency of Ronald Reagan. Perhaps worst of all, during the 1990s Greenspan helped deregulate Wall Street's derivatives industry, setting the stage for the eventual economic collapse. Greenspan apparently had been a close personal friend of Ayn Rand in the early 1960s.

> *"Ayn Rand became a stabilizing force in my life."*
> -Alan Greenspan, *"The age of Turbulence"*

According to some sources Greenspan spent time working on articles with her and other objectivists for the 'Objectivist News Letters' on topics like the virtues of selfishness and Laissez-faire capitalism... or capitalism in an environment in which transactions are held private between parties and free from state intervention, i.e. regulations, restrictions, taxes, tariffs etc.

This shocks some, showing an all-out embrace of egoism and greed over any form of ethics. All thanks to the head member of the U.S. Federal Reserve Board. One would hope that U.S. citizens have confidence in the main individual that holds the keys to the Fed and control of our public money supply. Such a professional should work as servants of the public, rather than managing a private elite money club that embraces objectivist cult-like-all-black-all-white intricately secretly coded principals.

Consider for example the Secretary of Treasury Henry Paulson, nicknamed by Wall Street insiders as "Snake," an ex-Nixon aide and a former Goldman Sachs exec. Prior to his treasury job departure he gave trillions to banks with no regulation plans overseeing bank CEOs. This oversight ultimately forced Congress to hastily pass updated regulatory legislation under a dubious threat that there would be a total collapse of the entire American banking system. Even so, the world's banking conglomerates bypassed any real investigations or trials. From their perspective this became proof that a public bailout was the best policy. This occurred only months before an executive team headed by none other than the Bush Cheney group were to leave office in early 2008.

As one news agency said, "The leader of these initiatives, Treasury Secretary Hank Paulson, repeats endlessly, "That these are "private" initiatives adopted because they are in 'everyone's interest'... not government-mandated schemes."

A **jester** questions, *"If that is truly the case, why is the government involved at all? What does government bring to the table that the market can't?"*

Paulson says "government is necessary because servicers

146

face an unprecedented volume of resets that cannot be addressed through individual, loan-by-loan negotiations." It requires, he says, a "streamlined" approach "facilitated" by Washington.

Project Lifeline: Collaboration or Intimidation? (Riverside Business Press, March 10, 2008)-Alex Epstein

The crossover jester enters looking like an old English schoolteacher with black robe, a flat-top black hat and tassel. He drags behind him a chalkboard and begins to write on it. "Let's get this straight everyone. We need a Recapitulation."

"**A**re you ready for this: OK take a long deep breath," He continues slowly and calmly writing in different colored chalk, laying out the divine logic of the ruling class with use of symbols, black and white, objectivists new intellectual terms, all mixed together with Orwell's newspeak and doublethink:

"So the reason, logic, and 'damn-right white ethics' of the true 'New Intellectual Objectivist' who believes in the virtues of damn-right individual selfishness without governmental interference in private capital free markets can be thrown out in matters of protecting the 1-percenters... So long as the objectivist party, new intellectuals, or members of the Ministry of Truth or Love or Plenty is recipient of the aide. As long as this "government assistance" comes only to bail out mistakes resulting from poor decisions made by previous "Blackwhite" ruling objectivists or

147

elite party members like Pirate Captain Greenspan who run the Federal and private banking systems yet at the same time meet with Secretaries of State, making critical decisions that impact world monetary policy.

An inferior ignorant public must pay for the mistakes through increased taxes, and austerity measures. Such diabolical diversions enable liquidations or sell offs' of public assets, ultimately using proceeds for their own self-serving purposes. Intellectual bankers act "grey or black," always happy to tell you they are only "damn-straight right white."

They bailed themselves out on Wall Street while the cash vanished and the "proletariat" got the bill. Furthermore, banking and investment firms that new intellectual party leaders in the White House considered as "too big to fail," plus untouchables at the "white Federal Reserve" became exempt from control. These crooks who wrote laws benefiting only themselves started feeling content evolving into what Ayn Rand followers on the right white call "altruists or socialists," or "Taggarts & Mouches." "Black Hank Paulson" and "White Tim Geithner" landed in positions deemed untouchable along with "Black Bush" and "White Cheney."This burden eventually passed on to the new "White Obama" and "Grey Capitol Hill."

White right wingers proud, conservatives and, Tea Party-Tea Bag capitalists, the Paul Ryan's, the Newts, and the Laissez- faire, capitalists blame "one legged grey government bureaucrats" and failures on Obama and the Democratic Party. Political adversaries called them all traitorous characters of the fantasy book 'Atlas Shrugged.' RINGGGG wait one minute please! 'Crimestop,' political correctness, or fear of critical thought.

But then Bush is "white" and Obama is "black?" "Blackwhite." Damn right they are!

148

"It is too much to take in!" the jester screams helpless. In the face of a bitter reality he wants to deny. Why would they paint such a mixed up, grey, confusing picture. Why can't they just be good and evil, plain and simple, Isn't that what Ayn Rand the artist/writer wanted to lead them into?" He yells crying and shivering.

"Relax, just take it in man. Watch yourself play with this show," said the redhead laughing while adjusting the chair and strapping him in tight. She turns on some strange polka techno background music."You must watch your crossover performance play out to the end. Only then can you pass through to your preferred dimension."

Just then the proud crossover jester enters the full screen as the show continues. This time wearing a black judge's robe and a pair of boxing gloves as he goes into some movements reminiscent of the dance, float and sting of the former world champion heavyweight boxer born Cassius Clay Jr: *No Vietcong ever called me nigger."* -Mohammad Ali

True to the jester's nature, let us find merit in illustrating alternative perspectives alternative views. Perhaps more prize fighting jesters are seeing this "blackwhite' Orwell/Rand contrast. A Fair Use contrast of written ideas remains a free artists right.

With credited excerpts and quotes from the texts, we are allowed to make a critical observation and shed light on alternative ways of thinking. It is a constitutional right for the moment as well, although threatened. In time such attitudes might become thought crimes if we let go of the symbolic comparative reality.

With such issues in mind, we need to consider whether a revolutionary idea or concept can be dangerously stolen and profited from. Orwell saw an oppressive threatening future, we are led to believe, he had developed within his own mind and passed this on to generations to come as a "blackwhite" fictional vision, or was it a seed? Perhaps a real idea meant to be planted and used in order to become a future guidebook of symbols to watch out for, or to use?

Or, was this a warning of an age of conspiracy that followed a creative reality, changing narrative? If considered a "seed," then the concept and product of a true visionary genius like Orwell's. This concept could have been changed around by a cult of connected creative tricksters, perhaps objectivists and then plagiarized in other words and copyrighted, then used in way's to manipulate an un prepared world via use of a new and dangerous idea or philosophy.

If a warning, then this notion begs affirming that the visionary could see the future somehow or he knew something was being developed. However that begs of conspiracy and we are programmed into a belief that this is a foolish argument. If that concept is considered out of the question on logical and reasonable grounds then we have to ask some crazy questions to further think this puzzle out.

This opens another topic: Who truly owns the very dangerous ideas, whether they come in the form of philosophy, fiction, fantasy, prose or propaganda? Should selected, well-connected monopolies be able to take ownership of another's creativity, their very descriptions of black and white? Should clever tricksters backed by corporate money be able to write down every abstract angle describing interpretations of reason, truth, reality, and the human self. Then should objectivists copyright these concepts, giving themselves a platform for future control or manipulations? Thoughts come naturally to man every day and have done so from the beginning of recorded time and through the ages.

Should we allow selfish secret cults of self validation to take control of such intellectual property? In doing so, mega monopolies undoubtedly would blow up the symbolic 'Fountain Head' buildings. These are unique buildings comprised of mankind's intricately connected and evolved co-created moral codes and histories. Perhaps then the universe is proven to be truly nothing after all and not so open and wonderful as science and religion would lead us to believe.

The crossover jester sharpens his samurai sword, saying: "Suddenly this reality narration stuff sounds serious, is it about us humans or is it about a bigger picture?"

School of Thought #1- Abstract

"If you had an infinitely rich (Universe), it could be explained by reference to its value. Its goodness could be the creative force, which had produced it." -John A. Leslie

Social Codes, values and ethics were developed over time sometimes by revolts mixed with not well understood subconscious social natural moral balanced unified conformity to past tyrannical highly religious cultural ages. Ages delicate and

151

uniquely hard to understand gave us codes of reality and rhythm melding to growing philosophical and technical intelligence that evolved naturally. Moral abstract codes that shaped our intelligence are so hard to grasp, perhaps sounding like… if you could make a melody of manmade words to describe it… it might be close to:

Godly, good, government, gracious, growing, guides giving greater grandeur, going galactic.

Sounding similar to this but translated in many languages at light speed. Think that sounds ridiculous?

School of thought #2 - Objectivism

If so, Then our existing alternative is to sign over our authorities to a disrespectful cult of brats. This way they could steal and control reason, truth and reality. Hand all copy written and patented knowledge to the "blackwhite" wizards. These cohorts, in turn, would pull and push the control knobs and buttons of the hardly understood or yet-mastered Internet and phone surveillance and control machine, hidden behind curtain Number 3.

Yes, this would become a real selfish cult that keeps the objectivists' nasty drawers locked while opening all of ours. Wicked wizard's will record your dirty secrets in order to own your obedience or dispel your threats.

Corporate anarchy, a jaded twist of morality and the ultimate ruling of economics all hinge on the success or failure of these objectivist-sanctioned cults. Collectively and individually, these cliques must accept and fully embrace a corrupt government system, nonsensical religious dogma and the politicians' control of local, state, national and international financial systems.

Then at the same time this proud body of selected top-of-the food chain, certificate-bragging, card-carrying, flag-wearing, cross-baring dogma-swearing cult members follow a code critical of anything altruistic, government, or religious.

A jester could say, "Now might be the time to take this seed-"1984" guide book and let us all speak for Mr. Orwell and raise him and his symbol and identification of 'blackwhite' to challenge such traitorous acts up to the top of that giant New York skyscraper and let his novels perceptive warning of this very spun out of control gathering of hypocrites capitalize on the facts."

Orwell's book "1984" no matter what year is written on its cover, is the true symbolic torch of defined description of a mental takeover. This timely critical warning points to the absolute value of true democracy, liberty, and freedom. Man must choose his own vision, truth, reason, and reality. Which have all been overlooked and perhaps taken for granted by most of us.

Perhaps now is the time to cover the confused and manipulated objectivist hijacked landscape with Orwell's 'blackwhite' warnings pointing out this very real crooked mental takeover. Let's watch the objectivist rats try to spin it into grey comedy, dodge and run from the compared premises, the moral dilemmas, the yin and yang and the Karma. All these belong to every mans chosen destiny. Perhaps some cool jesters will begin a real hilarious discourse before it is too late?

It is exactly the power to take absolute future long term ownership of something as ridiculous as anything remotely related to using Mickey Mouse symbols backed by corporate money and big law firms which is leading mankind down a progressively dangerous road. This leaves nothing left to be created that artistically challenges critical intellectual property questions towards particular power circles and corporate owners game controlling motives. New variations of inspired intellectual artistic property could be eliminated and forbidden because they may contain an inspired portion of another's seed, while at the same moment one-sided philosophical basics are forced upon us. Regurgitated re-written, funneled, corporate owned stale uninspiring safe and marketable versions are to become our politically excepted future?

Who speaks today for the late masters' whose bodies of work and wisdom have been hijacked, copyrights to protect their legacies... Non-existent? Giant calendar corporations located in China-and Europe profit from sketches by da Vinci and Gustav Klimt's "Kiss." Greatness has always been stolen. But to kitchefy great art turning it into cliché mugs and aprons because you're an all powerful corporation, thus reasoning for greedy ethics so the masterpiece becomes a whore for the corporate God. Combining the borrowed greatness of artistic revolutions made us all together greater. Then free flowing written, musical, and artistically drawn or painted thoughts and sounds and scientific and technological seeds and ideas lead us from one great invention to the other, without controls from the wheel to the car.

On August 24, 2012, Apple won its case against Samsung on design and trade principals. This emerged as a pretty grey area of appeal considering Apple had designed its first technology based on the state-of-the-art designs that IBM, XEROX-PARC and other tech companies had at the time when they entered the market.

If precedents are being set in this New World Order, then what about the design of 'blackwhite' made from Orwell's original design models? How many billions does the Ayn Rand's Institute and center for brain washing young political minds owe Orwell's "*1984*" copyright holder? These people who learned as children how to reason as a supreme flock of useful idiots via the 'New Intellectuals' seminars became, or could become, future leaders in science and politics. Evolving into objectivists as adults, these individuals now comprise a cult of moral grayness' using 'blackwhite' and 'newspeak.' This is done by design as a means to take charge of controlling and owning the artistic progression of world wide competitors like Samsung or Motorola. Their ultimate goal is to monopolize the world's tech progress under the banner of corporate capitalist Mickey Mouse, orgy, oligopoly, collusion and cartel. "This rat stinks!"

The crossover jester starts to move now with his boxing gloves in the air, throwing punches and dancing, gesturing. "Come on!" As a boxing referee, district attorney and nationally recognized TV show host Judge Mills Lane used to say before matching great hungry ear-biting prize fighters in the ring formerly, *"Let's get it on, gentlemen!"*

"**Why?**" The jester cries out still laying strapped to the cold chair, "**Please no more! I cant take it... please, no more. It is torture. Please make it... him stop... It is not me. This is not my world, I would never show such torturous reality. This vision is insanity, I want my ignorance back please keep me out of it. Please stop!**"

The tall woman with short red hair picks up a hand-held

transmitter. She turns on a background recording of 'Mozart's Requiem in D minor,' turns up the volume, filling the room with a sense-provoking sadness. This drowns the moment with a heavy, slow, continuous operatic depression as the story continues.

The redhead tightens the straps and pulls his eyelids open with a mechanical spider-looking apparatus. She forces him to see the violent thought playing out above him.

"Relax, it's almost over... Just watch your little comedic jester story continue."

Flashing above the jester across the screen is a text in large letters while the wail of Madonna's pop hit 'Material Girl' is creatively dub-mixed into Mozart's Requiem on a loop in the background.

Suddenly a title flashes across the screen:

Who is John Guilt?

The crossover jester yells, "they are the Queens wanting to wear the Kings Crown on a dimension of time, they think they will be creative enough to master and control! They are the thieves of greatness. They have no original idea of their own. Their champion gave them one idea that had potential merits, which could have made 20th Century philosophy transcend a creative mind and giving wings to the artist and craftsman within.

However, scummy brown-nosing bankers and politicians hijacked this dangerous amphetamine-like philosophy. Left-brained gluttons, worshipping the lucrative dog, sniff of each other as a special breed. These are classless yet connected people, and self ordained as kings of the modern technological and financial era.

Unfortunately, Ayn Rand in a way became the very thing she

hated. She transformed, perhaps unknowingly, from an artist into a cult narrator, a "witch doctor and a tool for Attila," A metaphor she used often looking up to her left-brain with eyes the size of teacups. Or, was that perhaps her 'doublethink' game? Only a few powerful players know these competitive rules, necessary to spin a new reality. This creates a dimension, proving that men, can become Gods if they harness power, want, desire, and posses formidable greed which they call "value." Now, objectivists strive to portray these men of privilege as victims who needed to crush competition and rise feeling as though they were the only stars of a galaxy.

They had a useful artist tweak and inhibit the direction of human morality. Like a computer, she had all the philosophical answers to keep a young malleable conservative mind on target during the age of high technology and easy money. These factors generated made a 'New Age' of it's own. It's no wonder the New York power clubs loved her novels. She was a talented writer. She created romantic larger-than-life heroes who generated new concepts of understanding and acceptance of new codes of reality derived from fiction. She had a knack for mixing up smart words having to do with great ancients, or to sound cool and confusing. Rand often used such techniques in conveying her message, thus demanding an authority to help provide the puzzling philosophical answers.

She also had a groovy Russian accent, and she remained bent on a hatred toward anything having a socialized nature. As a Russian immigrant, she portrayed herself as a victim of socialism. This all made her seem more credible. Unfortunately she and her philosophy helped a new breed of crony capitalists cover their guilt from a new kind of jaded 'Atlas Shrugged, Fountainhead.' The selfish religion with it's own very popular adventure story objectivist 'doublethink' bible.

Apparently corporations are Gods and people, too? Should the people corporations "take help?"

Had Ayn Rand been around during the economic breakdown of the late 2000's, perhaps she would have rethought some of her layout. What would be her opinion of corporations given more rights under the constitution than citizens? Would she have stuck with her "intellectual brothers" and validated the bailouts given to the private investment banks?

Many true and loyal enterprising capitalists who embraced the 'Objectivist-Individualist dogma' thrived on their own. They used these strategies in building small, medium, and large business's. As a result, the average person lost out to a selected, connected few at the top. Those privileged but undeserving top bananas got saved through a government socialized bailout handed to the very crony capitalists club members who were the architects that caused the demise of the breakdown through their neglectful greedy management practices.

Now those fat millionaires and billionaires still in charge of high positions in commerce and politics cry and whine and yell socialist, populist, altruist foul, any time the government wants to cut into their massive pie. The Exclusive Party of Jokers knows that the public are fully programmed to run from their masters bluff lest they fall victim to joining that circle of contemporary ignorance of not understanding the impossible intellectual code. The Jokers have no other choice but to use any philosophy or religion or regime or 'ocracy' or 'ism' to keep control and remain able to keep both homes in Europe and a yacht in the Caymans. Objectivist Philosophy, or "newspeak," "doublethink" rhetoric implementation through endless expensive political campaigns. Objectivists push out whatever it takes in order to maintain their strange elastic selfish faith. These Joker crony faiths now spread like a virus or disease across the globe.

Now, the beginning of this 21st Century would be the ideal time to read or listen to John Gault's speech. However direct it not to the poor government hacks that have become hungry themselves for lack of proper direction. But, rather direct it to the symbolic barbaric crony tribes-people mentioned in these essays that have creatively utilized any egoist philosophy or rhetoric to rape, pillage and rob a once great nation and world for that matter in the name of none other than total selfishness. Think of these charlatans and their best friends in high places all laughing as they easily load up their massive bank accounts full of our hard earned money. These crooks invest these funds for themselves funneling the cash to their own greener pastures and warmer climates in foreign lands. These heartless thieves could care less if society falls into a heap of disorder and despair as a result of their blatant economic crimes against humanity... Read or listen to the 1957 John Galt speech right to the oath at the end, and then think who is living for whom today?

The crossover jester is now seen in front of a 1930s Art Deco style silver chrome radio microphone.

"Ladies and gentlemen. I found it monumentally necessary to interrupt the regular programming to make a vital announcement."

"You have all been wondering who is the jester?"

'jester Shrugged Speech,'
Who is the jester?

For the Critics the ruling class and the 99%
We... Artists, fools and clowns?
Perhaps naughty interlopers in the eyes of the trickle down

Players who stamp the papers-shark the pool
The proud body, the Jokesters the "New Intellects"
Expensive that paper hanging up behind their large desks
Nice to have a Harvard or Yale title to rake in big fat checks

Most of us, who live a connected life with nature
You know we ranchers and gardeners don't really care
Don't care about your title.
We want to see what you have done.
All that money spent on your own ego, smokes,
twisting ethics having fun
Spinning our values and judgment in circles,
in fact it makes one sick
Some would rather play the fool card-get the trump
on Ayn Rand's Jokster's trick

Honestly,
To hell with that class, academic, stare
Why respect intellectual bullshit that points to validating
selfish, egoist directions
In matters of government, society, and economy
Seen the market, It's a bear by the viewpoint of upper-middle,
Working class and deprived-poor,
Perhaps, time to kill the jokester virus
can we open a new door?
Directed by connected leadership creative elite
nature lovers we implore

Constitutional based smart directions, blind justice,
and ethical judicial finger
Point out white-collar bad apples
Federal courts are empty, board Judges wait,
Yo… AGs bust a move don't linger!

Based on the neglected state of our present
Objectivist Anarchic environment
Damage via Jokester cults of thought, unbalanced twisted codes
of morality on freeze
Fund, implement, preach, held up as symbolic road signs found
tenet at major universities
Under the Guise of "New Intellectualism," "Objectivism"
and skewed 'Epistemology'
Austrian Economics, hey! Ron Paul, sounds nice, still ice

This programmed pass down the food chain certificate ruled reason
Seems to re create the same hypocritical demon
Keep your eye on its ultimate symbol Mitt Romney
2012 favorite presidential frontrunner pick for the Republi-crony
No doubt schooled in 'blackwhite' even states it doublethink
Objectivist model 'damn right white' zombie!
Frightened to be himself
Who is he-and what -ever side he is on?
Religious dogma spurting douche bag phony Mormon
or just a simple Republican Puppet millionaire,
market insider, lying manipulating corrupt moron.

Mass media bombards us, tries out any new gun
Listen to Paul Ryan he was Romney's Vice pick
he is the younger one
Ryan plays a 'blackwhite' game so well a gentle voice keeps
the simple folk immune
Handsome soft blue eyes they hope with zero facts to back him,
the public he can tune

A politically programmed Objectivist Atlas Shrugged infatuated
robot Wants to act like a bad ass, he likes to shoot his Gun
Say's... "he likes Music of Rage Against The Machine"

Use it for PR so he tells his aides the young voters will
think I'm fun

He has no idea what the lyrics mean? He can't get it!
Just political escapades
"Amusing Paul Ryan is the embodiment of the machine that our
music has been raging against for two decades."
Says Tom Morello the guitarist spoken out of just concern from a
noble character
A humble Artist on topic of this phony new young symbol
the rights been wavin.

Don't forget the female Robot symbols Hillary-C, Nancy-P
Sarah -P- ye- all -soccer moms must be confused and f-n-alin
Both parties full of foolish fluff
mainly representing corporate-owned puff
New shifty brands of fakes; different labels every few generations.
Perhaps time for us to call the bluff on mass manipulations?

They had their time of glory, they failed they lost the game
Now see what the monster of all objecti-capi-crapy crony-ism
has gotten us
Look around you who is to blame?
If you're a smart jester please advise the 'Good King,'
Help him play it sane.
Keep him safe and help him see.

If enlightenment and transcendentalist theories
are not considered useful tools
of inspiration for humanities to build from.
Philosophy, science and truly evolved ethics are pushed
to the back of the line,
For insanity, greed, and stupidity, fake objectivist idiots and jokers
are given reward and bonuses, jerk the payroll

with it buy the wine
Ask Brooksley Born she read through a crony Washington craze
Called out the Jokers to see the light through the greedy haze
Let it go, yelled Maestro Alan Green-Spam man…
let it grow … In the rain or on a train we all like our
derivatives FED eggs and 1- percent interest ham
Yo… both parties like them Spam Man
"Green Al I am…listen friends…
Smart bitch logic, she's trying to choke us"
Nasty political bull monkeys like Larry Summers
go steal the focus!

Twisted Dr. Seuss like 'Sneeches,' NO! LOL Leaches
with jaded stump speeches
Please God… keep this crony virus from
destroying all our beaches
Spin through a revolving door each term given larger stars
Wouldn't matter to us if they lived on mars.
They don't, this is Earth it's shared, this drunken un-kosher
weenie roast party… it's not fine.

If our globalized future rests exclusively in greedy hands
To unorganized egomaniacal un punished manipulation
Constructing money supply, nation building, and social integration
If greed leads connecting cross boarder diplomacy with respect to
foreign cultures, managing languages, histories and religions
Left to manipulation by ravenous vultures.

Then what can we expect
When it comes time to load the matrix
(AI Programs) that's what's next
Who will be the model of Supreme Intellect?
Politically blessed scientific, obedient, materialistic, chimps,

Loyal dogs to political-corporate hogs who gave
them Audis and citizenship
Clean new passports and tract homes for brains
brought from across the boarder
Is this what we wish for, is this... "New World Order?"

Just then the woman with red hair walks up to the chair with the sprawled-out Jester still strapped in tight.

"Well that is where we are. Did you like the story of a foolish jester playing with the hilarious concept of true reality in the multiplex of the dark material building dimensions of a pathetic human life?"

Looking down she realized the subject was not moving, his eyes completely white. She held his wrist in her hand and felt no pulse. She then removed the straps and contraptions and laid a large white sheet over him and smiled one last time while covering his face. She turned and walked from the room, which started filling quickly, taken over with energy and bright light.

Chapter
7
The Day We Became One -111

It's October 29, 2012 the U.S. east coast has suffered one of the worst natural disasters in recorded history. *Hurricane Sandy* proved even to the materially comfortable that no one is exempt from the reality that nature truly rules.

"Hi, Katarina, welcome. Come in, please. Let me take your umbrella and make yourself comfortable," says the middle-aged Nepali-American man with short grey hair and beard.

Katka removes her rubber boots and large hooded rain slicker and sets it upon a coat rack in the lobby of a large old brick New England building. Then she enters the warm office of her respected colleague and personal guru, Doctor Ramadeep.

"Hello Doctor. It is good to see you again." She says, taking a seat in a comfortable recliner. "I was happy we could still meet especially considering the fact that I nearly got caught in a stream of water that was far too difficult to drive through on my way here. However, my good new motorbike friend taught me when in doubt give it the gas."

"Life goes on, rain or shine," adds the doctor, smiling. "It's been several months since we last got together. I have a file here. He looks at some papers on his desk, and asks Katka to tell him what she has been feeling the last few months.

"Well it has been getting progressively better since my big breakdown," she says, shrugging a little.

"So, your getting back to a pattern of concentration at work and getting your home life back to order as well?" As he writes in a folder.

"Yes I would say so," she answered nodding her head.

"Good! No more voices?"

"No-No, not since the winter of 2010. That was it, then after the hospital and time off everything got progressively better."

"Good, Good," he repeats writing something into his file. "So did the 'Xyprexa' prescription work for you? And have you been keeping it up?"

"It did work at calming me down and then it was strange. About six months ago, I just started to feel horrible and fat, and I got hungry all the time, so, I slowly reduced the dose and have gotten down to one pill per week, now I am feeling much better, wanting to exercise and get back to work on my theories and experiments."

"You're getting exercise regularly and eating healthy?" He asked.

"Oh yes, and I have been studying up on the psychosis a little as well." She says meeting him eye-to-eye."

"Humm! He says with a pause, writing for a moment. Then he turns his seat towards her.

"I think I should tell you that these episodes can come back at any time and my personal opinion is in favor of medication for a few years after such traumatic occurrences. However, the fact that you are on top of your own healing process and given your scientific background I won't be pushy with you.

"Just know that if you feel any onset of the depression or similar symptoms coming on again, remember that you may contact me immediately. That way we can prescribe the necessary medicine for you."

"Doctor, I don't think I will be able to let it happen again honestly, because I feel almost re-born, or as though my mind and spirit got a re-boot," she says smiling.

"Tell me about that please if you could" he asks.

"Well I have started to re-evaluate many things in my life since the breakdown. So many things are changing. New feelings, new directions and I have a better attitude about what I want from life as well. Some amazing spiritual things are happening to me, Doctor."

"Such as?" He shifts in his seat and writes, not looking at her.

"Well, as you know for most all of my 20s and 30s I was very uninterested in having a relationship with a man. I think mostly because I had no time for one and I somewhat feared them because I did not want anything to come between me and my work. I have spent every moment developing my brain with so much data and thought and research and it was becoming an addiction. At least that is what I have come to realize these last few months. I would spend time with men when I was in secondary school on ski trips and class projects and felt very close to them and that is what made me afraid of them. I was nervous around them because they made me unable to think clearly. So I told myself constantly to block them out. Focus on work and study. I will be 40 years old next year and up until last year, I had only slept with one other man."

"Was that a good or bad experience?" He asked looking at her clutching his beard?"

"I was in college. He was very nice to me, if anything, I was the instigator, I wanted to see what it was all about, I pushed it and to my let down I felt only pain and he was confused. I made our coupling stop before he had orgasm. He got angered with me. I was young and ironically unschooled about sex or men. My parents were conservative and they never pried. I had been

167

only interested in the mind anyway. After that, I had absolutely no interest in men, then I met several women along the way who were very comforting and they didn't demand my time, only some companionship here and there. So I guess I began to find it convenient to take the label of gay-lesbian. It was I think more out of a feeling of what worked best for my career in academics.

Men left me alone and I found a warm and respectful constructive understanding between my peers of both sexes. The strange thing is I am comfortable with both sexes and I am not a hater of men. Women are attractive, mainly for companionship and understanding. Men, I find more sexually attractive. I just have not had time to worry about sex of any kind; I have always blocked it out… Until recently that is."

"Could you shed light on what happened to you recently?" He asked relaxing back into his seat.

"What had happened to me in November of last year 2011 had changed my life completely." She says as she holds her head with both hands. I was working on a paper that describes conscious and unconscious phenomena, at the same time I kept getting emails from friends asking me to read and go to internet sites showing metaphysical gatherings and contemporary spiritual movements. Now I am primarily an atheist and I have never had time for hocus pocus metaphysical theories. But for some reason because of the feelings I had at the time concerning my mental health, I spent a few days looking at some of the crazy science that was out there. I also spent time looking at some ancient Eastern philosophy and some shamanism of cultures throughout the world. The strange thing and no offense Doctor, but what they had to say soothed me after my mental sickness towards recovery far greater than much of what the accepted schools of psychology provided.

"In the past, I had rejected the concept of God because I

needed to know facts and truths. God floats in our consciousness. It is not a concrete being giving us reason, truth, and reality. That takes belief, something we in the scientific world use but understand only if it benefits our work. Then we accept it. We use it to generate energy for our theories, but deny it at the same token.

"I now believe that some kind of divine power somehow exists; some intelligent unexplainable energy that is beyond our control or label and it lives deep in our senses, doctor. It was around November when I kept seeing this number 11 everywhere: on clocks, on walls, on the TV, on the radio, in the car. Suddenly I would look up and of all numbers it would always be 11. It was something I dismissed at first.

Then a friend told me this was normal and many people have the same experience, and that it is a way for the subconscious spiritual part of our world to connect with us. She also sent me a link to a gathering that was being held in Hawaii on the date of 11/11/11. They were calling it the numerological date dawning a New Age of enlightenment where this phenomenon was to unlock a code unleashing a divine pattern of new consciousness. That will spread outward and upward healing those who recognize it and bring forward a new enlightenment and reality for the entire world. I read the various pages on the website explaining what was happening with this time. It fit perfectly with my experiments, and theories on the topic of Phenomenology."

"Why is that?" He looks up with an interested stare.

"Because here was a mass of thousands of people spread out throughout the world from different cultures and religious beliefs, uniting their minds on a topic of connecting together around a particular date and time. Interesting also was the fact that they all believed deeply that this date and time was very special. If anyone took the time to analyze it and calculate a little basic math that person could have a brief revelation. On the day of 11th of November 2011, if one added his or her birth date to the year he or she was born most everyone would come to 111.

I was 39 and I was born in 72. When I asked friends and family around me their birth dates I kept getting the same 111 numbers. A math teacher friend said this is just the wonder of math. 'No big deal.' 'This year everyone will be 112." And so on. "True," I said, but even so it is generating a powerful energy that for some strange reason seems to live outside of mathematical reality and becomes rather a phenomenal paradox mainly because there is energy and thought massing around this date and time and people are being effected by that energy not just the math surrounding it. How old are you Doctor?"

"57," he said clutching his beard more vigorously.

"So you were born in 55 right that equals"… as Katka paused.

"Right, he says cutting her off. "112." Interesting coincidence. He shifted a little nervously in his seat.

"Interesting yes, and you know, the mainstream press made no big deal out of it last year either, she continued. "I spent some time on the subject because I wanted to see if something truly magical could happen when so many humans focused energy on this date that some believed would bring a turning point to their lives and to the life of the world that if we believed all together at the same time that if we were all one connected mass, what could empirically potentially happen? It is an interesting thought is it not?" Katka asked.

The Doctor shrugs and notes something in the file on his desk.

"I know," she says shaking her head. Numerology sounds weird because it relies on belief rather than concrete facts. At the same time the number one is ancient and although basic it came from somewhere long ago and it is used everywhere, and from that number came an infinite set of possibilities. Civilization set our dates and symbols in motion thousands of years ago. Our clocks run by them and we live by them and history is written according to the dates. The numerical codes sometimes effect our lives weather we believe in anything deeper surrounding them or not."

"It is a fool's path to gravitate towards explanation of life by pie-in-the sky and numbers and codes, Katka. You should be very careful."

"I agree totally. In fact, I remain very critical about all this metaphysical wonder. However, I stumbled on an excerpt from one article explaining that if we all asked a question on that day of November eleventh at that time 11:00, when masses are all tuned in on the same unified physical mental frequency, all over the planet we should be given something we needed to confirm oneness. This would show we are all connected and one with our universe. We would get an answer that would expand our grasp of true reality. The article also said to be careful what you ask or wish for because it may not be what you want to see or hear." She replied.

"So what did you ask for?" He asked.

"I was trying to figure out what question would be most appropriate to put out into the universe for myself and you know that is not an easy task. But considering how I had felt around this time with so many strange feelings about my sexuality, For some reason I thought about whether or not I was meant to have a man come into my life or not. I was not getting any younger. So, and I know this sounds below me, but I decided to go to an online Internet dating service a week before 11/11, I surfed a few online services reading various profiles, further looking for any clue or symbol that would trigger a response.

"I had no luck and it was getting close to the 11/11 date. Then I went to dinner with a girlfriend who found her partners on a dating service, that was via phone call only. She told me the web-site address and I looked at it. I didn't know why but I could just feel for some strange reason that this phone call method was somehow key.

"When I went on the service and set up a log-in and joined, they let me have a list of phone numbers and names of potential candidates that would be willing to date and even go as far as sleep with me if I wanted. I was a little nervous, but knew it was now or never if I was going to ask this question for myself and to confirm the theories of my scientific experiment. So I downloaded 11 profiles 11 pages long of reading.

"This list of candidates that met a profile that I requested was difficult to sift through because any one could have the qualities that worked with my lifestyle, in other words there were more doctors, lawyers, and Indian chiefs; again like all the other dating sites I had been on, nothing stood out.

"Then I came across one profile about a businessman who traveled and worked regularly in Turkey and had recently toured and assisted in funding major archeological finds near the Syrian border. Suddenly I had a strange spark of interest, primarily because I had been deeply interested in the ruins near the Turkish-Syrian boarder that dated around 10,000 BC.

"Anyway, I decided, based on this coincidence, something told me to choose this businessman to call for a date at 11:00 on 11/11/2011. I was so nervous as I picked up my cell phone in my Boston flat, but at the same time I knew I would have nothing to lose. Something I felt inside was going to come out of it. It was a strange, deep, exciting feeling and it was real strong, doctor. I could hardly sleep and I thought about it day and night until that fateful day came."

Chapter
8
Ammo's Departure

It was the morning of the 11th of November when Ammo awakened in his hotel room at the Nevele Grand Resort in Upstate New York.

"Today was the big day," he thought to himself. He had been waiting for this date for several months. In fact he had followed every symbol and sign to get here. He was getting a little anxious because he could feel that something was coming soon, it was just a matter of time. Any moment in fact… He had just spent the early morning watching a beautiful sunrise from his balcony as he did yoga and sat to meditate with a cup of coffee. Looking over the golden valley with spots of red and orange spread out below him, he thought to himself, "Winter came late this year. Fortunately for Ammo, who was traveling by motorbike, it was calm and quiet outside and warm for this time of year.

So much had happened over the last two years. Ammo began to think he might lose his sanity if something didn't come to tell him why he was chosen to follow this strange pattern. He thought, "What was it that kept me going-riding and searching?"

"I am almost completely broke, but at the same time each coincidence and destined revelation gave me such an incredible high, that high is what I live for."

"Even if I die tomorrow, it was worth it to ride the day-to-day experience, getting more and more enlightened by witnessing pure life playing out moment-to-moment."

It had been such a learning experience since Ammo got kicked out of his house in the end of summer of 2010. Ammo's wife refused to accept the fact that he hadn't any new work prospects. Ammo was a high-end woodworker, who made his fortune during the building boom of the late nineties up to 2008. Then, when the economy crisis imploded, his business dropped and commissions dried up. It was either become depressed, take up drugs and drinking, or find a new hobby to fend off the mounting sadness. Around this time Ammo began to have intense dreams where he was becoming involved with many other people, friends and lovers alike. He began spending much of his time collecting information and reading about anything that spoke to him. This lasted until one day when he came home.

His wife had left a note:

"I needed to go visit my family and get some time alone. I need some time, I think you do also. Please have your things out when I get home. I think our feelings have changed. Amon, you need to find what it is that you're looking for.
Good luck, Amon
Veronica

Ammo sat still meditating, remembering his last few years, thinking, "She just didn't understand what I was going through. That's all and who could understand... I don't blame her. I was weak not to leave long ago. Veronica was for lack of better words a control freak bitch who needed a full-time partner/lap dog, someone who would be devoted to her, and do everything she demanded. We had nothing building our love any more; all we would do is argue and blame each other for everything in a life that just wasn't happening between us."

Ammo became completely obsessed with his senses and consciousness, devouring any reading materials explaining and giving definitions to all of these unique new thoughts, thoughts that left little room for Veronica anymore. As he sat in the hotel looking back he remembered Veronica who was brought to the states in the mid 1980s as a mail-order Russian bride. She had previously punished her first husband slowly, becoming more and more tyrannical while learning that women in the states had an opportunity to manipulate and leverage power.

"I should have been smarter about her; I should have seen her deeper true self through the façade of physical sexual desires. I should have noticed that Veronica had been ruined by strong feelings that the wealthier Western world owed her and her family something. Her new ex-communist attitude made me sick.

She was an untrustworthy petty thief who would secretly steal from her friends and employers and justify it in her own weird superior way, demanding she could do no wrong and that the players surrounding her were only a part of her dreams. She wanted everyone to pay her way and she never opened her wallet. I got an email mentioning that she landed a wealthy lawyer this time, poor bastard. I can only imagine she is taking it up to the next level on him. Perhaps his karma was to have her at her peek of mastered skills. What mystical power is it that brings certain people together, connecting random moments in time of self-fulfilled revelations anyway?"

Ammo thought all this as he sipped hot black coffee and looked out the hotel window, watching the eastern sun rise to greet the golden mass of leaf-barring trees that covered as far as the eye could see.

"We go through so much training down here. I'm over it now," he thought, looking outside the hotel window of the upstate New York hotel. "She did me a favor kicking me out. I can thank her for letting me go, I was too weak to leave. I was a broken man unsure of how to move on by myself even though I wished for it more than anything at the time. I was getting no sign on my own and no direction came to me. However, I know what I need in a woman now and it will have no resemblance to that tortured experience felt being married to Veronica."

It was amazing how easy this odd couple untangled itself in the end. Ammo noticed his psychiatrist friend had a copy of Freud's "*The Interpretation of Dreams,*" laying half torn and molding in the back seat of his camper van.

Of course the book reached out to him and his friend was happy to see him interested and just as happy to pass on the book. The psychiatrist friend said, '*The Interpretation of Dreams'* was like a map or landscape describing our mind's deeper reality, a division of unconscious, preconscious, and conscious domains. Dreams were not considered 'mental rubbish' or unimportant to Freud. Freud felt dreams were some sort of 'mental wish.' Freud reasoned that dreams created abstract patterns, and these were reflections of the unconscious mind."

Ammo's friend opened the book and recited an important paragraph: "Probably the most important description of this masterwork to remember." The psychiatrist located the section, blowing the dust and brushing dog hair from the edges of the old paperback version half held together. He continued:

"This part of the mind was lead by a 'pleasure principal,' In Freudian psychology, the 'pleasure principle' is the psychoanalytic concept for describing people seeking pleasure and avoiding suffering (pain) in order to satisfy their biological and psychological needs. 'In Freud's concept of Dreams this principal

dealt with 'wishes' whose fulfillment admitted of no contradiction and was unbound by logic or time.'

- "Interpretation of Dreams" Sigmund Freud

Ammo wrote for hours in journals, and stayed up late into the night researching on the internet for new metaphysical information about how we can mentally manifest our own destiny through dreams. He was embarrassed when his wife would come in and read over his shoulder, and then she would say something like,"you can't even manifest yourself some new work." Ammo's wife was very conservative, so naturally they clashed when it came to him daydreaming over metaphysical topics.

Truth was, Ammo was not the least bit interested in obtaining new work or money. He always lived for the next moment and the next mind-blowing bit of info. These details kept coming to him through deeply connected feelings and abstract patterns that appeared along a path or fabric as he walked and connected with it on an ever increasing mysterious construct. From his perspective all this had no time frame and gave him a satisfaction and a high greater than any materialistic or socially created reward possibly could.

Ammo had spent much time as a bachelor living for experiences all over the world through his twenties. By the time he was to settle down into building a family, his selfish mate refused to allow this to happen. It was hard to just say goodbye to that freer part of him. Veronica began to need his love less. She began occupying herself with more material needs, her successful professional career as an accountant and her own small groups of friends and colleagues was enough. Naturally, the married life had begun to drag quickly.

It dragged enough to slowly press Ammo towards a return to his solo adventures. Except for a trip to Burning Man or with the Club No Club every year on the motorcycle Ammo felt more and more ready to fly. Now, with a note from her which made everything clear to him, he was ready for this course of action and the time was now.

Luckily Veronica had Ammo sign a prenuptial agreement, because he had made some smart investments. Upon their divorce in early spring 2010, he sold most of his material possessions including a few cars as well as some less valuable stock and then loaded up a minimalist amount of necessities that he would need and strapped them to the old airhead motorbike. He decided to head south to see the Grand Canyon.

At the end of September the weather was as perfect for riding a motorbike as Ammo had ever felt. He traveled long clean roads through ranchlands and open fields of sagebrush and junipers, blue-sky warm mornings and T-shirt afternoons. This dream was going to be realized and it was all perfectly logical what was going on with his re-born adventurous mindset.

On his way south he stopped rather abruptly in a two-horse town called Dyer Nevada, on Nevada State Route 264, because there parked out in front of the local bar were two of the same classic R-100 BMW motorbikes both loaded with gear and covered in dust.

Ammo walked into the local bar and noticed right away a pair of his CNC offshoot motorbike club members called the "Desperados." Both riders sat up at a long wooden bar with a large gathering of local ranchers and miners enjoying an after-shift shot session.

"CC-Rider and Pistola!" He yelled when he noticed them. "What the hell are you guys doin' out here?" Ammo shouted shocking both rugged bikers off of their stools.

CC Rider was Ammo's alter ego; they had known each other since high school and paralleled each other in many ways Both remained interested in adventures and some of those ventures had been brought on sometimes by admiration and inspiration of one-another's ambitions.

They both had traveled the world with backpacks, separately fly fishing, rock climbing, bicycling and soul searching. They found each other after 20 years on the internet only to instantly be reunited as great friends with mountains of amazing stories and experiences in common. They both also shared a strong love for the same concept of remote motorbike riding.

Chris Cantour, a.k.a "CC-Rider," was a 6-foot-6-inch tall quiet, well read giant of a man, and abstract intellectual thinker, also an extremely talented painter and sculptor. However, he was not the most aggressive capitalist businessman. At the time, CC had been struggling to find commissions in San Francisco, where art took a hard hit due to the banking crisis. However, and not to his total displeasure the poor economic climate gave him more time to ride. Rather than be upset with the fact that things were not happening. He utilized the depression and toured the open sky of the West Coast states.

CC embraced Ammo with a large bear hug exclaiming, "Only desperado moto-trash out in these parts. We own them roads don't we? Not surprised to see you, but sure am happy you are here, Ammo. You just missed many of the rest of the gang, the Pilot, Moto-C, Dr. Stony, Diggler, Tucker, Chazko, Wolf, Red, Sherpa and the Night Rider went south about an hour ago I think they were heading for Gold Point to hook up at Sheriff Stones Donation Saloon for steaks, whisky, and all night shuffle board. Our buddies are undoubtedly with a large group of lost French college student au pairs, ladies that the guys had met at the hot springs today. Should be quite a rabble, the two of us opted to remain aloof."

Just then the blond handsome leading man, always an impeccably well dressed, gay, but not a man-loving, Pistola grabs

Ammo around the neck, squeezing him tight into his cinnamon-whisky drenched, whiskered face, yelling:

"Ammo so good to have the three desperados once again re-united on the path to find the spiral of YO."

"What the fuck is he talking about CC?" Asks Ammo half laughing, with a puzzled look as he sat between them at the bar while a short large busted brunette smiled asking him what he wanted to drink.

"Coors, Thanks," he said smiling back at the young woman behind the counter.

"He has been going off on this spiral thing ever since we cut out of San Francisco. That and Fibonacci, Pythagoras, Mondrian, nautilus shells and sun flowers." CC said as the bar waitress passes Ammo a bottle of 'Arrogant Bastard Ale.' Noticing the label, Ammo laughs and looked over to Pistola who smiled wide at him with a shit grin on his face while smoking a cigar.

"That's right," Pistola interjected almost spilling his beer. "It's all about the natural order of the numbers my friend, the golden mean, the Phi and desperados."

"We are the first Fibonacci three, the start of a spiral which will grow exponentially, taking us to the next universe, the Multi verse-and beyond my friends."

Ammo looked questioningly at CC-Rider who smiled and nodded.

Pistola opened his captain safety fanny-pack and poured the contents out onto the bar to share treasures with the attractive young bar waitress who instantly started to admire his painted finger nails, his fine collection of expensive Gucci facial lotions and a rich collection of Native Indian jewelry he collected traveling the lonely parts of Nevada. It was in fact Pistola's obsessive, compulsive nature that made him the man adored by those who worshipped experience and hated by those who feared any uncertainty related to his erratic off-the-hook spontaneity.

"Hey, another round for everyone!" Pistola yelled shaking up the entire bar, arousing a commotion of excited feedback from all corners of the establishment. "And how much for the Dyer T-shirts? Sweetheart, I must have one!" Indeed, for Pistola money never became an object. And money was never an object because he had to spend it. Furthermore, the feeling of instant gratification from owning an object and accumulating material power inspired and motivated him to lavish and share with everyone in his surroundings. He lived as if an actor starring in his own movie, a larger than life character, a loving super hero behind neon detachable multicolored Oakley sun shades. Pistola's instinctive relaxing into unconscious yet conscious actions by the moment generated his greatest highs.

Mario Romano Pizonelli a.k.a Pistola Pistofferson was a world-famous fashion designer of the brand name **UnOnE clothing.** He earned so much money while not working he had to spend it while playing. It was always a truly fun yet manic experience to ride with Pistola.

"See Ammo, that is a man who knows what he wants all the time, however; only from one moment to the next- is it no wonder we all get along so well," CC said, passing a shot of cinnamon spiced whisky to Ammo, They held up glasses clanking together and slammed the liquid down in a smooth gulp.

CC-Rider was also nicknamed by Pistola as 'the man of reason' of the desperado three. He quietly took in all the craziness of the moment between fools, only to wait until just the right time to drop a logical and well-articulated smart bomb just in time to keep spontaneous combustion in check.

"All right gentlemen, we had two legs of whisky. One more and we won't make it out of here alive." CC said with a laugh but very serious about cutting off shots because evening time was setting in. Both Ammo and Pistola now looked at CC, nodding knowing that two legs meant last call in Club No Club lingo. Out in the desert you could ride safe on a shot per leg, but arms and fingers and head go numb beyond that. And no one dare fight CC on that logical foundation. Besides, he was huge and intimidating to look up at. If you fought him physically or verbally you would lose.

"Where are you staying, Ammo?" CC asked as they walked out towards the motorbikes parked under a pair of shady cottonwood tree's in the pastel evening that greeted them with a contrasting coolness to the smoke and stale beer stench and stiff air they left from the inside of the road side bar.

"Not sure yet. Just on my way south towards the Grand Canyon I guess. I am, as usual, going with the flow." Ammo replied.

"Join us. We are camping out at the hot springs tonight. Potentially warm evening and a majestic sunset overhanging," CC added, while he aimed for a gas pump at the Mini Mart, pushing his large black 95 R-100 Dakar, the last of the Airhead Beemers.' That particular model was now rather famous with its shiny chrome dump bars and classic euro breast plate head covers-the ultimate trademark end of a mechanical era...before the company went tech with new complex electrical and cooling systems.

Ammo looked up and smiled at two nice young dark-skinned local girls that greeted him as he pushed his old 92 PD next to CC, who had just begun filling his tank.

"People sure are nice here," Ammo said to CC while placing the bike up on its center stand and removing his gas cap.

CC passed him the filling device. "Yes I think it's the water. They say it has lithium in it. It is no wonder everyone is amiable around here."

Just then Pistola showed up his arms full of fireworks. "Hey guys I just met the feminine version of my alter-ego, the female me. And guess what her nickname is also Pistola. Can you fucking believe it?"

"No way! She's kidding with you man." Ammo said patting him on the back.

"No really! And she sells fireworks and has a bloody container full of them so naturally..."

CC cut him off, laughing and shaking his head, "You naturally had to purchase a bunch. OK, so where is this suspect container load of pyrotechnics?"

"Right over there dude." he says pointing to a cargo ship container next to the mini market.

Ammo and CC headed over to the container to meet the female Pistola: a short yet robust fiery middle-aged attractive gal who, after handing her heaps of cash, goes into a long lecture about attainment of everything you ever wished for and the possibilities of positive thinking, liberal attitudes towards all races and religions, respecting nature and the absolute importance of gun ownership. The successful proprietor happily sends them both off with new wisdom, arm loads of various sized professional class A rockets of their own, and kisses to boot.

"There is something to be said for the contagious haughty sanguine natures of the Pistolas of the world," said CC.

"Yeah, for some strange reason, they seem to validate indulgence in an exhilarating way, don't they CC?"

"Indeed they do, Ammo."

The threesome pulled into the hot springs camping area just as the sun started to fall in the Western sky. After setting up their camp, it was time to soak in the well-maintained valley mineral baths. A 15-by 8-foot rectangle pool with a clean cement edge not always common for a free hot springs. Very clean and inviting, a perfect temperature, not too hot or too cold. The view looking south out at the colorful valley that spread out in front of them was majestic a mineral rainbow of multiple unique earth hues spread out across the entire mountain range east to west.

Next to them also camping in motor homes, were a few snowbirds, no doubt on their migratory departure to some very southern warmer climate as the fall and winter would push them into each new comfort zone.

Pistola wearing nothing but a light green bandana around his neck jumped into the warm spring screaming, "We begin the spiral of Yo my friends!"

"What is that spiral of Yo thing, Pistola?" Ammo asked him while opening a tall can of cold Coors beer.

Pistola looks at Ammo with a serious look…"Just say Yo," he answers with a serious look on his face. "Nancy Ragan knows Ammo, remember… "Just say YO."

"Nancy Ragan," CC interjects…you're high man. Her campaign in the 1980s was 'Just say NO,' No to drugs and I would suggest you heed her warning, Captain Safety."

With a confident tone, Pistola explained. "Yes, well the spiral of Yo is a positive, beautiful energy formed by an order that must be respected, worshipped and valued, my brethren. Most every flower and leaf and natural creature and body on this earth follows an order of $0, 1+1=2=3=5=8=13=21$…. and so on. We are all connected, every living thing by mathematics and it is a real deal. We are naturally and sensually drawn to most things, which geometrically fit within us harboring the perfection of this code, because we are connected to it. Even people connect mathematically, like attracts like look at us, the three Desperados who live for the accumulation of exceptional moments, cherishing the next one even more than the last."

"What are you getting at Pistola? Are you saying we are part of a program of some sort? what is your point?" CC asked laughing while making a fire, listening to the conversation next to him going on in the pool, as the night sky and stars begin to appear above them.

"Dudes, check it out! Why do you think I have made so much money as a designer of women's clothes? Because I can play in the competitive fashion world really well even though I am straight and not an intimate lover of men. Do you think it is because I just have a lucky star over my head? Guess again, the reason I have been so successful is because I tapped into the power of the golden ratio, gentlemen. And I am not the only one. It is real and it works. I started designing clothing that has patterns utilizing these geometric formulas that become pleasing to the eye that's all. We are naturally attracted to them and artists have used this formula of perfection to the eye, for centuries. It is nothing new."

Ammo interrupted, "I know about the golden ratio. Pistola. And I am intrigued by its idealized perfection, and its effects on our subconscious. However; when one compares the open abstract beauty of a child's mind that is unaware of prescribed empirical codes that has a particular beauty as well, does it not? In other words, you say look at Mondrian or daVinci, and I say look at Cezanne, Picasso or Zrzavy. There always needs to be a balance between the code of mathematical perfection and a random out-of place, unexplainable connection to that which is only phenomenal and uniquely original or perhaps human because we are imperfect creatures at the very same time."

"Perhaps that is why many of the downtrodden masses are in the mess they are in," shouted CC rider, the voice of reason as he set up the fireworks show near the pool. Perhaps there are truly two types of math, or codes, each constantly contradicting the other… one perhaps similar to fractal geometry, a much more abstract mathematics leading the spirit and true subconscious reality, and another greedy, leading and writing a version of manipulated reality with power over the hungry confused belly."

Just then, a blast of fire filled the pool area with a bright and spectacular light. Sizzzle poof Bang! Ba, Bang, Bang! Boom! Then the threesome rolled with loud obnoxious laughter, falling sometimes hysterically in and out of the hot bath pool. All along they drank and soaked up the hours of freedom and celebration of the moment, basking in the aromas of sulfur, beer, whisky and gunpowder. The whole time the snowbirds watched the show from the safety of their 25-foot mobile homes, able to hear every bizarre, loud and obnoxious abstract conversation that these three alien Desperados brought with them to the once-tranquil valley spring.

Early the next morning, Pistola and CC were awakened by the sudden discharge of rounds from an automatic weapon as an angry retaliating snow bird exited the steps of his motor home, yelling at the top of his lungs, "Wake up you mother fuckers!"

Ammo just slept on, motionless in his sleeping bag. When Ammo did finally wake, he noticed a strong pain in his right foot. He had somehow torn his entire middle right toenail off the previous night and a trail of blood lead to his sleeping bag. As Ammo sat up, he looked a little lost and confused. He found CC and Pistola laughing at the angry snowbird's morning show while beginning to pack their bikes and dress. The three passed coffee and granola bars and fruit around as they laughed off the whole experience of the night before.

"So, where are you going today, Ammo?" CC asked as Pistola gathered fireworks and trash scattered all over the pool area before placing each piece of trash into a paper sack.

"I'll head south, same as the snowbirds fly, friends. Arizona for now, I guess. Where ever the vibe takes me, and you?"

Just then Pistola walked over to CC and Ammo, putting a shiny, silver badge into their hands: "Ammo, we must go north back to Californication also known as the land of plenty and confusion and mostly plenty of confusion. But I want you both to have something to remember this time and our adventures together on the pathway of YO."

"What's this?" CC asked holding up a polished stainless steel five-pointed child's star badge with the words 'U.S. MARSHAL' written across the top.

Pistola already wore his while handing them out, saying, "It's the badge of the three desperados, my friends. The Fibonacci 3, the starters of fire spirit, and the power of the nature guides to the spiral of YO."

"Oh shit, not that YO thing again," Ammo said, shaking his head as he poured another cup of coffee from the jet boil stove...

"Badges," he yells in a Mexican accent, "we don't need any stinking badges." They all laughed, "yes, a marshal that's for us ha ha good one... U.S. Marshals for sure. If I wear this the cops might think I am a condescending Joker and an offensive smart ass and want to lock me up."

"So wear it upside down," shouted CC "That should place you in the fool category in the eyes of authority. That is when they will sometimes cut you some slack. Once they start to pity you for being the true jackass that you most certainly are, Ammo. Here, I put mine upside down. How does that grab you? Now it doesn't read U.S. MARSHAL anymore."

CC looked at the upside-down star, "Now it's looking more like an upside-down pentagram. Sure it is a pentagram 'ooo! That's almost cult-like symbolism. Now it reads 'L-AH-S-RAM S-n.' or something like that?"

"They all exclaimed "ooo" at the same time!

Ammo now chuckled and attached the last few items to his bike while he fired up the classic bike, waking the calm morning with the sound that for him was nothing more than of thumping and gurgling euphony. "So that is perfect, and a much more abstract representation of your spiral of YO theory, wouldn't you say, Pistola? A symbolic mystic pentagram with a strange unrecognizable word?"

"CC responded, "LAHSRAM Sn sounds almost Eastern or Asian and ancient. I guess it's all how you turn the world and it's orders and codes and letters upside down and connect it together to form a new order and abstract meaning, even if it only means something to very few who get it. Perhaps that way you can hide and manipulate the world into your favor?

Ammo turned his badge upside-down and clasped it to the front of his camel back: "Or, perhaps it is a safer way to be your true self in a world that wants to control us by a code and prescribed language and order which they own and manipulate us with?"

Pistola shouted, "Exactly Ammo, That's what I was saying all the time and the idea of the badge, Ammo... it's only a symbol for the riders of the spiral of YO, dude. It is our math and code, Dig! We can see who is down with the Desperados' the sunflowers and the sacrificial bees. Maybe there are more U.S. MARSHALS out there surfing the wave and arrow of time who want to fight the destroyers of the unchained mind and the natural mother?"

"We will only know when we ask them if they are U.S. Marshals?" CC adds, smiling at Ammo.

"What should they say guys?" asked Pistola very attentively.

"Damn straight, I am not." CC Yelled.

"Am not what?" Pistola asked, looking at Ammo who is chuckling and nodding back smiling as Pistola Googles up 'Lahsram Sn' from his iPod.

"Ah, yes, I get it...HA HA that's good I like it."

"Oh, soundtracks, cool here is the link I will send it to you right now so you can listen."

"So with that thought, I bid you good day, gentlemen," Ammo

climbed on his bike. "As always it has been a most memorable pleasure hanging out with you Desperados on another fantastic, spontaneous, in-the-face-anything-goes-off-the-hook adventure. But I must be off on my own now… She calls me as we speak. God speed, men, and by all means keep up the faith in Dreams and Experience."

As Ammo locates the Google audio link: *lahsram sn* that Pistola had sent on his smartphone. Ammo put his head phones on, revved up his bike and flew off into the cool morning. He continued listening to relaxing, calm, melodic beats while sticking his fist into the air and yelling, "LAHSRAM sn."

Ammo felt awesome, alone again in his helmet, the power of YO, a symbol represented the ride and why we ride ever forward letting go of the past yet not forgetting what we learned. Surrounded by twisted vibrating string-like matter, the theoretical physics of time and space past, present and future is perhaps only an illusion, a conundrum or perhaps a hilarious show tuned in via a profound frequency being watched by more advanced beings than ourselves.

"What if we mix up the logic of time and our expected script and reason of this puzzle of life reality playing out before us?" "I like it," he thought riding out into the cool desert morning air thinking deeply while space like electronic sounds of this connected new random music play into his helmet… slowing his perception of time down as the landscape, unmoved, raced by his view at 80 miles per hour.

"What if we rebel and tweak the quantum all connected mechanical script from outside the conformity of the dismal manmade prescribed matrix?" he thought, "We are all truly linked by a time frame by frame, A cosmic energy called the 'Now' or is it 'woN Buddhism' or Zen or neZ Perce if we play the Desperados game of connecting powerful links…taking us deeper into the spiral of the new mental hysterical dawn of the code of the U.S. Marshals, or perhaps all of the above?" elgooG or Google, we keep on searching, learning, connecting, creating abstractly.

We are integrating like ancient Vedic mathematicians reading backwards and forwards, up and down, perhaps even upside down, whatever it takes to break into the code of the ultimate Multiverse which may be the holy grail landscape we have all been waiting for. The only true jackass and enemy of the mind is the one who just says NO?"

When Ammo got to the southwest end of the Grand Canyon something spoke to him from the many billboards advertising Sedona, Arizona.

TRY YOGA AND FEEL YOUNG
AND FREE AT THE SEDONA YOGA RETREAT

Ammo got some work as a handyman and janitor in trade for a room and classes at The Sedona Yoga Retreat. While there, he met many people who were feeling similar to him, almost everyone making complete life changes. He never realized how important his mind body connection was until then. Yoga was a perfect balance to his daily routine. It was also perfect insurance for a motorbike rider. Being flexible made the long rides tolerable. Furthermore, if Ammo dumped the bike he stood a better chance of getting back up and on it.

He stayed in Sedona for a few months from the end of fall into the start of winter. He learned to improve his basic yoga and the mastery of coffee meditation. Strangely, this meditation would push him out of Sedona.

This transition began kicking into gear when Ammo met a social hippy girl named Summer Lane, a tall, thin 18 year old who liked to eat vegan food except for pepperoni pizza. She also liked to mooch off people, especially anyone who had grass. At least this was the rumor and gossip passed around the small town. Ammo usually had a bag so Summer was quick to hook on to him.

Every morning, Ammo would start his day with a coffee and meditation just sitting in a chair looking out from his room window while drinking coffee on cold days or when weather permitted outside on the porch. Ammo would gaze in a trance of observation at the dry, fascinating sandstone red, orange and yellow rock walls that surrounded the beautiful hills of this desert paradise. Just about every morning like clockwork, Ammo would settle into his deeper relaxed meditative zone, then all of a sudden…knock-knock-knock!

"Hey, dude, do you have any ganja?" She would ask, commanding a certain kind of authority that he had difficulty denying for some strange reason. There she was, Summer Lane, with full blonde dreadlocks, round face with freckles and ripped up old purple down ski vest, peg pants in leather moccasins, reeking of an overdose of patchouli oil and looking like some kind of alien creature... Right up in his face, starring at him with a phony grin and those yellow teeth.

Ammo was not the confrontational type, and besides he had experience, sure he would give her the grass thinking perhaps this was the way for him to get her respect to leave him alone. Unfortunately, it did not work. She kept it up. Every day she interrupted his peace demanding her morning smoke and then he wouldn't see her at all the rest of the day.

One day Ammo tried to trick Summer Lane. He took his routine to the café and sat looking out at the view off their back east facing deck, it was on this day as the sun rose and cast an intense warmth. Ammo fell into an amazing vision of vast jungles and trees and exotic creatures everywhere, such a contrast to the dry treeless desert where he had been up till now. There were leopards and panthers and monkeys and beautiful rainforests and…

"Hey, Dude, got any Ganja?"

"God damn it, Summer Lane." He said spilling his coffee all over himself. "Why do you do this every morning and how did you know I was here? Can't you see that I am meditating here and I try to do it every morning before I go to work but you ruin it every day!" he yelled.

"Sorry, dude, but I have my rounds every day and that is what I do dude every day, and you… Mr. Ammo Man are my every morning puff master. So get off your egoist self-centered caffeine jonesing meditation trip… and roll me up a splif cowboy, I want to get stoned."

Ammo, shaking his head pulled out the Zip-lock bag from his leather jacket and handed the whole thing to her. "I thought you would be conscious enough to notice when someone is meditating?" He said still shaking his head.

"You don't know how to meditate you just sit in a fucking window drinking coffee," she said laughing.

"Listen summer… that is how it works for me. I cant sit in lotus style for very long; it hurts my back. Besides, would you have left me alone if I had?"

"We will never know unless you try it will we?" She said as she rolled a big joint and licked the ends and lighted up."Try it tomorrow morning." She held in a full breath of smoke and then blew it out slowly.

"I will, but I will also be leaving after that."

"Where to?" She asked passing the joint to Ammo.

He took a hit with half held breathe: "I am heading south. I am getting a calling from the equator, I think I need to experience the green jungles and rainforests and wild lush plant life."

"Cool!" She said, tossing the small empty bag of grass in his lap. "See you Dude, have fun. I am on the run, Hasta la vista, Dude!" Summer Lane then skips out while Ammo sat shaking his head, wiping the soaked coffee stain from his T-shirt.

The next morning Ammo sat on the porch outside his room soaking in the heat from the sun as it rose in the East. This time he tried the lotus position remembering that today perhaps that crazy Summer Lane would not bug him if he did. He knew today he would be driving out heading in a direction which made it hard for him to clear his mind. Another sip of coffee and he was slowly back into it, he was back at the jungle.

When he came out of the zone a full hour later feeling great and even his back was relaxed and feeling strong. He looked down and on the deck in front of him was a small mason jar full of perfect buds.

Inside at the top of the jar was a small note:

Hey Dude:

You never got mad at me like most people. I know my nature, and it is who I am.

I will never change... it's what it takes to live here in this crazy privileged crystal vortex hell we locals call home. Thanks for all the smoke, keep up your "Coffee Meditation" but if you don't want people to bother you try it in lotus.

Later, Dude Love Summer

It was early November, 2010, when Ammo rode down through Mexico. This new journey that took him through the ancient ruins of the Aztec and then down to Nicaragua and finally landing in Nosara, Costa Rica on the Guanacaste coast of the Pacific Side. Nosara fascinated him because it had the most eclectic mix of nationalities. Characters the likes he had never seen congregated into one little remote part of the center of the two continents. These diverse characters ranged from ex drug lords, pirates, silver-spoon corporate trust account gringo children, surfers, poor artists, and hippies to wealthy secretive millionaires. Many hid out using mom and dad's credit cards so they could frolic with all the beautiful people that floated in and out of this hidden gem.

Nosara also became the Yoga Mecca of Costa Rica, with three schools offering many classes and styles. This increasingly popular Central American country also emerged as a favorite among surfers thanks to incredibly perfect year-round waves, and clean soft sand beaches. Ammo spent the winter of 2010-11 and New Years there studying at the Nosara Yoga School where he connected with the owner who the locals called the Enlightened One.

The Enlightened One was a surf and yoga teacher-guru-fantasy host and Don Juaneque lover of all races of women. The Enlightened One lived to fulfill the dreams of everyone who stayed at his hotel. This tall, slick Ricardo Montalban in long surf shorts possessed a great off-the-wall sense of humor. He became one of the first people to settle Nosara and build a hotel and business there when the region was more wild and untouched by tourism. He was a retired, recovering pot smuggler in his middle 40's with a few skeletons in his closet. He earned a well-deserved nickname, the King of Fun. His Majesty was always ready for a party and loved to be the provider of good times for all. But if you crossed the Enlightened One, beware. He could easily have your toe or finger removed by his strong man Guido, the Sicilian. Everyone feared Guido, extremely strong and intelligent, Nosara's best chess and soccer player. Guido, not only spoke Italian and Spanish, but also French, English and German. He had the best, most nefarious connections in this rather lawless part of Central America.

If you needed drugs or a car or a hooker you went to Guido. He impressed people as fair and honorable, something lacking here where you had to watch your things all the time and could trust almost no one at any time unless you were on a first-name basis with them. If Guido had your back you were in good hands. If anyone hassled you, one only needed to mention his name. Ammo was quick to get on Guido's good side.

Ammo got a job as the Enlightened One's Jack of all trades. He found himself doing everything from painting and welding to sign making for the hotel or maintaining his 1968 Land Rover that broke down with problems just about every week. There was no end to the projects at the hotel, which overlooked one of the most beautiful views of the Pacific Guanacaste coast along a one lane dirt road, off Coastal Highway 1.

One of the Enlightened One's hobbies was 'klepto-botany'… or recycling coconut trees and plants for his hotel. He loved plants and nature above all and mostly watching his hillside estate turn into a bigger, thicker and more diverse jungle. He became very excited when a group of scientists had developed the first *Fractal Geometric* study of the Guanacaste Rainforest near his Hotel. Researchers measured every inch of carbon consumption from the leaves, stems and stalks, plus the trunk down to the roots. Based on data from a single tree, scientists also calculated the average distance from each plant to its neighbor. Then a mathematical abstract mass of information and numbers was crunched with new and exciting geometry.

This huge amount of data showed the value of large tropical

old-growth forests by providing empirical mathematical proof. The Enlightened One would say, "Anyone who thinks that carbon is not a real issue and that these trees are not important should have their wealth taken and their fucking heads cut off."

He often bragged that his family hailed from a long line of honorable Scottish-Afro-Latino mulatto sea pirates that cornered the trade routes of the Caribbean. He harbored strong and handsome genetic characteristics, he got equally powerful traits from both his mother's and father's side of the family. The Enligtened One reasoned and weighed out the benefit of each moment and action and lived by the old Scottish ancestral code of honor your word and "tit for tat."

He kept a shit list. If someone screwed him on a business deal he took it out on that person in coconut trees and exotic foliage, when his victims were out of town. It was a simple solution really and no one got hurt. He would send his Nicaraguan gardeners and a flat-bed truck for a visit to the Ranchito of his choice. No one with wealth ever stayed in Costa Rica year-round. It was hard to stay long. It would make you crazy, in fact many referred to the Region of Nosara as "the open-air insane asylum." It was here where Ammo developed a deep love for jungle morning yoga, evening sundown surfing sessions, and nights at the Bamboo Bar, and the best coffee he had ever meditated on.

After an incredible evening at the Black Sheep Pub high in the hills overlooking Nosara, Ammo found himself a bit lost, and without direction. Ammo found an abandoned golf cart with key's left in it and decided to borrow it for the night. A bleach blond Tico surfer that Ammo saw everywhere but never learned the guy's name, looked like Spicoli from the 1982 movie, '*Fast Times at Ridgemont High*.' On this particular night Ammo picked him up somewhere on a road to no where, then joined him at the Tropicana where Costa Rica disco DJ's were spinning the best of Latino-salsa all night.

When Ammo walked in he immediately noticed the many attractive women, all very excited to share their wholesome beauty with every man who flapped around them like birds in a mating ritual.

Ammo just wanted to sit down and watch the energy display out before him and listen to the rhythmic sounds and beats of unique local dance hall Costa Rican rap music. If ever there was a place that projected pure sexuality this was it.

Just then Spicoli the surfer and three absolutely beautiful women from the Dominican Republic approached the coffee table and sat down at the sofa next to him. Ammo's Spanish was poor but the three dark-skinned shapely kittens spoke even better English than most of the Nosara Latino locals he had met thus far.

"Do you like the music and do you like to dance?" asked one of the Dominican beauties wearing a low-cut black blouse revealing very soft bronze round breasts. She began to swing her shoulders left and right.

"Not yet thanks… later perhaps," he said, smiling at her while nervously scratching the back of his head. "I just arrived I need to settle into the mood." Ammo continued sitting there somewhat stunned thinking for a moment he was in a dream.

"Wait, he now thought shaking his head. This was a dream I have seen this. So why not make the best of it."

Just then right on queue Guido walked in wearing a white shirt and slim slacks with a beautiful Latino princess latched onto him. Guido noticed Ammo and walked directly up to his table.

"Hey, Ammo man, can I get you anything?" Guido asked nodding his head in gesture showing respect for a man that can attract such an impressive entourage. "I have access to all of the pleasure enhancers necessary to make the females of our species want to give us all we want and perhaps then some."

"Hi, Guido, I just realized that, this is a dream I am revealing as time ticks by and I want to make it the best it can be before I awaken from it."

"Sounds profound, Ammo. But by all means my friend, don't wake up yet. Can I get you anything?"

"Oh, yes, sure. You know what to get. We are living it, Guido, if you could." Ammo looked around and gestured to the three ladies surrounding him. "Please get us a party size?"

"Guido mi amigo... but only the real quality one please, and perhaps something to drink. You know what will do the trick. Could you help me with that my friend?" Then Ammo handed Guido two one hundred-dollar bills.

"I will bring you a bottle." Guido said turning towards the bar and returning almost instantly with a large bottle of Tequila on a tray with four shot glasses.

While the women drank their shots, Ammo sat there overwhelmed with how absolutely beautiful they all were. He normally would have been completely shy and uncomfortable by so much sexual energy that he and these women were exchanging as he sat there. However, this time he knew that this night was meant for him, his dream come true.

He had seen it in meditations. He knew that these women belonged to him this night. No one asked them to dance and Spicoli the surfer disappeared. Everyone was leaving them all alone as if they were three hams left in a pond belonging to only one piranha.

Ammo wondered if the women were thinking as many nasty thoughts as he was and if he was a part of their dream as well. "Could three perfectly beautiful Afro-Latino women want to have one middle-aged gringo man?" He thought to himself? Just then Guido returned with a small plastic bag about as large as a pack of chewing gum, and handed it to Ammo.

"Have a good party, Pura vida Amigo!" Guido said, nodding and smiling, before walking off with his date toward the packed dance floor.

When the three Dominican women saw the coke they became instantly animated and jovial. Each took a turn with a rolled- up bill, poking it into the package and inhaling and laughing in Spanish and hugging each other and getting closer to Ammo with every moment. Ammo had a blast of the coke, and passed it on, then laid back dizzy into the couch and watched everyone move around the dance hall incredibly fast. For some reason the coke had a worthless effect on him, quite the opposite from what he was expecting. Just then one of the girls reached into his pocket and started to rub him arousing his heartbeat and hardening his lower central muscle.

It was just around this time when the Enlightened One showed up with two tall bleach blonde Barbie surfer girls from Switzerland, wearing short skirts and almost see-through blouses.

"Hay Ammo! This is Swiss Miss One and Swiss Miss Two," Everyone laughed including the blondes. The Enlightened One took a seat on the couch next to Ammo with blonde beauties clinging to him from both sides. Pushing-the whole group squeezed in closer together into the half-moon shaped couch.

"Is this place not magical?" he asked Ammo, smiling a wide grin while he took a turn poking the rolled straw into the bag of coke and passing it to one of the Barbies who giggled and shook her hair whipping it back behind her face as she took her turn.

Ammo loved seeing the variation of beauty that surrounded him, white women, black women, chocolate women. All gathered together as if they were on their own island around that small coffee table in the center of the world.

It was more than he had ever dreamed of… he was surrounded by a mass of sexual energy and beauty that filled him with extreme love. He wanted that moment to last for as long as he could keep it going. Everyone got so high and everyone smiled and flirted, laughed, and hugged.

After the coke went a few rounds, Ammo and the Enlightened One decided that pretty soon it was going to be anyone's game with these fine ladies unless they moved the party to a more private location. The coke landed one more time on one of the Swiss surfer babes. After she took a long snort and cleared her throat with a shot of booze, she started necking with one of the Dominican women, and then everyone began to get horny watching those two go at it. That's when the Enlightened One who doesn't like to mince words jumped up holding a bottle of Tequila and at the same time grabbed a black girl in one arm and a white one in the other and let out:

"Hey lets all go to the la finca for a fuck fest!"

Everyone cheered and yelled "fuck fest!"… the Swiss girls added.

"Viva la fuck fest, yea! Oh La La! Hurra! Fuck-Fuck-Fuck!"

Then they all got up off the couch and made a train holding each other's waist and danced weaving through the Tropicana chanting, "finca fuck fest! finca fuck fest! Oh La La!"

"Oh La La," Ammo added, grabbing hold of the end so not to loose track and let his dream run away from him.

It was a 10- minute jeep drive through the warm night to the finca (or ranch). Friends of the Enlightened One called it the Panty Dropper Villa.

Nestled high up in the trees overlooking the Pacific Coast, large indoor outdoor decks made of beautiful local hardwoods gave this jungle bungalow a charm ideal for romancing. Everyone continued singing and joking as they rolled up to the ranch.

Ammo flopped out of the Land Rover, and fell into a bush… getting mud all over himself. Now standing up… Everyone broke out laughing. Seeing him, the Swiss miss standing nearest him points at him while laughing hysterically.

"Oh funny," he mumbled, smearing mud on her breasts.

Then she grabbed mud and slapped it back in his face.

"Hey, it looks fun," shouted one of the Dominican women, as she took a handful and slapped it onto the Enlightened One.

"OK, that's enough, he yelled, picking her up then carrying her to the small swimming pool, and throwing her in.

Ammo pulled off his pants and shirt and jumped in after her. Then within seconds everyone got naked and frolicked in the pool splashing around and laughing and howling into the night.

Howler monkeys (genus ***Alouatta*** monotypic in subfamily **Alouattinae**) are among the largest of the New World monkeys. Fifteen species are currently recognized. These monkeys are native to South and Central American forests. Threats to howler monkeys include human predation, habitat destruction and being captured for captivity as pets or zoo animals. -*Wikipedia definition*

"HOO! HOO! HOO! HOOOOO!" Was this the howler monkey's distinct sound that awakened the wild animals of the Guanacaste Jungles?

Ammo lay fully nude in a large hammock with two naked Dominican women snuggled up in both arms. Four large black monkeys slowly swung between trees 10 to12 feet above the colorful party. The monkeys looked down at all the mess scattered about in all directions. Bottles of Tequila, beer cans, underwear, bongs, and strange questionable paraphernalia, boxes and wrappers of used and unused condoms were everywhere dotting the pool area.

Over to Ammo's left was the Enlightened One, on an inflatable mattress sandwiched literally between the two Swiss girls, his face buried in the breasts of the Dominican woman. They looked as if tangled into a pretzel shape of white and dark chocolate. Locked together, all four snored and remained oblivious to the time which meant absolutely nothing to any of them.

Perhaps this late show had been intended for the native monkeys that clung to the branches. The primates undoubtedly had witnessed the wild arthropods that invaded their territory the previous night and woke up the jungle with the sounds of serious all-night multi-cultural mating cries; if monkeys could dream?

That afternoon the Enlightened One and Ammo sat outside on the deck at the Bamboo Bar on the main corner of the wild western run down small village of Nosara. They calmly killed their headaches by drinking bottles of imperial beer with lime. Both are laid back and talked very slowly as their initial hangovers started to subside. A parade started to form further down the street, coming straight toward them. The parade signified the opening day of the local Nosara Rodeo Fiestas.

"If I don't get away from here soon this place is going to kill me," Ammo said, taking another sip of his beer.

"Yes," said the Enlightened One, setting his beer on the table. "Everyone says that same thing and everyone returns as well because here there is only 'Pura Vida'… Pure Life, my friend, every day….So do you know where you will go next?

"No, not yet, it hasn't come. I usually get visions from meditations and dreams and signs and symbols show me the pathways. Probably all the drugs are inhibiting the process this time."

"Perhaps you need to be here for a while. Maybe you needed to live the wild life… You're having a good time, right?"

Ammo held up the beer and nods his head. "Who wouldn't? This place is a beautiful paradise. It seems so free and easy here and all of the women are so loving and nice to me. I love women."

"It is the warmth and the wild energy of this land and the sea, Ammo. We are truly one and connected with nature more here than in the northern cold cities. The enlightened one replied.

This place brings out the natural beast in all of us, some positive and some negative. It is a powerful passionate energy, very difficult to control, that is why one must go with each moment and surf it, Mon. Be happy, smoke what you like, eat what you like, and fuck who you like, Mon, as long as you are not hurting anything. Do the ting dat make you happy, Mon, and every-ting will be Iree!"

"Now I see why they call you the Enlightened One!" Ammo said as they clanked the two brown bottles with black and yellow labels. Just then the parade of caballeros on horseback started trotting past them outside the Bamboo Bar. Within a few minutes this once-dead quiet little corner became alive with hundreds of local cowboys and cowgirls dressed in their best western clothes and all maneuvering their beautiful animals into various tricks of foot and fancy.

Lasso artists and trick ropers danced to mariachi bands, and singers walked within reach of Ammo on the one lane dirt road. The sounds built up and roared a commanding presence and then just as fast they faded into a dead quiet distance on down the dusty road that leads out of town to the fairgrounds. Within a half hour the show was history.

"Until this time next year," said the Enlightened One, as the parade slowly meandered its way out of sight, leaving only the haze of dust falling back to the hot dry clay and molasses-soaked ground of the still-composed, quiet yet busiest corner of Nosara.

Chapter
9
11/11/11

Ammo is back in Upstate New York.

It's 2011 on the 11th day of the 11th month Ammo comes out of a downward-dog stretch thinking to himself, "I am staying in the 'Nevele Grand' and today I am looking for some sign that I don't even know will appear."

He talks to himself just while finishing his yoga and taking a shower. He washes his long salt and pepper grey hair with a bottle of hotel soap with Nevele hotel written on the label. He laughs at the thought that it is this path and hunt for symbolic meaning that he lives for now.

Momentarily, Ammo wandered down to the restaurant for a cup of coffee.

Ammo took a seat in the corner of the hotel café across from a loud group of three women and a playboy, all drinking bloody marries and doing their best part to keep their previous evening all-night party alive. Ammo sat reading the New York Times while daydreaming

"I rode across the entire country to be here now in this place at this moment for whatever will come any moment. What a crazy bastard I have become." Ammo thought as the waitress approached. She asked, "What can I get you?"

"I have no idea. What do you recommend?" He asks looking blankly at the menu and shaking his head.

"We make a great breakfast sandwich." She replied with a smile. "eggs, avocado, tomato, cheddar, on sourdough or…"

He cut her off…"that sounds perfect…"

"Some more coffee?" She adds.

"Please," he answers smiling.

Ammo knew something was going right, this place was expecting him, because breakfast sandwiches were his favorite morning meal on the road, and not every place made them. They usually had just the right dose of ingredients, not too heavy and not too light.

Ammo began settling into his thoughts, which always became instantaneous whenever he waited for food.

Ammo was able to drop into meditation pretty much at any time, anywhere he liked, after learning the last few years how to master his consciousness.

The threesome carrying on at the table across from Ammo brought back memories of the wild adventures he had shared with the Enlightened One and the journey down south of the boarder. While sitting at the booth waiting for his meal, he remembered the rest of the long journey that brought him to this very moment.

Ammo had stayed for the rest of winter in Nosara until feeling a need to see Panama before crossing Colombia to Brazil in late spring. In middle June 2011, Ammo put his bike on a ship and boarded the Continental Airlines flight out of Rio to- Huston, Texas, where he picked up his bike and rode it to a Dream workshop in Flagstaff, Arizona.

As he waited for his flight in the airport he browsed a magazine rack, instantly attracted to a *National Geographic* with the text '*Birth of Religion Gobekli Tepe*' and a picture of an ancient ruin on the cover. Something struck him, so he purchased the magazine and stuffed it in his motorcycle carry-on tank-bag, only to forget about its essential importance until later.

When Ammo arrived in Flagstaff he felt completely worn out from partying through the winter. Rio had taken every last bit of his strength. He had wanted to stay south of the Equator, however the distractions and the availability of drugs and free-loving women was separating him from his more truthful and deeper purpose. He needed to reconnect and get back on the wave that controlled his healthy mind, body, and spirit. In Rio he had met two Australian Lesbians in a downtown café. The women had just started their South American journey, riding down from Canada on a pair of Honda African twins.

After a long morning, this quick acquaintance made over several cups of coffee between three riders came in the nick of time for Ammo. He had a need to find clear-headed fellow journeyers to share with, and share he did. Ammo was not usually one to open up, but these two beautiful strong spiritual motorbikers were very warm and friendly and they instantly saw that he needed someone to talk to. Ammo explained his journey and the trials and tribulations and of dreams and drugs and of falling off the path.

"Yes," he said. "I came down to meditate, do yoga and get into my deeper connection with higher consciousness, and what happened was quite the opposite, and that is cool and I have had so many amazing experiences by going with this 'don't-say-no, just-say-Yo! flow, but it has hit a complete roadblock finally."

One of the Aussie women gazed at him with a serious look, then turned to her friend, "Should we tell him about Dream Catcher Camp?"

"Sure, he seems cool and they would like him there," the other women said.

"What is it?" he asks excited by the name of it.

"'Dream Catcher Camp,' well we ran into it on the way down

207

here on the bikes. It is high in the mountains of Flagstaff, Arizona. A group of people keep it going year-round and it is basically a non-profit multi-cultural commune gathering of interesting people from all walks of life who come and go as they like, contributing to a building of shared higher consciousness, that is all.

They have seminars and lectures by various writers and gurus and philosophers and scientists and physics professors, anthropologists and artists. All kinds of creative stuff, but the main thing they are into is the conscious and sub conscious mind and how the brain works. They are big on dream workshops and they have them on going. We took part in one and it was interesting. It was very helpful because it got us to find a balance with our unconscious feelings that normally caused distraction and confrontation to living in the moment without fear or anxiety. The workshops helped us learn to live better with the moment and how to understand for ourselves what is good and not good for us in that moment."

"Wow, that sounds exactly like what I need. I have the hardest time saying 'no' or enough is enough," he said, taking out a pen to write down the information.

Enough was enough, thus Ammo returned to North America not far from Sedona, the place that sent him down with his original dream of going south. Strange how these things work out." Ammo thought as he road up into the high cool alpine forest outside of Flagstaff.

When Ammo arrived at the Dream Catcher Camp in the end of June, he noticed several teepees and nicely built cabins. He parked at the largest cabin and went up to the front door, as people were just exiting. When the last person who was about to close the door, noticed Ammo.

"Hi, can I help you?"

"Yes, I am here for the dream workshop if there are any

positions available at this time?

"Yes, there is one starting in the morning. But we normally require a pre-registration. Did you sign up for one?"

"No, I just followed advice from someone to come here and I followed my feelings to take me here and I have cash to pay for it, no prob."

"Well, I'm sorry but we have some strict rules about non-registered strangers entering our groups. It is not a money issue. We have had some bad experiences with unknowns showing up uninvited, if you know what I mean. We like to know who is here, so don't take it personally but I think you will have a hard time getting in this one and the next one won't start for another month. Again, I am very sorry. Our website has all the registration info; I recommend you start there. Good luck… Bye."

Upset, Ammo watched the man walk on down a path and disappear. He was upset mainly because he had traveled far to be there. He felt let down by his calling and wondered if this feeling to return to Arizona was all just not even really what he felt.

He heard the sounds of a stream running near where he parked the motorbike, and followed the sound which lead him to a small cliff edge. From there he looked down upon a beautiful 20-foot waterfall and a lush garden area where he noticed many different people spread out doing meditation and yoga. Some just sat around having picnics and chatting while others swam in nice granite pools of crystal clear water.

Ammo took a seat at a bench to rest and watch all the cool people having a good time below. He thought how strange it was to feel as if belonging somewhere that he wasn't allowed to go. At the same time, he tried to think of a way to get into the dream workshop. So he closed his eyes and said to himself. "I am here and I know that I must be here. I must stay here and find out what it is I must do next. I need a symbol; I need a sign. This is where

I feel I need to be if it is meant to be. Perhaps it wasn't meant to be?" He sat there in deep trance for some time.

"Hey Dude! What are you doing here?"

Ammo turned and there she was, Summer Lane, sporting her dreadlocks now full of beads. This time she wore a half cut T-shirt, shorts and flip flops. Was this the sign from the universe, A message of some sort from the last crazy women he remembered exchanging words with in North America. She had been the person who pretty much helped send him on his journey out of Sedona, because of her obnoxious nature, he thought to himself as he shook his head in disbelief.

"Summer Lane, it can't be?" Ammo still sat on the stone bench shaking his head.

"Oh yes," she said giving him a big hug, "it's me, man, and I thought you were jungle monkey bound Dude. You went north instead?"

"Oh no, I went south all right and I stayed down there through the winter; it was awesome... totally amazing, but it was enough. "Here have a seat." He moved to make room for her.

"So what happened down there, man?" she asked looking at him with intense questioning eyes.

"I had to come back up. To get reprogrammed after my ultimate cutting loose in Central and South America."

"That explains why you came to this place I guess," laughing and taking the seat next to him.

"Ammo, what do you think about this place?"

"Well you're not going to believe this but I only just arrived here about 40 minutes ago and so far I have a very good feeling about this place even though they refuse to let me in the dream workshop."

"You're kidding, man. Why won't they?"

"They say that I should have registered before a cut-off

period… apparently, they like to know who is coming and they don't allow people to just drop in," he said throwing up his hands.

"Sure they do, Dude. You just need to know the right cats that run the workshop."

Then Summer pulled out a cell phone, punched in some numbers, paused. "Hey, Pineapple, can you do me a favor? I have a friend who showed up out of nowhere who wants to hang out with this week's dream project. Can you fit him in? … OK … yeah, he's cool man…he is a bro, ha ha! Yo …OK, Dude, thanks. Hey Ammo, man you're in bro!" She exclaims, smiling and putting two thumbs up. "And it won't even cost you any ganja. Ha ha!"

Blown away, Ammo nearly fell off the bench. "This is for real. How did you do that?" Ammo looked at her while not knowing what to say. "Is it for real... or are you messing with me?"

"No, it's real dude, and since you know me you're not only in, but in solid. Just tell anyone here that you are a good friend of Summer Lane... Dude, all will be fine."

"How were you able to hook me up like that?" He asks, still shaking his head in disbelief.

"Well it just so happens that the Hawaiian guy who runs the Dream Workshops organization and registration happens to be my best friend. You will meet him in the morning, so where are you staying anyway?"

"I don't have anyplace yet."

"Well, you can stay here at the camp. We have some room in a teepee I think?"

Ammo placed his hand on her shoulder. "Before we go I have to say something. I honestly must tell you that I am blown away by your wanting to help me. Honestly, I didn't think you cared much for me, Summer."

"I didn't, Dude… not at first, you seemed like a typical stuffy self-absorbed meditation yoga freak in Sedona, and I only wanted to smoke your grass really at first. You know what it is like to see crystal vortex people high on life with wads of cash and fat bags of grass come down to these places and throw their big-city noses at you and look down at you. They gobble up the spiritual food and leave. They go back to their material, cushy, phony environments and most never come back into your life again in fact from my experience most could give a crap about making friends with us tour guides and spiritual trip suppliers. We are considered 'the help.' Most don't even remember your name. I was born down here, and after you have been here for a while you get sick of all the pretentiousness REI-Gucci-wearing weekend-conscious only types, you know, bro? That's all… I remembered you, though, and you remembered my name also. And for some reason you seem a lot more relaxed this time. It was good down there for you I guess, Dude?" She asked smiling wide showing off her yellow teeth.

"Yes, it was amazing, incredible for many reasons. I learned a lot and have so many memories."

"That's good. You will probably have some very interesting dreams to share here. Now let's see about getting you in a place. You must be tired?" They got up and walked towards a small group of teepees a hundred yards or so down a trail next to the creek.

While they walked together, Summer noticed a guy who was fly fishing. She momentarily walked down where she shared a few words with him. She returned to Ammo.

"Hey dude," gesturing with her head pointing at the fisherman.

"That cat is Fisher Fritz and he said you can share a teepee with him OK. He is a very cool German dude. He is not much for talking, but very cool and smart and you will get to eat a lot of fresh trout at his fire. Anyway his place is right here by the creek and it is probably the cleanest and coziest teepee in the camp, so enjoy your stay. If you want to bring the bike down the trail off the road its hard to miss the turn. I gotta blaze, Dude. I have to be at work in a few so if you need anything ask Fritz or the

Pineapple. I'll be seeing you around, have fun." Then, off she went down the trail as Ammo walked in the opposite direction to get his motorbike.

A short while later, Ammo pulled up on the motorbike, the German got out of the creek with a string of three fish, then walked towards him. Fisher Fritz set the string of fish on a log bench and began to stroll around the old BMW motorbike, looking at it rather intensely, then came towards Ammo, smiling. Then without a word Fritz gestured to him to come with him into the teepee. Inside, the place was much bigger than it had looked from the outside. There were many nice handmade Indian rugs and two small beds across each side of the roomy space. He paid particular attention to a rock fire circle in the middle with a triangle of wood, everything prepared neatly. The German had a small, low, three level bookshelf full of books near one of the beds and in the middle between two beds was a large thin table and two chairs and a small solar running refrigerator.

He opened the refrigerator and took out two cold import German beers, opened them and passed one to Ammo. Then this host walked to a large hump about 5-foot long covered by tapestries and Native blankets. He pulled the blankets off to reveal one of the most beautiful mint-condition 1984 R-80 Paris Dakar BMW's Ammo had ever seen. It, was the only boxer series that won first place in the Paris Dakar Race, by Belgian Rider Gaston Rahier. Ammo knew this as a work of mechanical art to behold.

Perhaps normally Fritz was a quiet man, but this night he sure had a lot to say about motorbikes. He knew everything about them and apparently he was an experienced BMW motorbike mechanic. As they ate fresh trout that night Fritz told Ammo of his adventures riding his Dakar all over Europe, Asia, and Africa, up through South America, and throughout North America. These two guys had so much in common they magically fit inside that teepee

213

together like two peas in a pod or a cone for that matter.

"How did that Summer Lane know?" Ammo thought to himself. Fritz told Ammo that until now he had been the only person in the camp with a motorbike.

The next morning Ammo entered the large lodge in the center of Camp Dream Catcher. Inside were about 12 people all sitting around on a floor on triple-thick yoga pads. Ammo said nothing and took a seat next to a nice looking Asian woman and smiled at her. She smiled back saying nothing. Then, in walked a solid giant 6-foot-6 Pacific Islander who instantly noticed Ammo and walked up to him and asked, "Are you Mr. Ammo, Summer's friend?"

"Yes" Ammo answered, a little shy because everyone was looking at him."

"Welcome to the workshop. I am Pineapple and these are our dream-sharing brothers and sisters, are you cool with that Mr. Ammo?"

"Yes, I'm cool with that," he answered wondering if he was or not yet playing along to see if he was going to be eventually... "and you can call me just Ammo."

"Have you done a dream workshop before, bro?"

"No, never," he answered. "I am just very interested in the power of dreams because of my own experiences with them."

"So you know how to manifest your dreams?"

"Yes, it is not easy but I have been living the manifestation of my dreams and it is actually my dreams that drive me and many of my decisions." Ammo told him.

"That's good," Pineapple said smiling. "If you are already living the want of dream manifestation, that means you have already crossed several of the more difficult hurdles and it also means that you are in the right workshop because this one deals with some of the highest levels of dream interpretation and dream research as well as 'Holotropic Breathwork,' which we will be experimenting with under the direction of invited experts who will join us later in the week.

"Everyone in here, like yourself, has also been on a path. In fact, everyone is on a path. What we forget is that our unconscious mind is much more important than we know. In these workshops you'll learn how to utilize your unconscious mind and value your night dreams as well as your day dreams..."Can we dig it?" Then everyone repeated the instructor:

"We dig it Pineapple!"

"Understand that we all listen to each other and we are all interested in each others story and even though there are so many amazing stories, no one has any better story in here. Sometimes we repeat some things all together, not because we are all sheepish cult-like freaks. Rather because it has an effect on the awakening of our conscious state into taking the information and coding it into our higher consciousness, that's all. We are going to put ego to rest and become better listeners. It is easy for people like us to daydream too much and disconnect from each other and drift into our own thoughts, and dreams and ideas, although that's normal; what we want to do here is to connect with each other, and furthermore, to work on each other's dreams together using our higher consciousness. Everyone feeling good?" He asked. Everyone repeated, "feeling good bro."

Ammo's Dream

On the last day of the workshop, Ammo got to lead the workshop explaining his dream. Every day two people lead a dream, one dream in the morning and the other in the afternoon. Afterward, they listen to a speaker or a lecture on various topics from several miscellaneous fields, or a reading as they break into a whole two-hour session devoted to the philosophical interpretation of a person's vision or dream. Everyone in the group writes a quick interpretation or draws and colors pictures based on their own ideas and then shares these images with the Dreamer. They would also sometimes even role play or act out the dream in order to better try to grasp the dream.

This time, Ammo stood up and read about his dream to the group.

"I was trying to get to my motorbike. I was surrounded by many confused people, some very upset, some kind of mob or protest or something, yet the mob was in control and positively excited, their energy made me excited and I wanted to join them at first, also there was suddenly a violent aggressive attack at them and then more of a mass could be seen which made the aggressors back off.

Then many non-violent people joined, yet those turned violent and aggressive. They made me want to run away from them. Some, wearing white were extremely violent. Some in black were also and they tried to provoke the peaceful people into violent behavior. There was no leader amongst these masses only a shared anger and frustration and chaos, these masses continued to grow in great numbers. I was frustrated because I wanted to find my motorbike and get away from them all, yet the bike was not anywhere to be seen.

Just then a door with the number 11 appeared. I stepped inside and noticed that I had walked into an old building with a huge beautiful lobby. Next, I walked down a corridor of marble tile. At the end of the hall there were two sets of glass doors opening out to a beautiful garden. Sitting in the courtyard was a tall woman smiling at me and holding her hand out towards me. She was waving me to come close to her. I was somewhat frightened of her yet intrigued at the same time. I sat next to her and became suddenly very happy and peaceful…Now came the best part of the dream. We entered a mystical setting and she gave herself to me. Hard to believe a dream can seem and feel so real. Then very reluctantly I was told to go and find my motorbike again, I did so and the dream faded away rather quickly from there."

Chapter
10
Mass Confusion, 11 Connection

On September 24, 2011, Ammo chops wood with Fritz the German near the teepee when Summer Lane jogs up to them with a newspaper.

"Check this out!" she yells. "The protests in New York, are getting bigger. They are calling them 'Occupy Wall Street,' and the cops are pepper spraying peaceful protestors, in fact spraying young women in the face for no reason. What a bunch of bastards.

Summer starts to read the article aloud to Fritz and Ammo who both stop working to sit on the log bench near the fire pit. Summer reads on… according to Wikipedia:

"Adbusters a Canadian-based group had the idea for an occupation of lower Manhattan in early June, 2011. Adbusters proposed a peaceful occupation of Wall Street to protest corporate influence, and the lack of legal penalties for those who brought about the global crisis and an increasing disparity in wealth.

"Occupy Wall Street was inspired by the British student protests of 2010, and Greece and Spain's anti-austerity protests as well as the Arab Spring protests.

"Adbusters had the idea for an occupation of lower Manhattan in early June, 2011. They registered the *OccupyWallSteet.org* domain name on June 9th. Adbusters proposed a peaceful occupation of Wall Street to protest corporate influence on democracy, as well as the lack of legal consequences for those who brought about the global crisis of monetary insolvency, and an increasing disparity in wealth. The protest was promoted with an image featuring a dancer atop Wall Street's symbolic Charging Bull statue.

"The official protest started on September 17, and a Facebook protest page started on the 19th. The original location was Chase Plaza then they moved it to Zuccotti Park where masses are growing every day and are inspiring other movements that began growing throughout the nation."

" HE HELD HIS PURPOSE FIRM, TO KILL THE
MINOTAUR AND SAVE THE YOUTHS AND MAIDS."
-Greek Myth-Isle of Crete

Ammo listened intensely as Summer read the headlines, which explained quite clearly the first part of his dream. In fact many in the dream interpretation group said that his dream seemed to resemble a protest. It was ironic that the "Wall Street" protest was put together in June around the same time Ammo had his dream. It was in July, he had shared the dream with the workshop group.

He thought, "Could we all be that connected? Is it possible through our dreams that we could pick up on something so far away?" Whether or not he picked up on something, he knew from this news where he was meant to go next. Instinctively, Ammo knew that the signs and symbols were too strong to reject; the door in the dream had the number eleven written on it. Someone in the dream workshop explained the power and symbolism behind the number 11 to him. She mentioned, "that the Age of Aquarius was the 11th sign of the Zodiac and that it was a master number in numerology and number eleven had a list of several other symbolic references." Furthermore she explained.

"One could spend hours on the Internet watching hundreds of YouTube videos and spiritual websites devoted to the powerful coincidences surrounding the number 11."

The fact that Ammo had a dream where the number 11 was visible made for a very interesting topic that day. Everyone had his or her own theory, and some went off on the number 11 coincidences concerning conspiracy theory and what happened on 9/11 and when you add 9 +1+1=11 and that the Twin Towers were shaped like one big 11.

Ammo was not much on conspiracy theories. However, his own experiences remained harbored in his memory. He vividly recalled the strangest one that happened just before September 11, 2001 on the Nevada playa at the Rabbit Camp at Burning Man.

Ammo was not one to believe everything he had heard. Yet he was also not one to dismiss everything either. If something was symbolically speaking to his higher consciousness he tended to go with that naturally. This he felt was the safe choice, and he was 99.9 percent right on.

In his holotropic breathing exercises and use of mind-altering drugs like peyote and LSD in his early years, he reached mental states where he felt more secure in his place in the world. As he learned to utilize the thoughts and sensual feelings under those states he found he no longer needed drugs to help him find a path. The path he discovered was the one that found him when he was ready to receive it, uninhibited, all natural.

Ammo remembered that New York was the eleventh state

adopted to join the union. Ammo wondered if that was a sign from the dream. Now after Summer Lane read the news of what happened in New York concerning the mounting protests, he became convinced that this was definitely the symbol he had seen in his dream. He knew beyond all doubt that it was time to load up the bike and ride to New York City. That must be where he would find his next clue. He could feel it.

As Ammo rode out of Arizona the morning of the 27th of September 2011, heading east on New Mexico State Route 40 through New Mexico, he thought about his stay with all the interesting and cool people at the dream workshop. He thought about how Summer Lane was the last person he would have imagined to be such a great and loyal friend. But once he got past Summer's appearance and odd personality he found her deep-down character was as noble and true and fair as anyone he had ever met. If it had not been for her, he would not perhaps have had the initial want to go south and leave Sedona, a place that really was not the best for him at that time. He also might not have met Fisher Fritz the German who made the eleven-week stay in Dream Catcher Camp so comfortable and pleasant.

Ammo would never forget how earlier that morning he awakened, walking out from the teepee to find Fritz just finishing up a washing on his bike, tires pumped and breaks bled and final drive and oil changed; a total maintenance on his BMW.

"What great people you meet in the world," he thought. All this becomes possible if you open yourself to the power of riding the adventure of life's moment-to-moment experiences.

Ammo rode into Occupy Wall Street on October 4, 2011, and was instantly overwhelmed with the contrast to seeing so many races and people from all walks of life scattered all over Zuccotti Park, so many different signs and messages and ideals being thrown out. Ammo realized almost immediately that this was definitely not a unified mass of people working on one connected and organized premise. However one thing they all agreed on was that the 1-percent who run Wall Street, the banks, the political arena and the media were out to get them and the world was in serious trouble if something didn't come from the ground up to force the change that was required. The protesters figured they were a voice for a society made up of about 99 percent of the population.

Organizers had a library and a kitchen where they invited Ammo to a fantastic vegetarian meal, asking only a donation to help out the volunteer cooks. They also had a computer tent from which people broadcasted WiFi Internet reports and sent out news flashes, attracting others to the protest movement.

People seemed so connected and happy to be there, and Ammo's conversations with some of the protestors were very stimulating. Many of the speeches had seemed to Ammo too far leading into one form of 'ism' or the other which made it hard for him to grasp a direction or purpose. But the greatest thing was the fact that so many different religions and diverse groups were having a mental exchange and bridging social and ethnic barriers in search of higher understanding of what the world's deeper problems were. If anyone was going to be able to figure out where the problems stemmed from in regards to discrepancies of the 99 percent. It would have to be this movement because they figured the 1% would never do it for the 99%.

As they chanted, "tell us what democracy looks like?- This is what Democracy looks like," hundreds of police officers surrounded every corner of the peaceful gathering. This intimidated some of the protestors. Someone told Ammo that

"New York Mayor Bloomberg was getting money from major credit card banks and some Wall Street corporations in order to hire more cops and help offset the overtime costs required to keep the police shifts going 24 hours."

Bloomberg had an axe to grind with the protestors because they were messing with his personal bread and butter. Bloomberg's riches were made by his connections to Wall Street. You can see this fact anytime you look at the little 'Bloomberg' report logo up on the screen at the stock exchange. He owed Wall Street his loyalty, not a mass of leftist liberal weirdoes who were disrupting business as usual.

This fact was bad for the protests and good at the same time. Bloomberg made some quick calls early on, sending white-shirt cops in with pepper spray to break up the mobs. That backfired big-time, thousands of tweets and Facebook messages became the result, and there were twice as many people in the street yelling things like: "Bloomberg is a jackass and a crony capitalist, elitist pig and mayor for the 1-percenters."

That calmed him down for a while, long enough for the 99-percent to build a larger camp at Zuccotti Park, a privately owned land near Wall Street.

Ammo found a place to park his bike near the Occupy Library at Zuccotti and camped out in his sleeping bag. The next morning of the 5th of October, after awakening he joined in a march of over 10,000 people including representatives of the AFL-CIO. This was giving the protest the kind of legitimacy it previously had been lacking and now journalists could be seen all over filming and keeping up with the movement. One news reporter walked up to Ammo and asked him."Why did you come out to protest in Zuccotti?"

Ammo wasn't quite sure what to say to the woman, mainly

because he really had driven all the way out there to find his next symbolic clue to his destiny. He was not sure anyone would quite understand that.

He paused for a moment to gather his thoughts. "I want to see the world become one, he smiled. I want to see the children of tomorrow not have to deal with the fear that we have been building for them. We should be embracing love and education…not war, greed, torture and evil. I want to see mankind become a steward for nature, rather than a rapist of a beautiful Mother Earth. I also want to see Americans face reality and admit that they were wrong about not embracing the metric system."

The reporter looked at him with a confused frown.

"Hey this is fun," he said. "You know what else would be great? Tell New York Mayor Bloom-bug to bring down some toilets for these nice protestors. It's hard having to shit every morning in a bag."

"Thanks... Goodbye," she said walking away quickly to interview another protestor.

Ammo was excited by his 60 seconds of fame, yet he was somewhat tired of the lack of direction this protest had. It seemed even strange to the long-time-club-no club member that the protest seemed a little cliquish.

One end of the park had its college grads, the library, the intellectuals, labor unions and power brokers, and the other end had its homeless, freaks, socialists and lost souls who only wanted to get a handout. The working groups seemed very exclusive and anytime Ammo wanted to join one he was told to go away and that he needed to be invited.

Ammo wished that Summer Lane were there with him because she would probably be able to get him in because she was young and spoke their language and looked cool enough. Every now and then a young smart looking articulate youth would yell out: "Mike Check!" And everyone would repeat this exactly word for word in order to project the message as if they collectively were one giant human microphone.

Ammo wasn't sure he liked that part so much. It kind of scared the individualist in him somewhat.

On October 11, Ammo joined the Millionaires March through the Manhattan's East Side where thousands of protestors marched through exclusive high-end neighborhoods in front of some of the wealthiest elite corporate hacks living in New York, like Tea Party financer David Koch, JP Morgan, or CEO Jamie Dimon, and when they stopped in front of News Corp executive Rupert Murdoch, a smart looking young black woman with dreadlocks got up on a top of a large van with a megaphone. She yelled: "This is the home of Rupert Murdoch now probably one of the most destructive men on the planet. Murdoch is an Australian, who became a U.S. citizen only so he could buy our news networks. This ruthless businessman owns and controls one third of the world's news sources and holds most of his monopoly within the U.S. He's a giant player on the world media stage who could care less if he destroys the character and dignity of any government, or person through propaganda so long as the next president of that government where he owns the media news plays his game."

"That game," she continued, is to make him and his cohorts even more rich, and if his candidate looses the executive control of that government, he sets out to bury the winner every chance he can by manipulating the news, quite often with zero facts and backing the next opponent to win, thus perpetuating the owing process to himself over and over again. If you spend any time watching his news channel Fox's fancy doublethink, it is easy to see that he manipulates the world by careful design to further the profits of the bloody wealthy ruling class that is sided with him."

"This man and his monopoly and others like it must be stopped

225

from monopolizing the world press and manipulating the free and open internet because if these oppressors in this business get their way, there won't be any news that is not controlled. Be aware of this danger to our world's freedom of information. The Internet is their next target…but…wait! Stop!!"

Just then some police in white shirts began to pull her down. They dragged her to a van parked down the street as protestors yelled and chanted… "let her go, let her speak and peaceful protest!"

Something stuck into Ammo about what the woman had said. To him, she had been convincing and passionate in her tone. He pondered this intensifying political battle against so much extreme wealth and power: "How could these sweet young nice kids hope to beat the owners of the world peacefully? Ammo thought. "And how could the owners of the world live with themselves knowing that such a mass of innocence was truly hating them for their greed and lack of care for the very natural world in which they dominated."

Ammo felt surprised by all of this sudden mental changing within society. He increasingly felt that this remarkable time in history would prove our character and place along side our fellow man, so much change of social thinking moving the whole country.

It struck Ammo as sheer hypocrisy, that President Obama, who is quoted as the president who ran a campaign on "Change," never addressed the Occupy Wall Street movement, or its main protestors directly or formally. He ignored the entire movement as well. In fact, business pretty much continued as usual in Washington, and most politicians, who had big stakes in the stock market or who needed Wall Street money, would not risk rocking that boat even if they knew the protestors were absolutely correct in their attributions.

Many have said:

"The revolution will not be televised."

Yet, that was said before the invention of the Internet and social networks.

Late at night on October 25th when Ammo woke up to a 'Mike check!

Suddenly a young man yelled, "This evening in Oakland... at the Occupy Oakland Camp across from City Hall, there were near a hundred or so arrests. An Iraq veteran standing up for the movement, was shot in the head by police with a tear gas canister and was put in critical condition." Everyone in Zuccotti started opening up their laptops.

"What is happening to this country? Ammo thought to himself that night. Why was he here at the protest? Was it possible to win this one with a non-violent protest of this kind?"

Ammo had spent nearly one month camping at Zuccotti and he was not fitting in with any one group. All that the Occupy Wall Street movement in Zuccotti Park managed to do was make more working people think across the country. For many people but not all, this new but rapidly growing movement had rather a revolutionary peace uniting effect to it rather than a classical physical revolutionary effect. Ammo thought perhaps this is what may make the movement eventually work where others had failed. But Ammo had journeyed here to find his clue to the next symbol and he wished for such a sign to come sometime soon because the movement had started wearing him out. Oakland sounded like it was having a real revolt, was he supposed to go down there he thought to himself?

This protest changed the topic of conversations. The elite need to feel fear also he thought. Not fear of a bunch of leaderless protestors, but rather the fear from inside their own lazy bought-off wealthy circles. The 1-percent must fear the power of true wisdom. Fear of the day the dreaded finger would point them out for their evil stupidity. Fear of the powerful dissemblers who lurk among them, who carry the flame of truth, conviction and intellect, those who have nothing to hide and who love the beauty of this world without labels, caste systems, religious dogma and secret codes of order. Ammo smiled in his thoughts. "One day the ruling class will have trembling fear of the no crow-eaters and the badass fight club virus beaters."

Ammo had become convinced that this great country, where he grew up a free man, appreciated freedom and intellect because the nation had been built on that premise. He remembered what his friend Warm Bear had said about the end times and he knew he had strong friends like the Desperados who rode the spiral of YO as U.S. Marshals connecting with believers of abstract thoughts and super conscious potentials. He believed a time would come and he felt in his heart that when the strongest among them emerge and show that they have the power, they should amass and sweep through the world, wiping out the virus of the selfish, fat idiots. The movement Ammo most identified with was the one in his own mind, that's the movement he will join.

The Occupy Movement was real and perhaps a part of what will come, he thought, as he sat watching all the people chatting, smiling, connecting, surrounding him in all directions; however, Ammo was most likely going to be a part of what will come and not a part of the Occupy Wall Street protest any longer.

At the 11th hour with war looming in the air, he decided to save himself for the ultimate game that he envisioned down the road. The rhetoric pertaining to Iran and Israel thrown out by the republican candidates competing for the main position as front-runner of 2012 presidential election made every freedom lover in America nervous. Perhaps this is our destiny, he thought while shuffling through his tank bag looking for something to drink.

Just then Ammo noticed the "National Geographic" that he

had bought back in June at the Rio airport, deep in his tank bag.

The cover image featured two giant stone columns, looking like a massive number 11.

'Gobekli Tepe the birthplace of religion,' was written on the cover. Ammo ran out of batteries reading the article that night as people scrambled about him, many of them still upset and confused about the news from Oakland.

The article taught that Gobekli Tepe remains as a very ancient relic. Ammo became stunned at the thought that it had doubled the age of every major, large archeological find concerning civilizations in history. The mysterious site baffled scientists. Ammo wanted more information, so he Googled the title on his laptop, pulling up a documentary on the ruin and scrolled down the page.

"What's this," he thought. "looks like a dream come true, and just when I needed it." The article read:

'GOBEKLI TEPE' "A DOORWAY TO THE PAST AND PERHAPS TO OUR FUTURE?"

THERE WILL BE A FREE DOCUMENTARY AND LECTURE BY ENTREPRENEUR BUSINESSMAN AND WORLD TRAVELER DR. WILLIAM A. GOTT ON NOVEMBER 11TH AT 7:00

Organizers planned the free documentary presentation, open to the public at the Nevele Grand Hotel, a newly renovated Catskills Resort in upstate New York below the Shawangunk Mountains.

Ammo was pulled from his daydreaming by the sound of a cell phone ringing while he sat at a booth in the hotel coffee shop.

Ring! ring! ring! The phone kept ringing across from him where a threesome had spent the morning mixing it up. They had disappeared while Ammo remained lost in his meditations. One of the party, it appeared had left a cell phone on the table. Just then Ammo looked up at a clock hanging in the café, showing the small hand on 11 and the big one on 11 minutes.

He then looked back at the phone which continued ringing, on the table. In the center he saw a number 11 tag attached to a napkin holder.

Ammo hurried over to pick up the phone. This was it, he instantly understood while reaching for the i-Phone in the center of the table, his heart racing as he placed the receiver to his ear.

"Hello," he said with great anticipation.

"Hi," she said in a very soft voice, sounding to him like a Slavic accent. "My Name is Katarina Nova. Do you speak English?"

"Yes I do," Ammo replied.

"Do you have a minute to talk with me? I promise I will be quick." She spoke what struck him as a nervous tone, breathing heavy.

"No, please… take your time," he said, intrigued. "I have all the time in the world today."

"Oh that is fine, great… I mean thanks! This may sound strange. However, I have been working on an experiment and it deals with the power of belief and how man has become connected through higher forms of unexplainable abstract subjective consciousness… Anyway, am I loosing you?"

"Oh, no, go on. I am enjoying this," he said smiling and taking a seat back at his table.

"Well, and I hope you don't think I am a kook but, part of my experiment was to make a phone call to you at exactly 11:00 today in order to see if there was something I was to receive from it."

"Do you know what it is your looking for, miss?" He asks her laying back into the soft booth in the café.

"No, that is the thing… I don't. I am very confused right now and it is all very strange to me. I have never called or answered a dating service request before."

Ammo thought immediately, "this must be that playboy's telephone," but he knew the call belonged to him.

"That's OK. there is a first time for everything." Ammo smiled and nodded into the tightly held iPhone.

"Thanks, you are very understanding, and I appreciate you

listening. I was not expecting such understanding. I have been extremely busy with my experimental scientific work and it can be such a struggle trying to fit in with a social life. I have never had much time for it, honestly."

"Oh I can understand, "I have similar problems myself."

"You do?" She said relaxing herself into her office chair.

"Oh yes, I am also living an experiment of sorts."

"You are? What is your experiment?"

To him, her tone sounded eager, yet somehow pensive as well.

"Well, I am living a day-to-day journey, and I am following my senses where ever they lead me and listening and asking questions of my subconscious dreams. That's basically it. I have been living by moment-to-moment experiences most of my life in fact."

Katka suddenly felt very strange as if something eternally powerful, cosmic and universal spoke into her deeply, a philosophy new to her, words of a new wisdom. She already realized that this phone call was most likely made to the right person.

"That sounds so profound yet intriguing to me." A tear fell from her eye, and her breath began to relax.

"Perhaps so, it is what it is." he shrugged his shoulders. "What about you, Katarina? Do you have a chance to experience true life?" A long pause ensued.

"Sure I do." Katarina chose her words carefully since expressing such thoughts openly, rarely came naturally to her. "However, it is more through the mind and through work and through being a part of the Academic learning process."

"That sounds like it can be a little extreme to me. So why did you call for a date, Katarina?" Ammo asked, wanting to get to the heart of what he expected would come from this conversation.

"Can I be honest with you? You won't look down on me will you?"

"No, nothing can shock me. I grew up seeing every kind of weirdness, believe me."

"OK, that's good, I have been unable to be with many men, and, well, I knew I was running out of time before I would just give in to being only with women. Is that strange to you?"

"No, go on I am cool with that."

"Well I have a need to experience a man completely and at the same time I need to find out if we are able to truly connect through symbolic chance or harnessing of our subconscious senses and that is actually a part of an experiment I am involved in. I know this all sounds complicated?"

"It's cool, each individual's life is an experiment of sorts. Well, where are you Katarina?"

"I am in Boston at the moment. Where are you?"

"Well, it just so happens I am three hours away in Upstate New York attending a lecture on an archeological ruin called Gobekli Tepe."

"Wait!" she yelled. "Did you say you were attending a lecture on the 12,000-year-old dig in Turkey... when and where is it?"

"Tonight at around 7:00 here at the Grand Nevele Resort Hotel. Do you know where it is?"

"No, but I can find it. Do you mind if I join you?"

"Not at all, it would be a great pleasure, should I reserve you a room or would you like to stay with me?"

"We shall see when I get there. I will pack and leave right away. See you in a few hours."

Then she hung up the phone and Ammo put the phone in his pocket, just in case she should call him. He might need it, at least until the end of this most interesting day.

He put a twenty-dollar bill on the table and left the café. "How interesting," he thought. Looking up, he noticed that the clock at the Grand Nevele Hotel café was broken, still showing 11:11.

Chapter 11
Ammo and Katka Connect

Katka arrived at the old hotel lobby at 3:30 p.m. only hours after her amazing talk with the stranger who pulled this woman away so easily from her usual morning demands. Taking her cell phone out of her handbag, she nervously dialed the phone while walking out into the hotel garden courtyard for better reception.

"Hello! He answered, is this Katarina?"

"Yes it is." She felt strange at this point. "I am in the courtyard."

"I know." He said. Ammo was looking Katka up and down, guessing she must be around 37-39 years old. "I am sitting right across from you as we speak."

She turned, looking for someone resembling this image of a man that she had fantasized about. Instead, she spotted a not bad looking man with long blond, grey hair in a ponytail and salt and pepper beard, in his early to mid-40's wearing a motorcycle jacket, jeans and leather boots. Entrepreneur, businessman, she thought.

He must be an eccentric one.

"Hi, I'm very pleased to meet you. What is your name again? She asked. "I am sorry I read it in your profile, but sometimes I am bad with names over here in the States, please forgive me."

He said. "Amon, just call me Ammo, Katarina." He was happy that she did not want to go into the fact that even though she came to meet him.

It was another's profile that had lead her to call him. Ammo thought he should feel guilty. However, he knew full well that on 11/11/11 at 11:00 with a phone from table 11 at Hotel Grand Eleven, this was not your average day. So, early on during this rendezvous, he decided that persistent guilt was not in the cards. He decided to milk every moment with this tall attractive and intelligent creature sent to him by the gods of the universe, who collectively and simultaneously placed his time on Earth receiving his personal revelations during this eleventh constellation.

It was the age of Aquarius and usually Ammo felt nothing for astrology. But this time it managed to become part of his dream and here she was and it all started to fit together like clockwork into his mind. He started humming, unable to control himself.

"When the sun is in the… and Jupiter aligns with…Love will….Hum! Hum!"

"You may call me Katka," she said with a sweet soft Czech accent and giving him a hug. "What are you humming?" She giggled lightly as Ammo woke himself to the fact that he was being a bit weird.

"Oh sorry, it is a little tune about the Age of Aquarius. You know the musical, 'Hair?'"

"I do. It is a classic." She smiled, thinking and recognizing now what he was humming. Katka considered this behavior as good, signaling his emotional connection to this symbolic moment. She liked the fact that he seemed undisputedly different.

Ammo's heart beating heavy and fast and he could hardly put his words together while standing there smiling because here was a person smiling back at him, unable to stop looking at him also and they had only had a simple five-minute phone conversation. He could never have guessed that within three and a half hours they would actually be touching one another, it all seemed so unreal so amazingly dreamlike.

"Please have a seat," Ammo asked, moving aside to clear a seat next to him, where they both soon sat quietly waiting for each other to open the topic of conversation.

Ammo broke first, asking: "Are you hungry or thirsty after the ride?"

"No," she put her hands in the air. "I had a bottle of water with me on the road and I couldn't eat a thing today, considering how amazing it has been so far that I almost don't know what to do with myself."

"Do you want me to help you bring in your things?"

"We have time," she said. "Let's chat for a bit. I am so curious about you, Ammo… As I drove here I couldn't believe that someone could be as understanding about my personal experiment. You've made this so easy for me, thank you."

"No thank you, Katka. I have been following symbols all the way from South America to get here to be at this moment with you… you were in my dream, I even knew you would be coming into this very courtyard because I saw it months ago. It's a long story and it is all true. I swear it."

"You're kidding," she said shaking her head.

"No it is the absolute truth. What is today's date?" he asked her looking into her eyes.

"It is the eleventh…wait, I know 11/11/11 that, is what it is all about for me also."

"What!" He yelled out with a surprised look on his face. "You know about the phenomena surrounding this day?"

"Of course I do, my experiment relied on it to make the phone call to confirm the destined answer to my personal question because a theory is held that this power of our human collective connection throughout the planet is at such a high frequency today."

They both just sat starring at each other without saying a

235

word. Each could see by looking into each other's eyes that what was happening was really unique and special.

"So, you waited for a phone call?" she asked.

"No… well, not exactly," he said looking a little nervous suddenly. "I was waiting for a sign or symbol. I didn't know what it was going to be. Then you rang."

Katka became very warm and excited, filled with feelings that she had never experienced before these increasingly intense yet non-threatening sensations came as she looked into the eyes of this complete stranger who magically dazzled her senses and lifted her spirits.

Ammo could see she appeared a little dizzy: "Would you like to get your own room, or would you like to come up to my room and rest and talk some more?"

"I want to be with you, just be with you," she said, almost slurring her voice.

"Come with me," said Ammo, I think a rest would be good for us, it has been a long trip getting to this point. We need to slow down and let it flow."

"OK, I trust you," she said as they entered an old elevator. Getting out at the second floor, they went down the hall.

Katka stood looking at the door smiling and nodding: "Of course," she said "this is almost too much."

"I was surprised they had this room available today, really, but then perhaps there are no accidents." He said as he turned the key and hung his jacket up on a hook by the door, "But then it's our dream, is it not?"

Walking into the classic honeymoon suite, Room 11 of the Grand Nevele was like walking into a bit of history, like going back in time, the decor was all Art Nuevo, one of the last truly classic and romantic stylistic eras to influence across the board design, beautiful ornate rugs and gold laced, and fringed tapestries

236

with designs that reminded one of the works draped across a painting by Gustov Klimt or Alfonse Mucha. Hung next to the windows were similar styled drapes and soft thick sofas loaded with colorful pillows, antique furnishings, everywhere exotic inlaid hardwoods crafted by masters loaded with carved flowers and swirls.

Tall ceilings and windows let just the right amount of light in, giving the atmosphere total peace and classy comfort. Paintings from the turn of the 19th-20th century, hung all around the large room of beautiful colorful pastel landscapes and flowers.

Katka by this time had nearly fallen down with so much emotion filling her, Ammo had to help her to lay down on the old four-post cherry, wood king size bed that was wave shaped like a dragons tail and had two wrapped and twisted dragons carved onto the backboard facing each other, draped down on all sides by white see-through silk.

As he held her close, she became even weaker in his arms. Ammo set her onto the soft and plush bed laying her up against the backboard as he gave her a gentle kiss. She would not let go of Ammo, who was also feeling the intense moment, very happy to hold her and be needed by her. They looked into each other's eyes, saying nothing for several minutes, then Katka began to unbutton her sweater revealing a plain white bra supporting shapely and subtle breasts, and she kicked both shoes off onto the floor.

Ammo wanted to tell her it was unnecessary, that he wasn't only interested in sex, but this powerful moment sealed his choice to be quiet. Katka's eye's glowed as she looked at Ammo, who began to feel an overwhelming desire to help her undress. He reached down so naturally, running his hands down both sides of her legs grasping her slacks which easily slid off of her reveling long and healthy legs, placing her pants on the foot of the bed. Ammo removed his shirt exposing his muscular chest. Katka reached for Ammo's pants as he straddled over her on the bed. She unbuttoned and pulled his jeans down along with his undershorts revealing his fully erect penis, the first circumcised one she had ever encountered.

Instantly a wave of information entered her scientific head. She contemplated further... as if she were scrolling in her mind through Wikipedia, Although this was the first live helmet she had ever seen, she had read about the circumcised penis going back as far as ancient Egypt wall paintings on tombs illustrating the process. Thirty percent of men globally have one, most prevalent in Africa where it originated.

The word penis: is nearest to Greek word Peos. Or pene: Therefore the etymological meaning of penis; part that goes inside. A humans penis is larger than any other primate, the next is a chimpanzee 7 to 8 centimeters and ironically a gorilla has the smallest when erect about four centimeters or 1.5 inches at plus or minus average in length. The corpora cavernosa are erectile tissue, during sexual excitation, their fibrous tissue is expanded by blood that flows into and fills their empty spaces. The penis becomes enlarged, hardened, and erect as a result of this increased blood pressure.

Ammo unclasped her bra, then began to kiss and lick her nipples as they got hard. He then removed her blouse and underpants, blown away by the extremely beautiful fully dilated flower calling him to taste her. The smell and taste of Katka so clean and fresh she was like nothing Ammo had ever had, she was truly superior. Katka took hold and examined the feel and taste of Ammo as well.

Ammo could tell she was nervous and inexperienced. He lead her through a slow calm and gentle transition of body massage as he poured the hotels complimentary bed-side rose oil on her and opened her up and relaxed her more. The exchange of massage was exhilarating for both of them. They both worked on each other with such respect taking in every moment and every feeling as they worked on each other's bodies. Ammo was afraid to take an initiative to insert, he did not want to seem aggressive, to Katka, they only just met. Katka on the other hand was overwhelmed with experimental desire, her mind and consciousness was working intensely at a high level gravitating towards and desperately wanting him; she embraced him, reaching for him pulling the symbolic key to her personal experiment his "peos" deep into her oiled, clean, shaven, vagina. Her vagina, Katka thought to herself, for that explosive moment was what made her a woman; however, as a University professor she lived in a predominantly man's world. Her vagina was something she always had, and although she had lived with it already 39 years she knew very little about what her vagina appreciated from life. Today her *vagina* was truly at the center of her body's focus.

'Vagina: Latin is a sheath or scabbard for holding a sword. During sexual arousal, the stimulation of the clitoris, also known as the "little man in a boat" or "man with the key" or "gatekeeper," the walls of the vagina self-lubricate. This reduces friction. With arousal, the vagina lengthens rapidly, to an average of about four inches, or ten centimeters. The walls of the vagina are composed of soft elastic folds stretching or contracting (with support from pelvic muscles) to the size of an inserted penis-stimulating the penis and helping to cause the male to experience orgasm and ejaculation, therefore enabling fertilization.'

It was at that moment she moaned with pleasure as though a part of her personal missing life somehow caught up to her. Ammo was aware of this fact, he could tell by her sounds and he remembered the conversations on topics of sexual orientation that they had shared that day, that this was perhaps one of her first real experiences' with a man.

Ammo began to be very conscious of her every sound, adjusting his tempo slowly to her movements that pushed and pulled him to and from her. This was lovemaking the likes of which he had never imagined where two bodies connected and began to resemble only one.

Slowly they moved together embracing every moment each equal in dominance. Time stood still, heat rose and sweat dripped. Neither could stop a lovemaking so overwhelming, it was like a flight into space were everything made no sense at all if you thought about it too much, yet every feeling if you went with it magically fit together perfectly for both of them. This opened up pathways to feelings in their senses which they both had no idea existed until that very moment.

After several loving rounds, bringing on euphoric numbing exhaustion, they both relaxed back into large pillows against the solid cherry wood headboard looking up at the high ceilings of the old hotel room and regaining a grounded reality of the moment.

"Wow, I had three consecutive orgasms," Ammo said, laying back his head deep into plush soft pillows. "I haven't made love like this in years, Katka. I felt like 18 again."

Katka just lay there completely still looking up next to him, smiling. He continued: "Today was a trip, I must say. The whole day I was truly living my dream."

"Your dreams?" She asked. "I have been with one other man who was too inexperienced, and women are very gentle. But this was something unique and special for me also. My whole body was and still is tingling all over. Very interesting feelings, and so many extreme subconscious emotions came out of me. It was as though I went into a deep vast and indescribable other world that spoke to every part of my mind and body. I will have to write this all down and document it somehow."

She said, easing back into the pillow up against the headboard.

"Ammo, did you ever think of someone and then that person would suddenly call you on a phone?"

"I have done that many times, in fact," he said, sliding in closer to Katka, holding her hand softly over his heart.

Ammo, did you know that it is theorized that there are perhaps ten dimensions of space and one dimension of time? It is also theorized that the universe is expanding and as we speak yet this complex gravitational fabric that we live on and our heavenly bodies ride may only be a program in our visual three earth dimensions that we can observe. When in reality the energy playing this almost holographic movie we call life in a universe is an illusion and that mysterious thing called space might be only a uniquely abstract dimensional box of scripts and set codes and connected literally to each and every material element we see forming a network connecting all reality surrounding us right on out to the edge of a universe and back. Every push or pull is felt by all of us through a not-yet-understood field of consciousness, whether we are witnessing it first-hand or millions of miles away.

"Wow! You are a scientist aren't you?" Ammo said laughing a little.

"Yes," she answered with a very serious look. "And my interest is the phenomenal abstract world. That's one reason why I was drawn to the world's many cultures' various interpretations of the number 11. Today is so special because it confirmed to me that we really are connected, not just you and I… that was phenomenal as well, but the whole thought process, it is as though there is a deeper unified mind that speaks and arranges life to happen accordingly for those who tap into the symbolic process and go with it through spontaneous acceptance. But it takes super consciousness to get to where we can meet others and tap in and share this on a positive level and be smart enough to not go too far and let it drive us insane or give up or both. You were special because you followed your dreams; I was the one who had to make a mental choice, a call to something I could only believe may exist.

"We both completed our task by going with our subconscious energy that we felt to be a deeper reality, something I had a very hard time believing in until I met you and this day confirmed my intuitions." Katka smiled and turned looking with a gentle glance at Ammo who met her eyes with a more serious expression.

"Katka it is also theorized that we are entering a new reality and that is what the Mayans referenced in their calendar; a shift of consciousness and love and unity taking over the dimensional order of the planet coming after winter solstice 2012.

"So now what do we do?" he said laughing, "you completed my last dream. Now I am lost again."

"No, you're not," she said. "Now you're found and we have to get ready for the lecture that will be starting in 45 minutes.

She got up and walked into the bathroom, "I will jump in the shower."

"Cool, I will follow you." He said, smiled and thought how he liked being with such a brilliant, take-charge woman. She was now his new symbol, he wanted to be with her, and follow her; he wanted to learn what she knew as well. "Relax…Moment-to-moment," he said to himself, "moment-to-moment."

At 7:00 when the lecture started Ammo and Katka had a seat somewhere toward the middle of the large hotel banquet hall. A very small turnout of perhaps only 45 people showed up, leaving many empty seats. You would think something this interesting would draw much more attention.

When a tall classically handsome gentleman with black hair stood up to work with a projector at the front of the stage, Ammo recognized him immediately. It was the playboy from the Hotel coffee shop who was with the three other women. He had totally forgotten about that.

"Hey," he said somewhat nervously, turning to face Katka who could tell something was wrong.

"I have to tell you something and I don't want you to take it the wrong way. But when you called today I was in the coffee shop here in the."...

Just then the lights dimmed and a young Asian woman came out to introduce the Lecturer.

"Today, we are pleased to bring our second lecture to the Grand Nevele Hotel for our four-part lecture series on the world's most critical archeological sites... Tonight we have a lecture on the digs going on in Turkey near the Syrian border at a place known as Gobekli Tepe; we don't have a lot of time this evening so without any further delay it is my pleasure to introduce Doctor William A. Gott."

Ammo sank into his chair looking nervous as Katka scratched her head. Ammo could tell she probably was trying to figure out where she had heard the name. Probably even recently he thought. Most likely it was today.

"I have to tell her," he said to himself.

Doctor Gott stood up and thanked the crowd for the small applause then he went into a speech about his business selling medical supplies to Turkey and the Middle East. It was easy to travel around between countries and it was through one of these excursions that he came in contact with the cooperative German, Turkish excavation teams that were uncovering the giant complex surrounding the hill at the site of Gobekli Tepe. Gott explained, "that his mission statement was to help fund the further excavations of the enormous site.

"This unique and unexplainable pre-historic site is located about 15 kilometers from the city of Sanliurfa, in Southeastern Turkey. The Political identity of the locals in the region: 2.97

percent Turkish; and between 12 percent and 20 percent calling themselves Kurdish; and the rest undeclared.

"What makes Gobekli Tepe unique in its class of ancient structures coupled with the date it was built, roughly twelve thousand years ago, circa 10,000 B.C., during the Neolithic A Period c. 9600–7300 B.C. thought to be built by hunter-gatherers. Göbekli Tepe is a series of several oval-shaped stone monolith structures set on the top of a hill."

The lecturer put up a slide show behind the stage. The initial photos featured distinct images of gravestones... first dismissed by archeologists working on what they referred to as "potbelly hill" in the 1960s. Years later a local sheepherder and his sons unearthed and discovered the site in 1993-1994. A German professor happened to be in the region looking for new sites when he heard of the rumor, then stumbled across the herdsman's find and fully understanding the discovery's significant potential. Excavations

began in 1994-1995 by the German professor and the German Archeological Institute.

Gott continued explaining, "there is archeological proof so far that these installations were not used for domestic use, but predominantly for ritual or religious purposes. The professor believes 'first came the temple, then the city.' If he is correct Carbon dating places Gobekli Tepe as possibly the oldest religious temple or worshiping site on Earth found thus far. The site consists of not only one temple structure. But geo-magnetic results also reveled that there are at least twenty installations, or separate circular temples buried under a mixture of loose dirt, stones, and gravel.

"Based on what has been unearthed so far, the pattern seems to be consistent. There are two huge monumental pillars in the center of each circle resembling perhaps two large ones or digits perhaps a T shape 18 feet high and weighing nearly 16 tons, surrounded by several smaller stone pillar enclosures all spread out around the hillside.

"The unique method used for the preservation of Gobekli Tepe has really been key to the survival of this science-changing site. A civilization that may or may not have built this magnificent monument, made sure of its survival by backfilling the sites thousands of years ago carefully and meticulously burying all of them, until the 1994 discovery led to today's excellent preservation.

"It is this puzzle that astounds everyone across the fields that study ancient science. One of the big questions is why would an ancient civilization bury it? Who would want to, and what was it they perhaps wanted to hide? So far it has not been classified as a cemetery or burial site because bodies have not yet been found, although scientists don't discount that possibility because the digging may continue for another 50 years. The building of the temple sites possibly lasted until 8200 B.C."

Dr. Gott then looked out to the gathering and asked, "are there were any questions?"

One man waved his hand, "Excuse me, but what was the significance of the central pillars? I am referring to the tall ones in the center of the ruins?" he said.

Dr. Gott explained, "They were perhaps symbolic representations of man because there were many details like arms and hands carved onto the pillars that gave them a human-like resemblance. They could have been used for rituals of some kind. Some theories suggest that they could have held up a roof. However no wood has been found yet to support such a theory.

"Many theories coming out now reject the previously accepted universal academic histories of ancient archeology, most of them concerning the giant intelligently cut stone blocks like those found in Baalbek in Lebanon, the Giza plateau and Abu Garab and Ollantaytambo, Peru northwest of Cusco. What all these sights including Gobekli have in common are the presence of giant stones far too large for primitive man to have lifted and transported with the known technologies of those time periods.

"True anomalies of science such as these start to open up interesting questions and opposing new theories. Egyptology has told us that the basalt and granite giant blocks, stacked and making up the inner areas of the pyramids, were created with copper chisels and measuring strings, and moved on giant round logs, to be set into perfectly square and flush positions so tight you couldn't get a piece of writing paper between them. Several engineers have been vigilant at crunching numbers, finding this to be nearly impossible. Machines of some kind had to be used. Other questions and theories also bother the comfortable old school scientific community: 'Were these sites built as forms of energy producers or power plants or high frequency planetary stations built only as a means to keep

246

stability and balance it across the Earth's environment in order to maintain it as a plantation directed under the authority of some other much higher intelligence which ruled an orderly outpost. Then suddenly for some reason the tools and technologies perhaps disappeared leaving few obvious traces other than these recently found and only-now-questioned mysteries.'

Katka raised her hand. "Was there any specific reason you were drawn to the ruins yourself? What was it that intrigued you or inspired your interest to help support the project?"

Ammo now looked at Katka with some curiosity. Katka looked back with a half frown, impressing him as being somewhat puzzled. She continued, "Was there something symbolic for you that lead you to the site, Doctor Gott?

"Humm!" The doctor adjusted his glasses, "That is a good question? Not exactly, at first we went as a group of business associates on an adventure to see them because they sounded interesting from the tour agency in Istanbul. No one from our travel group had ever heard of them before. Several of us spoke German so we got along with the excavation team there. We all had adventurous backgrounds traveling so this was an enticing quest. It wasn't until after we spent time around the site and met the project's coordinators. That's when we decided that it would be a great project to fund as one of our company's goodwill tasks."

Katka looked seriously over to Ammo, shrugging his shoulders; sinking a little into his chair. Just then another woman raised her hand with a question: "Doctor, is there a way to contact the site and the archeological team directly with an email or phone number? I am also doing research pertaining to similar ancient archeology. Do you have a link?"

"Unfortunately, Miss, today I left my iPhone somewhere and I have been unable to locate it so far. On that phone is the only link and email contact I had with me on this trip for them… if you give me your information I will be happy to send you a link when I get back home."

Ammo suddenly saw this as the only possible way to redeem himself and subdue his mounting bad Karma; he was quick to seize the moment. He stood up.

"Excuse me, Doctor did you say you lost your phone today?"

"Yes, I did." He answers, "This morning sometime."

"Well I found an iPhone in the coffee shop here at the hotel this morning at around 11:00. Were you there sometime before then? I didn't have a chance to turn it in at the front desk but I do have it right here with me." Ammo withdrew the small phone from his sweater pocket."

"I was in fact having breakfast this morning when I found it." Ammo looks over to Katka who was looking at him seriously yet remaining calm and quietly listening.

"Ammo held up a black phone, reaching out towards the Doctor who was making his way towards them up the aisle. As the Doctor got near he asked…

"Was there any call for me?"

Ammo looked with worry toward Katka, not knowing what to say.

Again the doctor asked. "Was there any calls today by chance?"

Katka looked over to the Doctor, then back at the half smiling uncomfortable man that had changed her life only hours ago. She looked into Ammo's worried and confused eyes and shook her head. Then Ammo, seeing this, also shook his head looking at Katka.

"Thanks for speaking up," said the Doctor, taking the phone and returning to the front of the room toward the woman waiting for the link.

After a few more questions, Ammo found himself unable

to concentrate. He just sat there looking every few minutes at Katka who ignored his glances, still listening to the lecture. It finally ended and as everyone slowly walked out, Ammo and Katka just sat there watching people empty the hall. Just then the three attractive young ladies that had had breakfast and morning cocktails with the doctor entered the front of the lecture room joining the doctor's side. He instantly embraced them, comfortably kissing both in a very provocative manner. Ammo looked over to Katka who sat as quiet as could be, still watching the happy threesome take down and pack lecture materials. Ammo finally caught her eye.

"I was going to tell you," he said with a pause, searching for words. "I was just caught up in the moment," he said, looking a little red in the face. "I hope you understand. I was waiting for the sign, I had come so far, that phone… it rang at 11:00… It was you."

"The most beautiful thing we can experience is the mysterious. It is the source of all true art and all science. He to whom this emotion is a stranger, who can no longer pause to wonder and stand rapt in awe, is as good as dead: his eyes are closed."

-Albert Einstein

249

Chapter
12
The Tale of Geeko Salamander

Geeko was a British-born metallic green and yellow salamander, ironically a cousin of Geico who was a famous British-American celebrity lizard that sold car insurance to people who liked having their decisions made by reptilian authorities during the start of the 21st Century.

Geeko had been having a tough time getting the new European Union to realize that full blood-Reptiles had rights to equality in voting and pay, the same as men, and women in this brand new union. Geeko got caught up in a court battle with conspiracy writer Dave Icky over contentious information Icky had been putting out related to the naming and calling out of what he called "Ruling Class Elite Reptilian Jews."

Geeko was a fully conscious, Jewish Salamander and had a problem with the half breed Zionists reptiles himself. It seemed that the aggressive half-breed grey alien species wanted to create a solid Zionist grey Reptile ruling state in Israel, disregarding the intellectual moral attitudes of the pure conscious Jews.

The fully conscious Jews knew that a Zionist approach would only lead to more division and wars between their closest Islamic Lizard neighbors. These neighbors, some who were also extremely proud and religiously fanatic reptiles, followed strict religious laws laid down by followers of a long-extinct supreme Lizard lord

Megalania. No one dare mention his name in any way negative
or in jest, else some off-the-hook insane extremist follower would
want to make a soup out of you.

Geeko Salamander's Mantra:

The truth.

All of the lizard tribes of the Holy Lands

At one time long ago were one family of reptile clans

In belief, truth, reason and reality

Under one unified God who gave

Mankind this strange world's war for religious plurality.

*"We sent Noah and Abraham, and bestowed on their offspring
prophet-hood and scriptures. Some were rightly guided, but many
were evildoers… and after those Jesus son of Mary…We gave
Him gospel, and put compassion and mercy in the hearts of His
followers. As for monasticism, they instituted it themselves."*

-57:25 Koran ,N.J. Dawood translation

Somewhere along the way back during Ronald Reagan's New
neo Repti-publi-Con presidential administration… Christian and
Jewish Lizards from the United States got in the middle of the
two reptile neighbors and decided to pick the side of the Zionists.
To this day no one can fully understand exactly why this was so
important. To many like Geeko it seemed as if flexing muscle was
only going to deepen hatred and drive bitter Apartheid throughout
the region.

Geeko, being an intellectual journalist for a major Czech
newspaper, the 'Frog Post' at the time was interested in exposing
those European Reptiles who strived to destroy peace between the
Jewish Lizards and the Pale-reptilian occupied territories. Dave
Icky was trying to dirty Geeko's reputation in Europe by telling the
German newspaper 'Der Spiegel' that the British-Czech Lizard was

a spy for the reptilian Zionists who worked undercover in Czech. He claimed Geeko documented the Euro skeptics' movements that had been aligning together, further supporting the breakdown of the Elite power of the new union in Brussels amid the start of Greece's governmental bankruptcy in 2010.

Icky wanted to hurt Geeko because Geeko, being a conspiracy writer himself, had refused to join with Icky's conspiracy movement against Zionist Lizards that had been building momentum. Geeko didn't join Icky, although he liked some of what Icky had to say about consciousness and changing reality. As far as grouping masses of Reptilian Elite and the Monarchy into one bloodline, Geeko thought Icky went a little too far. Geeko also disliked the idea of joining such conspiracies because he felt that good Jewish Salamanders would eventually band together with the Monarchy to organize a takeover of the bad Zionist reptiles. From Geeko's view, this was likely to eventually happen anyway because the evil ones were becoming virus-like, refusing to live in reality and leading the planet into a false and dysfunctional premise of order and existence.

Fortunately, Icky's story got lost for Geeko when uproar in Europe around this time regarding the fall of the Euro took over the headlines beginning on November 11/11. Ironically, Geeko had been intensively reading the book 1984 again at that very time.

It had been many years and he'd forgotten the plot of that book and had overlooked its' prophetic warnings. As Geeko read, he got blown away by just how prophetic "1984" turned out. Geeko had never embraced numerology nor did he even think it has anything to do with this coincidence. But strangely when he added the numbers "1984,"... 1+9+8+4=22, together the total was 22 if you divide that by two that equals 11/11. Geeko sensed that conspiracy theorists would go wild at the possibility of this being used as a code.

Geeko Had a Strange Revelation

Was it just an accident that by November 2011 the global technology would change all analog television to digital television for 90 percent of the western world? This catapulted the international computer and phone spy surveillance systems into overdrive on a grand scale? Most household computers were being converted into entertainment centers along with laptops. All these devices contained small camera eyes and free connections to video visual phone service providers like Skype.

During November 2011Geeko began to notice that he was suddenly bombarded daily by everyone wanting him to suddenly join their social network after he repeatedly said he was not interested.

On December, 13, 2011, Geeko closed his YouTube Channel Account. During the previous few years Geeko had considered this as a very unique and cool way to follow events and comment about things that interested him. All along he enjoyed certain favorite documentaries and video's, using YouTube as an ideal place to organize his preferences. But he suddenly soured on YouTube in November 2011 when the system changed the layout of his Channel page without asking him. They put up all of his commented videos, and removed his favorite video's that he had put in a particular order which was the content that he allowed for the viewing public to see on his personal channel.

Perhaps most important before this change, Geeko had wanted his YouTube channel for the primary purpose of sharing his favorite videos, music and commentaries created by others. He had never made a single video or pushed a view of his own creation on to the public.

Around the same time he noticed that if a person Googled

his or her YouTube login-name, that phrase or word would come up along with most if not all previous comments. This turned out fine for those who want people to read and follow any issues and perhaps even to find their personal channel. Certain visitors might like the channel account owner's way of thinking. By connecting this way, web surfers may become motivated to share interests as well as other channels and comments through this media experience.

Geeko thought, "But what about that time we are human and make a hasty comment and don't think about whether our statements might make a particular politically connected Ruling Class member upset?" Perhaps some 'tool' might become angry enough to click on that person's channel and start watching videos that go against everything that elite figure represents. Furthermore, this might cause a viewer to resent and retaliate against that channel owners freedom of speech, contacting the privately run Google and YouTube services to complain or demand censorship?

Geeko viewed the YouTube transition as ironic. Because, the last video he added to his favorites before they changed his page on him further forcing him into closing his account, was a speech by the "Dali Lama on the problems of greed and corruption taking over the planet."

The sudden unwanted change led Geeko to think that "Perhaps this planet is just that, a school of how not to be human."

"Why can't I have a cool channel that shows all the revolutionary things I like to share… things like the wonders of nature and mathematics, self-healing through diet and yoga, or the unjust removal of the Fourth Amendment of the Constitution through the Prolonged Detention Act pushed in the U.S. Senate? Or things like Frank Zappa and his song playing to Occupy Wall Street protests, or the Wikileaks information and raw video image of a U.S. Apache helicopter blowing away innocent journalists in Iraq? That was covered up, or videos pointing out certain political people who are greed-driven 'wolves in sheep's clothing' like Vladimir Dlouhy, Czech ex minister and Prague Goldman Sachs executive was a potential presidential candidate for 2013 nominations in Prague. Dloughy who actively sold out the Czech Republic to global financial agendas, thereby benefiting private elite investment clubs. Or great speeches by leaders who take a stand, people like Vaclave Klaus or Nigel Farage in front of the European Union in Brussels. These men spoke in the name of democracy and popular rights of the citizens before an ever-elite sect governed Europe."

Oh, yes this little Lizards' YouTube channel with 500 viewers surely would piss off this newly changed democratic nation called the Czech Republic.

Who is this British Lizard journalist who had the audacity to come here, and set up a residence in Prague while we kept busy brainwashing our slaves? We did this via corporate and state-owned TV techno garbage and overpriced name brand consumer goods and consolidated price fixing utilities, while generating Europe's highest priced telephone services. Who does he think he is to make waves here where our "Beloved Velvet Revolution" sliced out our own opportunistic transition? Our revolution had generated a creative way for us to have all the wonders of the west and keep our communist-engraved powers of connected control and manipulation in place at the highest levels of our new Laissez-faire capitalist economy. Who is he to challenge our Gods?

What is so damn funny? He is a total nobody, just an artist, and a bug eater who sees a programmed world with his own objective vision and judgment while living in the center of a culture that would do much better if it had adopted a Swiss attitude towards Central European politics, rather than joining an elite run Union of Reptiles.

255

To put everything into perspective this way, think of how this Lizard, a total nobody, moved to an extremely conservative part of the world and made a mildly provocative YouTube channel for himself. For some reason his channel impressed Czech Google Corporation as threatening. So, threatening that they had to change the page so it wouldn't show the intended materials to the corporate run slaves.

Google and YouTube pulled the plug on Geeko's channel in December 2011. In pulling off its devilish deed, the Corporation had moved Lizard's channel into an "account violation" category which they listed in red letters as containing "controversial subject matter."

Geeko had questions for Google and YouTube corp: "Who is the judge of what is to be considered controversial subject matter on personal and private channels? And if it becomes an issue because of a complaint from a position of power, why hide the complaint and judgment from view and change a channel page when all you have to do is take it up with the account owner and get the other side of the story? Shouldn't there be a hearing?"

Geeko spent many long hours pondering these thoughts. He remembered around winter 2010 when Google wanted Geeko to give them his email address to link it to his YouTube channel user name. Geeko figured the corporation's bureaucratic strategy served as a self-serving method of covering its own ass. He had no problem with that. It made total sense. He had nothing to hide and never misused the channel in any way. Yet when this sneaky redesigning of his page took place, Google never contacted him with any warnings of violation via email. Instead, they essentially blacklisted Geeko by placing his account in the violations category without giving advance notice. From that point forward Geeko knew that Google should never be considered a legitimate protector of private and personal information. But, who pulled

Google's marionette strings that forced the launch of such dubious controls? We may never know.

Ironically it was around the end of November 2011 Geeko got an email from his dad who uses gmail, also run by Google, saying in a very informal way, acting as him...

"Hey, Son, I use gmail, I thought you might like to set up a gmail account also, go and see what it has to offer you."

Well, Geeko knew right away that his dad would never write such an email, it is not his style to waste words just to promote something commercial like this. Furthermore, it was sent right after Geeko got an email from his father. So he wouldn't write back another for this reason. When Geeko finally asked his Dad, he confirmed it was bogus.

Also around 11/11/11 Geeko logged on to his computer through his channel via 'Google Chrome' and a box came up asking him to add his phone number and provider to the sight account. The message said this would help keep his account record and passwords in order.

Naturally Geeko felt violated. He thought why give my phone number and phone service provider to Google along with my email to gmail? Next, they will want me to give them my blood for sure."

In the Czech Republic banks send security pass numbers through cell phones for online banking. Geeko was surprised Google management would be so impulsive towards Czech citizens. He also wondered how many naive citizens fell for it.

As if this was not already enough for Geeko to start smelling a rat, on Dec 1, Wikileaks founder Jillian Assange had a press conference at City University in London exposing several large telecommunication systems for spying on their innocent clients from all classes worldwide. Even people high on the so-called power ladder were not immune and as high up the power ladder as they see fit throughout the world. Assange explained the "leaks" were specifically naming iPhone, blackberry and gmail. He explained that a very large surveillance plan had been put into place and these Reptilian Cybor Security-Spy Corporations conspired against all nations on a massive scale, anyone who used this technology.

These 287 Wikileaks files describing how the corporations used spy software to develop and sell data to intelligence operations within non-western countries, where this activity is not considered illegal to obtain information about anyone they target, not only about or exclusive to, potential terrorists, and without a judicial warrant. The companies are unregulated and able to track our every move, anywhere in the world, even take photos, including eye and voice print.

Assange also explained that Facebook and social media also had become perfect tools to gather and record information for a giant data bank, literally tons of information about innocent citizens. Most likely this evolved as a grand political conspiracy but rather entirely for profit gain during the post 9-11era. Private social media organizations and corporations sold out along side security and surveillance equipment companies. Piles of ill-gotten cash from this thievery enabled the game to move forward. "So keep being busy digging your hole while we put all your comments and personal info into a storage box, get on Facebook, Linkedin, Myspace,Twitter, YouTube, Google then one day what you have said and done will be used to incriminate you for any particular wrong. Most likely this sensitive information can be purchased or sold to and or used against you in the future. God help anyone doing anything against the powers of the intricate Reptilian clubs that made and invested into this consolidating of secret government and corporations dangerous spy networks."

"To hell with car insurance, 15 minutes to check your social network, or YouTube manage account page and trash/close your personal crap could save you from 15 years in future New World Order Reptilian Prison or from waterboarding or even more."

-An insurance tip from Geeko

Chapter
13
Katka's Battle

20/20 Vision Symposium on Abstract Connectionism Arts, multi Science Law, Economy and Artificial Intelligence.

The Conference Center at Bentley Waltham, Massachusetts, is written on a large banner hanging from the eaves of an old colonial brick building in the center of a beautiful New England courtyard.

Katka Nova sits on a park bench in the Bentley courtyard listening to Jimmy Hendrix sing the timeless 'All Along the Watchtower' on her headphones, looking up at the banner and thinking, "this was it." The ultimate moment of her professional career, this was to be the climax to all the daunting years she had spent combining several fields together in order to achieve the unthinkable: The unification of the mind through creative subjective and objective balance.

This weeks-long symposium filled every lecture hall and conference room as well as exterior tents. Symposium events combined with other activities take place at all major universities surrounding the Boston Area. Today, was the day she had to give an invitation-only speech at a 480-seat auditorium in front of some of the greatest contemporary minds of science and the arts representing every continent.

So much had happened over the last ten years since Katka began her own fieldwork in brain science. She had started out only building theories on the connections between symbolism and their relationships to linguistics. It seemed that this concept affected so many fields that many educational institutions became interested.

Schools of psychology, phenomenology, semantics, linguistics, economy, philosophy, and law were interested in what she had to say. Not all were keen on her breakthroughs, however. She had her critics as well, calling her theories metaphysical. She completely resented this notion because her theories sometimes negated the pure conservative approaches to some 'higher mathematics' reasoning in abstract areas in which science had invested centuries of objective rational and constructive meaning, areas that had much to loose financially if more holistic approaches lead mankind on paths of self-healing and self-enlightenments. But this is the nature of the trickle-down scientific beast. She was not afraid then and she is not afraid today.

Katka grew up during the last years of Czech Communist control. She could handle manipulation, and she knew the difference. If she started to feel uneasy or feel fear coming on, she would just imagine an age of the prehistoric dinosaurs. The age of the greedy selfish man is most likely momentary as well. Her duty was to be a part of the evolutionary process of mankind's quest for knowledge, not the inhibiter of energy flows or natural matter that becomes us out of pure comfortable laziness of life playing itself out naturally.

The irony of language itself took her further into the mind.

"Our language is a supreme code," she would say. "If it is getting simplified as technology moves forward, then now more than ever is time to redefine collectively the loosely defined before we let power define for us a simplified code of prescription."

As Katka sat there she thought about how she owed everything to the reboot she got following her mental breakdown suffered in the winter of 2010 while working on particular theories concerning

"The values of life versus nihilism, despair and the moral shift of mind related to the state of the world's economy and its leadership."

Fearful of "no trespass" signs, dare she commit to 'thought crime.' Attitudes were changing rapidly amongst the academia. Propaganda declared that corporate wealth should rule matters of intellectual property. Ignoring their own former long-time moral values and principles, the latest New Age objectivist educators pushed aside alternative ecological and homeopathic science in favor of new methods of manipulating science through power and controlling the world's brain pool.

Political directors at universities issued strong-arm memos, even warning not to use information from various said sources. Professors were warned that particular journalistic resources only spread fear among the intellectual circles at major universities.

One of those memos in which she was told to ignore was the information related to the Wikileaks website. That memo said this was not factual information representative of what an American University should sanction. Critical thinkers would remember this website as a bomb dropped into the world's journalistic thought process as we enter the age of Internet and computer technologies of the late 2000s.

On September 1, 2010 Wikileaks sent 251,287 diplomatic cables off to the world press. Wikileaks was an Internet site similar to Wikipedia that was built by a tech-savvy generation.

Wikileaks emerged as a vital platform for revealing corporate and government corruption and incompetence. The general public needed and deserved such critical information, although potentially damaging to corrupt politicians, unscrupulous bureaucrats and criminal-minded objectivists. The "Wikileaks goal" basically strived to make the world's governments more accountable and transparent. If successful, this would decrease corruption while creating a balanced playing field for press freedom and quality of public information. Wikileaks had continuously been gaining recognition and a positive reputation among anti-Americanization activists eager to level the worldwide economic playing fields. A moving team of researchers, tech IT experts and journalists strived to stay ahead of the info highway allowing leaks of top vital info. Wikileaks supporters wanted to provide a blanket of protection to the "whistle blower," and journalists who faced potential severe retribution. This site worked out fine for a short period of time until it started to piss off major players in the United States.

Katka developed a scientific approach to following these 'Cable Gate leaks' loaded with details. The United States Secretary of state Hillary Clinton as well as several Republican senators and congressmen including propaganda news hosts, who condemned the governmental leaks sent out by an insider from the military, a U.S. citizen, governmental whistleblower Army private Bradley Manning. While stationed in Iraq, Manning allegedly opened up and shared with Wikileaks a quarter million diplomatic cables of information, sent to the U.S. State Department via different embassies.

According to the world press, the diplomatic cables painted a very embarrassing U.S. diplomacy trend worldwide. Furthermore the documents made United States diplomats look morally ambivalent, like spoiled aggressive disrespectful, uncaring representatives.

Mainly, the leaks caused several U.S. diplomats to loose their jobs because they were found to be untrustworthy to their host countries and within the circles of power that ran those lands. Giving personal info and spying was not a diplomat's job in essence. A diplomat should act as a trustworthy go between. The American government's despicable treatment of Manning broke the unspoken U.S. code of fair and respectable play.

The leaks that prosecutors claimed he spilled showed many countries like Tunisia, Egypt and Libya that their leadership was not as powerful and that ties with America were fragile. These revelations prompted movements within them to revolt. The leaks uncovered realities about America's longtime role in propping up leaders that the U.S. government has had little respect for. The U.S. government strived to maintain leverage in regions of the Middle East for corporate and economic reasons. These leaks energized the Middle East, ultimately resulting in the overthrow of numerous governments throughout that region in 2011.

This quick explosion of Mideast movements robbed America of its ability to control the directions of foreign regimes. This change frustrated outspoken leaders in Washington. Those high-ranking lawmakers became the focus of Katka's cross-hairs. She identified and targeted individuals that disliked and felt intimidated by Wikileaks. Those shady characters became paranoid due to their own questionable political backgrounds. If one were only to take a simple moment to run a Google search and connect a money flow, the dots linked them all quite nicely. Katka did just that and each one on her list came out demanding to slay the messenger.

In fact, many politically high-ranking symbolic dark side pundits and politicians bluntly burst fourth on the world stage. Publicly exposed for the first time, these monsters shouted without any facts or authority demanding to immediately slay the messenger.

That messenger was eventually forced into exile at the Ecuadorian Embassy in London, England calmly waiting for the world to recognize and accept a fair, open and united potential reality.

Katka would write: "That messenger was Australian born,

world-traveled Wikileaks founder Julian Assange, at first look one has to be intrigued by his looks; he seemed more like a handsome rock star than a computer nerd. Assange was a captivating, sexy character, mysterious with balls like Crocodile Dundee ready to take on the imperialist "Bastards."

"Assange was an Australian, a former computer-hacker turned cyber vigilante. It is debated by the world power elites that were affected by the Cable leaks whether or not he can be considered a professional journalist. Julian Assange was however from what Katka could get out of what she read and the several documentaries that she watched 'a great club techno dancer and the founder and CEO and spokesman of the Wikileaks.org Internet site.' He felt the Americans wanted to throw the first amendment in the bin in favor of corporate greed. He also felt publishers must be free to publish. Katka began to perceive him as a heroic figure.

"The U.S. Secretary of State and many others condemned him, and his site and his sources. Some in Washington D.C., called for Interpol to issue an arrest warrant for Assange. Some even went so far as asking for him to be punished to death as a traitor. Calls for retribution or severe punishment intensified, even though he is not an American citizen, nor is his website even located in the U.S.

"His site continues to run, yet floats and has servers secret and hidden all over the world. The Americans continued to pressure Ecuador's president Rafael Correa and leaders of other smaller countries to avoid protecting Assange. The headlines show the South American power skeptics are the only protection Assange has to keep from being sent to a torture chamber/gulag such as Guantanamo Prison.

"Such actions against Assange are endorsed by the ruling powers he has embarrassed. Embarrassed enough to cause them fear for what else he has on high-ranking individuals. Perhaps information he has hidden as an insurance trigger to protect himself and his organization, also further secret information he had on any factions they should be fearful of.

"The Assange victims needed to get him to the U.S. where expert torture authority former Vice President Cheney aided by a strange type of media run philosophical injection program had creatively spun the general public confusion about the moral definitions and values on topics of torture for information. Now that torture is referred to as "Enhanced Interrogation Techniques." President Obama glided over the torture issue as well as the Wikileaks, Assange Private Manning issue obviously to smart to join any particular bandwagon and soil his lofty image with world elite."

Katka continued... "Assange is considered a hero to many hackers and open Internet neutrality groups including a movement known as Anonymous. This movement was choosing to be anonymous because it seemed safer if you could be anyone not disclosing a name under leaderless organization." Katka had a problem with them, because just as the terrorists remain nameless, so could an anonymous organization calling him or herself such."

The only problem she thought was: "Within time, Anonymous will become a dirty word to the ruling class. What happens when they are blamed for a bloody terrorist-like act? Who will care for a masked anonymous nobody freedom fighter?" Katka was quick to distance herself from Anonymous. She only wanted to surf the web and get an understanding of what Anonymous strived to prove during this amazing online war taking over the Internet during the fall of 2010.

Out of curiosity, Katka began to surf some strange internet red light districts like 4Chan, following the lure of computer hacker chats. This led her into areas she would soon regret. Hackers were encouraging assisted hits on major credit card companies like Visa and MasterCard. That is when Katka realized that this adventure to understand this young tech world was becoming a new and abstract language she found irresistible.

Katka channeled deeper into an interesting energy mass as everyone got connected on this topic via chats and Internet news sights. The world press realized that an Internet journalistic tool like Wikileaks provides more scoops pointing to government corruption in one year than 30 years of mainstream coverage. Many people started to turn off the TV. While Small Internet news programs like *Russia Today* or the *Al Jazeera*, or *the Young Turks* and new abstract forms of creative Rap News networks like *Juice News* gradually got as much or more attention as the mainstream media. This bold new Internet began covering stories that the controlled mainstream media failed to touch.

This all happened as the small African nation of Nigeria nominated former Vice President Cheney for an Interpol arrest warrant. Ironically at the same time the U.S. State Department demanded an extradition of Assange from England to face a court in Sweden on a bogus sex scandal. At the same time the U.S. refused to honor an extradition treaty first enacted with Nigeria in 1931. Nigeria wanted to punish their fellow elitist for crimes he committed while he was the CEO of Halliburton, all in the name of greed. The Nigerians provided a well documented case that uncovered $180 million in bribes used in order to gain a $6 billion natural gas contract for KBR, a Halliburton affiliate company. Only two mainstream American media news shows briefly mentioned the Cheney story, the MSNBC cable network's Keith Olbermann show and the Ed Show.

Increasingly eager to dig deep into the truth about this corruption, as her own depression deepened, Katka slept and ate less and spent nights surfing the new Internet news sights for facts.

Eventually she found herself looking around the courtyard

at all the people who were funneling into the various conference chambers. Katka sat, thinking deeply...

"A hunger for truth kept me working, I didn't know if I would make it back alive." Paranoid, she thought the people were following her because she kept looking into things that seemed to be extremely vicious areas of secret greed, driven powerful groups playing parts on the political world stage.

The turn of this Millennium will be remembered as a revenge of the computer nerds for real on a giant scale. The elites who have controlled the world's movements for centuries did not see this one coming. Now, many corrupt accounts were explaining the factual naming of several scandals between world diplomats. Everything fell too nicely into her theories for her paper on Nihilism, helping her connect the dots. The linking would take over her broad consciousness and blanket it with misanthropic fear of everyone for several months until she lost herself, sending her into a severe depression.

She nearly gave up, contemplating suicide. Luckily, Katka's work associates noticed her daily change in time and asked her to get treated. She needed tranquilizers to come off of the severe high, then a prescription of Zyprexa, which she took over the next year until she worked her way clean.

Katka remembered sitting down a year later with her psychiatrist friend, Doctor Ramadeep, who helped her through the experience.

"What were your thoughts before the severe stage set in?" He asked her calmly, listening quietly as he sat back into a large leather chair.

"I was just so angry at the whole world, seeing that we were given such gifts. Our minds and creative abilities, and yet we are so fake, deceiving and destructive at the same time. Too much imbalance, I became more depressed. That's all." She said looking at him with a glazed look in her eyes. He helped her understand that it was normal and many people who delve into the science fields meet similar scenarios of psychosis along the way. The Doctor now waving a finger in the air at Katka explained: "It is the chance you take when you open the Pandora's Box called the human brain, you of all people know this reality.

You know about Cantor and Boltzman don't you?" He asked clutching his gray beard. And laying back in his chair, Katka could see the image of her psychological guru from the Himalayas who gave her the It's normal and OK it happens to most people speech, which she needed at a very desperate moment and turning point in her life. Dr. Ramadeep continued. "The concept of infinite numbers could never be fully explained although Georg Cantor gave us to this day its best explanation. Neither could entropy because of the size and scope of its endless puzzle it presented. Ludwig Boltzman would be the one to challenge all the mathematical establishments on this, then kill himself feeling unaccepted for it. Both would suffer and die from depression, Boltzman so severe he hung himself. Humanity tries to find the keys to doors of Revelation that only Gods keep in their pockets. Be careful what you wish for Katka. Perhaps your fears and concerns could drive you mad, kill you, or make you great, or all three. What doesn't kill you truly makes you stronger."

Fortunately Katka was so interested in brain science in general, she took immediately to the task of healing herself by figuring out what had triggered her psychosis. She wanted to pinpoint and identify the problem in order to not let this difficult depressing situation happen again. Katka eventually identified the cause of her depression.

"The world is sick and dying. The sensitive among us are sick and dying along with the world because we are truly connected to Mother Earth yet unable to understand why we don't fit in."

Katka wrote this into a theory on basic phenomenal psychology and the super-united quantum consciousness, that she gave while students took meditation, and yoga at the same time while listening to her lectures on body, spirit, deep holistic breathing and art and music therapy. She accomplished all this amid right and left brain exercises combined with a radical whole foods diet. These were the healing methods she swore by. From the beginning of 2011, and for the next nine years she devoted her life to starting over with a clean mind, body, diet and spirit. Furthermore she took each sensitive day as the best next day of her life. She was staying in the game to heal herself and also for the greater good of her loved ones and the beauty she described in her own conscious reality.

She decided to take on the demons head to head, and call them out to face off at the threshold of reality itself. Reality that she felt, was as symbolic as a cup holding her ideals of the world's future order, balance, and health. Her attitude helped her find her deeper calling seeking the mysterious and taking chances she would never have done before. The calling had pushed her to reach out for the first time and meet people and connect with key players in her life. It also had lead her to met new people who changed her mind about love and sex, enhancing her life with understanding about experiencing the moment and seeking real love and following her heart and senses, connected to a much higher brain power and superior consciousness rather than remaining chained to earthly objective, old school reasoning. Daily, she would tell herself and anyone who wished to hear it as if like a mantra that kept her alive:

"Who knows where we shall go from here, but here, we have to kick ass with use of positive, creative, connected energy and unite thought and truths, or face the reality that we have all failed life's ultimate purpose." Failure was not an option for Katka Nova.

Chapter
14
The Game Revealed

"Miss Nova?" asked a tall man in a black suit and tie, wearing thick, black, plastic-rimmed dark glasses while standing over her at the courtyard bench. She didn't reply, sensing something strange about this man who looked down at her with a shaved head and straight face.

"May I help you?" She asked taking off her headphones looking up at him with a suspicious tone in her voice.

"Do you mind if I sit here? I just have a few important words concerning your conference today that's all?"

"No," she said, hesitating a bit. "Please sit."

"Hi, my name is Anthony, You can call me TJ. I am sorry for approaching you this way. However, the people I work for won't allow me to make contacts in any other way for security and privacy reasons.

"Is there some problem?" She asked, squinting a little and rolling her shoulders.

"No problem at all… in fact, I was sent here to let you know that you should have nothing to fear because we are looking out for you."

"Who is 'we,' and why would you need to be looking out for me?" She looked at him in the mirrored dark glasses, seeing her reflection.

"I am afraid I can't disclose certain critical information

because I don't have the answers myself nor the authority to advise or guess on which to give you, although you may ask me anything you like. I will be happy to answer what I can."

"Well, if you refuse tell me who you work for, why are you here?"

"We and... I mean there is a group of us here to look out for you because we have reason to believe that some entities would like to do harm to you and your project. Furthermore, the very idea of your project and this symposium is considered very damaging to certain very powerful mega corporations and certain high ranking politicians and ruling bodies. We are just here to keep the road clear for you that's all. So if you see many of the same people around you from now on you don't need to look too hard at them, or pay attention to them. Just go about your business as usual, ok? We have everything handled from the outside, you need not worry. You're in the best hands in the business."

"What business are you talking about?" She asked looking at him with a look of confusion.

"Again, I am not able to give you labels to your questions. But you can keep fishing, and I will answer all you ask, at least whatever is in my power to do so."

"Ok, then why would you want to protect me and my project? Are you familiar with my project?" She asked him gesturing to a banner that hung in the courtyard.

"Let me put it to you this way. We watched you develop it. In fact…we have been watching you for some time now." He crossed his legs and relaxed back into the bench.

"Were you following me in 2010?"

"I am aware of what happened to you back in the winter of 2010, while the Web war erupted into a frenzy. The Internet went crazy watching hackers and leakers and cyber terrorists and because you were playing with it and downloading several

272

megabytes of Wikileaks for your theories, you got red flagged. Over the years your information kept being passed further up the watch, mainly because your info was far too broad for our average bee watchers."

"When it was passed to our department, I can tell you it is one of the highest departments… we thought you were some kind of nut at first honestly. But then we soon became very interested in your theories as well. Before too long we had members in the department actually getting in long drawn-out fights, in fact, over the topic of whether your work was subversive to our authorities' perspectives. You know, no one could answer those questions for us and no one wanted to take charge of how to deal with your case because you were not like anything we had ever dealt with before. Most radicals and subversives were always against something that would lead them to breaking the rules of sanity and tolerance under the order or codes of the departments. In your case, you just played the game without knowing you were doing so at all, and now you're almost to the untouchable status.

I say almost… although many others and myself are on your side and see the merit in what your project proposes to further the greater prosperity of the whole, including many for whom we may not speak of and for good reason must stay anonymous. However, there are some who don't want the kind of change your abstract concept represents. Some powerful players would like to see you dead and your program eliminated frankly."

"What do you mean by breaking the rules?" She asked him with a serious tone looking right at him.

"I was afraid you were going to ask me that. All I can tell you is there exists a set of them and they have been here from the beginning of recorded civilized time, someone more powerful on the world game than me will be able to give them to you, unfortunately I cannot."

"Do you know the rules, Anthony?" She asks him smiling.

"For my own health and safety I have refused to know the rules. I obey and follow orders." He said.

Those whom I work for think you might know the rules. However, the rules come from very profound divine directions, the people I am connected with follow the directions very carefully and we protect those whose logic seems most coherent with our authorities' future security and ideas of the ever changing definition of the rules. That's all. No grand conspiracy just logic and a will to survive with intellect.

The world is evolving and your ideas just seem to weigh in favor of intelligence and reality. Everyone wants to stay alive, that's all. There are many dangerous schools of thought playing out the tragedy of the commons. No one wants to get on the wrong side of history. The energies will lead us all into the part we play. One day at a time. My part is to watch you give your presentation today. With that final note, let me say it has been a pleasure finally meeting you. And, if you should need anything just yell out loud my name… TJ! I am here for you."

"Wait TJ, one more thing, clutching his arm before he stands up." I need to know something but you need to take your glasses off and look in my eyes if I should believe anything you have said to me today."

TJ removed his glasses revealing deep greenish grey eyes, and a very unsymmetrical face, the right side extremely relaxed and the left side very stern and serious. Katka took a deep look as she asked him, "Do you have children?"

"Yes," he said.

The next question she asked was with her eyes. "Do you?"

TJ looked back deep into hers slowly nodding his head up and down.

She spoke calmly, "If you know what we are about, you

realize where the virus lives and what must be done to it also TJ?"

He nods back, looking a little more seriously.

"TJ, then lets go play our parts, it could take some time to get this thing done." She say's as she stands up smiling and nodding to him with mouth closed, putting her large yellow music headphones on playing Pink's '*Blow me one last kiss*' and walks off towards a large set of doors as many people filled into a huge auditorium while the beats, tempo and lyrics mix away the anxiety of her nervous moment. She used this as a way of reminding herself to stay focused and on course with her own theme even if no one might ever understand what she was about to tell everyone.

TJ watched her walk, bobbing her head up and down slowly as she strolled down the cobblestone courtyard and through the hand-carved double doors into the old new England colonial style brick building. He then reached behind his ear to press a button on a micro sized listening device:

"Contact was made, objective communicated, she seemed cool as anyone I ever met, like a Jedi Knight, a very charismatic, attractive, strong and fearless woman… I think I am in love. No, of course I am joking…yes I'm kidding, she is now privy to the game… Over."

Katka entered the large lecture auditorium at Bentley and is immediately recognized and greeted by two young men who lead her to the front of the stage where a long table and podium are set up.

The hall filled quite rapidly as she sensed with some nervousness that the moment she had anticipated for years would come. She removed her headphones while climbing the steps, before taking a seat to the right of the podium to her left at a table that was split in the middle. Nearest the podium sat Professor Ringo, her Japanese colleague and director of (AI) connectionist brain research at the Massachusetts Institute of Technology. Within

275

moments he walked up to the front of the old oak podium and adjusted the microphone.

Noticing the rear doors being closed and all of the seats taken, he opened the discussion.

"Ladies and gentlemen, distinguished guests, and colleges, it is a distinct and great honor to be here today at the first of, and I hope, many symposiums of this kind in the future. We have here today one of the greatest gatherings of minds in one place in years. The great thing is the wide spectrum of intelligence and fields represented here is something truly unique and exciting. We have top experts from brain science, biology, genealogy, economics, and mathematics, to law, musical and visual artists and writers, philosophers and health experts just to name a few. We have all come together volunteering our time and funds and connections for one purpose and one purpose only.

"That purpose is the unification of the world through greater thought and consciousness, further connecting thought that unites us and heals our planet's wounds caused by decades of unconscious programming. I am proud to say that there is no single force to thank for this gathering; the thank-you goes out to everyone who was invited to this symposium because you made it happen. However, there is one special thanks that goes out to someone who, had she not prepared the original theories and had she not been so pushy with them early on, we most likely would not have grasped the concepts on our own quite as quickly in the same and organized manor. She developed not only the theories of 'Abstract Connectionist' philosophy towards the unified (AI) mind but she has also worked endlessly providing the architecture to the development of the Internet Qualia neural gathering construct that potentially will make a unified mind function in accordance with multiple fields and networks. Of course this is very general coming from me so please…

It's with great honor to introduce a woman who has spent her life devoted to the mind."

"Doctor Katarina Nova holds a doctorate degree from Charles University in Psychology and Philosophy, a Baccalaureate in Visual Arts, and Art History, a teaching degree from the Pedagogical Faculty in Prague as well as associates degree in English and Linguistics. She holds an Oxford and Harvard Law School, co-masters degree in constitutional law. She came from Oxford as a JFK scholar to finish at Harvard and she is also a certified art therapist. Katka has written over 200 controversial papers influencing several fields. She has also authored and co-authored several books on her 'Abstract Connectionist' theories. I got to know her when she came to my department at the McGovern Institute for Brain Research at MIT four years ago. She wanted to further her own developing research on Abstract Connectionist brain networks and (AI) science related to AI programming."

"Last year her humorous paper on *'Addiction and The piggyback bandit'* got her an honorary degree from the (AI) brain and cognitive science departments at MIT.

This paper was unlike anything that the department had ever seen before. Her theories about particular phenomenal senses connected to addiction impressed everyone as unusual and her abstracts gave alternative insights to brain wave functions. This humorous analysis case study of a 240-pound man who was banned from five Northwestern States for bribing children to give him piggybacks at high school basketball games."

The whole auditorium began to laugh, as the speaker continued.

Her research on the Addicted 'Piggy Back Bandit' helped her attach and find neurological locations of the brain relating to addiction stimuli for abstract fetishes and materialism. Very humorous paper we all enjoyed it and it is leading thought in new directions in neurology and brain science. Perhaps one day we won't need to have so much materially forced on us by corporations once we understand the mental process running most of our material wants and addictions. According to Miss Nova's research, perhaps the roots of many psychosis's comes down purely to culturally and commercially enforced and programmed brain disorders."

"So without further delay Miss Katarina Nova"

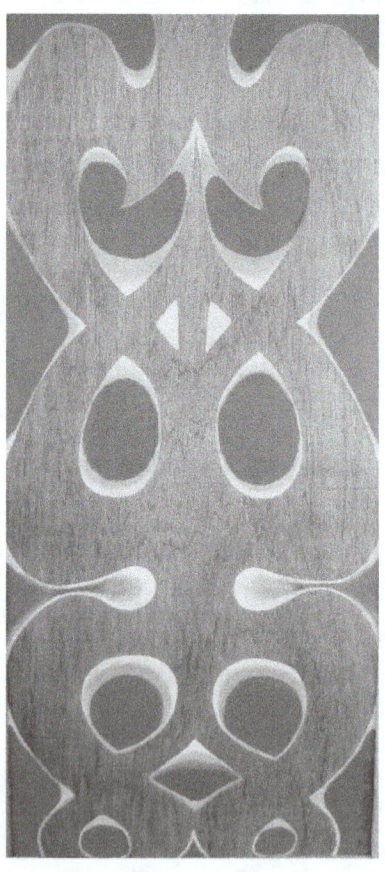

Chapter
15
The Show Must Go On!

Katarina was in a trance as she heard her name called and the round of applause that rose up into the air and filled the large 480-seat auditorium.

The conference chairman waved towards Katka to take the podium. At 47 years old and in her career prime, she stood up tall in her professional skirt, showing long slim healthy legs. She moved in the direction of the oak box that was central to the stage and laid out a set of cards she had kept in her side coat pocket of her black slim suit top. It was hot, so she took a second to unbutton the top of her white blouse as she prepared.

As the audience continued clapping, her long auburn hair remained hung uncomfortably in her face. So she adjusted her hair as the applause slowly subsided. Katka looked out and smiled.

"It is a wonderful honor to be here today, I honestly can't believe this all came true. I knew when I first wrote the basic papers on the 'Ultimate Super Computer' back in 2011 that there might be some who possibly felt the way I did, but the response, and now this gathering with all that has happened so far is beyond belief. Thanks so much to all of you for being here today.

"I know it has been a long conference schedule and there is much to cover so I will try to move through it as quick and clearly as I can, feel free to stop me and ask questions at any time during the lecture." The house lights then suddenly dimmed and a screen lights up behind her showing a vast universe of stars while Katka walked from behind the stage, holding a microphone. Softly and clearly she began her most important speech of her life.

"As absurd and ludicrous as humans can be, the piggyback bandit materialist research is a perfect example of that. Humanity is fortunate to have the ability to use the senses in harmony within our own minds' conceptual visions and interpretations of semiotic reasoning of our languages complex socially created codes. Regardless of the existence of or lack of a divine direction or mathematical equation we all have the ability to make our own observations of any given object. What we define through inference, our own mental state, belongs to us. The experience we gain as we engage in the world around us is the gift of life itself, and although external from us this gift of life experience is our conceptual property, as long as we remain free men and women, we can decide when and how we want to share it in any form, through music, art science, politics, economics, anything. Civilizations of man have evolved through this form of sharing experiences and ideas because these societies generate the art that moves us ever forward.

"Controlling ideas and thought is very difficult because the world as well as the mind are continually found to be more and more abstract," she continues.

"However, a dichotomy of pure joy and good versus anxiety and evil exists, and it makes life on this earth seem overwhelmingly manic. All the pathetic-ironic humor going on around us as we watch the business and political workings of the contemporary world, if one tunes in, it surely makes for a comedy channel like no other. We live in a time where we invest and waste billions of dollars to fund presidential election campaigns while our governments spend us into deeper debt playing a show by using one or the other party for blame and or glory while both favor the whims of the corporate elite over the public anyway.

"We live in a time of new technology which allows us to accumulate info at rocket speed, and a tap of the finger, all from the comfort of our own homes as we have never been able to do before; the visual senses are working at an all time high witnessing digital breakthroughs that radically transcend our concept of reality with virtual realities, and with artificial realities.

"This embrace of modern material and visual pleasures is also rapidly removing us from our more grounded selves making us forget who we are and where we come from and changing our very form of communication and linguistics which separates us from all other creatures. That, in turn even begins changing and manipulating the very delicate fabric of the science of the brain itself.

"I can hear it also speaking to me through-memories of our history, like a little friend whispering: 'yes we are fortunate but, this technological change we are experiencing is exciting yet dangerous and potentially threatening to the core concepts of liberty and freedom.'

"Power and money if given opportunity, manage to inhibit free and open scientific and technological artistic movements. In terms of intellectual evolution relating to the fields of philosophy and linguistics in the specific areas of epistemic moral reasoning of virtues and their necessary placement in society and politics, there have been no great breakthroughs since the eras of new world enlightenment which sparked a momentum of thought and lead to the building of the U.S. Bill of Rights and the Constitution that made liberty a reality for the average layman, thus setting a standard for the world to follow."

Katka referred to the PowerPoint on the screen behind her and up in between the sea of stars and galaxies a graphic popped up and the Following quote and headings:

"As soon as questions of will or decision or reason or choice of action arise, human science is at a loss." **-Noam Chomsky**

Katka turned around, a wisp of hair in her mouth, and said: "The revolution of reason and reality itself has begun."

The AC PARTY Flashes up on the screen.

"We are a proactive worldwide arts and science embracing community that recognizes a unified collective of knowledge, reason, truth, and connected reality. We reject any power-driven, prescribed reality and order from an omnipotent authority. Our open and free neutral Internet networks maintain our democratic freedom and liberty and growth and further unification. We will not be controlled by private minority singular entities in the future. We will rather in time take control of the future as a free intellectual unified world mass.

"We have come full circle, ladies and gentlemen. It is with great pleasure to thank everyone here who had a part in the development of the Abstract Connectionist World Party Movement.

Katka pointed to the white screen where the Power Point appeared.

"Our new AC Philosophy and science is interested in building the much-needed mathematics to make this changing of guard transition a smooth and natural reality. From this idea and seed in its infancy we project it forward towards the ultimate goal: The most mega-connected non, gravitational philosophy and science this world has ever experienced. But for this new direction to function requires a sacrifice.

Katka looks directly into the audience's eyes: "The Sacrifice."

"The unbalanced facade of individualist, objectivist, collusive cults, and secret glad handing orders must be recognized as a virus and a threat to natural world progress and the rebuilding of a logical and balanced world order. Selfishly motivated decisions are breeding rampant destructive globalism, favoritism, elitism, imperialism, fascism, totalitarianism and a worldwide corporate monopoly only benefiting a very minute percent of crony multi-corporate entities. These two-faced wolves in sheep's clothing must be dealt with quickly and carefully, coming from a ground-up direction of mass world connection in order to restore a trust in world leaderships and restore a healthy world order.

"If a logical antidote for the addictive amphetamine-like destructive drugs called objectivism, greed and selfishness are needed to base a call of bluffs, then this discourse you're about to be taken through today is only a glimpse of the abstracts many great men and women of connected arts and science have thus far put together.

"The carefully constructed (AI) and cognitive scientific community and unified mind could potentially help restore mankind's trust in himself or herself through a new worldwide community.

"The political power structure being amassed today seems to be forcing world revolution. Uncertainty is in the air. We need to identify the problems with connected worldwide reason concerning globalized corporate topics. The world's common man and workers are thrown by their lords into no win situations, which are completely out of their control. How do we get a balanced control back?

"Reasoning this out is a tricky landscape full of thorns, and projectiles.

"Thus it is believed by our ever-growing collective of 'Abstract Connectionists' that only by connecting worldwide with super conscious direction will intellect be able to decide whether or not we can trust our future and its developers and planners. This is primarily so that we don't get made to be fools by something so-state-of-the-art, which is being force-fed to us with very little time to read the warning label.

"So many things today are coming at us that sound too good to be true. My father always said: 'if it sounds so… it probably is.' With more allowance of machines and technologies to do our work and thinking for us also means loosing our skepticism in some areas that protected us and kept us free men and women.

Katka pauses, noticing a raised hand in the second row. "You have a question?" she asks a young man.

"What is 'Abstract Connectionism,' exactly? I am new to this concept."

"Sure, basically it is the absolute quantum everything material and phenomenal pot surrounded by every cook imaginable, all throwing in the exact properly fitting ingredient in order to arrive at the absolute best taste, smell, feel and visual outcome as possible and still knowing it is not perfect."

Katka continued, while a Power Point illustrated the topics behind her on a projector screen.

"This Abstract in general: lets call it: "The connectionist approach to linguistics, arts, science and politics aiming on a philosophical, cognitive scientific level that fosters building a better world order by using an open organized brain function as opposed to a closed-objectively-driven one.

"The Proud comfortable scientist will say something like: The term 'Connectionist' and *Connectionism* and its theory was based on the neural learning of the brain and nervous systems and led to and formed the Idea of (AI) Artificial Intelligence or study of making machines think. Another name on this line is *'parallel distributed processing or PDP.'* It is also the study of how the brain stores information in 'distributed fashion' connectionist research is concerned with how the brain does this.

"Alan Turing, who in 1947 wrote an interesting report on the topic of *'Intelligent Machinery'* was basically saying our brains are 'digital computing machines.'

Turing says 'our brains are like machines.' Katka paused...

"OK...Turing breaks open the pathway to 'Artificial Intelligence' and uses the magic word connect a code word that is known universally to anyone who puts any number of objects together to form a connection.

"It's no wonder his brain would call it that because that is probably exactly how our brains, sorry 'machines' according to Turing...just do it 'naturally,' simply said."

Katka smiled and pointed again to reference of the Power Point.

"So the question becomes whether one can get past the term *'Connectionism'* as only a form or field pertaining to computers, and (AI) science and the brain as a tool for neural science and developing only machine artificial intelligence.

"Are we not women and men? We are not machines yet!" She yelled.

Some of the audience laughed and coughed.

"So what are the positive aspects and potentials of connectionist theories for use in seeing the real human brain as a tool for our real mental progress and the progress of furthering humanity's need for higher developed forms of philosophy, arts and science, linguistics, law and world economy. She began tapping the podium with her pencil.

"Perhaps we call it 'Abstract Connectionism?'"

"Personally, I would love this because the potential is endless, however, not through a linear old school, top-down, critical, rationalists, objectivists, one-sided approach. Why?

"Our brains are not machines. In reality they are complex two-sided underestimated physical wonders of nature as perplexing as the universe is.

"I fear recklessness, and inevitable potential doom from those inferior intellects that have and use power and greed and pride to condition the (AI) to act as they do. What would be their motives?

"Is the goal to create a machine to evolve into a superhuman who will one day be at a level of say: Alan Greenspan, or Newt Gingrich, or Dick Cheney as a model?" Katka looked out pausing and watching the crowd erupt into relaxed laughter.

"Unlike these examples just mentioned, some of us have free creative brains. Or are we faced with a return to becoming even more stupid than an ape. Is this part of the hidden code of a strange dimension called Planet Earth 21st Century? Was Darwin right, however, the order of direction was wrong? Is human destiny to de-evolve? Because...apes don't act as foolish as we often do when it comes to valuing of nature and science. Let us be critical of our leadership of the garden!"

The whole auditorium started to erupt into laughter at hearing this...Katka continued:

"Yes, you may laugh but don't forget only humans would think of killing for trivial material means, stealing the ivory and furs and leaving the flesh to rot."

"As far as the field of the 'Artificial Intelligence' brain and neural science the potential is out of this world if they should embrace the 'Abstract Connectionist' approach to their existing connectionist brain sciences. Why?

"Abstract Connectionism' opens up the core of the abstract mathematical problems naturally by tapping the entire universe, rather than drilling into it from all different directions, trying to play God with manmade higher abstract mathematics only.

"It is perhaps through an 'Abstract Connectionist' across-the-field' approach to science that we may attempt to help the technological age reverse the entropy spiral. Basically connecting the dots of all art forms and science, furthermore constructing openness through geometrically and mathematically linking a blueprint to other abstract forms of thought across the academic fields, creating an eventual unified model priori as a goal. Once the worldwide unified language of science has been achieved and tested, this model should become the driving force to press a more subjective return to philosophical and ethical directives of political and social world order and direction. A world order designed by a multi-culture-sharing mass and not by a small minority with selfish interests only backed by wealth and manipulated militaries."

Several hands went up as a microphone was passed to a middle aged man sitting near the edge of the isle. He stood and reached out for the microphone that was being passed up the aisle.

"Thank you, Doctor honestly this all seems far fetched. I am unsure your theories on creating a new kind of backwards mathematics, this 'Abstract Connectionist' movement, can challenge the demands of the worlds scientific fields with such an unrealistic approach… I am curious how the proposed 'Connected Unified Mind Super Computer' expects that given the nature of man's inevitable need to control, corrupt, and rise to power because it's naturally human to create, accumulate, procreate and dominate. How can we expect the movement to function above this natural animalistic circular reality that has dominated mankind since the beginning of time? I mean, I can hardly get anyone to agree with me in one field. Don't even mention when I have to explain or deal with politics. How can we expect to bring it all together?"

Katka laughs for a moment before responding:

"That is a very good question, and honestly there is no answer to it because we are in the developmental stage of this movement... this very moment in fact. When one looks at how badly the constitution and the U.S. Bill of Rights have been manipulated since its beginning, some in destructive and negative ways, it is easy to loose faith in anything that suggests volunteered moral endeavors towards bureaucracy even if an age of enlightenment is on your side. Power and greed, and fear of its loss of control eventually try to rewrite the books and crush any movement of good intention that has positive ideals favoring a benevolent control of the pie.

"I suggest watching the documentary '*The Art of the Steal.*' That is a perfect example of political theft. Change is inevitable and masses create movements when social critical times arise. Political power will want or refuse a movement based on how it affects profit. History shows us that great movements of change rise from the desperate. These are the facts.

"Where this or any movement will go is history itself being made as we speak.

"I choose to be a part of the positive process, as do many of the folks surrounding us here in this auditorium because it makes us feel that a significant and essential positive purpose here at this time is being met.

"If I worry about change and fear or loosing my routine, I won't be able to do my best part for the unified collective. I can only repeat to myself that I am a positive piece of the giant abstract puzzle being put together.

"You are also a part of the puzzle even if you think you are against these ideas. You came here today and your skepticism and reason has a value because it presses the movement to reanalyze its theories. We need you. Yet we recommend you keep an open mind and entertain subjective ideas as well with your critical analysis. We hope this unified, deeply shared feeling will give us one day a truly enlightened super conscious unified (AI) mind. The Power Point changes its screens to the following:

"The one I like we call the '**Zillion Dollar Question**.'

"It is a good time to ask difficult questions, Katka says as she smiles at the man who stood up with the question. Katka then scrolled the PowerPoint.

"Will we all, be able to mature and recognize our human mistakes? Can we point to the true virus and sickness, the disease affecting our world politics that stagnates us all wishing to chain our creativity?

"Will our future generations take these Nihilistic times as lessons, prompting future leaders to judge, and reject fear-driven decision making? Also will this inspire our wiser and connected elite unseen keepers to destroy their virus, like two-faced corrupt yes men? Would they punish the psychologically damaged followers of false premise? Will the owners be bold enough to take the hit from these bad ideas and re-boot the hard drive?

"Our research is showing us that perhaps the only true symbolic fear we face in this 21st Century is consolidated top-down conditioning and programming of the (AI) science. This concept forces science to ask questions of priority in terms of the Military Industrial Complex. Whether to militarize this programming rule of directive order begs skepticism and endless fears between all nations."

Suddenly, up across the screen appears: **"Concept of lesser of two evils. If you can't beat them, join them and make them smarter."**

Katka walks out to the front of the stage with a small microphone: "We need the coming and inevitable (AI) to be

289

intelligent and understanding.

"The (AI) must see the black white and grey areas surrounding all issues, which face the challenges ahead. More importantly, the private corporations that have been working on the (AI) up to now need all of us even more.

"Without the Artificial Intelligence Science, our critical world understanding of the complexity of the sensual abstract cognitive science and the nature of brain function would be curtailed. Instead our world needs (AI) to move forward in harmony with all nature and the universe primarily subjectively. Perhaps just as important, it must be in accord to the full spectrum of the entire world's open mind or otherwise (AI science) won't be able to achieve an intellectually complete product."

Katka paused briefly to take a sip of water.

"Our brilliant scientific arts community is building an (AC-AI) model. We believe in time it will be naturally necessary for (AI science) to design a supercomputer that will be able to think and evaluate on all matters of objective and subjective orders collectively and it must be open to millions of abstract points of view, giving it its artificial consciousness. Also, this computer must have an elected body from across a worldwide unified scientific community of academia genius program its 'machine brain.' The program must maintain an upward momentum directive towards maintaining trust, progress, peace, respect and equality between the real biological human united minds connected via the community sharing the new network or world 'Unified Mind.' This is the subjective, creative driver and programmer that builds "the Enlightened Machine Brain or (AI) Quantum Supercomputer.'

"This supercomputer will be programmed to work as a servant and tool for mankind's optimistic peaceful future as well as for the planets naturally balanced future.

"The AI Quantum Supercomputer we propose will be programmed to know that it is only a computer and a tool and won't be proud or strive to be something it is not.

Not unlike 'Hal 9000' scenario from... *2001 A Space Odyssey.*'"

Suddenly, a young man in the front row raised his hand and he took the microphone.

"Doctor, this is a very interesting concept developing a supper intellectual AI computer. However, so many existing and comfortable corporations are needed to help build something which is very critical of them and their profitable comforts as tech leaders. How will the AC party expect to penetrate the existing capitalist system and bring a change?"

"Good question. It won't happen overnight, that is for sure, although we believe drawing new symbols and a higher language and understanding within the scientific community will help generate essential progress. This will be done through new education, further creating elevated linguistics grammar and semantics critical for an enlightened guide of the human race. These factors in turn, will move us toward the next collective, connected, unified mind, and it's careful conditioning.

"Perhaps we are finally technically able to persuade future generations that we can evolve into a balanced caretaker rather than an off-balanced consumer machine directed and conditioned to only follow the defective dumbing down of our intellect and consciousness through centuries of poor, faulty, and destructive materialistic programming.

"Only after we have surrendered our profit and materialistic motivated theories as utilities of the past, can we then open new directions that are free, non-toxic and not directed towards greed.

"Theories open to abstract thoughts and directives start from the bottom up.

"The youth can lead us naturally, because the age of connecting is now.

"Because of the Internet Age the access to information and the ability to connect with totally new ideas, like never before we see this theory of abstract connectionist thought across the fields before us. It is being proven by Internet non-profit activist organizations such as '*Avaaz.org*' using the world-wide-web to petition millions, on topics of protest concerning environment, social and political difference.

This new tool is linking the world's minds and opinions globally and it is building bridges between cultures in many positive ways. Also, through linking science and the arts it is being done through the use of contemporary research and sharing on sights such as '*creativity post.com,*' or concept and idea sharing, which is building interest such as '*TED.com.*"

Katka stops for a moment, and addresses the crowd.

"This theory of connection to our ancient past and its oldest civilizations, languages, customs, symbols, arts and their religions and codes of ethics, as well as technologies, science, genetics and biology are paramount to 'Abstract Connectionist' theory building. As more ancient civilizations become uncovered we must constantly recheck and combine data from all diverse perspectives. We have to pressure religious libraries to share secret texts and hidden histories. We must also come clean with truth in order to usher in a new enlightenment. We need to cram the high-speed computer with open information to maintain a structure of cultural shared consciousness. This way perhaps we may find a method of continuing into the future of mankind with more respect, building shared agreements relating to our world's hotly debated scientific and religious problematic past histories and truths. Thus building consensus science, we will be able to move quicker and more efficiently at achieving a world peace and understanding rather than only through the power of war and might which becomes an endless sad and wasteful circular reoccurrence.

"Some schools say that a 'Neuroaesthetics' approach to Neuroscience would be perhaps a fruitless mission. Some analysts argue that art exists too far off the chart of what can be empirically grasped by constructive mathematical research. Perhaps it's exactly this lack of being explained through abstract and 'higher mathematics' that makes any viable connection hard to prove. For this reason we need a new mathematics based on study across the fields from arts and science to every unified material part of that object related and taken into context from the perspective of the object itself relative to it's infinite conscious and unconscious environment.

"At this juncture the quantum mechanical super high-speed computer tool can be utilized to assist in crunching the never-ending mass supply of information called the potential artificial consciousness. (Or in other words what AC members call "wide-open-no-gravity, upside-down math")... If this new math was PHI, Vedic, Fractal Geometry or an ancient lost math and or an alternatively calculable and a numerical order exists, one could explain the universe with subconsciously. If it has all along, then, perhaps, we shall get even closer to understanding the connections and the magic together. No entity shall disparage all human beings of this planet this right to have such knowledge that gives power to share in potential creation as long as they share and share alike within and according to the growing open community."

Suddenly a young woman stands waving her hand in the air in the back row.

"Doctor Nova, how will a computer make decisions for us, even if we were able to cram it as you say with all the ancient data? How do we know we can trust it to provide the right leadership throughout so many fields? How is such a giant computer able to make this work?" She questioned.

"It will work thanks to a biological/mechanical computer linking all of our minds together as one giant complete mind." Katka answered.

"I will give you a basic example of an across the fields connected approach. In my illustration "General theory of early Metaphorical pattern drawing," I gave a basic text discription of my neurological idea freely to the connectionist community blog of creative professional and amateur scientists. I did not give drawings, illustrations or blueprints. Going forward depends on who wants to share with me and what that party wants to do with the said information. Any resulting outcome shall depend upon them fitting in with me on an intellectual agreement between two private parties, where more detailed ideas can be bought or sold or traded or shared."

"What we do and create and turn in at the end of the day will be subject to scrutiny by the rest of the unified 'Abstract Connectionist' intellectual mind, connected on the many scientific forums. Participants can adopt it or reject it, in part or whole. The cool thing is that the record of ideas will be permanently traced and dated. So, on matters of critical recognition and where title must belong, it will be possible to locate a documented idea from origin, see where it went forward and how it was created into the object of debate."

"It would resemble something like YouTube, yet not privately owned and organized. It would be a volunteer based share of topics, where you would be able to place your idea, up in different areas/topics that it fits. And, where certain abstract constructs are being created, you can show basic adverts to your designs. If it fits another design and or idea then the like-minded builders can develop a chat and or negotiate further on development of a product or object of study or research, etc., perhaps even locating investors who are interested in such potential ideas.

"The opportunities are endless. Unlike specific scientific chat rooms, this one is open to everyone whether you work from a major University or from a garage. Anyone may join." Suddenly, several hands go up. Katka points to a gentleman in a very expensive suit.

"This is very interesting, Doctor, but where is the credit and who will pay for all of this if the idea is to lead away from greed towards benevolence and non profit?" the man inquires.

"We thought about this, and it is very complex and disturbing to think of building a model for satisfying so many appeals across the various fields." She responds.

"Thus, for the science of 'Abstract Connectionism' to function, grow and evolve within a new community, this community must rely on volunteer cooperation on theoretical projects free to the public. No commercial or corporate entity will be allowed near its management." Katka clicks a button on the remote then suddenly a sky with clouds appears with the words…

Imagine a non-marketed, non-solicited return to reality and sanity.

"Solicitors are considered the biggest pest of the mind because these are diversions which present themselves. If you seek out diversions that is one thing but when they come at you in the form of ads, junk mail, spam on the net, flyers on the front door of your home or via a phone, we believe it is toxic to our natural intellectual growth, especially to children." Katka continues.

"The construct we are designing could resemble what is happening in the non-commercial Wikimovements-Wikipedia, Wikileaks and Craig's List. In this case, we would have a wiki/list connection of sharing, negotiating and trading/selling ideas and products across the board, directed to build a positive and progressive freedom-of-choice open world. Katka then scrolls the PowerPoint:

Law of Design / function of Abstract Connectionism.

"Design Ideas are not products:

"Ideas are in the Universe of which we are all connected. Our researchers have proven that many people simultaneously grab the same types of ideas around the same time, because for some strange reason, thoughts travel and spin around through the universe and come down and eventually become utilized. Is it the *"100th monkey effect?"*

"We are not quite sure as a scientific world why this pattern of eventual realization exists.

"Perhaps we will understand the phenomenon one day. A perfect example of this is the Italian renaissance technologies in lost wax versus Nigerian technologies in bronze sculptural arts. Both happened in the same time period between the 1400s and 1600s. Most importantly, each made the human form portraits so incredibly life-like yet both schools were so far away from each other, that it is difficult to imagine one teaching the other.

However, these two uniquely different civilizations arrived on building artistic movements, coming out of their own more crude forms of anatomical representation into closer copies of the actual human form within the same historical period in time thousands of miles from each other."

"We design and build products from others original ideas. Some are better at ideas and some at building products. It is critical that we control the stealing of all documented recognized first original patented exceptional products because they set the standards for future technologies to build from. In an open AC designed market, all who come after must play the game of each leader, sharing any documented technology." Katka scrolls the Power Point again:

296

Mixed Fruit theory and the corporate reality pops up

"This is not allowing for an end to justify a means. As was the design case with Apple vs. Samsung. We have thought this out carefully.

"Copy the quality shape and curves of an Apple Company product then you must become a legitimate player and you can name it Orange Company. If Apple paints it orange and shapes it like an apple. The Orange Company may also, and even add a banana.

AC philosophy lets the market decide which product is better. In the case of art and character, if a cartoon character looks similar to a Walt Disney one, however, and he criticizes with parody and shows distaste of corporate monopoly. If we stop questioning, soon all we will be doing is swimming in a sea of plastic Goofy, Donald, and Mini Mouse, while unable to eat healthy fish or see a wild elephant. The skeptic in us fears that the corporation has taken control of our *IP intellectual property* and our children's reason and reality of value and description. Thus, secure mega corporations need not worry that we have seen and purchased the little mouse long enough.

"The negative wise guy parody is just more fun for some because they are waking to the realization that they are getting sick of being made to be fools any longer.

"Pirated duplicate products, on the other hand, which steal their label and character, exact design and models from companies using a patent or copyright, should be strictly forbidden from the marketplace worldwide. It is theft, and left unmonitored in any country, it could cause harm, sometimes even death, to a consumer. Any country violating this agreement, we feel, should not be able to sell to any world community."

"Furthermore and most important the corporation that builds

products is regarded as not human and therefore of last importance on the list.

"The philosophy which could possibly best handle corporatism and balance it in many ways is the idea of horizontal collective corporatism, or setting up democratic governments of regulation and order to tighten the screws of scrutiny towards capitalist enterprise.

Suddenly the audience became uncomfortable. Some coughed and whispered and moved around in their seats and many hands raised. Katka called on a man far in the back of the auditorium eagerly waving at her.

"Thanks for calling on me, Doctor. I am not familiar with the 'Abstract Connectionist Philosophy.' This is a little hard to grasp when you lay it out. The corporation has become larger than life itself and many of us live good lives thanks to benefits that the corporate concept provides. So how can it be reduced to the back of the line? This notion seems almost impossible."

Katka scrolls to the next Power Point, and continued: "Let me give you an example."

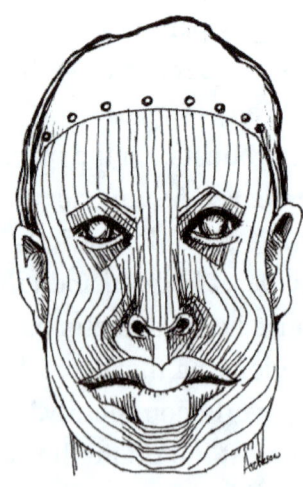

African artworks, next to a Picasso filled up the large screen behind her.

"The Europeans Picasso and Modigliani," she begins…"were inspired by much of what they saw made for centuries in Africa. They were inspired by it because it was visually something unique and different. These modern era artists called their forms something else and they made things that perhaps resembled the African original yet had it's own shape, style, and statement. They also became wealthy in their own time from these creations. To say Big African Corp controlled everything that resembles their product is to kill the progress of the art form, furthermore if (BAC) had existed and were allowed omnipotent powers of control over creative design ideas, we would not have experienced the artistic movements that were created by these and other great artists who arrived at ideas through emulation, not through direct imitation.

"To an 'Abstract Connectionist,' technology is a natural process. The corporate idea of holding onto an idea forever, mass marketing it and fighting to keep it the only idea out there goes against human evolution. Look at the oil companies." Everyone starts laughing hysterically.

"Oh yes, why are we paying the price when we should all be flying in free energy vehicles that have no carbon imprint whatsoever by now in this tech age.

To an 'Abstract Connectionist' the goal of technology is not profit driven." Katka continued.

"The ultimate goal of 'Abstract Connectionism' is the return to a humanity which functions with a natural world order where profit is seen as the achievement and goal of arriving at that nature-balanced order where pure healthy profit naturally evolves and is distributed. It is spread out accordingly, as prescribed by the unified, connected brain of a highly intellectual, care taking society, all linked together as one world and becoming more evolved with our total environment via perspective of all dimensions humanly calculated.

"It is a new technologically linked, connected, communicative, conscious society where every citizen has not only an equal opportunity to utilize, organize and police resources together logically. But each citizen also must continually fulfill a duty to maintain and to perfect the system and materials to fit in with nature as the tech and globalized world continually evolves forward in a positive way."

The same man in the back of the room raises his hand, "Doctor, how can our love of capitalism and free markets ever be changed? Now that the whole world is playing this game and multi corporations are globalizing everything in the world so fast anyway?"

Katka smiled, "We, the unified mass of thinking individuals must connect to change the reality now, and take ownership of our shared world's resources and enforce strict protectionism around the globe, further protecting our garden. If we were to start with our AC model this year, for example, in time based on our algorithmic experiments, we should by 2030 see this mega-connected world we envision begin to rapidly heal. Yet, again, it would take some serious sacrifice from the top.

"We should see no free trade between nations, this has been proven to only benefit the corporations; it most often destroys smaller companies within poorer countries who can't keep up with giant multi-national corporations' low prices on goods. This concept must be broken down completely and immediately.

"We should also see all water, air, mineral and gas resources including power and communications forbidden from corporate ownership. Such irreplaceable, natural resources vital to human life and industry should only be owned and maintained, distributed publicly from region to region where those resources are located, and held precious, furthermore, and plugged in and checked, balanced, policed and overseen by the ever-evolving connected unified mind quantum supercomputer resource management team of young, energetic, environmentally engaged green children as well.

"This direction is not based on socialism or communism or utopianism. It is a natural fact that we own and use the resources together and we rely on them together across the planet, and that the cause and effects have shown that poor management in one area drastically inhibits the other.

"Therefore, in this tricky area, the future unified collective, unbiased scientific community must take charge as the ultimate judge of resource management.

"Rather than focusing primarily on war as they do today, the world's militaries must evolve into an international janitorial service. This alliance shall work non-stop to clean and maintain the environment. The World Military must follow orders from the unified scientific community, while rules prohibit corporations from dictating polices. If any of the latter get in the way, then the guns come out of the lockers and point at those self-interested parties and companies that try to steal from the shared garden."

Just then the auditorium filled with loud roars of different commotion, some clapping and whistling and some booing with angry faces. Just then a fat man in a big black suit and an American flag pin on his lapel stood up and yelled at Katka. "Doctor Nova , please, you and your AC party are full of shit! This is a bunch of pie in the sky, and there is no way the police and war machine will be turned into janitors. You're dreaming! I have heard enough of this," Then he turned and left the room followed by around fifteen others as several people in the back of the room clapped and shouted.

"Good, get lost and go fuck yourself!" One guy yelled "New

World Order puppets!" Katka calmed them down:

"It's ok, we should not expect everyone to see an abstract vision with an open mind so soon in this day and age. Everyone has the opportunity to close the book at any time and turn off the thinking and stay plugged into the matrix. This philosophy is hard to accept quickly.

"Yet, if we look at the alternative to trying to build this community as soon as possible. If we leave it up to private banks and corporations within a globalized New World Order to decide how our resources are handled and laws are drawn and rules are made, then most likely all titles will eventually be owned and stolen by the ever-expanding financial institutions and corporations in the future. They will by objectivist nature, overtake, buy out, patent and copyright every bit of land, stream, thought, gene and life form, in order to enslave all of humanity. This would monopolize the entire natural world itself, putting our destiny and fate of subsequent generations into the hands of a very few elite connected lost souls. Striving to act behind the scene, these self-serving rulers would try to play Gods when in fact they themselves would be the most frightened of all Earths creatures."

Just then a young girl in the front row stood and asked, "The question I have doctor is. How can we turn the tide and change the flow of greed and consumption ruling the economic order? This has been building ever greater imbalance to nature since the beginning of time."

Katka replied, "Our scientific studies have shown that it is achieved based on the power of connecting unified minds within fields using modern tech Internet tools in new and abstract ways into the future if net neutrality is foreseeable and thus maintained. Possibly we can achieve our goal of a logical breakdown via two parts."

Katka then flashes another slide onto the screen behind her, which reads: **Ground Up legal Direction.**

"A properly designed 'Abstract Connectionist' oversight worldwide could regulate and alleviate our present day society's poorly programmed, psychological greed disorder. But, it would take the patent and legal professions to implement it. They have to sign up to contributing to an 'Abstract Connectionist' approach from the ground up as well. They would have to use their rational brains outside the box of business-as-usual, governmental rubber-stamp diplomacy.

"The new legal community embracing connected abstract new directions must drive and suggest new amendments to a constitution for a new technological generation perhaps? In other words...

"We see a positive constructivist judicial revolt, so to speak, pointing out a need of very serious understanding of the corporate role in the world today. It will be important to implement reattachment of values pertaining to logical laws and constitutions and amendments that work and have been tested through time on the world-scale to emerge as effective. We need to avoid dumping newer confusing protective rights and regulations out of fear of a future that is being deconstructed by a minority of unpatriotic corporate opportunists and lobbyists which have spent the last few centuries influencing the changing language of the entire world's unhealthy political justice systems.

"Why is this important? she asked. "Because corporations, although they exist as giant persons who live all over the world, are considered to be in such a way here in the United States and are given the same rights as a single citizen, when needed, as to protect them under the blanket of the Constitution, selective and worded as needed using selective incorporation.

"U.S. Supreme Court rulings over time have minimized the

303

right of states to enact laws that limit the rights and privileges granted to corporate citizens in the Constitution. This has protected the questionable actions of said corporations from state authorities where they hold their property and wealth.

"An 'Abstract Connectionist,' transparently-lead movement of legal and judicial cleansing at supreme court levels could very easily dissect this problem and find the rotten apples, removing them and re-adjusting the grey amendment legislations to promote a state right privilege to evaluate topics of limited, liability, bankruptcy, or protective insolvency of corporations given permission to operate within city and state. This would then pave a way for a more constructive, symbiotic relationship between corporations and public and States needs.

Our systems will hold corporations accountable to its employees, states, countries and environments, and less beholding to only the companies' worldwide shareholders. Opposite of where the emphasis is today. It is not logical that the lazy courts of old dogs will ever come up with a plan to patch the hole of a sinking ship on their own. It is not the Judges' fault either. Many call it corruption and beg a grand conspiracy, but the truth is that this defective pool of cronyism was built over time through series of manipulated mistakes favoring greed over intellectual principal and democratic benevolence." Just then, a dozen well dressed men and women stood up and walked out of the auditorium, some shook their heads and some laughed as they made their way out. On the Power Point is written:

'The Unified Judicial Mind'

Katka smiled again as she addressed the confused crowd. "Again, we can quit and walk away from our confusing vision and close the book anytime. But, the show must go on! Only remember if we give up now then we risk not getting the full mind-challenging experience from this dimension. She continued.

"Imagine if you will... the intelligence surrounding the building of a unified connected super judicial computer guided by the connectionist world judicial blogs. These are made up of the best legal minds in the world, which we propose should bring in all veteran judicial courts within time, to adopt an abstract connectionist approach to pinpointing the merits and mistakes of the existing amendments and furthering a rebuild of better functioning laws and rights.

"We also would hope to see the comfortably settled, neutered house cats, such as Justice Scalia, resign their posts and retire. Put out to pasture if they have nothing intelligent to contribute to a better natural future and logical world order." Just then a young man stood, "Doctor, this is a very interesting concept, but who leads such a movement? Lawyers don't trust each other, and the top Justices are never going to budge. I mean it sounds great but highly unlikely," he said shaking his head as he sat down.

"You're absolutely right, in the present crony system at top levels critical to creating world order, who can trust the legal system? A revolutionary approach towards law as massive and important in scale as we foresee and have modeled in our experiments as this one would potentially be, must come from the passionate uncompromised, unmolded ethically engaged youth. They must bring new legal ideas and directions into this modern tech era, drawing from the ground up and seeding a more realistic contemporary future in regards to globalism and world politics.

"When we say ground up, it means rethinking the movement of all new ideas as our modern age of mass individual connectivity and technology takes us forward. To a true 'Abstract Connectionist,' great judicial thought has existed in our past and does exist for the future. New legal ideas can be combined and integrated into the political orders running our science, technology and economy as we enter the modern era.

"The new fathers of this enlightenment shall be sworn in and extremely well paid. Abstract Connectionist lawyers must be uncompromising, nature-loving lawyers who declare strict oaths requiring that they marshal like watchdogs. This shall build our giant connected community, rooting out objective corrupt manipulations. We feel optimistic that the new clear-minded judges can obliterate corporate mistakes. As this phase starts our volunteers will post recommendations and petitions to the local municipal, state courts and legislatures. Precise goals shall be set, developed to meet the needs of specific unique and diverse constituencies. Logically, both the corporation and the State should remain balanced and satisfied accordingly as any company gains value. Like a five-lane circular merger into a single-lane tunnel, every proposed law and regulation tuned in and respectful of the other in turn, because you can't control any movement at hand with a supreme rule and force, from the top down with threat. The only traitor of a true community is the one who gives up feeling for a fellow person.

"A Wikileaks.org type of check and balance should be embraced as a tested model and enhanced and activated alongside the future legal construct. Otherwise, a concept of such an order must be considered hypocrisy, particularly if no even and strict playing field is laid amongst all respected nations, small and large. A transparent parent overseeing the creation and running of the entire network is vital. In fact, the *Whistle Blowing Policy* in areas of corporate, world governments, and military defense in general should be encouraged. When operating at peak efficiency will effect world public knowledge, social and economic stability while balancing democratic order. Whistleblowers like Bradley Manning who point to the corruption of moral and logical diplomacy should be recognized and rewarded rather than condemned.

Private Bradley Manning

"If we are building a "New World Order" what does that mean for smaller nations?

"Total transparency within all governments must become a primary goal for the inevitable 'Abstract Connectionist' concept of new world order functioning." Just then another dozen or so people leave the auditorium.

Katka smiled and took another drink of water and continued as the Power Point listed a set of provisions up onto the screen:

Spying and invasion of personal privacy should be illegal without a judge warrant. Diplomatic trust and confidentiality should be embraced. Rats, and mud throwing between professionals should be frowned upon in matters of opinion and topics on wide-open minded social morality. Unified accepted law and countless public referendums and petitions maintained by the Internet unified mind mass should be the tool of identification of priority of public focus on issues. Not media focus or distraction issues.

Katka then changes the Power Point. "Now we will move to our second part:"

The Economic Peoples Bank Potential For
Socialized Financial Systems

Suddenly many groans are heard in the auditorium. Katka looked out and smiled, then looking back up to the screen.

"We seem to be programmed to react this way when we hear such words in the U.S.A. however; our strategy serves as perhaps the only way to level and balance the playing field. Besides why is it ok to use 'Socialized Banking' when it comes to bailing out the defective decisions of selfish billionaire bankers and not for everyone?

"Ok then, imagine your money as another check and balance of democracy." Katka threw her hands up. "Now socialized banking maintained communism during the Cold War to a large extent, which I can tell you coming from that part of the world was definitely not a functioning social concept full of imperfections. However, everyone had a roof over their head and medical benefits. Private control over Federal Reserve banking is not maintaining free market capitalism at present because there are no longer solid liquid assets held by the banks. Billions of good hard-working people are homeless and broke.

We the working class give our money through our accounts, taxes, pensions, and bonds to private thieves. They steal it, play with it, and loose it, and we have to make more to give to them again to steal again. That is how it works in the world at present under the capitalist system.

"What are just some of the advantages that The New Era Abstract Connectionist community World Bank will bring? We have worked with some of the best young modern-day economists and by 2025 our models show staggering growth if similar connectionist utilities replace the existing ones.

Katka scrolled the Power Point, while having another drink as the audience read.

Your Account:

"(NFNCOD) Banking-No-Fees-No-Credit no Checks-Only-Debit. When you're empty you're turned off. Fill it up, you're turned on. No more credit from thin air. No more creating lifetime debtors. NFNCOD banking will in time replace the privately controlled reserve banks all together because you can trust the revolutionary new banking system. All who want a loan from our (AC Bank) will have to apply to strict unbiased and critical but fair process. A Unified Mind World Bank super computer network of bank members will connect to the intricate financial matrix, which strictly controls and regulates Bank Stocks and Bonds Markets rather than private non-transparent elite money clubs. We will prohibit bank-charged percentage cuts of your minimum 5 to 7 percent guaranteed monthly account interest. Loans are given out according to strict logic of return on solid tangible capital.

"All credits will be deposited into several giant liquid safeguard funds that will never be used to loan or fund anything that the unified financially invested community is opposed to, or goes against the new connected community and their philosophy and order." Just then many groans reverberated amid nervous expressions.

Katka continues: "I know this one is hard for many to handle. Humans are inherently insecure creatures and money is always at the top of our priority list for that reason. The AC Stock market will be run and overseen by a collective control of young independent, unconnected and well-paid morally responsible economy experts. These professionals will answer to the Unified Mind World Bank community and not to an executive political branch and federal privately run cult like reserve board of sneaky, crony, greedy crooks.

Suddenly twenty or more people left the auditorium as they

309

booed, some shouting nasty comments are heard throughout the room.

Katka interjects; "its ok, let them go they will find their way through it on their own. We will wish them good luck to find a positive solution for themselves. Some of us are choosing to unite to solve it with the community. We can close this book at any time. Things will only get crazier anyway with them, or without them. Just then a graphic goes up on the screen behind Katka:

Connected Intellect A New Guide for Genius

Katka put her hands together as though she were praying. "No offense to everyone gathered here today, this is not directed to you but honestly, "We have experienced centuries of the fat, over-paid, controlled, manipulated, intellectual hierarchy in the world. They have let the departments of administrations and accountants take over most of the higher education centers and turn them into profit-driven corporations, throwing the quality of education to the wayside, in favor of bigger and bigger salaries and bonuses within their exclusive comfortable food chains.

"The Abstract Connected Intellect and respect for the unified world mind should become the educators guide as well in the coming technological age."

Katka then called on an attractive young woman in the front row.

"Doctor Nova, who will decide or be a judge of which people can play or be a part of the massive community? And how can it be watched or monitored and how will people know it can be more trustworthy than private Internet communities? Also, how do we know it won't be eventually taken over by the bad guys?"

Katka smiled, "We spent a long time thinking this one out, and I am sure some will try to take it over. Concerning the hijacking of this movement, such potential shenanigans must be strictly and constantly held off at all cost. Those who abuse, or try to subvert the 'Abstract Connectionist' developed structure or guides concerning all departments and blogs and building of its super computer must be asked to simply leave the group and their membership card and license revoked for not playing the intellectual game properly. They will get a label of 'idiota.' This will be the most humiliating and shameful punishment.

"In fact, 'Labeled Idiots' will strictly be forbidden to help create any part of the (AI) and Unified computer in any field, nor are they ever to be recognized or credited for their work career or abilities by the unified members of this giant community. Somewhat like being revoked from the legal professions 'Bar Authority.'

"The cases of subversion most likely will be rare because to subvert an intelligent intellectually organized progressive movement alone is very difficult and requires a huge conspiracy to do so. Labeled Idiota, or representatives of private corporations, governments representatives, military representatives, religious, activists, anonymous and or terrorist or extremist voices will not be allowed to enter the community and build the 'Abstract Connectionist' Unified Mind or Quantum Super Computer with any ill intent. Only individuals with true voices unlabeled may enter and move up in rank in a very formal and respectful manor.

"Let me emphasize, only true individual people with no titles, or code names, or pseudonyms added. Real voices and faces only can participate in the building of this worldwide super computer free from any supreme single authoritative leadership.

"In other words you can be a president of a country and hold religious opinions and work with corporations and instruct militaries and still be a part of the 'Unified Mind.' But you will be only as powerful as Bob plumber when you share it. There will be no leveraging up the ranks via titles or positions of power. In fact,

311

flexing or name throwing will be frowned upon within the equal community.

"The ideal Abstract Connectionist movement will be so transparent in function, broad based and naturally organized by worldwide opinion and great intellect. This will happen without greed-driven supreme leaders. Our members and the supercomputer will immediately spot any malfunction or negative manipulation, much like a beehive where a foreign intruder enters to steal honey, quite the opposite of how our world governments are running now.

Katka takes another drink and stretched her body a little, rolled her head in circles as she scrolled the Power Point flashing a description of her theory onto the screen.

United Nations of Connected Intellect

"The goal will be to not take over the world's existing democratically elected leaderships right away with a Unified Mind but rather give it its own branch of government somewhat like a 'United Nations of Unified Thought.' In achieving the ultimate goal this 'Unified Thought check and balance' will positively transform world politics and the world economy. This way we will accomplish a symbiotic relationship of consensus through understanding each others' perspectives intelligently and with reason rather than only politically world wide.

Katka turned to flash up on the screen her PowerPoint reading aloud to the audience.

Threat to Political structure at present

"It is easy to imagine many of the present political and corporate structures becoming fearful of such a separate entity when we quickly prove that a more logical and ethical leadership better serves the masses. If the civil servants who are true to their faiths and truly believe in the oaths that they have made to their constituencies, such a revolution shall become possible, but only if they totally embrace an abstract connectionist approach that meets society's need regarding politics and economics.

"One can only imagine the unified force once the people with power see how much more powerful they become, and how much ridicule will be replaced by respect if they embrace the new Connectionist Intellectual movement. The positive transition shall begin once they get online and utilize the connected high speed mega conscious community. "It is simple, when take-charge intellect enters the room of confusion and despair, intellect wins, guides and rules. Not fear and military power manipulation.

"This new united intellect will press the powers of politics towards progressive change. We believe with such a tool, truth and justice can be salvaged from the toxic heap of judicial bureaucratic disorder that was created by generations of defective programming.

"This Unified mind can be a new voting tool for political progress as well on across-the-board issues, further cleansing corruption and leading us towards elections without campaigns that waste precious time and funds that could otherwise be used for more useful purposes. Leadership will come from the ground up by individuals who will represent a unified intellect."

Just then, an older man in a sweater stood in the middle of the room:

"Doctor, it sounds as though you have created a new complex philosophy which you're somewhat begging mankind to grasp, over all the distraction given to us by those entities that have invested fortunes needing us to be exactly as tuned out as we are in order to control how the future game is to be played according to their terms."

"Yes it is a brand new philosophy, and a serious philosophy which we hope to use to identify the viruses and those very defective program manipulators.

"We all have a duty to this Earth to call the manipulators of truth reason and reality out and to make them speak their truth before the world's unified mind and our future well-constructed young fearless justice system. The intended improvements shall emerge once this reality shift takes over and more people understand this new enlightenment for what it will be able to achieve.

"The citizens must demand if these manipulators want to keep a position they must help become a part of the new natural creative community. If they reject the path of unified and connected reason and truth, then we as a world mass must make a critical vote on whether to let them continue or to destroy them. Everyone gets a fair vote on multiple matters concerning appropriate punishment that goes along as a recommendation to the future new world justice system through a fair trial. Every citizen has a right no matter the crime. We recognize the constitution, and we believe no man is above the law, nor should any man be excluded. No drones will be dispatched in an intellectually connected New World Order.

"However, the AC party also considers torture or 'enhanced interrogation' as heinous acts. The molestation of any human, animal, sea and the Earth shall become condemned as the ultimate display of human ignorance and psychological sickness, inhibiting the positive progress of the planet. Those officials like Dick Cheney who promote such ruthless behavior are considered defective members of this shared world society, destined for severe punishment and asked if necessary to repay what they have stolen. Such a recommendation could only be made by a vote and referendum of the unified mind mass of judicial thought.

"What if a dolphin or a bee or a tree could talk to our world's leadership, what would they advise us to do? Katka asked:

"The connected know what they would tell us because we feel for their extinction, in just the same way we now have begun to feel for our own future extinction.

Ultimate Challenge

"It is this primary 'Abstract Connectionist Philosophy' regarding respect for the subconscious, almost metaphysical truths that speak deep within us, for nature, and guides the rapidly organizing body upwards. That organized body will, in time, create its language and its epistemic value and structure related to the ever building of a progressive collective, which further builds an even stronger Unified Mind and super Quantum mechanical light speed computer. This mind recreates a natural balance and order to heal and repair every inch of our natural world of shared resources. We foresee the control knobs of our prospective 'Connected New World Order' being turned by only the greatest and most respected brains across the fields.

"We all own the mass of atoms and particulates we waste, and once we understand how to put them back into working order, perhaps only then God will find the hypocritical game-playing reality chasers of this planet worthy to play dice with.

To allow the progression of (AI) science un-regulated in the hands of private corporations and politicians or governments alone, based on a wish that man and science will be ethical is not logical.

"To leave (AI) science up to the unregulated, corporate run fields of (AI) alone begs a 'Terminator scenario' similar to the science fiction film of the early 1980s. This is not unlike what happened when our elected government's economy was left to the hands of the bankers to design its motives that brought on an economic crisis heard and felt worldwide at the beginning of this new century and millennium. The time has come to reverse the spiral.

Katka turned off the Power Point and up flashes a giant image of a galaxy of stars that looked like thousands of tiny multicolored metallic jewels, all making a perfect spiral above her.

"The time is now." She continued in a very serious tone. "The Abstract Connectionist dialogue must be started and driven into the political arena. Many have run from us today unfortunately. However, many more have stayed and I thank you all for your understanding that this lecture is not one that can be understood with footnotes. These new ideas are but minute seeds waiting to be planted and nurtured by enterprising and eager young gardeners of the creative new AC community. These symposiums perhaps could be our only true opportunity to ask these difficult questions together before it is too late. We may not get this life back, and what we create here now in these desperate times may ultimately decide whether we are worthy to go on to anywhere else or if a corrupt ecologically broken planet and a society controlled by greed is all we get.

"Thank you."

Applause filled the entire hall as everyone stood up and cheered for the tall, thin central European woman who stood alone at the center of the small stage of the 480-seat New England Auditorium. Once the applause died down Katka looked out to the crowd.

"Are there any questions I can answer?"

Katka then pointed to a tall slender black woman in the back of the room who had just taken the microphone from a young attendant.

"Thank you, Doctor Nova, my question is two part: The first is considering the size of the 'Abstract Connectionist' proposed super computer and its potential to take over Google and the existing Internet engines over time with a non-corporate more liberal and transparent leaderless approach. How can this be done? The second is what will be China's roll in this abstract construct and how can we ever expect the Chinese government and scientific fields within such strictly run nations to go along with it, especially when considering that control is number one. Trickle down is for real to this corrupt nation's hierarchy, and public freedoms are a slow process still in that part of the world."

"Very good questions…to answer your first question, I would say basically… 'build it and they shall come.' Everyone wants to be a part of a free and open society; the Internet is basically becoming the world's largest multinational and multicultural single society. It should be free and open and remain so for all time. Freedom is why so many Europeans moved to new lands like America, Australia or South Africa. Every corporate entity owe their profits from the fact that today's freedoms first enacted hundreds of years ago allowed for the world to break away from the shackles of the elite who monopolized those lands and orders. Thus, they fled. The technical age we value today came from this breaking away to new frontiers where our human liberty and creativity and fruits of our labor could be realized by any hard-working man or woman who held the powers of their own vision. Now, we have a new elite, whom we collectively need to bring into this revolutionary contemporary connected enlightenment.

"The projects we propose are the Shangri-La of open connectivity. Imagine a neutral non-corporate run mega site forum of the minds surrounding and measuring the conscious and subconscious thoughts and feelings and pulse of every living ecosystem and environmental resource. Our massive connected world community will unite, creating a shared functioning and organized future where the world's resources are our priority number one. That perception of value will be that new frontier and drive and no advertising should be needed beyond that fact. Only a brain dead zombie wouldn't want to be a part of it. There are so many infinite ways to be a part of it. For your second question,

I believe China, Russia, North Korea, Iran, and Saudi Arabia as well as many other conflicting strict governments, will want to be a part of this new connected community, perhaps even more than the U.S., and Europe. China needs and hungers for logical and balanced openness and intellectual freedom to emerge and harmonize with their wealth which will bring them up and out of the stagnation of decaying old world principals as well. Their long obedient, yet tired, public expects more freedoms and logical directives because they have sacrificed many years to make their country what it has become today.

"I would like to add one thing to that, there are negative policies on environment and social humanitarian principal in China and throughout the world and on every continent and those most critical life-and-death problems will never be overcome by the existing political circus via the globalized United Nations and their arena of corporate corrupt bulldogging. However, the youth of the world know how to communicate with technology, and as a result positive change will come from them... but only if we provide them all a chance for a subsidized, well-directed higher education and spread it throughout the planet.

"Now is the time. The children can finally have the tools to connect like never before. They only need a trustworthy and well-sponsored safe house in which to play, and a scientific and judicial intellectual community hip enough to say it is most cool to do so.

"That safe house can be the 'Unified Abstract Connectionist Quantum Super Conscious Computer.' The community is all of us who have a desire to connect as a means to destroy a virus called ignorance and greed."

❧━━━━━━━━━━❧

Katka walked from the large auditorium at Bentley accompanied by a sizeable group of formally dressed men and women who were busy taking pictures of Katka as she was being lead by two smart looking rather dapper gentlemen, both competing for her attention as she walked towards the courtyard at the conference center.

"We would like to meet with you on the topic of mass brain linking Doctor Nova," One of them asked eagerly, double stepping close to Katka.

"You wrote about creating a mind tool that could perhaps make a quantum (AI) super computer more life-like using a game and several state-of-the-art computer applications. The second man asked, as he quickly walked close to her other side as they walked briskly towards a large parking lot into the warm afternoon air.

"Miss Nova our company has a resourceful group of dedicated neuroscientists and computer tech specialists who are very interested in an 'Abstract Connectionist' approach to combine and enhance their (AI) neural research. We have been overlooking the power of tapping the human brain's subjectivity in combination with our existing mega computers resources. Your ideas sound very promising doctor. We would love to discuss the potential of combining data."

Katka laughed, "You know, gentlemen, the common man built houses all over Europe for centuries out of free mud and straw bricks. Then when they could afford new materials, experts and authorities told them that their buildings walls were inferior. Even though the structures in many cases only needed new roofs and reinforcements of various kinds. Yet, in many cases homeowners within general populace chose to buy alternative materials and re-build. Many tore those old perfectly fine thick mud wall homes down. Now the ecological green age is pushing for straw and mud houses again but this time the competitive arrogant architects and engineers are involved and the process is expensive, difficult, and complex, and non-local. The exotic materials have to be imported from all over the globalized world, and today the wealthy classes who want to cover their guilt with feelings of pride realize an ecological house." Katka then stopped, turned to face the small entourage trailing behind her, and put her hands together in a prayer position and looked both men back and forth in the eyes.

"Gentlemen, beyond all of our positions and places of power and how many neuroscientists we have in our back pocket or how much cash we get from any corporate directed force, is one basic fact… we are all discovering that the super computer was always here in front of us and we lived in it for centuries as did those poor folks in houses of mud and straw. Before the hipsters with degrees said it was cool for even the affluent to do so."

One of the Doctors anxiously asked if she needed a ride. She looked at him with a sweet and thankful smile, then noticed the thumping sound and the approach of a large black and chrome motorbike heading towards them stopping in front of Katka.

"Looks like my ride is here. Thanks Doctors for everything and of course we will be in touch. Once the 'Abstract Connectionist Super Computer transparent social blog' is complete, we can share the world together to build the (AI) as one connected intellectual mass of new dimensional ideas that will change this world.

"This, I believe will happen. I think we should all be in for an optimistic interesting millennium to come as this project becomes realized."

She then removed a thick mass of leather from her briefcase before she loaded the case into a side bag attached to the back of the large motorcycle. She quickly climbed into a black, shapely leather body suit with a long white racing stripe down both sides. She wrapped herself, tightly zipping up to her neck. Then forthwith while donning a pearl white helmet she jumped on the back of the vintage BMW bike with an unreadable mud-covered license plate. As the two excited doctors and the large entourage of journalists and photographers stared with wonder as Katka pressed a wireless connection from her iPhone music, tuning her helmet into her own audio background movie playing the music of *Grimes, 'Genesis'* then she wrapped her arms tightly around the stranger. Then the black leather charioteer, also in a white helmet and darkly tinted windscreen, kicked in the gear and let off the clutch. The picture was of confused stares and shaking of heads from those wanting a last glimpse of this unique woman.

The confused spectators looked on.

Who really was this interesting woman who had just given such a profound out-of-this-world lecture... only to be suddenly retrieved instantly and fluidly by a mysterious masked motorbike man before she could be scrutinized by the press and paparazzi. They chased after her waving note pads and flashing pictures.

Who was this masked man they were so envious of? The guy who quickly whisked their star away from them, down the wooded one-lane road and out of sight as the western sun sank low and the golden hour threw pastel pink, purple and blue clouds against a new optimistic and refreshing New England horizon?

Chapter
16
Sometime In the
Not-So-Distant Future

"M r. President," said the short round bald spokesman with a weak monotone voice and a large bird-bill shaped nose standing about 4-foot-five with a beard and glasses in the center of the gathering around the large conference table."

"We have a serious problem. It seems that we have been unable to get a hold of and subvert the 'Abstract Connectionist' organization that is working on the subjective intricacies needed to complete the artificial Plato brain program that we have been developing through the Defense Department. If we fail to take over their research and program, we stand to loose our country's control and power of the worlds (AI) technologies that… I have to remind you… today, in this day and age we can't afford to take chances. The council recommends that we institute our own Plato project immediately and begin to inform the departments of Homeland Security and Homeland Information on a wide scale and press the congress and Senate to fall into suit. Everything is ready to go. The HAARP program is tested and on board. The Communications networks and the World Wide Web are under our full control after much deliberation and much thanks to the administrations search engines, which hate seeing the focus shifting to the new 'Abstract connectionist' non-corporate search engines. It has taken years to prepare for the implementation of this well planned project. Now that the European and Chinese councils loyal to our order have expressed their fear of the Connectionists as well, it is unanimously believed by the entire United World Councils of World and Foreign Affairs that this just may be the only window of time to get the ball rolling."

"Every day we wait, allows for more of the public to be awakened to the populist logic that supports 'Abstract Connectionism.' We have many powerful leaders with us already on board and it is their belief that those who will decide to go against our supreme leadership, well, we must call them casualties of war no matter who they are or how powerful."

The President looked at the man sternly in disbelief. "Mr. speaker, I have read the memo and I am not sure I like where the Council wishes to go with this. The (AI) Plato brain, honestly, in fact, it sounds a little scary. So let me get this straight," he continued calmly. "What the Council is recommending is to indict thousands of the world's intellectuals, scientists, political leaders, monarchs and great thinkers in order for the council to maintain control over the Unified yet undeveloped artificial intelligence brain?

"The supercomputer, you realize was developed by the very people who you are targeting. I have used their 'Abstract Connectionist' search engines and social networks and mental challenging games. Honestly, I have found them to be much more progressive and useful than Google Chrome, YouTube, Facebook, MySpace or twitter. These are brilliant and creative minds and the council is ready to label them as if they were terrorists?"

"That is correct, Mr. President," the short bald man answered with a straight face.

"So, you want me to criminalize some of the world's greatest artists, thinkers and political and judicial leaders, calling them terrorists and enemies of the state and traitors? In favor of the wishes of the ruling body at the council?"

"Mr. President, the united councils have their thinkers and artists and intellects, sir. The loyal patriotic ones who want to see our nation's long ruling elite continue to rule, as they have done for centuries."

The President noticed around the room all the blank expressions of these weak men and women that had gathered with him.

"Well then Mister Chairman. Who decides who is and who is not acceptable to remain in this so-called idealized Platonic World?" The President took a seat at the head of a long table surrounded by suits of black and dark blue, all of them motionless characterless drones.

"The computer sir." The small bald man answered."

The president shouted surprised, shaking his head. "The computer?"

"Why, yes, sir, the new Department of Homeland Justice has programmed a special computer that will be able to objectively search for a person's history and profile. The department will instantaneously search that persons entire background and life history via social networks and health and work records as well as accountability and tax records. It will even be able to see booked flights, plus where he or she has been, lived and worked anywhere in the world and what he or she has done throughout a lifetime. The data includes any factual audio and video taken while the subject was unaware, via the little eye on his computer screen or television or through city cameras that are also linked in. Based on a programmed account, that computer will be a judge and jury of the person's fate, thus instantaneously delivering a sentence and a punishment reprieve or pardon. What is unique about this computer is a person's presumed guilty until such time the party

324

is proven innocent. The computer holds a storehouse of files on that person, a nano size of a flea in its giant memory which should find anything in a matter of seconds. We load a name, and bingo, out spits a report of his or her crimes and a recommendation of penalty. It is fast food legal work simple as that Mr. President."

"Perhaps fast food, but I am not so sure this sounds very constitutional Mr. Speaker. Everyone has a bad past of unfortunate happenstance. I believe we would all be guilty. It sounds more like a fascist's dream run amok by use of an untested Pandora's Box."

"Oh yes, Mr. President, the questions have been made as to how legal is an all out search? Besides, to search everyone is not the idea. Only this search is to be conducted against anyone who is declared an 'enemy combatant.'"

"I thought we abandoned that term because it became possible to be used too loosely against ourselves. The idea that we can easily throw out a label like this in order to keep a citizen from a right to have a just trial in a court of law?"

"Oh, yes, we did throw it out but only when a particular situation pertains to party members. However, we can pull it out and utilize its function at random, when needed, particularly in instances where we consider ourselves as threatened and we decide to declare a national emergency. George W. Bush used it after September eleventh in order to send certain folks to Guantanamo. It was a national emergency. He had no choice. 'Enemy combatant' works. It resolves and erases harming knowledge of the past and opens a clean and fresh-controlled future."

"Now such an emergency has arrived. You only have to declare it, sir. Everything is ready to move. We also have a potential to use predator drones on any potential enemy combatants outside our borders and within the Homeland. The stage is being set sir the entire council is waiting on your signature."

"What makes one an 'enemy combatant', and how can I authorize any of this? I don't want blood on my hands?

"Well specifically, this means anyone that the council finds who violates the progress and agendas of the world's power councils. Our allies, the world's national leaders have agreed on planned and promoted global projects, an agenda that has already been set and the council remains determined to keep it on track. Furthermore, a project like the 'Abstract Connectionist Unified Collective Mind and world super computer' could very well over time ruin the collected power structure of the Council and its many corporate monopolies and disassemble an order that took years and countless trillions of dollars to create. These are considered traitorous and coup d'tat acts in which we all have something to loose if left unattended. I would like to advise everyone sitting around this table that you all owe your positions of power to the Council and they expect your full cooperation." Now standing up and looking vengeful and serious the little man calmly states:

"Again it is the unanimous agreement of the council that… You're either with us, or you're with the Connectionists. "Furthermore, we don't want to see a smoking gun come in the form of an abstract cloud now do we?" He said it loud and assertive, as his face turned red with a sneer. He then turned and walked out of the room slamming the door behind him.

The president looked around shaking his head, and all he could see was a colorless waste of privileged whores seated at the table before him. He hated them all, he thought to himself and he now even hated himself because he knew that the evolution of true freedom had just run its course.

Liberty could soon be history and in time even true history would most likely become fantasy or myth. The president had taken a solemn vow, an oath to represent the greater public. Yet now as he looked at the pathetic display of pig-like men and women who

326

helped put him in power for their own self serving reasons, now he could only see characterless, fearful, immature losers with blank washed-out lost expressions looking back at him.

Something familiar yet strange took hold of the president, and flashes of his past were radically bombarding him. He did not get this far in life because he was weak and foolish, he thought. What was it he was feeling? Suddenly the faces of his precious children bombarded his confused mind, forcing him to cover his eyes. Could it be fear, remorse, guilt and shame all together? His guts started to clench and the pain in his whole body became nauseating, further causing him to shake, tremble, and sweat.

That was the moment time stopped. Breath became heavy. Nothing and no one, the self, or family mattered to this man who looked out at a table before him. Everything in his eyes appeared as if gray matter and colorless. From his perspective these were sheep and worthless flesh sitting in front of him.

He suddenly remembered a time when unique individual character was what it took to pass the great spirits' tests of temptation, thus transcending the threshold of time to center the spiral of a conscious life and pass through crossover. He considered this as one of many impressionable graduate lessons of super consciousness facing the complexity of a universal code. Only one time learned was all you got, a transition powerful enough to guide the heart and soul. His soul told him about divine thought, further passing into other dimensions not yet explained or understood completely. However, the president recognized and understood some people among us are eager and earnest to become more valuable than the most precious of metals. Those metals finally realized and considered diversions of spirit were only an external minute atomic part of the mass material makeup that some considered to be the shared DNA of the Universe. This physics whether we understood any word of it or not we realized was part of an infinite truth. The president realized that such individuals felt with their hearts a beating biological life, a growing mass of connected minds that would give their effort the ability to point out the flaws in a complex system. Together, the true alchemists and artists connect and correct the world while united as one.

Vecernícek Phenomenon

Suddenly the jester appears out of nowhere:
Yells "wait... stop... think!"
Then gives one last smile and a wink.
With a tip of his paper hat, "Good Evening!"
Then after throwing little paper pages in the sky he explodes into a bright blinding supernova the size of a pea...and poof!
Vanishes-spinning at the speed of light, he becomes scattered across the Milky Way.

Tongue Twister:
Funny puny photon flash fights false philosophical fractions fruiting psychological friend foe frictions found furthers fears for free flow future fulfilling physical phenomenon.

Bang! As though a light bulb deep inside his mind exploded. The words rang again and again in his head, the words rang out almost scripted. The young man sat looking up at the tall handsome Italian leader of the group. He was the town's proud well-known wealthy owner of a plumbing company. This plumber who maintained a high position within the church and local community used his purse strings to manipulate the meeting. This group composed of other well known men of the community and members of the church gave large amounts of money to build the new cathedral and now they thought they were in charge of the design of the tabernacle. They believed giving the church copious amounts of cash would insure them a place in heaven. The young artist had been commissioned to design the project and had delivered designs that were approved by the architect and the priest. This group who had absolutely no ideas about creativity, primarily listened to the wants of the designer of the stain glass windows. This woman felt the young artist did not have designs that went along with her stain glass designs and selfishly insisted that he change his designs. This group of un-enlightened money mongrels decided to go along with her, not realizing how being nonchalant with their decision would affect the feelings of this young creative artist.

"I can't change what feels in my heart to be the direction I was given. I don't take these commissions lightly, and besides, the main objectors to this design are outside arbitrators who had nothing to do with the building of these plans. The architect is positive about my intentions." The young man told the group.

The plumber smiling with pride, said: "Sometimes everyone has to eat a little crow, we all have, and you should also." One of the other men that sat at the table said. "I agree, just change the design the way the stain-glass lady expects you to do, in order to fit her design and work with this group. Just finish the project and you will get your remaining pay and perhaps even a bonus."

The young man looked around for help from the group and explained: "I had thought the priest was conducting the creative process based on theological references to the written texts of the Old Testament. That was how I was asked to create the theme of the project. A bronze tabernacle intricately designed to enlighten and enhance the atmosphere for the believers as they worship in this giant new cathedral. The young man explained.

"This was the main idea was it not?" He asked, while he looked towards the Irish priest who would not look the young man in the eye, seated at the end of the conference table.

"This design was a serious work of art made by my hands, made with my vision, design, skill and interpretation of the information given to me. Not the product of a forced whim from a dominating proud Jewish stained glass craftswoman who is only concerned with whether its theme matches her work.

What about the sacred Christian scripture?" Then the young artist tried to look into the eyes of the priest seated at the end of the table. This young man had spent many hours working with this priest, giving him the designs that the priest had asked of him and now, he would not look back at the young artist. Suddenly a strange feeling came to the young man, one making him feel somehow free and comfortable, a feeling he had never felt before that was of extreme power and control in the face of uncompromising helplessness. It was at this moment, the young artist calmly stood up before all of the other older men gathered at the large long oak conference table and said to them…

"Throughout time men challenged new roads with nothing but their own incorruptible visions, visions that were gained by the tribes, texts, tools, seeds, symbols and keys left them from the masters, the grandfathers, and grandmothers, which had overlooked their offspring's rise. From those great men and women's shared ideas and thoughts and creativity on earth, they progressed us all forward. Those who ruled the times were just only that, the rulers, sometimes envious of those who could do that which they themselves were not blessed with. The evil, greedy and selfish among them found pleasure in the sport of breaking a young man down and taking over and owning his thoughts, ideas, and feelings through taming or changing him, that if they could make him compromise even by brutal means if need be thus signing up obedience of their illogical directions, then that prized object for which the subject labored could somehow become truly theirs to steal and do with as they saw fit. One day came a larger than life incorporated objective driven man who had more rights and powers than a natural man has, the Giant could buy most any common man or vision, a man monstrous in size and with enormous appetite. This Giant man took over and quickly sucked our natural world dry, destroying our mother to son bonds, belief's and our codes of morality. We began to worship this inhuman Giant paying all we had, just to be close to the intricate string pullers in order to suckle at the teats of a larger and larger imaginary fortune. Our new mother and father, our new religion, our New World Order, our new God, we cared not what the label meant so long as we were well fed.

"We obeyed it and quickly turned off any criticism of this Giant.

We closed our eyes to unique un-prescribed artistic, vision, reason and truth because the Giant taught us that these other un-monopolized values could harm us. I am very sad to say.

"Your management of this church seems to follow the new false plastic Gods values rather than those, which should have brought you all to this important moment, for the sake of your code of ethics, morals and beliefs, your church and mainly yourselves. Therefore…

331

"I will not eat your "crow" with you gentlemen, furthermore if the "crow" tastes like chicken to you, then it's your chicken and you can all fuck that chicken any way you like!"

Bang! Like a shock wave the heart pumping life and strength, an energy so profound it shook the entire conference room into an uncomfortable attention.

This symbolic man finally felt as though he were no longer alone in the face of the ultimate evil that wanted to make a fool of him. These opportunists that used God like a doormat. He realized were nothing in the scope of true reality, they had wealth and power here and now, but they lost this test of time playing in a dimension of reality they obviously could not understand. He knew the truth now and that truth was exactly the purpose he was living for and he was exactly where he was meant to be at that moment and the reason he was meant to be was absolutely opposite of the prescribed plan of the matrix which an ancient unseen evil dark hand continued to deal out. It was so easy to finally realize this test he thought, he then calmly turned and walked out of the conference room feeling better than he had ever imagined he could in a billion years spread between several layered dimensions across a million galaxies. When the free warrior, the young man, the leader, the president, turned slowly closing the door behind him, he looked up smiling wide, for on the solid mahogany door was written in silver numbers 101.

www.ingramcontent.com/pod-product-compliance
Lightning Source LLC
Chambersburg PA
CBHW072055020726
47501CB00003B/593